Lorde of Chicago

A NOVEL BY: G. Y. RiGGS

Copyright © 2021 G.Y. Riggs All rights reserved

This is a work of fiction. The characters and events portrayed in this book are fictitious.

No part of this book may be reproduced, or stored in a retrieval system, or transmitted in any form or by any means, electronic, mechanical, photocopying, recording, or otherwise, without express written permission of the publisher.

ISBN-978-1-7365444-1-9

Paperback Version

Printed in the United States of America

To Elizabeth G. and Jackie B. - Thank you for the endless hours of hard work helping a dyslexic structure coherent sentences. This book wouldn't have been possible without your patience and contributions

To my "Readers/Proofers" - Kathy K., Quentin K., John B., Chris H., Lee G., & Chris Y. for reading through multiple drafts and giving me great feedback

And to Patty - for forty-four years of putting up with me. I love you and always will

TABLE OF CONTENTS

Section	Page
Prologue	
Chapter 1 – Sunday	*1*
Chapter 2 – Monday	*12*
Chapter 3 – Tuesday	*47*
Chapter 4 – Wednesday	*91*
Chapter 5 – Thursday	*139*
Chapter 6 – Friday	*165*
Chapter 7 – Saturday	*228*
Chapter 8 – Sunday	*253*
Field Notes	*i*
Map of Greater Chicago	*viii*
Map of the Loop (Downtown)	*ix*

PROLOGUE

Welcome to Chicago. It's May of 1932, and since you'll be spending a week here there are a few things that it might be helpful to know. To this end, you'll find some Field Notes at the end of this journal that will give you some helpful background information. If you have any questions, you might find some answers there.

Also, you'll soon discover that Chicago is a pretty big place, so there are a couple of maps at the end of the Field Notes that can help. During the coming week you might want to refer to these maps from time to time – just so you can find your way around town and not get lost.

Well, that pretty much covers the basics. The rest you can figure out on your own. Be careful, watch your back, don't take any wooden nickels, and have a great week. Oh, and if things in this city don't seem to operate as they do in the rest of the country, just remember – **This is Chicago!**

CHAPTER ONE

SUNDAY

There's money to be made from the evil men crave -Anonymous

Evening

"God I miss Paris," lamented the gangster as he looked out of the brothel's grimy rain streaked window. The thug had been part of the American Expeditionary Force in France during the Great War, and for six months after the armistice his unit had been stationed ten miles outside the French capital, awaiting orders to return home. During that time he made twice weekly visits to the city and grew to love everything about it. Nowadays, he all too frequently found himself in situations similar to this one, procuring young-ones for Frank and dealing with scumbags like the Fat Man. All the while quietly yearning for a return to his beloved "Paname".

The atmosphere at Leonard's, the Goose Island whorehouse he was standing in, perfectly match the mood of Chicago, which was still reeling from the double blows of the '29 collapse and the ascendency of the Outfit. The old industrial building which housed the joint was filthy, as one might expect. It also reeked of cheap cigarettes, rotgut, sweat, sex, and opium. The look and smell of the place mingled with the sounds of rain on the tin roof, and the constant honky-tonk coming from an out-of-tune piano in the front parlor, creating an air of desperation that seeped into everything, and everyone.

The gangster was biding his time by cleaning his fingernails, while he waited for the owner of Leonard's to make an appearance. The thud of heavy footsteps from down the hall heralded his approach, and once Patty Calhoun entered the room it didn't take a fancy college degree to figure out how he'd gotten his nickname. He was of average height, but tipped the scales somewhere close to 370 pounds. What was unusual about his bulky appearance, however, was that his large round stomach didn't droop down over his belt as it would with your typical fat guy. Instead, as if by magic, it seemed to float out in front of him, like he was hiding a medicine ball under his shirt. He had a broad face, twisted nose, and a thick mustache. The few strands of hair that were still on the side of his head had been swept across the top in a ludicrous and vain attempt to convince both himself and others that he wasn't bald.

The Fat Man had started in the Chicago rackets 28 years and 200 pounds earlier. He had been one of the "Northsiders" who had survived the gang war, and his retirement plan had been to take control of Leonard's. When he was younger he had assumed that running a whorehouse would be fun. So after killing the house's namesake, as well as the man's wife and son, he had planned to spend the rest of his life counting his cash and fucking whores. Unfortunately, keeping the money flowing was always a headache due to the typical problems every small business man faces – cash-flow, accounting, marketing, suppliers, employees, kickbacks, runaways, payoffs, and eliminating competitors. And as for sex, with both his age and weight constantly increasing, his inability to keep it hard made that dream a delusion. In the end, Leonard's turned out to be a trap from which he'd never free himself. He knew his life was "circling the bowl" and with each passing day his anger and resentment grew.

Upon the Fat Man entrance into the "bedroom" his eyes were immediately drawn toward the large powerfully built thug casually leaning against the window frame and cleaning his nails with the tip of a stiletto knife. Besides the size of the guy, the thing that stood out about him were his cold piercing gray eyes. These now looked up from his fingertips, and focused squarely on Patty. From his dress and attitude the man looked every inch an enforcer for the Outfit. To make matters worse, his "Mediterranean" complexion suggested he was Sicilian and, as every Northsider knew, those goombahs were the worst.

"I paid last week," the Fat Man declared with a bitter tone in his voice. Since the Outfit took control Calhoun, like everyone else, had to pay weekly for "protection". Every time he forked over his dough, it fueled his anger. "So what do ya want 'pizan'?" he asked with as much scorn as he could muster.

"Her," was the gangster's simple reply as he moved to the center of the room. He used his knife to point towards a young girl wearing a dirty white chemise and sitting on a brass bed that dominated the small space.

CHAPTER I - SUNDAY

She was a pretty, blonde, blue-eyed, Nordic type – just the kind of fresh-faced kid that stepped off a Greyhound several times a day in Chicago, and exactly what Frank had wanted him to find. These girls ran away from home towns all across the northern mid-west, lured by the glamor and excitement of the big city. Sadly, and far too often, they ended up in a place like Leonard's. The gangster then added, "And I need her for the whole night." Reaching into his pocket, he peeled off a ten spot from a large roll of cash and flipped it towards the bed. The girl showed no interest in either of the two men haggling over her. She'd been given a pipe just twenty minutes earlier and was still drifting through an opium cloud.

The Fat Man tensed as he watched the sawbuck land on the bedding. "Go fuck yourself," he said as he pulled the whore up and dragged her behind him. "This joint ain't for waps." The gangster could see the spittle spew from the man's thick lips as he hurled his insult. Calhoun started to smile, but the full force of the gangster's icy gaze halted it halfway up his face.

"I didn't say she was for me," he said softly. He continued his penetrating stare as he added, "she's for Frank."

The sound of the front parlor's off-key piano suddenly stopped. The silence added to the tension in the room. "You dagos are all the same," complained Calhoun, "you think you can just take anything you want." As the Fat Man's rage grew the gangster glanced towards the open hallway door. From the movement just outside it was clear that Calhoun's muscle was now waiting in the corridor.

"Look," explained the gangster calmly, "neither of us wants trouble. I just need the girl for the night." As he spoke, he took another sawbuck from his roll and tossed it on the bed. "And like I said, she's not for me, she's for Frank."

The Fat Man swallowed hard. That was twice now this prick has dropped the name Frank, he thought to himself, and he was all too familiar with who he was referring to. Frank "The Enforcer" Nitti was Al Capone's right hand. It had been Frank who had organized the Saint Valentine's Day Massacre. "Why the fuck does Frank want one of my girls?" asked the Fat Man as his voice began to rise again. "He's got his pick from all the whores in Chicago."

"I know," replied the thug calmly, "and he has me and a couple of the boys do the picking for him. Now if you want me to go back and tell the man that you don't want him to have one of your girls, it's no skin off my nose." With that, the gangster folded his knife and put it back in his inside coat pocket. Then reached down to pick up the money he'd placed on the bed.

"How do I know she's for Frank?" Calhoun was now sweating as he grabbed the arm of the young girl and dragged her back to the center of the room.

The gangster turned towards him and let out a heavy sigh. "Oh, for Christ sake, I don't want to play games," he said wearily. "Just phone the man. I'll give you his number at the club." The Fat Man thought for a moment then held up his hand to signify that the call wouldn't be necessary. He knew if he made waves he'd draw unwanted attention from Frank. As his old boss Big Jim had been fond of saying, "there are old gangsters and there are bold gangsters, but there are no old bold gangsters." Calhoun intended to get old, and he realized that mixing it up with Frank Nitti wouldn't be much of a fight – it would just be suicide.

"Twenty bucks ain't enough for the whole night. She's one of my best earners." His words now signaled that the negotiations were finally underway. "I want thirty."

The gangster smiled. "You and I both know that twenty is twice what she's worth." His eyes locked on Calhoun's, and he could see that the man's rage was starting to build again. He waited a couple of seconds before throwing a fin on the table. "I'll do twenty-five, but that's it."

Calhoun stared at the money and then back at Nitti's enforcer. After a long pause his body seemed to shrink slightly. "Fine, take the bitch, but I want her back here by 8:00 tomorrow morning, and you tell Frank no scars. I don't care what bruises she has, bruises heal, but scars are forever, and if she's got scars I can't sell her as fresh. You got that?"

The gangster looked directly into Calhoun's eyes and smiled briefly. "You want me to tell Frank that, do you?" he asked mockingly.

"Fuck you," shouted Calhoun as he shoved the girl towards the gangster. After a moment he added, "now get the fuck out of my place."

Aware that Patty was mercurial, the gangster grabbed the young woman's arm and moved slowly but deliberately towards the bedroom door. Once in the hallway, the Muscle that had been standing in the corridor moved to block his path. The gangster tensed, the full power of his dark stare now bore directly into the eyes of the large man blocking his exit, causing the man to take a half step back. Without turning his gaze away from the Muscle, the gangster called back to Calhoun. "You want to get your goon out of my way, before something very painful happens to him?" Without looking at either of them, Calhoun mumbled an obscenity before waving his hand. Quickly the Muscle stepped aside, letting out an audible sigh of relief as the gangster passed.

The young woman and her new escort continued down the corridor and into the front parlor. As they entered the noisy, smoke filled room, the piano started up again. The gangster picked up his trench coat and tan fedora off the rack and continued down the steps, out into the cold, rain soaked night.

It was nearly 11:00 by the time the hoodlum pulled his car up to the brown two-story brick building on South Morgan Street, just off Roosevelt Road. As he got out of the car, a middle-aged black woman came out from the building holding an umbrella. The rain was still heavy, and the woman rushed to shelter the young girl.

"What took so long?" she asked clearly annoyed. "We've been waiting for over an hour."

"It wasn't that easy finding the right one," the man replied defensively. The three of them then dashed through the rain and into the building.

The young woman was still somewhat dazed from the effects of the opium and, despite the gangster's trench coat draped over her shoulders, she was soaked and shivering from the rain. "You poor dear," exclaimed the older woman as she got out a fresh blanket from the hallway closet. The woman removed the trench coat, wrapped the blanket around the girl, and sat her down in an arm chair by a glowing fireplace. She handed the gangster back his coat and quickly kissed him on the cheek. At that moment a door flew open and an elderly priest rushed into the room. He was thin, stood five foot five with short gray hair, glasses, and dressed just as you'd expect a priest to be dressed.

"What took you so long?" He was clearly annoyed.

The gangster glared at him with his cold hard stare but it had no effect on the priest – it never did. He shook his head and sighed. "Jeez, Frank, gim'me a break will ya. I got here as fast as I could."

Surprise spread across the girl's face as she looked up at the priest. "You're Frank?"

"Yes, my dear," he replied with a smile as he knelt down beside her. "I'm Father Frank Lorde and you're at St. Jerome's Church. This kind lady is Miss Ella. She's a dear friend of our parish." Father Frank was clearly worried about the girl and asked, "How do you feel?" The young woman didn't answer, but instead she just looked more confused.

Miss Ella brought over a cup of hot tea and placed it on the table next to the girl. "Drink this dear. It'll warm you up."

The priest took the girl's hand and said softly, "You get to start over, LeAnn." As he spoke the young woman began to realize that she was free of Leonard's and of the Fat Man. Tears slowly welled up in her eyes and her lower lip began to quiver. "You've been through a terrible ordeal," said Frank, "but your life from here on out will be what you make of it."

"Make the most of it, child," added Miss Ella, as she tenderly stroked the girl's head. At that moment, another man walked into the room. The girl looked over at him, mouthed a word, but wasn't able to make a sound. Tears flowed uncontrollably down her face.

"Baby," said the man as his voice trembled and tears formed in his eyes as well.

"Oh, Daddy," the young girl cried out, her voice breaking. She sprang from her chair into her father's outstretched arms. While the two embraced, the gangster stepped back towards the door, put his hat and coat on and quietly left. As he walked out of the parish rectory he heard both the father and daughter expressing their regrets and their love.

Once outside, he pulled up the collar on his trench coat, lit up a Chesterfield and stepped out into the cold rain. As he approached his car, he heard the rectory door open. Looking back, he saw Father Frank standing under the covered doorway. "You did a good thing tonight, Joe," Frank said with a smile. "Why don't you stay for a while? I know the girl's father wants to thank you."

Joe shook his head. "I can't. I gotta be somewhere."

Frank hadn't expected him to stay, so he waved his farewell, adding, "I heard you missed today. I trust you won't miss next Sunday as well."

Joe rolled his eyes as he called back to the priest. "I didn't wanna miss today, but I was out looking for the girl."

After leaving the rectory, Joe drove back to Halsted Street and continued south until he reached the Union Stock Yards in the New City section of town. It was nearly midnight by the time he arrived, yet the area was still a beehive of activity. The stock yards were a collection of slaughter houses, meat packing plants, rail yards, and animal pens, stretching out as far as the eye could see. It had become virtually synonymous with Chicago. The smell of the yard was so strong that it could be experienced almost anywhere in the city, depending on which way the wind was blowing. Joe, like most everyone else in the windy city, had learned to ignore it for the most part.

He parked on Exchange Avenue, next to the main gate. Assuming he'd have to wait a while, he shut off his engine, lit up another cigarette, leaned his head back, and tilted his hat so the brim covered his eyes.

There are times in everyone's life when something impacts one of their senses in such a way as to generate an intense memory. Perhaps it's a particular scent that instantly recalls an image of your mother, or hearing a song on the radio that brings back the memory of a lost love. As the heavy, wind-driven downpour beat against his windshield, the sound triggered Joe's memory of the fateful night, on his seventeenth birthday, when Father Frank finally explained to him how he had ended up at St. Jerome's orphanage.

The rain struck against the rectory's windows as if tapping out an urgent message in Morse code. Joe entered the padre's office, but didn't sit in one of the wooden chairs that the boys always used when called in to see the priest. Instead, the Father steered him to one of the two upholstered chairs that faced each other next to the fireplace. The ones that were always reserved for guests. The priest then sat down in the adjacent chair and began to tell Joe his story. As he sat there listening Joe's stomach began to churn, and he felt as if the very ground under his feet was giving way. In an instant, everything he thought he knew about himself changed. Try as he may, he couldn't comprehend what he had just heard.

After leaving Frank's office, Joe walked back to the dorm, packed the few things he owned into a rucksack, and ran away from the only home he had ever known. He walked miles through rain soaked streets to the Stock Yards where he hopped an empty freight car headed east. After a week of riding the rails, he found himself in New York. He had lived all his life in a big city, but he wasn't prepared for the Big Apple. He felt as if he had landed in a foreign country. With no job, money or place to live, he wandered the streets of Manhattan, living the rough life for over a month. Perpetual hunger drove him to steal some food from a corner store and a beat cop caught him. After sitting in jail for several days he was brought up before a local judge who gave him the choice of a further 90 days in jail or joining the army. He chose the latter and was immediately hauled off to the recruitment office.

Because Joe had been left at St. Jerome's when he was just a few days old the priests had selected his name. He kind of liked the name Joe but had never cared for the surname they had chosen for him. Consequently, when he stood in front of the army recruiter and was asked for his last name he paused for a moment before giving the only name that popped into his head. Two days later Private Joseph Lorde hopped off a train in Yaphank, New York, and started basic training. Joe would soon regret not choosing the 90-day jail term because eight days after arriving in Yaphank the United States declared war on Germany.

The sound of metal repeatedly striking the glass of the passenger window pulled Joe back from the past. He looked towards the sound and saw a black man with slim build and average height wearing a dark overcoat and a gray tweed flat cap. The man was holding a pistol and signaled for him to open the door. Joe looked at the gun and sighed, then leaned across the car, unlocked the passenger door and watched as the man jumped in.

"Where did you get the gun?" Joe was obviously upset by the presence of the weapon.

"It's Arthur's. He doesn't know I have it."

"Well, you shouldn't have it, Sam. Those things can get you killed."

"If things had gone badly with the Fat Man tonight you'd have been real glad I brought it with me," Sam replied. He flashed one of his trade mark smiles that all the ladies found irresistible, but Joe just found annoying.

"Well, you don't need it now." As he spoke Joe grabbed the gun from him and began to unload it.

"What is it with you and guns? You have to be the only private dick in the world who hates guns."

"I've told you a million times, it's not guns I hate, it's bullets."

His smile flashed once more. "They kind of go hand in glove, don't you think?"

Joe finished unloading the pistol, handed it back and changed the subject. "Thanks for the heads up tonight. I wouldn't have known that goon was in the hallway if you hadn't stopped playing." Sam nodded in response while stuffing the gun and bullets back into his pocket. "But what's up with that piano? It sounded like every other string was out of tune."

"Yeah, it played real rough," Sam agreed as he shook his head in disgust. "As much dough as Leonard's rakes in you'd think they could spring for someone to tune it."

"Everything go all right after I left?"

"Yeah, everything was jake. The Fat Man did a lotta yelling, but the con held, he never caught on."

"I owe you a sawbuck for the last two tonight." Joe took out the roll of cash he had been flashing at the whorehouse and peeled off a ten dollar bill. As he did, it became clear that the remainder of the roll was actually cut up newspaper.

Sam waved his hand. "Don't worry about it, Joe. I know you did this one for Frank. Besides, I got paid by the house for playing the last two nights and made six bucks. You get the girl out ok?"

"Yeah, she's back with her dad. Lots of tears and hugs, but the hard part for them is still ahead."

"It was a good thing you did tonight, helping that girl."

"If I hadn't agreed to help I would never have heard the end of it." Sam knew that Joe always felt uncomfortable with any type of compliment, so he wasn't surprised that he acted as if he'd been coerced, but he also knew that the guy had a big heart and it was one of the reasons he liked him. "Thanks for playing there tonight. I appreciate the backup."

"Well, you keep bluffing like you do and one of these days your luck's going to run out. Did you do the knife bit? The one where you clean your nails?" Joe gave a rare half-smile and nodded and Sam shook his head disapprovingly. "Now that's exactly what I'm talking about. You couldn't hit the broad side of a barn with that knife. Let alone actually get it to stick into something you're aiming at. Hell, Rose is better with a blade than you," he added.

"You and I know that," replied Joe.

"Don't forget Rose. She knows it too."

"Ok, fine." Joe was annoyed at the interruption. "You *and Rose* and I know that, but the Fat Man didn't, and that's what I was counting on."

"You take way too many chances, Joe. You always do. You need to be just a little more cautious. One of these days someone is going to call your bluff, and when they do you'd better hope I'm packing Arthur's gun."

"You sound like Kat," replied Joe. "I owe you one for tonight."

"Did you spring for the tickets?"

"Yeah, I got three on the first base line just above the dugout."

"Then we're square." Sam opened the passenger door and started to get out but the smile on his face disappeared as he turned back to Joe. "You just be sure you're there on Sunday."

"Cut me some slack, will ya? I've only missed one Sunday all year."

"Two! You missed two," Sam replied sternly as he held up two fingers. "And when anyone misses we're all in Dutch."

"It's not like I wanted to miss it. I actually enjoy Sundays," he explained earnestly. "I was stuck on this case. Anyhow, relax I'll be there." Then he added, "Did you hear if the Sox won?"

"Afraid not, they got swept by the Senators," Sam responded as he jumped out of the car. He tossed a wave goodbye and ran through the rain towards a black Chevy coupe parked across the street.

Joe watched as Sam climbed into the car and drove away. Sadly, he repeated Sam's last few words softly to himself, "Swept by the Senators," while shaking his head in disgust. Then he started the engine, shifted into first, and pointed his roadster in the direction of Warren Street.

CHAPTER 1 – SUNDAY

[Case Epilogue] – LeAnn and her father returned to Black Earth, Wisconsin. As soon as they got home LeAnn fell ill. The local doctor was called in and he had trouble diagnosing the problem because he had never seen the symptoms of drug withdrawal before. It took nearly two months for LeAnn to recover physically from her ordeal at the Fat Man's whorehouse, but the psychological damage took much longer to heal. Slowly she regained contact with her old friends, rejoined the local Lutheran Church, and eventually started dating a local boy she had known since she was five. After they were married LeAnn settled down to the life that she had thought she never wanted. She had a husband she loved deeply, a nice home, four beautiful children and eleven playful and energetic grandchildren. She died at age 90, a contented woman surrounded by her family and at peace knowing that she had made the most of the second chance she had been given.

Three weeks after Joe rescued LeAnn from Leonard's, Patty "the Fat Man" Calhoun was trying out a new girl and smacked her around a bit. Unfortunately for him, he messed with the wrong girl. The next night his new whore got hold of an ice pick from the bar in the front parlor and, while Calhoun was working at his desk, she jammed the pick through the base of his skull and into his brain. It took him thirty agonizing minutes to die and the entire time he lay on the floor with his body convulsed in spasms the young woman stood over him and smiled. The girl then set fire to the Fat Man's office to cover her crime. The embers from the fire drifted over to a nearby grain elevator and the grain dust exploded. By dawn twenty thousand spectators had gathered to watch sixty-five engines and two fire boats fight the blaze. What would be called the "Great Goose Island Fire" burned for several days, consuming dozens of buildings, and wiping away all traces of Leonard's.

CHAPTER TWO

MONDAY

May your coffee be stronger & your Monday's be shorter -Unknown

Morning

Joe woke to the sound of the couple next door locked in the throes of passion but, since both were dedicated Reds, passion was always reserved for politics. She was a Bolshevik and a member of the Communist Party, and he was a Menshevik who had never joined the Party. Joe didn't think their political philosophies were all that different, but the two of them found endless issues to debate and argue over. This morning it was the noise from one of their heated exchanges that caused him to open his eyes. Their shouting lasted for another five minutes until finally fading away. It was at this point that Joe suddenly caught a whiff of lavender. He had smelled the same fragrance in his office last Wednesday, and as he rolled over in bed he found himself staring into the barrel of a Savage 9mm semi-automatic pistol.

The 9mm was being held by Avaj Patel, a short, fragile looking man of about forty with delicate features, black hair, and a thin moustache. The little man wore an impeccably tailored gray pinstriped suit with black and tan shoes, a tan waistcoat, and a blue tie with a matching monogramed handkerchief tucked perfectly into his suit coat pocket. Patel had come into his office and offered to pay fifty dollars to have a package picked up from a Greek sailor named Kyranos who was arriving on the tramp steamer "Carlo". The ship was scheduled to come through the lakes and dock at the Navy Pier last Friday night. When Joe had asked him why he didn't pick up his own package, the dapper gent had spun a story about being afraid to meet the ship and needing someone to act as his intermediary. Joe thought the guy's story was hinky, but he took the job because Patel was offering way too much money for a simple pick up and

CHAPTER 2 - MONDAY

it made him curious. Now his client was sitting in an old armchair in his bedroom looking about as threatening as Toby the Pup, but nonetheless pointing a gun at his head. "How did you get in here?" Joe asked more out of curiosity than any real concern.

"My original intent was to pick the lock on your door." The little man spoke flawless English, with a slight accent that was hard to place. "So imagine my surprise when a sweet silver haired old lady offered to unlock it and let me in."

"That's my landlady," Joe explained as he shook his head in disgust. "She'd open the door for Jack the Ripper if she thought he was 'nice'."

Joe shifted his weight in the bed, startling Patel. "Please don't make any sudden moves, Mr. Lorde," he warned. "I would hate to have to shoot you this early in our conversation." Joe swung his feet from under the covers, placed them on the floor and now sat directly in front of Patel.

"Don't be a twit, Avaj. You can't shoot me. I'm the only one who knows where your package is. If you shoot me you'll never find it." He focused his glare directly at the little man. After only a few seconds of looking into the cold eyes in front of him, Patel turned his head. Joe rose out of bed, stretched and yawned. Then, dressed only in white boxer shorts, he staggered to the washroom.

"I told you not to move," complained his startled client.

"Correct me if I'm wrong, but we agreed to meet in my office this morning at ten, didn't we?"

"Yes, we did," admitted the little man as he rose from the chair and followed Joe towards the toilet.

"So what are you doing in my flat at 7:45?"

"I believe you have the package that you agreed to pick up from Mr. Kyranos ..."

"If you believe I have it," interrupted Joe, "and we're supposed to meet at ten, then again I ask, why are you holding a gun on me at 7:45?" He scowled at his client through the reflection in his washroom mirror and again Patel turned away. Joe grabbed a toothbrush, wet it under the running faucet, sprinkled it with tooth powder, and began to brush his teeth.

"I have been attempting to acquire the contents of that package for quite some time. In the past, others who I've hired have, shall we say, altered their plans, once they obtained possession. I came here this morning to make sure you didn't end up altering your plans as well."

"So what's in the package that's so damn important?"

The client hesitated for a moment and then began his explanation. "I am from Patna in the Indian State of Bihar. Patna was the capital of the great Gupta Empire. The item you picked up for me contains an important artifact of my people. It dates back 1,400 years to the beginning of that empire. It was the property of the first ruler, Maharaja Sri-Gupta, and priceless to my people. At the same time, there are collectors of antiquities who would pay dearly for it. One such collector was the Emperor Franz Joseph of the old Austro-Hungarian Empire. Because of his well-known love of antiquities, the item was given to him as a gift by Queen Victoria on his birthday in '91. At the end of the Great War the Austrian Empire collapsed. The Hapsburgs monarchy, that ruled the empire, fled Vienna for Switzerland, taking all their valuables including this item with them. The item was one of many things stolen from the Hapsburgs in Zurich, and two guards were killed during the theft."

"I remember that robbery – it was headline news. The thieves stole most of the Austrian crown jewels as well."

"Yes," agreed Patel. "Nothing that was stolen was ever recovered. The item you now possess disappeared at the time of the robbery and only recently resurfaced. It is my sacred duty to my people to recover it. So, if you don't give it to me this instant, I'm afraid I must search your rooms. Please put your hands up and sit in the corner."

Joe continued to brush but responded in a garbled voice. "Like I said before, Avaj, you can't shoot me, so I really don't have to do what you tell me."

The little man now appeared both angry and confused. "You have to do what I say. I'm holding a gun!"

"And a very nice one it is too," mumbled Joe while still brushing. "I haven't seen a Savage 9mm since the war. By the way, they have a tendency to jam, usually if you try to fire them when the chamber is empty." He spat into the sink, then began rinsing his mouth out with water.

CHAPTER 2 - MONDAY

Patel was at a loss for what to do next and followed Joe as he walked back into the bedroom. "I order you to sit down over there," he shouted and pointed to the armchair with the barrel of his pistol. With the gun briefly pointed at the chair, Joe reached out and grabbed it with his left hand, while connecting to Patel's jaw with a hard right. At the moment of impact, the little man released his grip on the 9mm, collapsing unconscious to the floor. With the threat neutralized Joe immediately unloaded the gun. As he did he noticed that there was no bullet in the chamber. The gun's magazine had been loaded but it wasn't ready to fire.

Patel continued to lay motionless on the floor as Joe did a quick search. In the man's pockets he found some loose change, a key from the Congress Hotel, a brass money clip with two hundred dollars in it, and two passports, one French and the other British. He put everything back in the unconscious man's pockets and walked back into the washroom. After shaving, he opened his small closet and picked out a clean white shirt, a red striped tie, and one of his two "normal" business suits.

Joe owned four suits in total which was quite an extravagance these days. Only two of the suits were for everyday use, while the other two were for "special occasions". He used one when posing as a gangster, just as he had done the night before at Leonard's. It was a double breasted dark blue pinstriped suit that he had bought at the Hub a few years back. Whenever he wore it people just assumed he was part of the Outfit, and there were times when it could be quite useful for people to jump to that conclusion. His other special suit was an English cut gray vicuna that he'd gotten at Marshal Fields about three years ago. It had cost more than his other three suits combined and was impeccably tailored. Typically he only used it when he had dealings with Chicago's upper crust. His suits, however, weren't the only thing he changed when he dealt with the different groups in the city. He was a chameleon in mannerisms and speech as well, and he tended to speak at whatever social level he found himself.

Once dressed, Joe walked to his kitchenette. He took out an ice pick from a drawer, opened his ice box and chipped off a couple of chunks from the large block that sat at the top of the chest. Then he took the chunks and wrapped them in a small dish towel. Patel, who had been lying on Joe's bedroom floor for about twenty minutes, eventually staggered to his feet and walked into the main room of the apartment. Joe was sitting at the small counter that separated the kitchenette from the rest of the main room, drinking a glass of milk and smoking a Chesterfield. The little man sat down on the stool beside him and Joe handed him the dish towel with the ice wrapped inside. Patel gently placed the improvised icepack against his sore chin.

"I fail to see why you found it necessary to resort to violence," he complained.

"You were pointing a gun at me, Avaj. I don't like it when people point guns at me."

"I just want what I paid for, that's all," replied the client defensively.

"Unfortunately, I can't give you the package. I heard yesterday that the Greek sailor you arranged for me to meet was found dead early Saturday morning."

"What?" Patel was clearly startled by the news. "Kyranos is dead?" Without waiting for an answer he asked, "Have they caught the killer?" Joe said nothing but instead just stared at the little man. Patel's expression changed and he now looked frightened. "Wait … you think I had something to do with that?" he asked excitedly before adding defensively, "I can assure you I know nothing about that poor man's death."

"Maybe you do, maybe you don't, but I hate coincidences. So before I give you your package I want to make sure that it, and you, are clean."

"Clean?" he queried, confused and clearly insulted by the use of the word.

Joe sighed and explained, "Let me rephrase … I want to make sure that you and that package had nothing to do with Kyranos' death."

"Ah," replied his client, satisfied with the explanation.

"Now, I need to finish getting ready for work, and you need to leave." He pushed his client towards the front door, handing him the mahogany cane, trilby hat, and gray coat that were draped over a tall stuffed chair in the main room. Joe opened the door to the hallway then gently shoved the little man out of his apartment.

"So we will meet at your office at ten?" Patel asked meekly as he put on his hat and coat and pocketed his gloves.

"No, we can meet later in the week. I'll leave a message at your hotel."

"But we had agreed to meet this morning," protested Patel.

CHAPTER 2 – MONDAY

"Yes, but that was before you came to my flat and held me at gunpoint. Oh," Joe added, "speaking of guns ..." he reached into his suit pocket and pulled out the Savage 9mm. "I believe this is yours," and handed the pistol back to his client.

"Thank you," said Patel, clearly startled that he was getting his weapon back. He took it from Joe's hand and quickly pointed it at him again. "Now we will go back inside and you will sit in the corner while I search your premises," he said with as much authority as he could muster.

"I told you before, Avaj, you can't shoot me because if you do you'll never get your package."

"You're right in that I can't kill you, but I can shoot you in the leg, which is what I intend to do unless you do as I say." Then, in an attempt to frighten his much bigger opponent, he pulled back on the bolt to chamber a round, aimed his pistol up towards the ceiling and pulled the trigger. CLICK ... The weapon failed to fire. Patel tried again to pull back the bolt on the semi-automatic, but it wouldn't budge.

While the frustrated man examined his gun trying to figure out why it hadn't fired, Joe took out the 9mm bullets from his pocket and showed them to him. "I did warn you that they tended to jam. Wiggle the trigger back and forth a bit, while you pull on the bolt," Joe advised. "It'll clear the jam."

He did as he was told, freeing up the bolt. Then he looked meekly at Joe and said, "Clearly Mr. Lorde, I underestimated you."

"I get that a lot," Joe replied before closing the door in the little man's face. His client could be heard mumbling to himself as he slowly walked away from the apartment.

Joe went back to his bedroom, opened his top dresser drawer, and took out a package wrapped in plain brown paper and tied with twine. He hadn't intended to open it, but after hearing from the police about the dead Greek, and now this incident with Patel, he'd decided it was time to find out what all the fuss was about. He cut open the package and found a hard black rubber ball wrapped up tightly in pages of *To Vima*, an Athens daily newspaper. The ball was slightly smaller and a bit heavier than a baseball, and encircling the outside was a raised band. Inside the band there were three rows of symbols. These symbols were small and the same black color as the rest of the ball, making it difficult to see them clearly. He checked his watch and was surprised to see that it was well past 8:00. He put on his trench coat, grabbed his favorite gray fedora, and pocketed the rubber ball before heading to his office.

Joe lived a block west of Union Park, on Warren Street, in a one bedroom apartment on the second floor. It was a pleasant neighborhood with tree lined streets and narrow freestanding stone and brick apartment buildings. A thin layer of dust, from last week's black blizzard, had covered everything in the city for days but the previous night's heavy rain had finally washed it away. The morning sky was a dense steel gray and there was a strong wind blowing from the north. The wind's direction meant it was cold, but it also meant you couldn't smell the Stock Yards. He made his way to a brown Ford Model-A Roadster that he'd bought for four hundred dollars two and a half years ago. It was the first car he'd ever owned, as well as the first one he'd ever driven. He liked it because it was a ragtop, and because it was brown rather than black, like almost every other car. He climbed in, fired it up, engaged the gear, and released the clutch, then smoothly pulled away from the curb.

Chicagoland was as flat as a pancake, and the city's streets were laid out in a giant grid. This made driving around town fairly easy. Virtually all the roads ran in a straight line, with most running either north/south or east/west. There were some streets that ran at an angle, like Lincoln or Ogden, but there weren't many, and the few that did still ran in straight lines. Horse drawn wagons, hand carts, broken down jalopies along with slow moving trucks and Speed Wagons could all cause traffic to back up. Because of the grid layout, if the street you were on was jammed, you could usually find an empty one that ran parallel, just a block or two away. Chicago had a north side, a west side and a south side, but there was no east side, because Lake Michigan consumed the entire eastern half of the map.

Every morning on his way in to work, regardless of which route he took, Joe passed numerous "shape-ups" with crowds of men milling outside the factories that had managed to stay open. Most of the time, he tried not to look at the faces of the men who waited, because their plight hit too close to home. Since he opened his business in '28 he'd done all right, but he was all too aware that the only thing separating him from the men in shape-ups were a couple of months of bad luck.

Halfway into the office, he pulled up to Woolworth's and bought two black rubber balls. They were lighter than the ball in his pocket and also

CHAPTER 2 - MONDAY

slightly bigger, but not so much that you'd notice. Along with the balls, he bought a magnifying glass and four lollypops. He didn't know what kind of lollypops they were, but he was pretty sure it wouldn't matter.

Joe's office was in the Reliance Building at the corner of Washington and State streets, in the heart of city. Banking, retail, brokerage, large companies, government institutions, entertainment, and the arts all occupied just a few square miles of land that was pressed up against the western edge of Lake Michigan and bounded on both the north and west sides by the Chicago River.

Within this central business district, there was an elevated rapid transit system, known locally as the "L", which ran thirty feet above ground. The trains that ran on the "L" served the northern, western, and southern areas of town. They all converged on the city's central core like spokes on a giant wagon wheel that, thanks to Lake Michigan, had been sliced in half. The hub for these spokes was a section of the "L" that was seven blocks long and five blocks wide, and encircled downtown Chicago. This loop of track resembled a giant toy train set raised three stories above street level. When the transit trains entered the core of the city they spun around the central business district before heading back out into the suburbs. There was no other city in the world that had an elevated train system quite like Chicago's. This distinctive transit "Loop" became synonymous with the core of the city and gave the district its name.

Joe arrived at the Reliance Building just before 9:00, crossed its small art deco lobby, and headed towards the elevators. One of the cab operators was an affable guy named Paweł Wiśniewski, but everyone called him "Pudge". He was universally loved by all the building occupants except Joe.

"Morning, Joe," said Pudge with an oversized grin on his face. Joe cursed his luck. With three elevators in the building, he had only a one-in-three chance of getting any particular operator but for some reason he always got the cab with Pudge. As usual, the operator delivered his greeting with way too much enthusiasm. "Great weekend, wasn't it, buddy?" Pudge was a small dark haired Pole, with a weathered face that made it difficult to guess his age. He was also in a perpetually good mood which grated on Joe's nerves. What really set Joe off however, was that Pudge was an unabashed and fanatical Cubs fan. To any Cubs fan, there were few weekends better than one where the Cubs swept a three game series while the White Sox lost three games. Joe was a Sox fan, a fact Pudge was well aware of. "We swept them Dodgers. I tell you, pal, this is our year," he continued, with the size of his grin undiminished. Sadly, it looked like Pudge might be right, a month into the season and the Cubs were off to a great start. The Sox, on the other hand, were already seven games back of the Yankees.

"Here you go pally, sixth floor, have a great day."

"Fuck off," mumbled Joe under his breath as the elevator doors closed behind him.

There were a number of small offices located on the sixth floor. Joe walked down the black and white tiled hallway until he reached a wooden door with a frosted glass panel that read "No. 603 – Argonne Detective Agency" in stenciled black letters. Entering the office he saw Kat, his secretary, sitting behind her desk just to the left of the door.

Ekaterina Moroscova or Kat, as she was known, was a tall, statuesque blond who despite her fifty-one years still possessed the poise and bearing of her youth. She was a snazzy dresser and typically wore clothes that showed off a figure she was rightfully proud of. From birth she had lived the life of privilege and wealth in St. Petersburg, Russia, but her idyllic world crashed and burned in '16 when her husband, an officer in the Russian army, was killed in action.

After the revolution, and the fall of the old order, Kat's life continued its downward spiral. To escape the Bolsheviks she, along with her twelve-year-old son Michael and father-in-law Feodor, immigrated to America in '18. Soon after they docked in New York she lost Michael to the influenza pandemic. Then, in the winter of '24, an old family friend convinced Feodor that they should to move to Chicago. Three months after stepping off the train their friend had swindled them out of everything they had left. Feodor died a week later. The doctor told her he had succumbed to pneumonia, but Kat knew in her heart that the old man had simply lost the will to live.

With the last remnant of her past life gone, Kat's life seemed to end as well. In order to get the money to bury Feodor she borrowed from a loan shark, and was forced to spend months doing "things" on the street in order to pay him back. The memory of those times still made her cry late at night. When her debts were finally cleared, she survived by cleaning washrooms and scrubbing floors.

CHAPTER 2 - MONDAY

In November of '28, Joe decided to start his detective agency and he advertised for a secretary. Before the crash jobs were more plentiful. Consequently, he couldn't get anyone to take the job because he couldn't guarantee them that they'd get paid after the first few weeks. Kat had never worked as a secretary, and wasn't quite sure what they did, but decided to answer the ad anyway. In the end, they took a chance on each other and it was the best thing to happen to her since the start of the Great War.

Besides doing his scheduling, filing, and correspondence, Kat handled all of the billings and collections. What she really loved about the job, however, were the cases. Embezzlement, robbery, blackmail, philandering husbands, cheating wives, missing persons, and an occasional dead body – it was all fascinating. From the start, Joe always discussed the cases with her, and was genuinely interested in her opinion. For the first time in a long time she felt needed and wanted. She was never sure how or when it happened, but at some point over the past few years she'd emerged from the darkness that had overwhelmed her for so long, and began to live again.

"How did it go last night?" she asked. Her English was flawless but her Russian accent was noticeable. "Did you find the girl?"

"Yeah, she was over at that damn whorehouse on Goose Island."

"Language, Joseph," responded Kat. She detested swearing and was quick to admonish anyone who transgressed. Then she asked, "Will she be ok?"

"Hard to say. What she's been through tends to leave deep scars."

"The poor thing," she said. She then shook her head and shuddered slightly as she suppressed memories of her own. "Did you have any trouble?"

"Not really, but the Fat Man was there."

"I thought you said he wouldn't be there." Kat was clearly upset.

"No, I said I didn't *think* he would be there. It was bad luck, but it worked out ok."

"You were playing 'the gangster' again, weren't you?" she asked in a disapproving tone.

"It was the only play I had," he explained.

"Oh, Joseph, I do worry about you." Whenever she called him Joseph he knew he was in for a lecture. "You're reckless and take way too many chances," she said sternly.

Joe Lorde stood six foot four and was a muscular two hundred and thirty-five pounds. He had an olive complexion with short wavy black hair and intense gray eyes, with a prominent scar just above the left one. Women were attracted to his "rugged good looks" and the sense of strength and confidence he projected, but those were traits that had developed over time. In his younger years he'd been tall, skinny, and riddled with acne. And the many rejections he'd received during his feeble attempts at meeting girls had convinced him he was anything but good looking. Even today, when he looked in the mirror, he still saw that awkward kid looking back at him.

His complexion looked Mediterranean in origin, and his stature and bearing, along with his cold piercing eyes, were extremely intimidating. It was his gift that he could fix an intense stare on virtually anyone and make their spine turn to jelly. When people first met him, they immediately assumed that he was nothing more than hired muscle. He was, however, keenly intelligent and would always try to use his head instead of his fists to get out of a jam.

From the day she met him Kat had never seen Joe intimidated by any person or situation. Nothing seemed to unnerve him. He always seemed to be in control and supremely confident. He was also a man who played his cards close to his vest and rarely smiled. When Kat first started working for him he seemed cold and hard, but over time she came to realize that he was much tougher on the outside than he was on the inside.

She walked over to the coffee pot that sat atop an electric burner on one of the five wooden file cabinets lined up against the far wall. Kat had never gotten used to the weak coffee Americans drank, and Joe also disliked a "weak brew", so the coffee she made for them was very strong. She filled her cup and then poured one for him. "You're going to bluff once too often, Joseph, and I'm afraid of what will happen when someone calls that bluff." She handed him a mug and put a copy of today's *Chicago Tribune* on his desk.

CHAPTER 2 - MONDAY

"No worries, Kit-Kat." He only called her Kit-Kat when he knew she was upset with him. "I'm indestructible," he added as he sipped his hot coffee. "You know that."

"No one is indestructible," she snapped and then shook her head disapprovingly. Her Russian accent was even more noticeable, as it always was when she became excited or upset. "You're just as destructible as anyone else."

"How was your weekend?"

"You're trying to change the subject."

"Yes, I am," he admitted. "So how was it?"

Realizing that he was going to ignore her warning, she decided to give up her lecture on his habitual recklessness, for now. She sighed, and replied, "It was very nice. Thomas took me to the Biograph and we saw *Red Dust*, with Gable and Harlow, it was delightful." Thomas was Kat's neighbor, a widower who lived in her building. Joe was pretty certain they were an item, but she never offered any details and he wasn't the type to pry. It didn't surprise him that she had gone to see Gable's new picture. She adored him, and Joe was pretty sure she'd happily sit for two hours and watch paint dry as long as someone flashed a photo of Gable every few minutes. "It was a double feature," she added, "we also saw the new Charlie Chan film."

"Any good?"

"It was ok, but they never give you the clues you need to actually figure out for yourself who did it."

"So what's in the news?" he asked. Kat read the *Trib* first thing every morning, as well as the *Daily News* in the evening, and would typically give him a rundown on the headlines while they drank their coffee.

"The Tax Strike is still going on. All those business men are refusing to pay the city and the *Daily News* says they're running out of cash."

"That must be giving Bill Daily fits. Anything else?"

"Hmmm," she said as she picked up the *Trib* and quickly scanned the major stories. "The Japanese are continuing their invasion of China. Their occupation seems so brutal," she added with a shake of her head. Then she jumped to another story. "It seems some poor Russian émigré snapped and shot the French President dead, in Paris." Kat was about to tell him more but stopped when she noticed a small brown paper bag from Woolworth's on his desk. She reached into the bag and pulled out two rubber balls. Joe then took what he'd gotten from the late Mr. Kyranos and rolled it across the desk. Kat picked up the wobbling ball and examined it.

"That's what Mr. Patel hired us to pick up from that Greek sailor I met Friday night," he explained as he sipped his coffee.

"The meeting at the Navy Pier?"

"That's the one. You see the markings on the ball?" he asked as she held it up to the desk lamp. "Do you think you can copy them onto these other two balls?"

"The ball from Kyranos has raised markings," she observed. "Any copies I make won't have raised markings."

"I know, but they should look enough like the original that I can pass 'em off from a distance."

"It's very hard to read these symbols."

"That's why I also bought this," he said as he took the magnifying glass out of the paper bag.

Kat studied the markings through the magnifying glass. "How exact do you need them to be?"

"Not all that exact, just so it looks the same from a few feet away."

"I'll have to use blue ink. If I use black you won't be able to tell there's anything drawn on the ball. I can make the copies, but it'll take me a couple of hours. What's this about?"

"At this point I'm not sure, but I'm guessing someone really wants that ball," said Joe, "maybe even enough to kill for it."

Kat looked up, surprised by the remark. "Kill for it? Who was killed?"

"Kyranos was shot dead early Saturday morning."

"You think he was killed for this ball?"

"I don't know, but I don't intend to give it to anyone until I know for sure."

Kat took the four lollypops out of the Woolworth's bag. "What are these?"

"Lollypops, they were giving away free samples."

"They were giving them away, were they?" Kat repeated, but clearly didn't believe it. She knew when Joe did something nice for someone he'd never admit it. "I've never seen this kind before. It's called a Tootsie Pop," she said reading the label. Kat unwrapped a red one and put it in her mouth. "Not bad," she smiled, and continued examining the ball. "Don't forget," she added as she walked back to her desk and sat down, "Mr. Patel will be here at ten."

"Actually, he stopped by this morning and we rescheduled the meeting." Joe sat in his office chair and lit up a cigarette. As he took a sip of coffee, he picked up the baseball he always kept on his desk and began to toss it straight up and catch it.

Kat stood up from her desk and walked back into his office looking surprised. "He came to your apartment? How did he know where you live? You're not in the book."

Joe continued to toss his baseball as he talked. "I'm not sure how he knew, but when I woke up this morning he was pointing a gun at me."

"A gun!" Kat said excitedly as she sat on the edge of his desk and crossed her legs. "But he seemed like such a nice little man." Then she thought for a moment before asking "Why was he there in the first place?"

"He wanted that rubber ball."

"So what happened?"

"I convinced him to let me keep it for a while." Joe put down his baseball, took out the 9mm bullets he'd removed from Patel's gun and poured them onto his desk.

"I hope you didn't hurt him." Kat knew that when Joe used a phrase like "I convinced him" it usually meant there had been trouble. "He seemed so frail."

Annoyed at her reaction, he frowned as he looked up at her. "I tried not to hurt him, but he was pointing a gun at me."

"So, if he's not coming this morning, when is he coming?"

"I told him I'd leave a message at his hotel later this week about when we could meet."

Kat jotted down a reminder to contact Patel in her pad before picking up the rubber ball Joe had gotten from the dead Greek. "What's so special about this?"

"I'm not sure. Patel was trying to feed me some bull about it being an ancient artifact from India that was over a thousand years old."

"How do you know it isn't?"

"If it was that old it would be made of unprocessed natural rubber which is white. Plus, look how perfectly round it is, clearly this was machine made. After you make the copies I'm going to take the original over to Marty. I'm guessing those symbols are a code, and you know how much Marty likes a puzzle. What time is Mickey coming in today?"

"He'll be in sometime after three."

It was nearly three years ago that the young red headed Irish kid with big ears, a face full of freckles, and a boyish grin had gone door to door in the Reliance Building looking for work. For some reason that Kat could never understand, Joe had taken an instant liking to the him – something she had never seen him do before, or since. Mickey was the oldest of four and had quit school when his father died to help support his family. Joe agreed to pay him four bucks a week to be the office "runner". He also convinced Father Frank to go to bat for him at De La Salle, an all-boys Catholic high school over on South Wabash in the Douglas section of town. So now, thanks to Joe, Mickey would graduate from high school this spring.

"Patel is staying at the Congress Hotel, and I think Mickey has a friend that works as a bell hop over there. Ask him if he can have his pal keep an eye on our client. Usual stuff, comings, goings, visitors, that sort of thing. Tell him there's a duce in it for his friend."

Joe snuffed out the butt of his Chesterfield in an ashtray on his desk. He got up from his chair, grabbed his hat and coat, tucking the copy of the *Trib* that Kat had given him into his pocket. "Since I don't have to stick around for a meeting at ten, I might as well go see Walt. I probably won't get back until after lunch."

Kat called out as he was half way out the door. "Don't forget about the Steiner murder. Father Frank asked me to remind you, and you might want to have a look at today's *Trib* because they did an obit on him."

Joe felt like someone had let the air out of his tires as he shook his head in disgust. "I didn't forget, I wish I could, but I didn't." He was convinced that this case Frank had him chasing was a loser, but he was trapped and he could see no way out.

It was last Saturday afternoon when he got a message from Frank asking him to come over to the parish as soon as possible. When he arrived, he was surprised to see Miss Ella there as well.

"Hello, Joseph," she said with a warm smile before pressing a kiss on his cheek. As soon as he saw her, he knew that whatever it was Frank wanted, he'd been worried Joe wouldn't do it. That was the only reason he would have brought in Miss Ella – he needed the extra muscle. From his earliest memories of growing up at St. Jerome's there had always been Miss Ella. She had been a volunteer who worked three nights a week to cook and help with the cleaning. From a very young age he'd been assigned to assist her with those chores. She was kind and loving and, while Joe was growing up, she was the closest thing to a mother he had known. He also knew that she was an extremely determined woman who never took "no" for an answer.

Immediately after Miss Ella greeted him, Father Frank introduced Mrs. Sofia Porcini, a local member of his parish. The middle aged woman sobbed and in a thick Italian accent begged for his help. "Mrs. Porcini's son Torre was arrested today," explained Frank. "He's accused of robbing and killing Fritz Steiner, the city's chief engineer, late Friday night."

"My Torre's a good boy," cried his mother, "he never do nothing like this." As Joe listened to the woman's plea, he wished he had a nickel for every time some parent had told him that their hoodlum kid was a good boy. He imagined somewhere Al Capone's mother was proudly telling anyone who would listen that her son was a good boy.

"I'll be straight with you, Joe," said the priest. "The boy's been in some trouble before."

"Wow, that's a shock," Joe replied sarcastically.

Frank was used to Joe's snide comments and ignored his remark. "But it's all been kids' stuff."

"Maybe he's all grown up, Frank," he replied warily.

"But my Torre he's a good boy," repeated his mother. "He would never do what the polizia are saying."

Joe pulled the priest aside and spoke in a hushed tone. "Look, Frank," he began, his frustration clear in his voice. "You have me look into these kinds of cases all the time, and the only thing I ever prove is that the kids are guilty." There were only three people in the world who could intimidate Joe and as one of them stepped back from the discussion another stepped forward.

Miss Ella had a soft, warm face and an engaging personality that masked an iron will that lay just below the surface. She had been quite thin in her younger days, but middle age coupled with the success of her laundry business had conspired to add a few pounds. She was five foot four inches tall with straightened black shoulder length hair that was now laced with streaks of gray. "Joseph," she began, "I have known Mrs. Porcini for over twenty-five years. The two of us have gotten down on our hands and knees night after night and scrubbed the church floor together. I am not going to sit by while this dear lady's only child is railroaded into prison."

"I'm sure he won't be railroaded, Miss Ella," interjected Joe feebly.

"You and I both know how the police operate. Once they've arrested someone they'll stop investigating. This poor lady has no money for a lawyer, so her son won't stand a chance in court. Now I know you don't want to see this innocent young man go to prison simply because there was no one to help him, do you?"

"No ma'am," was his weak reply.

"Good. Then it's settled." And it was. As a first step he agreed to see how strong a case the police had.

Early Sunday afternoon Joe managed to catch up with Burt Callahan at the 1st Precinct over on Harrison and Clark, in the Loop. Callahan, the detective assigned to investigate the Steiner murder, was a man of few words and even fewer thoughts. Joe had a long history with him, and none of it was good. Any time Callahan had the chance to stick it to him he would. Like many of his fellow officers, his convictions and morals could easily be set aside for a slight fee. After Joe slipped him a fin he was happy to sum up the facts of the case.

CHAPTER 2 - MONDAY

Fritz Steiner, the city's chief engineer, was found dead in an alley near the corner of Randolph and Canal streets, just a few blocks east of Haymarket Square. He'd been stabbed twice and a young man had been spotted running away from the murder scene. There were no eyewitnesses to the actual crime, and none of the people who lived nearby heard anything, yet the case seemed fairly open and shut. Both the dead man's watch and wallet were stolen. The police found the wallet on Torre Porcini when he was busted. The engineer's watch had been pawned at a shop nearby and the pawnbroker identified Torre as the one who had hocked it. When the cops picked him up Torre had a knife on him, which they believed was the murder weapon. The final nail in the coffin was that two eyewitnesses identified the kid as the one they saw running down Randolph and away from Canal Street just before the body was discovered.

The building that housed the Coroner's Office was attached to the Cook County morgue in the Hospital District, west of the Loop. It was late morning and still cold and windy when Joe parked his roadster next to the old two-story brick building on Polk Street. From the outside the building looked more like a warehouse than a morgue. Joe entered through the main entrance on Wood Street. Then he walked through the sterile cream-colored hallways paved with white linoleum, towards a small interior office with a name plate identifying its occupant as Dr. Walter Dorfman. Walt had been with the coroner's office for five years, but his relationship with Joe went back to their days at St. Jerome's Orphanage.

Joe poked his head inside the open office door. His friend was huddled over his desk, reading a report while a Lucky Strike hung precariously from his lower lip. "You got a minute?" he asked.

Walt put down his fountain pen and gave his visitor a half-hearted smile, followed by a heavy sigh. Joe knew what was bothering him, he'd been dating Jodie Reynolds for over eighteen months and last weekend he finally went up to Lake George to meet her family. Undoubtedly, Walt wanted him to ask about the weekend, but the last thing Joe wanted to do this morning, or any morning, was listen to someone talk about their love life. He was never comfortable discussing feelings, whether they were his or someone else's. As he stood in the doorway, he tried to think of a way to get out of the inevitable conversation. When Walt gave off another heavy sigh, Joe realized he was trapped. Reluctantly, he asked, "How was your weekend?"

"Ok, I guess, but I felt I was being shown like a prize bull at the state fair. They brought out the whole Reynolds clan to meet me and let me tell you there are a lot of 'em. I counted at least sixty people."

"I'm sure they all loved you." Joe was hoping that they had now covered the subject and he could steer the conversation towards the reason for his visit.

Walt sighed yet again. "I think Jodie's father thought I was there to ask for her hand." He shook his head. "It got a bit awkward towards the end when he realized I wasn't."

"I thought you did want to marry her?"

"I guess so. Sure …," he replied, "but I wasn't ready to ask him about it. Can we not talk about marriage? It's making my palms sweat. Let's change the subject." It didn't take much to make Walt sweat. At five foot nine, he was very heavy set with short straight black hair, dark brown eyes, and an olive complexion. He had a thick mustache that curled down slightly on both sides of his mouth and a perpetual five o'clock shadow. When he was in his last year at the orphanage, he weighed about one hundred and seventy pounds. Every year since he'd left, he'd put on a few extra pounds, so that today he weighed close to two hundred and sixty.

"Alright," agreed Joe, relieved that he didn't have to talk any more about Walt's personal problems. "You have any dead Greek sailors staying with you?"

"Well, I did a Greek sailor earlier today," Walt mumbled through the cigarette still perched upon his lower lip. Then he paused and looked nervously at his friend. "Wait … that didn't come out right."

Joe gave a slight smirk. "Can you let me see him?"

"They wheeled him back after I finished, let me check the 'guest list' and see where they put him. The guy's name was Kyranos, right?"

"Yeah, that's him."

Walt scanned the list and found him on the second page. "Right, here he is. Drawer C3." He stubbed out the remnants of his cigarette and led Joe out of the office. They walked down a long hall to the refrigerated storage area known as the "cooler". Inside, the temperature was kept at about forty-five degrees. This was warmer than the individual storage drawers, but still too cold to stay in for any length of time without a coat. Along the entire far wall were rows of small wooden doors with stainless steel hinges and latches. Letters ran horizontally across the top and numbers ran vertically down the sides so that each individual cooler drawer had an address corresponding to a number and letter.

"Here we go," Walt said, as he opened a drawer and rolled out a slab with a body covered in a white sheet. He took the clipboard that was attached to the gurney and pulled back the sheet. "Here's your dead Greek." Joe took a close look the man's features and confirmed that it was the same man he had met down at the docks last Friday night.

"Looks like your pal here was shot four times from a distance of about fifteen to twenty feet," observed Walt. "He was hit by four .45 caliber slugs, one to the chest, one grazed his head, and one minor wound in each arm. The one in the chest was the fatal shot, the others didn't even bleed much."

"How many shots were fired in total?"

"Sixteen. At least that's how many shell casing they recovered at the scene."

"Wait … someone was throwing that much lead from just twenty feet with only one real hit!" Joe said in amazement. "Could there have been two shooters?"

"It's hard to believe you could find two guys who were both such terrible shots. If it was two shooters, based on the angle that the shots were fired from, they would have to have been standing shoulder to shoulder. I think it's far more likely there was just one shooter firing two .45 caliber pistols."

"Blazing away with a piece in each hand?" Joe shook his head in disbelief. "Who shot this guy … Tom Mix?"

"Doubt it, I've heard Mix is a much better shot. One thing's clear, whoever shot him couldn't hit water if he fell out of a boat."

"You sure it was just two guns that fired all those bullets?"

"It sure looks like it, but give me a little more time and I should be able to answer that question for certain. I have a few tests I want to run."

"Was he robbed?"

"He was definitely searched," replied Walt. "You can see from these crime-scene photos that he was flying some Hoover Flags." Joe examined the photos that were attached to the clipboard and could see the victim's turned out pockets. "But it doesn't appear to be a robbery," continued Walt, "he was still wearing a wrist watch and a signet ring when they found him. It seems likely someone was looking for something." Walt then glanced over at his friend. "You have any idea what it was?"

"Possibly."

Walt pulled the sheet over the dead Greek and pushed him back into the wall. "Anything else I can help you with?" he asked, as he closed the cooler door.

"Well, now that you mention it, I'm working on another case and I think the victim is one of your 'guests'."

"You're a busy boy."

"Do you have the autopsy results for the dead city engineer, Fritz Steiner?"

Walt looked through his list. "That autopsy is being handled by Tony Palletti."

"I thought you said he didn't know shit from Shinola?" said Joe, surprised.

"He doesn't."

"Then do me a favor and take a look at both Palletti's report and the body, will ya?"

Walt glanced at the "guest list" and then checked the hallway to make sure they were alone. "Ok, but we'll have to be quick about it. There'll be hell to pay if I'm caught checking Palletti's work."

The two men walked over to the drawer labeled G4 and Walt unlatched the wooden door, pulled the slab out and reviewed the autopsy notes on the clipboard. As his friend studied the chart, Joe pulled back the sheet. "This all looks pretty straightforward," said Walt, alternating between reading the chart and examining the dead man. "The cause of death was a pair of knife wounds that entered just below the ribs. Palletti may be a twit, but even he couldn't mess that up. The guy died from one of the stab wounds. I can't be certain which one was the actual cause of death, but either by itself would have been sufficient to kill him. Whoever did this either knew how to handle a knife or just got lucky. Either way, it was two quick thrusts just under the rib cage into the heart with a long thin blade."

"Is there anything else in the case notes that sticks out?" Joe asked.

Walt studied the chart and the body more carefully, referring back to the autopsy notes several times. "According to the report, the killer was left handed. Based on the angle of these wounds the killer must have thrust the knife twice on the right side of the body like this." Walt demonstrated, using Joe as the victim. "From what I see here, I'd have to agree." Walt slid the body back into the cooler and the two men walked back along the linoleum floor towards Walt's office.

"Thanks for the help."

"Happy to be of service," Walt replied, as he lit another cigarette.

Joe moved towards the main entrance, but stopped when he heard Walt give out yet another deep sigh. He turned back to the office, took out one of his Chesterfields, lit up and took a pull. "You know you'll never find anyone else as good for you as Jodie," he said and then slowly blew out a stream of smoke. "Sometimes you just have to stop thinking with your head and use your heart." Joe's words hung in the air for a moment before he added, "I'll see you around."

Walt took a drag from his cigarette as he watched his friend leave and smiled. He did love Jodie, he thought to himself, and he really did want to spend the rest of his life with her. Maybe it was time to take the plunge.

It was just before lunch when Joe arrived at the corner of California and 30th streets in South Lawndale and parked his Ford in the visitor's lot of the Cook County Jail. It was an imposing structure with just a few windows, and even fewer doors. It took him fifteen minutes to go through the entry process and then another twenty minutes before Torre Porcini was finally brought into the cavernous visitor's hall. There were long rows of tables with benches on both sides, and one of the guards pointed to where the two of them should sit. During the first few minutes their discussion was pointless as Torre tried to act tough and refused to answer questions, but when Joe got up to leave the kid cracked.

"I didn't do it, Mr. Lorde. I swear ta ya I didn't kill the guy. The bulls are trying ta pin it on me, but I'm innocent," he insisted.

"Everyone in this joint is innocent, kid, ya haven't figured that out yet?" Joe replied in a sarcastic tone. "Ya say ya didn't kill the guy. Fine, but ya gotta level with me and tell me what did happen."

The young man hesitated and then said, "I was walking along Canal Street and I looks down this alley and I sees this guy laying there not moving. I says ta him, 'hey mister, you ok', but he doesn't answer so I goes over ta him and I sees he's all dead and stuff. So I scram outa there. I didn't take anything I swear."

"Look kid," Joe was clearly impatient with his client. "That line may play with your ma and the padre, but ya go ta a judge and jury with that malarkey and ya might as well hand them the rope ta hang ya. Now they gotta witness that swears ya pawned the watch and there's cops that'll swear ya had the dead guy's wallet on ya when they arrested ya. I'll give ya one last chance ta be square with me but if ya don't come clean I'm outta here."

"Ok, ok, I lifted the stiff's wallet 'n watch," admitted Torre, who was now visibly scared. "Look the guy was dead – I figured he didn't need 'em anyhow. It was easy dough. I'm being square with ya, all I did was take the stuff. I never killed nobody. Ya gotta believe me, I'm a patsy," he pleaded.

"Look, you've been lying ta me so much you're gonna have ta do more Hail Mary's than Judas Iscariot," Joe said. "Why should I believe ya now?"

"Cause I'm telling ya the truth." Torre bowed his head and after several seconds he added in a hushed voice, "and if ya don't help me no one will."

Joe took out a pack of Chesterfields from his coat pocket and quickly tossed it at the unsuspecting kid. Torre instinctively reached out and caught the pack with his left hand. Joe shook his head and motioned for the kid to throw it back, which he did again using his left hand. Joe continued to stare at the young man for several more seconds until finally he let out a sigh and left the visitor's hall.

Heading back to his car he had a nasty feeling in the pit of his stomach – the kind he always got when he had to break bad news to Frank. But this time it was going to be worse, because this time he had to face Miss Ella too.

Afternoon

CHAPTER 2 - MONDAY

When Joe arrived back at his office Kat was still working on making the copies of Patel's rubber ball. She had a table top radio positioned on a small stand just behind her desk, and he could hear muffled voices coming from the speaker. It wasn't music and it didn't sound like the news either. "What are you listening to?"

"It's a radio program called 'Day Dreams'," she replied as she continued to work on the ball. "It's a daily drama, like one of those new radio serials that play in the evenings, but it comes on in the early afternoon."

"I thought you wanted that radio to listen to music and news."

"I do, but I like to catch up on my show every day, its only on for fifteen minutes. I have one of the balls done," she added with a smile and happy to change the subject. "But the other one will take me at least another hour."

"I need the real one," said Joe. "I want to get it over to the professor this afternoon." He took the original off Kat's desk. Then leaned over and examined the copy she'd already finished. "This one dry?" he asked.

"Not completely, so be careful with it."

He picked up the copy and compared it to the ball he'd gotten from the dead Greek. The original was definitely heavier, a bit smaller and its markings were raised, but from a distance he thought it might just fool someone. As he was studying the two balls, Sid Schacter walked into the office.

Joe first ran into Sid a few months after he started his detective agency. Like all who routinely passed him lying semiconscious in an alley, Joe had assumed the old guy was just another bum. For as long as anyone could remember Sid had been a drunk who hung around the Cook County Courthouse. Joe would have never given the old rummy a second thought if one afternoon he hadn't spotted one of the courthouse lawyers giving him some money in exchange for a set of papers. About a week later he witnessed another attorney do the same thing. His perpetual curiosity led him to ask around and it was Billie Breslau, a *Trib* reporter, who told him the story. According to Billie, twenty-five years earlier Sid had been an excellent young lawyer. Then tragedy struck when both his wife and baby died during childbirth. A local beat cop heard the news and made a wisecrack about there being "two less kikes in the neighborhood". Sid had been within earshot and clocked him with a hard right. He was disbarred and spent two years in jail. When he was released he slid into a bottle on skid row, but still managed to earn some drinking money by drafting appeals and motions for a number of lawyers in town.

He stood just five foot five and weighing in at one hundred and forty pounds, but throughout his life he'd maintained a determined and combative nature. When Joe's agency started getting more business than it could handle, he offered Sid a job as an investigator, but on the condition that he'd give up the sauce. Joe hadn't really expected that a guy who'd spent twenty years inside a bottle would be able to crawl out, but he'd wanted to give him a chance. At first Sid suffered terribly from the DT's and the shakes, but he was determined not to squander this opportunity. Over the past four years he'd fallen off the wagon only three times, and always on the same day, February 19th, the anniversary of the death of his wife and child.

"Hey boss, I checked out the witnesses on the Steiner killing, like ya asked." As Sid spoke, Joe put the balls down and turned towards his investigator, who was now in his usual spot on the couch opposite Kat's desk.

"And?"

"Well, I talked to the pawn broker and he was positive that the kid he saw in the lineup Saturday afternoon was the same one who pawned the watch in his shop Saturday morning."

"What about the two eyewitnesses who saw him run away from the scene?"

"I've only been able to track down one of 'em so far," Sid explained. "But he told me he had no trouble picking the kid out of the lineup." Joe shook his head, exasperated by the prospect of telling Frank and Miss Ella that yet another teenage hood would be lucky if he ended up spending the next thirty years in prison.

Kat could sense that was Joe disheartened. Hoping there was some better news she asked, "Did Walter have any information about the late Mr. Steiner?"

"Yeah," Joe replied. "It seems that Steiner was killed by two thrusts just under the ribs." Joe pulled Sid up from the couch. "The killer was standing in front of Steiner and shoved the knife in like this, with two quick jabs," he explained, as he demonstrated using his retracted stiletto on Sid. "Which means the killer was left handed, and unfortunately the kid is left handed as well."

"Well, I guess that pretty much closes this one," said Kat sadly. "Hopefully his age will keep him from getting the chair. Did he confess about the wallet and watch he stole?"

"Yeah, but he swears he found Steiner dead in the alley and stole the stuff from a stiff."

The room fell silent for a minute but then Sid spoke up, "It's kind of odd don't you think?"

"What's odd?" replied Kat.

"There were people living all around that alley and you would have thought that if someone was being mugged he would have called out for help or made some kind of noise. According to the cops, no one heard a thing. If Walt's right, and Steiner was stabbed on the right side of his body by a left handed killer," continued Sid, "he would have seen his killer coming at him. So why didn't he shout or make any noise before he was stabbed?"

An idea popped into Joe's head, and he turned towards Sid, "Let's try recreating that attack again." Sid moved to the far right of the office and slowly crossed the room. As he did, Joe stepped behind him and put his left hand over his investigator's mouth. He yanked him back, stabbing him twice, but this time, because he was behind Sid, the thrusts came from his right hand.

"Quick and clean," observed Sid as Joe released him. "And since the killer was standing behind his victim, he could use his right hand to stab Steiner and his left to cover the guy's mouth. That would explain why no one heard anything. If the kid's left handed he couldn't have done it. You'd have to be right handed to kill someone like that."

"But the kid did take the watch and wallet off Steiner's body," said Kat, "which means Steiner didn't die in a robbery. He was killed for another reason."

"So if the kid didn't do it, and it wasn't robbery, who killed him and why?" asked Joe. The room went quiet again as all three tried to figure out a scenario that fit the facts.

Eventually Joe turned to Kat. "I'm going out for a while," he said. "I need to talk to Marty about this rubber ball. If there's a code on it, I'll bet he can crack it."

"What do you want me to do with this other copy I'm making?" she asked, as Joe was leaving the office. "Should I try and finish it?"

"Yeah, use the first copy as a guide to finish the second. The symbols are so hard to read I doubt you have to be all that accurate." Then he added, "When you're done, keep them both out of sight."

"What do ya want me to do, boss?" asked Sid.

"See if you can track down that last witness on this Steiner murder. We might as well touch 'em all."

The sun was beginning to peek through the clouds as Joe parked his car on 59th Street, south of the University of Chicago campus. The wind was still coming out of the North, which meant the smell of the Stock Yards was faint but noticeable as he entered the University's Central Quad. In the center of the Quad, Joe noticed a crude stage had been erected on the lawn. Above the stage was a banner that read "Peace Pledge". Several hundred students were gathered in front of the stage, listening intently to a young co-ed as she began to speak. Joe stopped well short of the crowd and stared at her. With strawberry blonde hair, white skin, and soft faded freckles, she radiated beauty from the stage. She had an inviting smile and a pure sweet voice that carried easily across the Quad and captivated her audience.

"It's your duty to say 'no' to war," cried the co-ed. "We have all gathered here today to send a message to the corrupt governments of the world that we will no longer fight in their imperialist wars of conquest and aggression. Mankind has progressed beyond war and this 'Peace Pledge' will ensure that the senseless slaughter of the last war will never be repeated." The young woman began to lead the crowd in an oath never to fight in a war. As the crowd joined her, Joe gazed at the beautiful co-ed and was struck by how closely she resembled his former fiancée, Wendy. It wasn't simply her looks that reminded him of her. It was also her smile, her voice, and the way her beautiful shoulder length hair fell in soft curls around her face. There were so many similarities it was startling.

Before Wendy, Joe had never believed in love. Sure, he believed that a mother could love her child, and someone could love a puppy. He thought "romantic" love, however, was nonsense. All of his previous relationships with women had centered around lust. He'd never come across anyone or any reason that made him doubt his conviction that the concept of romantic love was a fairy tale. He firmly believed that it had been concocted over the centuries by writers, dreamers, and fools. The moment he laid eyes on Wendy everything stopped. When she looked back at him and smiled, all that he thought he knew about love and life was altered forever. As he got to know her, he discovered so many things about her that he found appealing – the way she walked, her laugh, the smell of her hair, the touch of her hand, and her gorgeous green eyes. Wendy cast a spell over him that he was powerless to resist. When he realized that she cared for him too it created a sea of emotions within him that he hadn't known he was capable of feeling and had no idea how to control.

Joe had returned from Paris so that he could come to terms with his past. Once he'd faced it, he had always intended to go back. He loved the "City of Light" and felt at home there. He'd never planned on staying in Chicago but then he'd never planned on falling in love either. Love changed everything and suddenly he yearned for the things she wanted. Marriage, a home and children, all things he had never imagined for himself. For a short while he tried to control the changes that were sweeping over him. After the first time they made love, however, he willingly surrendered his heart to her, and to his new life. When she said that she'd marry him he was enveloped by a feeling of joy and contentment the likes of which he had never known.

Two weeks before their wedding Joe finally told Wendy about how he'd ended up at St. Jerome's Orphanage. At first she seemed to accept it, but three days later she walked out on him. He nearly drowned in the wave of despair that swept over him, and there had been times when he felt certain that he would never come up for air. It had been three years now since she'd left, and he could no longer remember the last sleepless night he'd had. As he stood in the Quad watching the young woman on the stage, he was surprised that her intense resemblance to Wendy didn't dredge up the pain of her leaving. Instead, it just brought a smile to his face.

When the crowd finished the Peace Pledge they erupted into applause. As the young woman descended the platform, another student quickly took the stage and began to speak. Joe's eyes followed the co-ed as she moved through the crowd towards a tall, thin, good looking man in his late thirties or early forties. The man was dressed like a typical professor with a worn tweed coat, a white wide brimmed fedora hat, and a cane he clearly didn't need but carried for effect. The co-ed approached him and he whispered something to her. She giggled her response, kissed him on the cheek, and headed North across the Quad towards Rosenwald Hall.

Joe walked away from the rally and headed south to Ryerson Hall. When he arrived, he climbed the front steps and entered the small wood-paneled lobby. He quickly glanced at the building directory before ascending the large open staircase to the third floor.

Martin Russell was the newest associate professor of mathematics at the University of Chicago. Marty had served with Joe during the war, but he had not been part of the original contingent that landed in France. He was a replacement who had arrived later in the year. Typically, veterans ignored replacements because they tended to get killed within a couple of weeks of showing up. At six foot five and two hundred and twenty pounds Marty was hard to ignore. As a young man in combat, his body had been all muscle. Some of the men in the unit had tried to nickname him "Moose". Marty made it clear that he didn't like the name and most agreed it was wise to respect his wishes on the subject. Joe and his two pals Chance and Rick had taken a liking to the replacement and decided to look after him. Marty often told friends that he wouldn't have lasted a week at the front without their help.

"What do you think?" Marty asked, with a silly grin on his face, waving his arms around to show Joe his new office. He'd worked hard to get where he was, and Joe knew how much pride he took in becoming an associate professor at the university.

Joe glanced around his friend's office, clearly pleased for his success. "Pretty impressive."

"It's just an associate position," said Marty, still grinning. "There's a long way to go before I earn a full professorship and then of course, there's a little thing they call 'tenure'."

"Eve must be pleased." After mathematics, Eve was the other great love of Marty's life. While math had given him purpose, it was Eve who had given him love, a home and three children.

CHAPTER 2 – MONDAY

"She is, but she's upset at you because you said you'd come to dinner last week and then canceled ... again."

"Sorry about that but duty called."

"So, are you going to tell me why you're here?" Marty knew that Joe hated small talk and always liked getting to the point.

He tossed him the rubber ball he had gotten from the Greek sailor. "I have a puzzle for you."

Marty held it up to his desk lamp and began his examination. "It looks like a plain rubber ball."

"That was my first thought as well," agreed Joe, "but someone might have been killed for it last Friday, and this morning I had a guy stick a gun in my face trying to get it. So the question is, what's so special about this ball?"

"It certainly doesn't seem remarkable. What are these markings inside the center band?"

"I think they may be some kind of code."

"A code? Interesting." Marty reached into his desk and pulled out a magnifying glass. "Did you notice that some of these markings are raised quite a bit while others are nearly flush?" he asked as he examined the ball closely. "You say someone might have been killed over this?"

"A sailor that came in to the Navy Pier on Friday," replied Joe. "Look, I gotta to run. You want to see if you can make any sense out of those markings?"

"Sure, let me work on it for a while. I'll ring you later and let you know if I find anything."

"Thanks. And tell Eve I'm sorry I missed dinner."

"No, you're not," said Marty, without looking up from his examination of the ball, "but I'll tell her you were anyhow."

Joe walked to the door, then turned back and asked, "Did you get a chance to speak to the Dean about Mickey?"

"Sure did." Marty looked up from the ball and continued, "The Dean says he's reviewed the kid's application and the university is going to offer him a scholarship, but it's only going to cover tuition, nothing else."

"That's great, Marty, thanks. I owe you one."

"You don't owe me anything. The Dean had already decided to give Mickey the scholarship before I had the chance to speak to him. He told me that he had never seen a scholarship kid with so many strong recommendations. His exact words were 'Mickey had more fire power behind him than the Maginot Line'. You want to let him know he's in?"

"Could you have the school send him a letter? I'd prefer he didn't know I was involved."

"The kid should know you went to bat for him," said Marty, not surprised by Joe's response.

"Nah, he'll feel better about it if he thinks he did without any help."

"Ok, Joe, if that's how you want to play it. Do you know how he's going to pay for his books and living expenses?"

"Not yet, but I'll figure something out."

Retracing his steps back down to the lobby, Joe found a pay phone, dropped in a nickel and placed a call to the office. "You got anything for me, Kat?"

"Mr. Gibbs' office phoned and he wants you to stop by first thing tomorrow," she replied. "He wanted to know if 8:30 was ok."

"Tell him 8:30 is fine. Did his secretary say why he wanted to meet?"

"No, but my guess is he wants to talk about the bill we just sent them."

Joe really hated billing issues. It was by far the worst part of the job. He would rather stare down a gang of angry hoods than face one billing issue. "Ok," he sighed. "Anything else?"

"No, that's it. Where are you off to?"

"According to the *Trib*, there's a viewing at the Steiner home this afternoon. I'm going to drop by and pay my respects to the widow. I'm hoping I'll get the chance to talk to her about her husband and find out if anyone might have had a reason to kill him. It's a long shot but it's worth a try."

Joe left Ryerson Hall and headed back across the Quad. The Peace Pledge rally was still underway, so he stopped well short of the crowd to see if he could spot the young co-ed he'd seen earlier. When he didn't see her, he turned to leave. As he turned he noticed an elderly woman had moved up next to him. She looked about seventy and was short in stature. She had a black broad brimmed hat atop gray hair that had been pulled back into a bun, and wore a simple long black dress, which had been her trademark for decades.

"It's a beautiful sentiment, don't you think?" said the woman with a smile.

Joe looked over at her and uncharacteristically returned her smile. "Peace is a wonderful concept," he agreed. "How are you, Miss Addams?"

"I'm fine, Joseph," she answered, still smiling. Jane Addams had been a force in and around the Chicago area for almost fifty years. Her accomplishments were so numerous that it was difficult to remember them all. Perhaps her most enduring legacy was as a founder of Hull House, one of the country's first settlement houses. Alone, pregnant and scared, Joe's mother had found shelter at Hull House. It was there, a few months later while taking a night class, that she'd gone into labor and given birth. Joe had never heard the story until Frank had told him on the night he turned seventeen. He hadn't known anything about his family or that it had been Jane Addams who had brought him from Hull House to the orphanage when he was just a few days old. All through his childhood, Jane had been there for him and, as with Miss Ella and Father Frank, there wasn't anything he wouldn't do for her.

"So what brings you down here?" he asked.

"I heard about this rally, and I knew I had to come down and give my support."

"You don't think they're being a touch naïve?"

Jane turned to him and smiled. "Naïve? Well, maybe, but then that's what they said when we first started fighting for a woman's right to vote. I don't think any war is worth the price, and I'm sure you'd agree that 'The Great War' as they're calling it now, was anything but 'Great'." Jane had been a pacifist all her life, and had been deeply upset when she learned that Joe had enlisted in the army.

"I'm sure it doesn't hurt their cause to have a winner of the Nobel Peace Prize attend their rally," he observed.

"I'm still not sure why they felt I deserved that," she said modestly. "By the way, I never had the chance to thank you properly for your assistance with that problem last month."

"I was happy to help." It had taken Joe over a week to track down the runaway kids, but he'd managed to bring them all back safely.

"I'm afraid I've lost track of all the times I've asked for your help over the years, and I've never had the chance to pay you. Surely you must be owed something, even if it's just to reimburse you for your expenses."

"No, Miss Addams," he replied with a half smile and a tip of his hat. "I'm still trying to repay my debt to you."

As he finished his sentence, a tall, neatly dressed young man came over to Jane and held out his arm. "I'm afraid you'll have to excuse me, dear boy," she said as she took the young man's arm, "but I believe I'm supposed to speak now." She seemed very frail as she clung to the student's arm. She took a step with his assistance, then stopped and turned back towards Joe. "Now, I expect you to come by sometime soon. It's been far too long since your last visit and I do so enjoy our chats."

"I'll try and come by sometime next week." He bent down and kissed the old woman's cheek. "And thanks for writing that recommendation letter to the Dean for me."

"Nonsense," she replied with a smile. "I was happy to help your young man."

Joe watched as she was escorted to the stage, showing a tremendous contrast between strength of will and frailty of body. He examined the young men who'd gathered around the stage and noticed that they were all dressed in a similar manner. It was as if they were wearing some kind of uniform, right down to the same type of brown shoes. He realized that if Mickey was going to fit in he would have to dress accordingly, and that would cost money.

Joe's next stop was up in Lincoln Park, at a German enclave in the city's North Side. These ethnic neighborhoods were a great example of what made Chicago ... Chicago. There were enclaves for just about every race and culture randomly scattered all through the area. In fact the city was nothing more than a patchwork of small ethnic communities, with many having their own churches, newspapers, banks, social clubs, gangs, grocery stores, bakeries, and butcher shops.

It was late in the afternoon by the time he pulled up to the Steiner home – a tall, narrow, three-story, red brick house on North Birling Street. As he was walking in he saw the *Trib* reporter Billie Breslau walking out. Both tipped their hats as a sign of recognition when they passed.

The two hours he ended up spending at Frau Steiner's turned out to be of minimal value. At first, she'd declined to talk with him but when he began to speak in German she quickly warmed up. She then began flooding their conversation with detailed accounts of her husband's gardening exploits. When it was over, Joe had learned only two bits of useful information. The first was that her husband was responsible for overseeing the construction of the new World's Fair site. While he didn't talk much about his work she could tell that he was very upset about something. She assumed it involved the local trade unions and their demand for more jobs. The second bit of information was that she and her husband had been kicked out of the local German/American Club. They had belonged to the club for twenty-five years, but had fought the club's merger with the Nazi controlled Friends of Germany. For that they had been expelled.

Evening

It was well past 7:30 when Joe stepped out of Berghoff's on Adams Street in the Loop and headed south down Wabash. Before prohibition Berghoff's was known for serving good beer and mediocre food. Now they were known for serving good food and Near-Beer, which, at its best, never quite rose to the level of mediocrity. Joe continued down Wabash, made a left at Van Buren, and after half a block took another left into a grimy alley. As he entered, the darkness obscured everything in front of him. The only thing he could hear were his own footsteps and the faint sound of music off in the distance. He walked slowly down the alley, allowing his eyes to adjust to the darkness. As they did, he spotted a large dark figure standing about twenty-five yards away. The glow of the man's cigarette was the only visible light. The figure quickly reacted to Joe's presence by shifting his position so that he blocked the doorway that was directly behind him. When Joe approached, the man he gave him the once over, smiled and stepped aside. Upon entering the Friar's Club, Joe was immediately enveloped by its sights, smells and sounds. The joint wasn't very big, just a dimly lit room with a badly worn wood floor, a long bar at the back, and a small stage in front. The warm stagnant air was made up of a blueish-gray cigarette fog mixed with the smell of booze and sweat. The joint's atmosphere, however, was electrified by the sounds coming from the stage. There was no doubt about it, the Friar's Club was a real speakeasy, not a blind pig, and it served up an honest drink and the best jazz in town.

There was never a crowd on a Monday night, so Joe had his pick from several small tables off to the right of the stage. He sat down and tossed his hat and coat on an empty chair next to him. What made Mondays so special was that it was the night when virtually all the other clubs in town were closed. Now, if you were a bartender, a waiter or a cigarette girl and your joint was closed, that meant you had the night off. But if you were a musician, you didn't want the night off, you wanted to play. So, if you were a jazz musician in Chicago on a Monday night, you jammed at the Friar's Club.

It was Sam who had first told him about Monday nights several years ago. Now, as he looked at the stage, Joe could see him playing piano as part of a quartet. The waitress stopped at Joe's table and served him a scotch. He hadn't ordered it, but the bartender had poured him one as soon as he saw him enter. Joe sipped his drink, took a long pull on his cigarette, and listened to Sam kick out. There was no doubt about it, the man could really tickle those ivories. He had a fantastic technique that produced a smooth sound. Joe could think of no better way to end a Monday than listening to him play.

CHAPTER THREE

TUESDAY

Money is like love; it kills slowly and painfully the one who hoards it, and enriches the one who turns it on his fellow man -Kahlil Gibran

As the sergeant blew his whistle for the first time, up and down the line the sound of hundreds of other whistles could be heard. Standing in the trench, on a cold gray morning in late October, Joe leaned against a crude wooden ladder, listening to the roar of the Allied shells landing several hundred yards in front of their position. When the barrage finally stopped an eerie stillness gripped the battlefield. That silence abruptly ended when the German machine guns opened up. The thought of tens of thousands of bullets rushing towards him sent a cold shiver down Joe's spine. To steady himself he looked over at the reassuring faces of his two friends and took a deep breath. Joe had met Chance and Rick on his first day at boot camp. The three of them quickly formed a friendship that had only grown stronger with time. Over the course of their six months at the front, they had saved each other's lives countless times and now trusted each other implicitly.

Joe felt a strong hand rested on his shoulder. He looked to his left, into the freckled face of his buddy Chance. "You ready to give 'em hell, Chicago?" yelled Chance, as the tracers whizzed just inches above his bright red hair.

"There are so many bullets, Chance," Joe replied, his voice calm but troubled. "I really hate bullets."

"Ah, come on, Joe, you know you're indestructible," he replied. The young Irishman's boyish grin and big ears forced a smile out of his friend.

"You two watch yourselves," warned Rick, who was now standing to Joe's right, holding his BAR. "You keep your heads down and keep moving forward." Rick's face was tense and his eyes showed determination. "This war is going to be over soon and it would be a hell of a shame to catch a bullet now. I'll see you both at the rendezvous point."

Suddenly the second whistle blew and a massive roar rose from the line as tens of thousands of men climbed out of the trenches and advanced on the German positions. In an instant, Joe found himself running through hundreds of yards of "No Man's Land" while machine bullets knocked the men around him down like bowling pins. Ignoring the carnage, he raced through the morning mist towards a large tree stump directly in front of the first German trench. This was the rendezvous point that the three of them had agreed to earlier. Joe smiled when he threw himself between his two friends who'd already taken cover at the base of the stump. Somehow, they'd managed to come through yet another charge across No Man's Land. Chance laughed and patted his friends on the back, and Rick gave them both a thumbs-up. The relief that had swept over Joe instantly turned to terror as he watched what happened next. Slowly, Chance poked his head up to get a better look at the German positions, and Joe screamed in horror as a bullet tore into his friend's skull, killing him instantly.

Morning

Joe sat on the edge of his bed, his heart racing. He was covered in a cold sweat and his throat was sore, which meant he'd been screaming in his sleep again. He sat quietly for several more minutes until his pulse and breathing finally slowed. He had been through nightmares about the war many times before, but the one with Chance was always the worst. Looking over at his clock, he noticed that it was already past seven, so he pulled himself away from his bed and dressed for work.

Chicagoland in May could have weather that was anything from snow showers to thunderstorms. Stepping out of his apartment building this morning, Joe was greeted by a cloudless sky, a fresh breeze and a warm spring sun on his face. Descending the building's granite steps, he tipped his hat to his neighbors before lighting a cigarette and heading for his morning meeting with Theo.

Theodore Gibbs was a partner at Ismay, Little & Burle, one of Chicago's most prestigious law firms. Their clientele were all well-heeled, and the cases Joe handled for them typically paid very well. He'd first met Theo in France a couple of months after the Armistice was signed in late '18. Joe and Rick were waiting for orders to be shipped home when Rick got into a fight with a drunk American officer who was trying to rape a young French girl. Unfortunately for Rick, the officer was sober enough to remember him and the next day he pressed charges. Since the US was still technically in a state of war, the punishment for assaulting an officer was death. Theo had been assigned as Rick's legal counsel, but despite his best efforts Rick's conviction was never in doubt. Fortunately, Rick's timely escape kept him from being shot, but Joe always respected Theo for how hard he'd fought to save his friend's life. After the war Theo became a partner at Ismay Little. When he heard that Joe had come back to Chicago and opened a detective agency, he contacted him to see if he'd do some work for his firm. Since then Joe had done quite a few jobs for Theo, and the two men had come to trust other a great deal.

It was 8:20 by the time he pulled up in front of the Carbide Building on Michigan Avenue, just south of the river. As he approached the entrance, he noticed a crowd had gathered around the Harris Bank building across the street. Banks in Chicago didn't open until ten, so he wasn't quite sure why so many had gathered so early.

Joe walked over to the lobby attendant, tilted his head towards the bank, and asked, "What gives?"

"It's a run on the bank," answered the attendant. "I got wind of it late yesterday and pulled my dough out just before they closed. If ya got money at Harris, ya better get it out now, while ya still can," he added. Runs like this one had closed over thirty banks in the Chicago area during the past year, and they seemed to be happening more frequently. Harris was always considered one of the strongest banks in town and it was hard to believe they were under pressure as well. Lately it felt as if the entire country was going to hell in a hand basket, and Joe wondered if it was ever going to end.

Walking through the large ornate lobby he headed to one of the building's six new automatic elevators. What made these elevators "automatic" was that there were no operators in the cabs. Instead, you simply pushed a button for the floor you wanted and the elevator went there all on its own. The first time Joe had ridden one he had been alone in the cab, which he found unsettling, but after using it several times he learned to appreciate the fact that the elevator wasn't going to drone on about the Cubs.

The law firm of Ismay, Little & Burle had its offices on the 23rd floor. Joe stepped off the elevator and checked his appearance in the reflection of the shiny brass doors. He was wearing his expensive gray English tailored suit because he knew that appearances were important to Theo's clients.

It was exactly 8:30 when he entered the office but Mary Simons, Theo's private secretary, asked him to wait for a moment because her boss wasn't quite ready. Joe took a seat across from her, picked up the morning paper from the table next to the chair, and began to skim the headlines.

Mary looked up from her desk and tried to make eye contact with the cute guy sitting a few feet away. Unfortunately, and just like the other times he'd come to Mr. Gibbs' office, he had his nose buried in a newspaper and wasn't looking up.

Mary's mother had always told her that it was a man's duty to find a job and a woman's duty to find a husband. Consequently, a woman was obliged, both to herself and her unborn children, to find the right man. Regrettably, a "smart match" wasn't always easy to come by and getting the wrong guy was the surest way to ruin a girl's life. Sadly, Mary had seen it happen all too often. Several of her girlfriends had settled for love without considering their husband's future prospects. They ended up paying the price later on. Mary was determined to make a smart match, love would be nice, but it was only one of several factors a girl had to consider. Mary was twenty-four and very attractive, with light brown hair, beautiful dark brown eyes and a knockout figure. She was the prettiest girl in her neighborhood, but was also the only one over twenty who wasn't married. While no one was using the term "old maid" just yet, her parents were starting to worry.

Upon coming to work at Ismay Little four years earlier, Mary's plan had been to catch a young lawyer. Over the past two years, however, she found herself drawn more and more to the tall, dark, good looking private detective sitting just a few feet away. Everything about him she found attractive. Even the scar above his left eye seemed to add to a look she found incredibly appealing. From her conversations with his secretary she'd learned that he was a great guy who was single. Based on the invoices Joe's agency had sent over for payment, she also knew he'd be a good provider. There was no doubt in her mind he'd be a smart match, and from the way he made her feel, she was certain she'd get love as part of the deal.

CHAPTER 3 - TUESDAY

Mary tried two more times to make eye contact, but after a couple of minutes decided that she couldn't keep Mr. Gibbs waiting any longer. She picked up the phone and pushed an unused button before saying, to no one, "Mr. Gibbs, I just wanted to remind you that Mr. Lorde is waiting." Glancing over at the private detective, she smiled and added, "Yes, sir, right away. Mr. Gibbs will see you now, Mr. Lorde."

Joe entered the spacious and well-appointed private office. As he did, Theo Gibbs rose from his desk and walked over to greet him. In his mid-forties and well dressed, Theo was tall, lanky, and sported a well groomed mustache. He also had thinning dark brown hair with a small bald spot towards the back of his head. Joe always thought the bald spot made him look a bit like a monk.

Joe had assumed that the purpose of their meeting was to discuss a large bill Kat had submitted, but if there was a problem with it, it wasn't mentioned. Instead Theo had something else he wanted to discuss. "Cyrus McNulty will most likely be dead within the week," he began, as he sat back down at his desk. Joe had, of course, heard of Cyrus McNulty, most everyone in the country had. He was the founder and chairman of International Auto. Up until '25 it had been called McNulty Auto, and through most of its history it had been a small manufacturer of cars and taxi cabs. All of that changed in '20 when Cyrus invented the first practical "Self Starter" for a car. Before Cyrus' invention, starting a car required hand-cranking, which was difficult, and sometimes even dangerous. Joe had almost broken his arm back in '28 when a crank he was using to start an old Model-T violently reversed direction after a backfire.

In the early twenties the income from Cyrus' starter began to surpass what he made from the sales of his cars. By '25 he decided to concentrate all his efforts on building starters for other car manufacturers. That's when McNulty Auto changed its name to International Auto. Within a few years half of the cars sold in North America had one of Cyrus' starters. As a result, he went from being a mere success to one of Chicago's wealthiest businessmen.

"I'm sorry to hear about Cyrus," replied Joe as he sat down, "but I'm sure you didn't ask me over here just to tell me that."

"No," admitted Theo. "It seems he has a slight problem, and he's going to need your help. You see, this law firm has represented Cyrus for many years, and we drew up his will. The problem I mentioned is that up until Sunday we were under the impression that he had only one heir – his son."

"Up until Sunday?" Joe asked skeptically.

"Yes. Sunday afternoon a young woman came forward claiming to be Cyrus' illegitimate daughter. She says her name is Emma O'Donnell. Coincidentally, O'Donnell was the surname of a young maid in the McNulty household about twenty-five years ago."

"So, let me get this straight," said Joe. "Cyrus is on his deathbed and by pure chance a young woman happens to come forward claiming to be his long lost daughter? That's a bit of stretch, don't you think?"

"That was my first thought as well, but as strange as it sounds, she might be legit. She has a birth certificate she only recently discovered that shows her father to be one "Cyrus McNulty from Chicago". She says her mother had always told her that her father was dead. When she found Cyrus' name on the certificate she decided to come to Chicago and look for him."

"Does Cyrus know if he fathered a child with the maid, or is he too far gone to be able to provide any information?" asked Joe.

"Cyrus is a very sick old man but, he's still alert and hasn't lost any of his mental faculties. He confirms that he did indeed have an affair with a housemaid back in '06. Her name was Maggie O'Donnell and the affair lasted for the better part of a year. Eventually his wife found out and forced him to end it. He told Maggie she would have to leave because his wife was going to ask for a divorce if she didn't. Cyrus gave her five hundred dollars to start over somewhere, which was a lot of money back then."

"It's a lot of money now," added Joe.

"After she left, he never heard from her again, but he did hear a few months later that she might have been pregnant. The birth certificate that I mentioned shows the young woman's mother was Margret O'Donnell from Fort Wayne, Indiana. That's where the maid was from, and where she returned to after she left Chicago. The date of birth fits the timeline as well. Cyrus also says that the girl is the spitting image of the maid."

"Is that it?"

"No, actually, there's quite a bit more," replied Theo. "Cyrus felt extremely guilty about sending the maid away. Seems he actually cared for the woman. His wife passed away three years ago, so he no longer has to worry about her feelings. Interestingly enough, his will does allow for additional heirs to be provided for. I asked him about this yesterday and he said he wanted to make sure that any future heir that came forward was protected. It seems he was thinking about Margret O'Donnell's child all along."

"Another thing you need to know is what will happen to his estate after he dies," continued Theo. "Cyrus made a lot of enemies, and not many people will mourn his death, not even his only son. I think his conscience has weighed heavily on him, so a few years ago he set up the trust and rewrote his will. Between you and me, I think he may be trying to buy his way into heaven. For whatever reason, he put virtually all his money, which is about ninety million, into a trust that benefits three local charities."

"Ninety million," repeated Joe, letting out a long low whistle. "Not quite Rockefeller, but pretty damn close. So if he's leaving all his dough to charity, then what exactly do his heirs get?"

"Well, to be precise," answered Theo, "he's already given his money to charity. Virtually all his assets were transferred to the trust right after it was set up two years ago. But if you're asking what's left for his heirs? They'll get the remaining assets that were left out of the trust. That would be things like the McNulty mansion and all the furnishings, the local bank account, his late wife's jewelry, the cars, the yacht in Newport, and a townhouse in New York. All totaled, it's worth just over a million, but that's a conservative estimate. It might turn out to be a lot more than that."

"Well, for most people a million bucks would be a fortune, but if you were expecting ninety million you might be just a bit upset."

"I'm willing to bet Cyrus' son, Vance, would agree with you," said Theo. "It's no secret that he's angry about the trust and feels that the money is rightfully his. Vance has been estranged from his father for many years. His mother's death only served to reinforce that separation. He moved out about five years ago, and now lives in the New York townhouse I mentioned. Throughout his life his mother indulged him, but his father was always disappointed in him. Cyrus has kept his son on an allowance. It's extremely generous, but I gather Vance deeply resents him for it."

"Does Vance know about this woman who claims to be his half-sister?"

"All he knows is that a woman has come forward claiming to be Cyrus' illegitimate daughter. Cyrus asked me not to discuss the matter with him, and so he's aware of no other details. I believe that Vance is refusing to acknowledge the woman in any way. He won't meet or even talk to her."

"So, if this woman's claim holds up, Vance will end up with a measly half a million dollars," said Joe.

"Yes, but that's not all he'll get," said Theo. "The heir becomes the chair of the McNulty Charitable Trust and is entitled to a yearly stipend of $65,000."

"So, not only does Vance fail to inherit $90 million, but he has to split the $1 million he thought was his, and also split the $65,000 a year salary from the trust?"

"Well, you're half right," corrected Theo. "He'll have to split the $1 million, but he won't have to split the $65,000 trust payment. If this young lady is found to be an heir, she'd become the co-chair of the trust and be entitled to the same yearly payment of $65,000."

"What exactly does this board do?"

"It has complete responsibility for the trust. Cyrus set up the initial investment and disposition strategies, but the board will oversee the performance. It will also have absolute discretion to make any changes or adjustments, as they see fit."

"So besides Vance, who else makes up this board?" asked Joe.

"There are three other members. One is appointed by each of the three charities that benefit from the trust. Each of these members has one vote on the board. The chairman of the trust's board will have two votes instead of just one. Cyrus specifically gave the heir two votes so that the board couldn't be deadlocked on any issue, there would always be an odd number of votes."

"The whole thing sounds fairly complex," said Joe.

"I suppose it does, the first time you go through it. But as trusts go, it's fairly simple. We've set up a lot more complex structures than this."

CHAPTER 3 - TUESDAY

"So, what do you need from me?"

"Cyrus needs us, or should I say you, to look into this girl's claim. If she turns out to be legit, then he wants to acknowledge her before he dies, so Vance can't try anything after his death."

Theo handed him a manila envelope. "Inside are some typed notes from my interview with both Cyrus and this girl who claims to be his daughter. There are also a couple of photos of her, as well as a photo of her birth certificate. Unfortunately, this is all the information I have. I assume our standard fee arrangement would be agreeable?" he asked, referring to their previous arrangement of thirty-five dollars a day, plus expenses. Joe nodded his head in agreement. "In addition, there's a bonus this time. Cyrus has authorized a payment of five hundred dollars if you can definitively prove or disprove the girl's claim. The bonus goes to a thousand if you can get the proof before the old man dies. He's expecting you at his estate up in Kenilworth sometime this morning. The address is in the envelope. I know it's short notice, but the old man doesn't have much time left."

"One final question," Joe said, as he looked up from the envelope. "Why me? Cyrus McNulty has more money than God, why not hire the Pinkertons?"

Theo was aware that many of the obscenely rich routinely used the Pinkertons as their personal army. Cyrus had used them back in '25, when his workers went out on strike. They'd blocked the plant's gates preventing anyone or anything from crossing their picket line. The police, who had been at the plant to maintain order, were suddenly ordered back, and the Pinkertons stepped up. The papers called what happened next the "Lake Michigan Massacre", because when the dust settled, there were seven dead, including two who were just boys.

"Not after what happened in '25," explained Theo.

Joe nodded in agreement and said sadly, "I remember that one. It was front page news, even in Paris."

"Have you ever heard the saying 'Behind every great fortune, there's a great crime'?" Theo asked. Joe nodded his head in response. "Well, Cyrus' great crime was how he broke that strike. The Pinkertons just did what they were told, but the old man always blamed them for what happened. I think by blaming them it was easier for him to live with himself. No," said Theo firmly, "Cyrus would never use the Pinkertons again."

"Okay, Theo, I'll get over to the McNulty estate this morning."

The two men stood up, said their goodbyes and Joe left the office. While he waited for the elevator Theo's secretary, Mary, rushed up to him.

"Mr. Lorde," she said, slightly out of breath. "I'm sorry, I was supposed to give you this after your meeting with Mr. Gibbs, but I was away from my desk when you came out." She handed him an envelope and Joe glanced inside and saw a check.

"Thanks, Mary," he said with a smile. "I appreciate you catching up to me."

Mary looked into his gray eyes and smiled back at him. It was the first time he'd ever smiled at her and she suddenly felt weak at the knees. There was also a strange feeling in the pit of her stomach, like she'd just stepped off the coaster at Riverview Park. Joe was about to say something to her when suddenly there was the sound of a bell, the elevator door opened, and several people got off.

"Tell Theo I'll try and give him an update on this new case sometime later today or tomorrow morning," he said. He then stepped into the cab and the door quickly closed.

Mary lingered for a few moments in the elevator lobby before walking back to her desk.

In the elevator cab Joe shook his head and thought what a shame it was that Mary wasn't interested in him. There was something about her he found so appealing. Once back in the ground floor lobby, he spotted a payphone in the far corner and decided to check in with Kat. She answered the phone on the second ring.

"Any messages?" he asked.

"Nothing since last night. Did you remember your meeting with Mr. Gibbs?"

"Yeah, I just finished up with him a few minutes ago."

"Was he upset about the bill for the Webber case?"

"I guess not. His secretary gave me a check for the full amount."

"I think she has a thing for you, by the way."

"Who, Mary?" Joe was clearly surprised by Kat's remark. "Nah, I was just sitting by her desk for a few minutes waiting for Theo and she never said a word to me."

"Well did you speak to her?"

"Sure ... well ... I think I did."

Kat let out a deep sigh. "Birds fly not into our mouth ready roasted."

After listening to Kat's proverbs for the past few years, both Joe and Sid knew precisely the points she was trying to make. They both agreed, however, that it was a lot more fun to give her a bit of grief about them. Joe smiled to himself and waited a few seconds before replying, "You want me to cook a bird?"

She let out another sigh before giving up. "So if Mr. Gibbs didn't have a problem with the bill, why did he need to see you?"

"He has another case for us, and I need to get up to Kenilworth this morning. I'm not sure I'll get back 'til after lunch. Is Sid in his usual spot? I need to talk to him."

Kat looked over at her co-worker who was lying down on the couch across from her desk. "He's right where you'd expect," she replied with a smile before handing him the phone.

"Hey boss, whaddya need?"

"I talked to Frau Steiner late yesterday and she said that her husband was running the Exposition project. Seems he ran into some problems with the unions. Can you check out the union angle for me? See if you can find out what they thought of Steiner and if they had a reason to knock him off."

"You got it, boss."

"Thanks. After you check on the unions, I need you to check out a group that the Steiners had a falling out with. They're called the 'Friends of Germany'."

"Aren't they linked to those Nazi bastards?"

"Yeah," Joe replied. "It seems the Steiners weren't pleased with the direction their old German club had taken. From what I know about Nazis, they don't like anyone who disagrees with them."

"No problem boss. I'll check them out as well, but I might need Mickey on this one."

Sid rarely asked for help with any investigation, so his request for Mickey caught Joe by surprise. "I guess so," he replied, "but what do you need him for?"

"Well those brown shirted swine aren't particularly friendly to those of us who are circumcised."

Joe felt like a twit. Sid was right, of course, he couldn't send him to talk to a bunch of Nazi goons even if they were the home grown version. "Sorry Sid, go ahead and take Mickey with you. He can pose as a potential recruit, but you two be careful."

"Will do."

Joe hung up the phone, headed back across the lobby, and out through the main entrance. As he left the building he could see that the run on Harris Bank was in full swing. The crowd feared that the bank would run out of cash. If that happened, Harris would be forced to close and only those who'd managed to get their money out would avoid losing some or all of it. The customers who had arrived late were now trying to push and shove their way to the front. Consequently, the somewhat orderly atmosphere that existed earlier had given way to a near riot. With every passing minute the size of the crowd grew. Joe could see fear in their eyes as the crowd began to turn into a mob. The situation escalated when several mounted policemen showed up. Joe now worried that things could get out of hand, so he picked up his pace and ran to his car. The last thing he needed was for some nervous flatfoot to peg him as a trouble maker and take a swing at him. Once he got to his car, he fired up the Roadster, pointed it in the opposite direction of the bank and floored it.

The route to Kenilworth headed north, paralleling the lakefront. Just outside the city, he passed a large group of Bonus Marchers on their way to Washington. Joe had a lot of sympathy for their cause, and if they were successful he'd be in line to get a payment of about $800. Also, along the route he passed a couple of Hoovervilles. To Joe, this new name for a shanty town dripped with irony. He found it impossible to reconcile the man who had done so much to help Europe's poor with the president who now seemed incapable of doing anything to ease the plight of his countrymen.

CHAPTER 3 – TUESDAY

Forty minutes after leaving the Loop Joe reach Kenilworth, a town built to be an enclave for the rich and powerful. It was located well north of the city, and nestled against the Lake Michigan shoreline. When compared to Chicago, struggling with the Depression, this town was bathed in prosperity and offered a surreal contrast.

Joe turned on to the estate's long gravel driveway, passing through a dense layer of trees that shielded the property from the road. As an obscenely rich industrialist, Joe had expected McNulty's mansion to be impressive, and it didn't disappoint. The main house was one of the most extraordinary homes he'd ever seen. Built of white stone, and looking like a picture on a European postcard, the massive four-story structure had a huge front portico in the center, supported by four towering columns. The driveway ended in a large circle at the front of the house. In the center of the circle was an elaborate fountain, surrounded by a magnificent arrangement of flowers. Joe wasn't much for gardening, but even he had to admire the beauty of the layout.

He parked his car next to a Duisenberg, walked up to the two huge wooden doors that formed the entrance, and pulled a cord to ring the bell. A maid quickly greeted him, took his hat and coat and ushered him into the large ornate two-story entry hall. She left him standing there alone for several minutes. Eventually she returned and escorted him to an impressive drawing room, where old man McNulty's only son was waiting for him.

Vance was a tall, lean, good looking man in his early thirties with light brown hair and eyes. He was wearing a pair of gray slacks with a casual white cotton shirt, and draped over his shoulders was a light blue cashmere sweater. He gave off an air of sophistication and superiority, looking much as Joe had expected. His demeanor, however, was unexpected – he was both gracious and hospitable.

"Mr. Lorde, it's a pleasure to meet you," he said as they shook hands. Joe was startled by how soft the man's hands were. "Mr. Gibbs told me you'd be looking into this case. Thank you for coming. Please join me for some coffee." He rang for the housekeeper, but when no one responded immediately he turned to Joe clearly embarrassed. "You'll have to excuse us. I'm afraid we are very short staffed at the moment. The help know that they'll be let go after my father's death, so quite a few of them have left for other positions. It's funny really," said Vance with a smile, "there are so many people out of work nowadays you'd think we'd have no problem getting staff, but obviously we can't hire just anyone." As he finished this explanation an older housemaid entered the room. "Ah, Sophie, would you be an angel and bring us some coffee?" The housemaid nodded before quietly leaving. "I understand from Mr. Gibbs that you are fully aware of our current situation," Vance began, "and I've been told that I should feel free to talk openly with you."

"I imagine you must be very skeptical of this woman's claim?"

"To say the least," he replied with a slight chuckle. "But if her claim is true, which I seriously doubt, I don't see that there's much I can do about it, do you?"

"I have to tell you, if I were in your shoes, I don't think I'd be as understanding as you seem to be."

"It actually doesn't impact me as much as you might think. As Mr. Gibbs must have told you, I'll only inherit a fraction of my father's estate, and I've known that for some time. Father wanted to avoid any unpleasant scene after his death, so he told me about the charitable trust several years ago. I would be lying if I didn't admit that I was upset when he told me." His voice sounded bitter, despite his best efforts to hide it. "But the truly important thing for me is that after he dies, I can return to New York and resume my life." As Vance talked, the maid returned with coffee. "You see, Father wanted me to build cars or motors or whatever it is his company makes, but his world holds no interest for me. Instead, I've built my life around the arts. I suppose I've inherited my love of the arts from Mother. She adored the theater. She was also a major patron of the Pavley-Oukrainsky Ballet and the Chicago Symphony. Father, on the other hand, had no interest in the arts," Vance explained in a bitter tone he made no effort to disguise. He poured Joe some coffee and then continued. "He's a hard man, Mr. Lorde. Don't let his tryst with the maid fool you into thinking he's some kind of poet, because he isn't. As a father and a husband, he was a dismal failure. When I was just a boy, he told me that the only education I would ever need I could get on the shop floor. Mother, however, didn't want that sort of life for me. She saw to it that I had a proper education at the finest schools," he said with pride. "When I graduated from college I tried to live here in Chicago, but I found this city to be a cultural desert. I fled to New York after only a year. The truth is, Mr. Lorde, Father disapproves of me because of who I am, but I disapprove of him because of what he let himself become. Mother understood this. She was the one who insisted that he buy the townhouse in New York, so I'd have a suitable place to live."

Lance took a sip of his coffee and then continued. "When Mother died, I found myself without any source of funds. By that time, my relationship with Father was so strained that the last thing either of us wanted was for me to come home. So we agreed that I would stay in New York and receive an allowance. You may wonder why the annual payment from the trust is sixty-five thousand?" Then without waiting for an answer he replied, "It's because that's what my current yearly allowance is from Father."

"Of course, I had hoped to contest his will after his death, to right the wrong he's done to me. Unfortunately, there's a codicil in the document that will keep me from doing so. It states that if an heir contests any portion of the will, that heir will be cut out, and get nothing regardless of the results of the contestation." The bitterness of his words gave his voice a harsh tone. "In other words, the mere act of contesting his will leaves me penniless. So, if this tart from New York is Father's bastard child, I'm in no position to object. If I make a fuss I'll lose everything."

"The truth is, after dear Papa dies I'll turn my back on this god forsaken town, and return to New York. I'll have enough cash to purchase my own townhouse, and I'll have plenty of money in the bank. To be honest, that's something I've never had before. So you see, my father's romp with his Irish whore won't cost me forty-five million, as most people assume. I was never going to get any of that money. Actually," he added with a smile, "if you think about it, the person who will truly be upset when they read the will is his bastard child. The terms of my father's will are private and won't be revealed until after his death, so undoubtedly this poor girl is blissfully unaware that she won't inherit forty-five million. If her claim to be an heir is upheld, imagine how disappointed she'll be," he said still smiling.

Just then a nurse came into the room. "Mr. McNulty will see you now," she said to Joe. Vance excused himself and Joe was led back to the main hall, up a magnificent hand-carved wooden staircase and then down a long paneled hallway. The master bedroom suite of the McNulty mansion matched the opulence of the estate, and was two or three times larger than Joe's flat. The walls were covered with dark wood paneling. There was impressive crown molding surrounding the ceiling and on top of the parquet floor was the largest Persian rug Joe had ever seen. The center of the room was dominated by a massive four poster bed. On the right side of that bed lay Cyrus McNulty, looking every bit the dying seventy-year-old man that he was. He wore a gold smoking jacket with black trim and was so thin and frail that he seemed to sink deep into the huge bed. Cyrus dismissed the nurse with a wave of his hand, leaving Joe standing in the doorway. The old man was clearly used to giving orders and having them obeyed. He barked at Joe. "Are you the private detective Gibbs told me about?"

"I'm Joe Lorde," he replied as he walked into the bedroom. "Mr. Gibbs has asked me to speak with you about verifying the claims of an additional heir to your estate."

"How long will it take to clear this matter up?" demanded the old man in a weak voice.

"That's impossible to say. We'll get started right away but …"

"That's not good enough, Lorde," interrupted the tycoon. He coughed several times before adding, "If you can't get me the answers in a day or two, perhaps I should get someone else."

"Mr. McNulty, it would suit me just fine to finish this quickly, in fact I have a significant financial incentive to do just that, but I am not going to promise you something I can't deliver. If that's what you're looking for, I suggest you call the Pinkertons. I'm sure they'll be happy to take this case."

Joe turned to leave the room but, as he expected, Cyrus called out. "Mr. Gibbs said you were an honest man. I've lived in Chicago for the last fifty years, so it's been a while since I've dealt with one of those. Clearly, I'm out of practice." Joe turned back towards the bed and took a seat next to Cyrus. "As I'm sure you were told, I'm dying and I don't have much time left." His voice was even weaker now and much less harsh. "I need to know if this young woman is my daughter."

"Well, perhaps we could start by you telling me about the woman you had the affair with twenty-five years ago."

Cyrus pointed to a drawer on the nightstand next to him. "Could you take out the book that's in there?" Joe did as the old man asked, and handed him a letter-sized brown book with gold trim. The frail man grabbed it and pressed it with both hands against his chest. "I have kept a journal my entire adult life. Until I told Mr. Gibbs about it yesterday, no one else knew about this, not even my late wife. You are now the second person I've told." The old man looked fondly at the book he was holding. "My father once told me that people who have secrets like to write them down. I suppose that's why I kept a journal. I had a lot of secrets to keep. These are my private thoughts and I never intended for anyone to read them. I have given strict instructions to Mr. Gibbs that all my journals are to be destroyed immediately upon my death. The book you just handed me covers my life in '06. Until I looked at it Sunday, I hadn't read any of these pages for over twenty years. It took me a long time, but eventually I managed to put Maggie out of my daily thoughts. This was one year I never wanted to look back on," he continued sadly. "Reading these entries again has reminded me just how much I loved her. I didn't know what love was before I met her, and I know I never loved anyone after she left. I'm sure you find that hard to understand."

"No," responded Joe with a slight nod of his head. "I understand exactly how you feel."

"She first came to work for us in early '05, but our affair didn't start until the winter of '06. Neither of us ever expected the relationship, but there was no denying that we shared an intense attraction from the moment we first met. When it started it was truly magical, but of course our relationship was doomed from the beginning. She was a good Catholic girl who didn't want to have an affair with a married man, and I ... I was consumed by my desire for success. Inevitably, my wife found out about us. Looking back, I realize that it must have been easy for anyone to tell that I was in love. Everything changes when you're in love." He looked into the eyes of his visitor. "Did you know that, Mr. Lorde?"

"Yes," Joe replied sadly. "That's one lesson I've learned."

"I was so much in love with my Maggie I wrote a poem to express my feelings. It's here in my journal," he laughed but then the laughed morphed into a deep cough. "Can you imagine me writing a poem?" he continued, after catching his breath. "I can say with complete certainty that it's the only one I've ever written. That's what love does to you, Mr. Lorde. It turns you into a poet, and a bad one at that. When my wife confronted me about the affair, she demanded that I end it. I was a successful businessman back then, but I wasn't the wealthy and powerful man I so yearned to be. A divorce would have destroyed my reputation and I would have been ruined. So I did what she asked. It's hard to believe, even for me, that I chose money over love, but at that point in my life I would have made a bargain with the devil to get what I wanted. Perhaps that's precisely what I did. I sent Maggie away and paid a bitter price. When I told her she had to leave, the only thing she asked was if that was what I truly wanted. I assured her it was, so she kissed me on the cheek, told me she loved me, and left. I never saw her again."

"I understand you gave her some money to get started somewhere else?"

"I did, but a few weeks after she left I got five hundred dollars in the mail with no note or return address, just a Fort Wayne postmark. I had my man George drive down to Fort Wayne, and I told him to make sure she took the money. He told me that she refused. He also told me that he thought she was pregnant. When my wife found out about George's trip, she was livid. She threatened to leave me and tell the world what I had done to her. To avoid a scandal, I swore that I would never make contact with Maggie again, and I never did. It's funny, really. Years later, when I finally achieved the wealth and power that I had sacrificed everything for, I discovered that it didn't bring any happiness or fulfillment at all. I had held the real treasure in my arms years before, and I turned my back on it."

"What can you tell me about this girl who claims to be your daughter?"

"Emma?" as he spoke her name Cyrus' gray face showed a faint sign of life. "She reminds me so much of my Maggie. She has her eyes, her hair and her wonderful smile. When Maggie entered a room it was as if the sun had just broken through the clouds. Emma was my mother's name and Maggie had told me during our magical year together, that if we ever had a girl she wanted to name her Emma."

"Why didn't you try and get in touch with Maggie after your wife died? You could have tried to rectify things when you had the chance?"

"The truth is, I was afraid," replied the old man sadly. "You see, my father left when I was just two years old and I grew up hating him. I watched as my mother grew bitter over the years. I was so afraid that Maggie would have grown to hate me for what I had done. I was also afraid that my daughter had grown up despising me, and I just couldn't bear that. I did make provisions in my will for another heir however, and once I was gone Mr. Gibbs would have received my written instructions to find Emma."

The old man seemed to have sunk further into the bed and was now struggling for each word. "We're almost done Mr. McNulty." Joe said by way of encouragement. "Do you know where I can find Miss O'Donnell?"

"I told her she could stay here while we look into her claim. I turned out the love of my life; I wasn't going to do the same thing to my daughter. I knew that Vance wouldn't be pleased, so until I know for sure, I felt it best to keep her at the guesthouse. Have you met my son, by the way?"

"Yes, I talked to him downstairs when I was waiting to see you."

"I'm sure he gave you an earful. I'm afraid he doesn't like me very much, but I suppose I've given him plenty of cause," he said sadly. "He lives in New York, you know. He's always been more interested in the theater than in real life. The last I heard, he was auditioning actors for a new play he wants to produce. Unfortunately, my impending death dragged him back here."

"One last question. I'd like to speak to George, the man you sent down to Fort Wayne. Does he still work for you?"

"No," replied Cyrus sadly as he shook his head. "George was with me for over thirty-five years, but he died two years ago." Cyrus' voice had grown soft, and he now sounded extremely tired. "You'll have to excuse me, but I'm afraid I have to rest now." His eyes began to close, but he forced them open and looked back up at his guest. "Find out the truth for me, Mr. Lorde," he said with in shaky but hopeful voice. "Tell me if this is my little girl."

Joe got up from the chair and started to leave the room. As he reached the door, the nurse came back in. Gently, he tugged her sleeve and whispered, "How long does he have?"

"It's hard to say," she replied softly, "but I'd guess no more than a day or two."

Joe walked back through the long second floor hallway and down the staircase to the ground floor. When he reached the entry, the housekeeper handed him his hat and coat. "Can I ask you a few questions?" he asked.

The woman, in her late fifties, looked skeptically at him before replying sternly, "I'm not sure there's anything I can do to help you."

"Do you know if anyone remembers Maggie O'Donnell? She worked here twenty-five years ago?" he asked.

"I don't know anything about that. I'm afraid you'll have to ask someone else. Now, if you'll excuse me, I've gotta get back to work."

"How about George?" Joe asked, as he tried again to get some information out of the woman. "The man who used to work here. He died a few years ago?"

"Yes, sir, I knew George, but not all that well. Now, I don't mean to be rude, but these floors aren't going to clean themselves, so I need get back to work".

Joe wasn't surprised by her attitude. He'd gotten the bum's rush before from the people who worked for the rich and powerful. They typically didn't want to risk losing their jobs by spilling family secrets. He realized he'd have to come at this from a different angle. Fortunately, he knew someone who had a gift for getting people to sing like canaries.

Walking out of the house, he spotted a young man working in the flower beds that encircled the fountain in the center of the circular driveway. "Excuse me," he said to the gardener. "Can you tell me where the guesthouse is?"

"Just take the driveway back towards the main road, and when you pass a large stand of trees, you'll see another driveway off to the left. Follow that, and you'll be at the guesthouse."

"Thanks." Joe headed for his car but stopped and turned back to take another look at the young man. He was in his mid-twenties, tall, and good looking, with a very dark complexion and a lean muscular build. "What's your name?" he called out.

"Adam," replied the gardener.

"Thanks, Adam, I appreciate your help." He made a mental note to himself that the gardener was definitely a problem.

Following Adam's directions, Joe arrived at the McNulty guesthouse. Like the main house, it was built of white stone in a classic style, but scaled down so that it resembled a large city bank building or a small town's courthouse. Joe rang the bell and a young housemaid answered the door.

CHAPTER 3 – TUESDAY

"I'd like to see Miss O'Donnell. My name is Joe Lorde and I'm here at the request of Cyrus McNulty." The maid ushered him into the main hallway and took his hat and coat.

"Would you please wait here," she instructed. "I'll let Miss O'Donnell know you're here." She climbed an impressive curved staircase that ran up to the second floor and disappeared from view. As he waited, he couldn't help but admire the large entry hall. Both the curved staircase and the floor were all laid with rose colored marble, and its outer walls were a beautiful gray granite. Most impressive, however, was the ceiling height. Built in an atrium style, the main hallway opened to a second floor landing some fifteen feet above the lower floor. There was a polished wooden banister that ran up along the marble stairs and continued straight across the open second floor landing.

After waiting for a few minutes, Joe heard a soft sweet voice call out from the top of the staircase. "You must be Mr. Lorde." His eyes instinctively moved towards the sound and became transfixed on a young woman slowly descending the stairs. From both the photos that Theo had given him, and Cyrus' description, he'd expected her to be pretty, but neither prepared him for the vision that now approached. "Pretty" didn't adequately describe her at all. Emma O'Donnell was exquisite. She was the kind of woman that caused a man to remember what he wanted, or what he'd lost. Cyrus had also said that she brought sunshine wherever she went and, as if on cue, the large entry hall seemed to light up as she descended the staircase.

"It's a pleasure to meet you, Mr. Lorde." As she spoke his name, she flashed a radiant smile. "I'm Emma O'Donnell. Please join me in the drawing room." She reached the bottom of the staircase and Joe followed her across the hallway into an adjoining room. "Would you like something to drink," she offered, as she sat down on the sofa. "Some coffee, perhaps?"

Joe shook his head, "I'm fine, thanks."

Emma was about five foot four with a smooth white complexion. She had strawberry blonde hair that fell in soft curls onto her shoulders, and clear blue eyes that sparkled like gemstones reflecting sunlight. She was wearing a white dress that showed off a perfect figure. When she spoke, her compelling eyes looked directly into his and she tapped the cushion next to her. "Please come and sit down," she said with a smile. Joe instinctively did as she asked. "I understand that you're going to be checking my background to make sure my story is true."

"Yes, Miss O'Donnell. I've been hired to try and confirm your identity."

"Please," she said as she reached out and briefly touched his knee with her hand. "Call me Emma. May I call you Joe?"

"Of course." His reply was accompanied by an involuntary smile.

"Mr. Gibbs said that you'd need to ask me some questions, so please ask me anything you'd like." Joe noticed that her voice had a soft lilt to it and she had a way of changing its inflection that he found quite appealing. He proceeded to ask a series of questions related to the information he'd gotten from both Theo and Cyrus. Their talk lasted forty-five minutes, and during that time he never got the feeling that she was hiding anything or trying to be evasive. When their conversation ended, he got up to leave, but wished for a reason to stay longer. They continued talking to each other as they walked out of the guest house and towards his car.

"Will you be coming back anytime soon?" she asked. The tone of her voice made it feel more like an invitation than a question.

"I'm not sure," was his initial response before adding, "As I collect more information I'll almost certainly have more questions."

"Oh good," she began, but then she blushed slightly and corrected herself, "I mean of course. And if you need me, I'll be here or up at the main house. You can come by anytime."

Joe was smiling again though he didn't realize it, and responded, "Ok ... well ... yes, I'll ring you before I come back over."

"That would be lovely," she said, as she flashed him a smile that felt like another invitation.

Throughout his life, Joe had always prided himself on his memory. At meetings or interviews he never found it necessary to take notes. He could always remember any event or conversation in detail days or even weeks later. After his interview with Emma, however, the only thing he could clearly recall was the woman herself. Now, as he drove back to the Loop, he found himself trying to remember something of value from their conversation. But while he struggled to think of anything useful, he could remember quite clearly the smell of her perfume, the shape of her lips and the funny way her nose crinkled when she laughed. He felt like an idiot as he realized that he didn't know any more about her now than he did before the interview. Once back in the city, he headed to the Green Door Tavern over on Orleans Street to grab a bite to eat. He used the time to write down everything he could remember about his meeting with Emma, which wasn't much.

Afternoon

Joe made it back to his office after lunch, but just forty minutes later he grabbed his hat and coat and headed for the door. "Where are you off to?" asked Kat.

"I need to see Walt. We came up with that theory of Steiner being stabbed from behind by a right handed killer and I want to see if he thinks it holds water."

"Any chance we could get paid for this one?" Kat always preferred cases that involved money.

"I don't see how," he replied from the hall as the door closed behind him.

It was 1:40 in the afternoon when Joe arrived back at the coroner's office on West Polk. It took him a few minutes to find his friend, but he eventually caught up with him in the cooler.

"You again?" Walt asked, as he was pulling one of the stainless steel "slabs" from the wall.

"I'm afraid so. I want to run a theory by you on the Steiner murder, and see what you think."

"Ok, shoot." There followed a fifteen-minute discussion on the theory that Steiner had been stabbed from behind. Walt then pulled out the dead city engineer from slot G4. After carefully reexamining the body, he eventually agreed that the man might well have been killed the way his friend had suggested.

With his theory validated, Joe said his goodbyes and began to leave, while Walt returned to the corpse he'd earlier retrieved from the wall. When Walt pulled back the sheet that was covering the body Joe caught a glimpse of who was lying on the slab. Stunned, he stood frozen for several seconds, unable to take a breath. There on the table, was the young woman he'd seen on campus the day before, leading her fellow students in the Peace Pledge. As she lay there lifeless, the beauty that she'd radiated the day before was still evident, despite the bruises on her face and the surgical marks from her autopsy. Walt noticed Joe's expression and couldn't figure out why his friend was reacting as he was. He knew that Joe had seen dozens of bodies here in the morgue, and regardless of their condition he'd never shown much of a reaction. He then looked back at the dead girl and finally noticed the intense resemblance to Wendy. He had known Joe's ex-fiancée and remembered what her leaving had done to him. Gently, he put his hand on his friend's shoulder and said softly, "it's not her."

Joe finally took a deep breath and replied, "I know," before slowly exhaling. He then explained, "It's just that I saw this girl yesterday. She was speaking at a rally on campus."

The two men quietly stared at the co-ed for several moments before Walt broke their trance by noting, "The resemblance is uncanny."

Joe gave his pal a faint smile, "You should have seen her yesterday."

Walt was about to continue his examination but looked at his friend and suggested, "Maybe you shouldn't watch this."

"No ... it's ok," he replied. "Do you know what happened?"

"Well, her name is ... was Genevieve Ericson," he began, "and she was shot in the back of the head last night." His examination progressed. "If you look here," he pointed to the back of the girl's scull, "you'll see the point of entry." Walt looked back at his notes and continued. "We recovered the bullet and it's a very unusual caliber, a 7.65mm. You ever hear of a pistol that fires a round like that?"

"I can think of one in particular, but it's a European make. I haven't seen one here in the US."

"Luckily, we've recovered the bullet intact."

"What's the significance of that?"

"It seems there's a new test you can do," he explained, "if a bullet is recovered in decent shape, it's now possible to match it to the specific gun that fired it. So if we find the gun, we might be able to tie it to the person who killed her."

"How's that possible?"

"It's something they're calling 'ballistics'. Ness, the G-man here in Chicago, was telling us about it just last week. It seems that each gun makes a unique set of marks on a bullet. All you need to do is take the

CHAPTER 3 – TUESDAY

gun you think is the murder weapon, and fire a round into a tub of water. Then you fish out the slug and compare it under a microscope with the one that killed this girl. If the markings on the two slugs match, you have your murder weapon. Elliott said they've set up a laboratory outside DC where they're developing all sorts of scientific tests that can be used to solve crimes. This 'ballistics' thing is just one of them. I talked to the Chief of Detectives and told him about it. He's given us the green light to use this technique whenever we can. Since the bullet that killed this girl is in good shape, we should be able to do the test, assuming someone finds the murder weapon."

"This doesn't sound much like your line of work. How come you're doing it?"

"Because you need a microscope to compare the slugs and we're the only city department that has one," he explained. "The CoD said he was ok with doing the tests, but he wasn't going to spend any of the city's coin on microscopes."

"You know, it's funny," Walt added, "typically, when someone is shot in the head the slug is too badly damaged to analyze, but this time it was intact."

"Do they think it was robbery?" Joe asked.

"Not likely. She had four dollars and change on her, plus a watch and a silver necklace." Walt looked at the autopsy notes again before adding sadly, "But it does look like she was raped ..." He pulled the sheet further back exposing the girl's heavily bruised lower torso and continued his sentence, "... and I'm guessing more than once, so it's a good bet there were multiple attackers."

"Anything else?"

"No, that pretty much sums it up." Walt covered her body with the sheet and rolled the slab back into the cooler before adding, "She didn't deserve to die like that."

"Nobody does," Joe said with sorrow evident in his voice. Then he turned to his friend and asked, "Are there any leads?"

"No, from what I heard she was found in an alley just north of Madison and Union in the 'Red Belt'. There are no hard clues yet and no one knows why she was in that neighborhood." The two men silently left the cooler and headed back down the corridor towards Walt's office. As they walked, Joe's thoughts were about the young vibrant girl he'd seen at the Peace Rally the day before.

When they reached Walt's office, he turned to Joe and said, "I've been giving it a lot of thought and I think it's time I popped the question."

At first Joe wasn't sure what his friend was talking about, but then he realized that Walt was planning to ask his girlfriend to marry him. "That's a big step," he commented while walking slowly past the office, hoping to avoid a long conversation.

Walt stood in his doorway, lit a cigarette and asked nervously, "You think I'm doing the right thing, getting spliced?"

Joe spun around to face him, while continuing to slowly back pedal towards the exit. "I think it doesn't matter what I think," he responded. "It only matters what you think, and I'm guessing you think it's the right thing to do. Now the big question is, will she have you?"

"Why?" his friend replied, now clearly nervous. "Did you hear something?"

Still heading for the door, Joe shook his head, flashed another weak smile, and replied. "I didn't hear anything you chucklehead, but you do have to get the girl to say 'yes', don't you?" Walt didn't say anything. Instead, he simply nodded in agreement and went back into his office while Joe made his escape.

The beautiful blue sky that had started the day had slowly given way to clouds and showers. Joe drove his ragtop through the wet streets and over to South Indiana Avenue. During the past twenty-five years this part of town had seen a large migration of Blacks from the south. Because of the influx of new residents, the area had become known as the Black Belt or "Bronzeville".

Walking along Indiana, he reached a three-story building with a storefront on the ground level and offices on the upper two floors. He entered the building through a side door off the street, and went straight up the stairs to an office lobby on the second floor. This was the home of *The Chicago Defender* – the largest and most influential Black newspaper in America. *The Defender,* as most called it, was a weekly that had become a powerful force in the lives of Black Americans all across the country. It had a staff of nearly one hundred, and among them was a "Cub" reporter named Rose Hughes.

CHAPTER 3 – TUESDAY

"Hi, Princess," Joe called out as he entered the office. Rose looked up from her desk and flashed a dazzling smile. She got up from her chair and crossed the room. As she moved towards him, Joe was struck by just how beautiful she'd become. He had known Rose since she was a baby, and her awkward teenage years gave no indication that she would blossom into the stunner that she was today. She stood five-six with a slim build, brown eyes and a soft clear brown complexion. She had beautiful black hair, that she took great pains to keep straight, and perfect teeth that enhanced her smile. Regardless of their race, men's heads couldn't help but turn when Rose passed by.

When she reached him, she gave him a hug and a peck on the cheek. "Hi, handsome," she responded, still wearing her infectious smile. "What do you need me to do?" Her mood always brightened at the thought of getting out of the office and working on one of Joe's cases.

To most people who met Joe he seemed cold, detached, and very scary. To the few who thought of him as a friend, he was a rock that they could always depend on. But only two people had ever thought of him as a warm and open person – one had been Wendy, the other was Rose. Joe and Rose were deeply fond of each other and always enjoyed spending time together.

"Princess, do you think I'd only come here because I need you to do something for me?" he asked in mock pain. "I'm hurt, truly hurt."

"I think you only call me 'Princess' when you need me to do something for you, and you came at one o'clock because you know Papa takes a long lunch with Aunt Edna every Tuesday. And it doesn't take Sherlock Holmes to figure out that the only reason you would want to avoid Papa is because you need me to do something on one of your cases." Besides being beautiful Rose was also keenly intelligent and had finished at the top of her class at Howard just two years ago.

"Well," said Joe, as he reached into his pocket, "it might be that I came here to see if you were interested in going to the double header on Monday," and he flashed three tickets. "First base line, just above the dugout."

"Oooh," squealed Rose as she grabbed the tickets from him. "Yes ... yes ... yes, and Sam will be so pleased it's the Giants' turn," she added while hugging him. It had been a long tradition that Sam, Rose and Joe would alternate games between Joe's team, the White Sox, and Sam's team, the Giants. "Does Sam know yet?" she asked excitedly.

"I told him Sunday night."

"When you had him playing piano at that awful place," she responded with an exaggerated pout.

"Sam hasn't been shooting his mouth off about that, has he?" Joe was clearly concerned.

"Don't worry," she replied with a giggle. "No one's going to tell. By the way," she added, "you are going to be there on Sunday, right?"

"Why does everyone keep asking me that?" complained Joe. "I'll be there. Now let's change the subject. You have any free time today or tomorrow?"

"Here it comes." Rose always pretended that she was doing him a favor, but the truth was she found Joe's cases much more interesting than writing puff pieces about the "Bud Bilken" parade. When she started working at *The Defender* she had hopes of becoming an investigative journalist. Now, after a couple of years, she was beginning to think she'd never get the chance to do anything of substance.

Joe pulled up a chair and Rose was almost giddy with excitement. "Have you ever heard of Cyrus McNulty?" he began.

"The millionaire?" she responded in astonishment as she sat down across from him.

"Daddy Warbucks in the flesh." Joe replied.

He then proceeded to fill her in on what he knew about the case. After he finished Rose sat back in her chair. "Wow! So she never knew her father until she met him on Sunday?"

"That's right."

"Can you imagine …?" she stopped abruptly when she remembered how Joe had grown up. "I'm so sorry," she said concerned that she'd hurt him.

Joe smiled. "Don't worry, Princess, you didn't hurt my feelings."

She smiled once again and continued, "So what do you need me to do?"

"The staff is reluctant to talk to me, and I was hoping you could coax some information out of them." As Joe had the gift of intimidation, Rose had the gift of empathy. Whenever she talked with someone they always ended up pouring out their life story to her. Information flowed towards her like water downhill. For Joe, on the other hand, information flowed more like beer from a keg. Invariably he had to smack it a few times before anything came out of the tap.

"I know that the McNulty's are short on help right now," Joe explained. "I think they would be interested in hiring someone to work in the main house. If you go up there you might just get the staff to open up a bit."

"I get it, you want me to play the maid again."

"Oh, hell no!" he replied adamantly and with a look of horror on his face. "We're not doing that again. I thought Arthur was going to kill me when he found out about that. Just so we're clear on this, under no circumstance are you to take a job as the McNulty's maid. You're just going to act like you might take a job there."

Rose laughed. "You're splitting hairs, aren't you. Somehow, I don't think Papa would see much of a difference."

Joe ignored her comment. "I need you to talk to the people there, and find out what they know about Maggie. Also, try and find out if anyone remembers George and his trip to Fort Wayne. Oh, and also be sure to ask if they think Emma is legit."

"I could get away on Thursday, but how am I going to get up to the McNulty estate?"

"I'll have Sid drive you."

"That'll work," she replied in her usual chipper voice, before adding, "Now let's talk about my fee."

"I was thinking the same as last time, a dollar an hour."

"Last time you were doing a job for Father Lorde, and I knew you weren't getting paid. This time, you're working for Daddy Warbucks. I want three dollars an hour."

Joe's eyes went wide. "Three dollars! For Christ sake, Jean Harlow doesn't make that kind of dough."

"Careful," she replied with a devilish smile. "I'll tell Kat you were swearing."

"Be reasonable Princess," he replied.

"All right, I'll do it for two-fifty."

"That's a lot of dough for a couple of hours work."

"Don't forget the time it takes to ride up and back," her eyes sparkled as she continued her negotiations. "I want to be paid for that as well."

"I'll give you two-twenty-five, and that's it."

Rose could tell she'd pushed him about as far as he was willing to go. She paused for a moment to make him think that she was considering his offer before replying, "Deal." She then spit in her right hand and held it out, just as she always did before they sealed a bargain.

Joe was about to grab it but stopped and added, "Wait, there's one more thing. I need you to stay away from the gardener, some guy named Adam."

"What do you mean?" She was clearly perplexed by the request.

"I've been warned by Cyrus himself that their gardener is a Lunger. They tell me his condition is very serious. Because of his tuberculosis he's been quarantined at the estate, and no one is to go near him for at least six months."

Her face showed her concern as she asked, "Oh, the poor man, is his condition serious?"

"It must be. I hear Cyrus will have a provision in his will to send him to a sanitarium out west."

Rose smiled and said sympathetically, "That is so nice of Mr. McNulty to take care of him like that."

"Well, it's important that you keep your distance. I'd never forgive myself if something like that happened to you," he said as he locked his eyes squarely on her. Ever since he was a young boy, Joe had been able to influence or intimidate people with his stare and it worked on virtually everyone.

She giggled in response. "You always look so funny when you stare like that." Unfortunately, it never worked on Rose.

"Come on, Princess," he said, frustrated that she wasn't taking this seriously. "You're going to have to swear to me that you'll stay away from the gardener or you can't work this case."

Rose sighed and then raised her right hand and pledged, "I promise not to go anywhere near the gardener." She then spit in her hand again, before they shook.

"Good," he said. He kissed her on the forehead and added, "I'll see you Thursday." He headed for the exit, but as he reached the front door Arthur Hughes unexpectedly entered the office.

"Joseph, what a pleasant surprise." He grabbed Joe's hand with a broad smile. Arthur stood five-eight and weighed in at about two hundred and ten pounds. He had a very dark complexion, short hair tinged with plenty of gray, and an energy level that few fifty-eight-year-old men could match. He was wearing a brown suit, with his trademark red bow tie, and white Panama hat. There were two other distinguishing characteristics about Arthur. The first was his large upper body, which he'd developed in his early twenties after taking up professional wrestling as a way to pay for college. The other was the large Cuban Coronas cigar he was constantly smoking.

Arthur had been one of the first employees at *The Defender*. He had started as a young reporter, just a year after it was founded in '05, and was now editor of the city desk. "To what do I owe the pleasure of this unexpected visit?"

"I just dropped by to visit my favorite gal."

Arthur's smile disappeared and he continued to hold Joe's hand but tightened his grip. "You didn't come here to involve Rose in one of your investigations again, did you?"

"No, sir," Joe lied. "Absolutely not. I came over to tell Rose that Sam and I are taking her to the Giants game next week." Arthur looked over at his daughter and she waved the tickets in the air, then gave her father a broad smile.

"Excellent," he exclaimed as he released his grip. Joe flexed his hand several times to restore the circulation. "I think the Giants are going to have a fantastic year. Certainly a better one than your White Sox, I can tell you that." Arthur was a big fan of the Chicago Giants and *The Defender* reported extensively on the Negro leagues. "I wish I could go with the three of you. Now, come over to my office, have some coffee, and tell me what you've been up to."

The two men sat down and began to talk. Typically, they would cover a wide variety of topics during one of their conversations. This time, however, Arthur's mind was focused solely on the Democratic convention, coming to the Chicago Stadium in just two months. Arthur, like most black men his age, had been born and raised Republican. After all, it had been the Republicans who had fought the Civil War and ended slavery and it was the southern Democrats, or "Dixi-Crats", who suppressed civil rights throughout the south. This year, however, things promised to be different. The Northern Democrats had heavily courted the Black vote. Consequently, their candidate, Franklin Roosevelt, had the backing of men like Arthur and newspapers like *The Defender*. Joe and Arthur continued to talk politics for almost an hour before Arthur's secretary reluctantly interrupted them to remind him that he had a staff meeting.

Forty minutes later Joe arrived back at the University of Chicago and poked his head into his friend Marty's office. "Any luck cracking the code?"

"No, if there's a code here I haven't been able to break it," Marty admitted. "I gotta say, I'm pretty stumped. I might be making this more difficult than it is. I hear one of our new physics professors just arrived from Germany, and he worked on their codes during the war. I'm going to see him later today and pick his brain. You know, if you had rung me I could have told you this over the phone and saved you the trip."

"Actually I need to talk to you about something else. Did you hear about the graduate student who was killed?"

"Sure, it's all over campus. People are pretty bent about it. Are you looking into the girl's death?"

"At this point I'm not sure."

"Well, I don't think the cops have a clue," he said sadly. "If you got involved, then maybe they'd have a shot at catching her killer."

"I saw her yesterday just before I came to see you."

"No kidding," he replied, clearly surprised, "where did you see her?"

"She was speaking at the Peace Pledge rally on the Quad. After she spoke, I saw her talking to a man that looked like he might be a professor. He's in his mid-40's, good looking, graying hair. He was wearing a gray tweed jacket, a white fedora and carried a cane that I'm pretty sure was just for show."

"That sounds like Professor Maximilian – don't call me Max – Somerfield," said Marty.

"He doesn't like the name Max?" replied Joe.

"Positively hates it. From what I hear, you got two choices," explained Marty. "You can call him Professor Somerfield or, if he lets you, Maximillian, but you can never call him Max. There's a story around campus that a few years back one of the graduate assistants referred to him as 'Max'. Sadly, the professor got wind of it and had the poor devil's assistantship yanked. The kid had to drop out of school."

"He sounds charming."

"Well, the ladies sure seem to think so. He's got more notches on his bed post than any other guy on campus, and that's saying something."

"Where can I find Romeo?"

"Why?"

"I'm going to pay the good professor a visit," Joe replied.

"Really?" The worry in Marty's voice was obvious. "His office is over in Rosenwald Hall, across the Central Quad." Marty pointed out the window towards one of the other campus buildings. "The guy's a full professor in the Sociology Department and quite active on the faculty committee. He also has a seat at the Round Table over at the Quadrangle Club. He's one of the most respected professors on campus. Both well published and tenured. He would be just the kind of 'friend' someone like me could use if I ever wanted to get tenure."

"I just want to ask him about this dead girl," Joe said defensively.

"I'm not going to ask why you're interested in this girl's death or how Somerfield might be connected, 'cause I know you won't tell me and I'm guessing I don't want to know. Do me a favor, will you," the tone in Marty's voice reflected how nervous he was. "If you're going to drag Somerfield into your investigation, please keep my name out of it. Having him as an enemy is a headache I don't need."

"I promise, your name will never come up," Joe replied. He waived to his friend as he headed out the door, adding, "and ix-nay on the ax-may," which forced a smile from Marty.

From Ryerson Hall, Joe walked across the Central Quad to Rosenwald Hall, which housed both the schools of Economics and Sociology. Once inside, he asked a student where he could find Professor Somerfield. He was directed to a large private office on the third floor, with a wonderful view of the quad.

Joe knocked on the frame of the open door and entered. Standing in the large wood-paneled room was the same man he'd seen talking to the murdered co-ed the day before. He was next to an attractive young blonde who was sitting on his desk with her legs crossed. Her skirt was hiked up well above her knee and the professor's left hand was inching it even higher. Joe's knock startled them both. The blushing co-ed quickly pulled her skirt down, hopped off the desk, grabbed her books, and left the room. The professor, clearly annoyed at the interruption, snapped at the intruder, "What do you want?"

"I'm sorry to bother you, Professor, but I've been assigned to look into the death of Genevieve Ericson." Using the phrase 'I've been assigned' was one of Joe's favorite tricks. When people heard it, they typically jumped to the conclusion that he was a cop, and became more cooperative. Of course he was always careful to never actually say he was with the police. Impersonating a cop was one of the most reliable ways to get a beating in Chicago.

The professor stiffened and crossed the room to shake his visitor's hand. "Yes, of course, such a terrible tragedy. Please come in." Joe took out his notebook and a pencil, and acted as if he was going to write down what the professor had to say. People expected cops to take notes, and he found that it was best to act accordingly.

"I understand you knew the deceased?" he began.

The professor took out a cigarette from a wooden box on his desk, lit it and took a long drag before responding. "Yes, I knew Gen," he blew out the gray smoke from his lungs and continued. "In fact, we were 'an item', as they say." Joe was surprised by his admission and Somerfield could tell from the look on his face, and smiled. "I'm not ashamed of my relationship with Gen, detective. To use the popular expression, we were both free, white and twenty-one. On top of that, there was a strong mutual attraction, and she wasn't my student when we were dating."

"How long were the two of you 'an item'?"

"Just a couple of months actually, and then it was over. I believe she recently started dating another man, and I heard he was also about my age. Some women just prefer older, more experienced men," he said, unapologetically.

"Do you have any idea what she was doing at Madison and Union streets yesterday evening?"

"I understand she was working in the 'Red Belt' on her thesis. Most likely doing field research, gathering data on the local population's social behaviors, that sort of thing." Joe was familiar with the Red Belt. It was where most of the leftist organizations, like the communists and International Labor Defense Union, were located. These groups were there to recruit from the poorer neighborhoods that comprised the district. "I'm afraid I never saw a draft of her paper, so I'm unsure how far along she was on her research," he continued. "I haven't seen or spoken to her for several months, but I do know that she was interested in the condition of the lower classes. Her thesis involved researching their social norms and practices. She believed strongly in the inherent goodness of people and felt passionately that the poor needed society's help."

"What about you, professor, don't you believe in helping the poor?"

"What I believe is irrelevant, detective. I'm just telling you what Gen believed. You see, she was a dedicated communist and the cornerstone of their belief is that, eventually, the masses will rise up and seize power. Based on that theory, any help given to the poor now will only delay the changes that are coming."

"By 'changes' you mean a revolution?"

"Look," replied the professor with a smile, "You and I may not believe it, but to the faithful, like Gen, the revolution is as inevitable as the dawn of a new day. She believed she was a 'good solider' to the cause, and saw herself on the front lines. Of course, good soldiers don't question orders, they do what they're told. That, I'm afraid, was something Gen was uncomfortable with. She broke with Party doctrine and discipline when it came to the plight of the poor. To be frank, her political beliefs were of no interest to me. As an academician, however, I was concerned that she was having difficulty remaining detached from the subjects she was studying. Any good sociologist knows that you can never get personally involved because you'll lose your objectivity, and this skews your analysis. Sadly, she cared too deeply about the masses to be a first rate sociologist.

My guess is, she tried to help some poor soul she was supposed to be studying and he turned on her. It's a dangerous area she was working. It's not called the 'Blood Red Ward' for nothing."

"Do you know where in that ward she was conducting her research?"

"No, I'm afraid I can't help with that. I understand that one of the local missions gave her a closet to use as her 'office' but I'm afraid that's all I know."

"Thank you, professor, I appreciate your candor."

"I'm always happy to cooperate with the authorities, detective. I was very fond of Gen and I truly hope you catch that poor girl's killers. Please let me know if there is anything else I can do to help."

Joe descended the steps of Rosenwald and stopped once he reached the small ground floor lobby. He had to decide whether he should continue looking into the Ericson girl's death. He had several cases right now, and really didn't have time to jump into another one. Yet the vision of the young co-ed lying on the morgue's slab continued to haunt him. After considering the issue for a few moments he decided that he just couldn't let it go. He spotted a pay phone in the corner and placed a call to Kat. He needed her to check the phone book for any missions in the Red Belt. He had to wait for about five minutes and deposited an additional nickel. When she got back on the phone, she told him that there were two missions operating in the Red Belt, and gave him their numbers. He got lucky with his first call.

In Chicago all the early US presidents have roads named after them. These streets start in the Loop and run through the city in an east/west direction. The exception to this is Jefferson Street. For some reason the road named for the third president is west of the Loop and runs in a north/south direction. Being outside the Loop makes Jefferson Street a less than desirable address, and Joe often wondered what the man did to get banished from the Loop.

It was late in the afternoon by the time Joe parked his Ford on Jefferson next to a three-story brick tenement that was the Salvation Army Mission. Located in Chicago's Red Belt, the Mission was surrounded by old and dilapidated three and four-story brick buildings. To say the area was a slum was like saying the stockyard smelled. The statement might be true, but it did little to prepare you for what you'd experience upon arrival. A popular saying since the crash was that "prosperity was just around the corner". Clearly no one knew which corner it was lurking behind, but Joe was fairly confident it wasn't anywhere near this stretch of Jefferson.

On the ground floor of the Mission there was a combination meeting and dining hall in the front and a "soup kitchen" in the back. The second and third floors housed the men's dormitory, and on the fourth were the Mission's offices, along with quarters for the staff. A line, comprised exclusively of men, was wrapped around the outside of the building. These were the souls that waited patiently for a bowl of soup, a chunk of bread and the word of God. Joe went inside and after searching for several minutes found the man in charge.

"Your rank of 'captain' signifies what, exactly?" Joe asked.

"The Salvation Army is an army of God," he explained. "Our enemy isn't any nation of course, but Satan, and all his works. In this divine army, I have the privilege of holding the rank of captain." He was a tall, gaunt, and deeply unattractive man of about forty. He had a weather face, crooked teeth, dark brown eyes and thinning but matching hair. He was wearing a black military style uniform with a white shirt, a thin black tie, and captain's bars on his collar.

"I've been assigned to look into the death of Gen Ericson," explained Joe, as he took out his notepad and pencil. "Did you know her?"

"Yes," he replied sadly. "I knew Gen. She was very popular here at the Mission and in the neighborhood as well. It's hard to believe that anyone would have harmed her."

"I was told that she was using a closet as an office here at the Mission."

A surprised look spread across the captain's face. "Yes she was, but frankly I'm amazed you knew about that. Gen asked me six months ago if I could spare some space for her to work. To be honest I wasn't crazy about the idea, but she was very persistent. In the end, it was a lot easier to give in to her than to continue arguing over it," he said with a half smile.

"Would it be possible to see it?"

"Of course, just follow me." Joe was led up a narrow and well-worn wooden staircase toward the fourth floor. "As you'll see, the term 'office' is an absurd exaggeration. She always called it that, and she asked me not to tell anyone about it. She used to say that it was our little secret. I think she was afraid that some of her university colleagues would make fun of her if they knew she was working out of a closet. I did offer to give her a little more space, down in the basement, but she said she didn't mind the cramped quarters." Captain Miller paused for just a moment and looked back at Joe with a deep sadness etched on his face. "She was a lovely girl, Mr. Lorde. I pray you find the person who did this to her."

Joe had seen that kind of anguish on a man's face many times before. Undoubtedly, the Captain had been in love with the beautiful co-ed, but he seriously doubted that Gen ever knew. He then asked, "Did you know what she was working on?"

"I believe she was doing some kind of study to help the people in this ward. She eventually became very involved with some neighborhood issues, and was trying to organize the residence."

"Was she in her 'office' very often?" Joe asked as the two men continued up the stairs.

"She'd been working constantly for the last several months, and that included most every day these past few weeks."

"Did she have any men around, boyfriends, that sort of thing?"

"No, at least no one I saw. She did mention a couple of times over the past couple of weeks that she'd had a late date the night before," he said disapprovingly. "However, she didn't say anything more and I didn't pry." The captain opened the closet door and pulled a string that was dangling from a single bare bulb hanging from the center of the ceiling. Instantly a dim light filled the "office" whereupon he quickly stepped out so that Joe could enter.

"You'll have to excuse me, we'll begin serving dinner at five and I need to talk to people as they arrive. It's part of my ministry. Will you please turn off the light when you're finished?"

"Yes, of course, and thanks for your help," Joe replied as the captain left.

As advertised, the space was a closet. There was just enough room to hold an old roll-top desk and a chair on rollers. On the back of the door and opposite the desk, Gen had mounted a map of the ward. On this map she'd drawn a grid, and scattered throughout the grid were colored pins. Joe opened the file drawer on the right side of the desk and started to go through her papers. Most consisted of interviews that she'd done with people in the area. Each interview had a grid reference which seemed to indicate where the interview took place. These grid references matched up to the colored pins on the wall map. He then found a bound black journal with red trim. There was no label on the cover, but the first page read "Field Notes". The book appeared to be a kind of diary containing a daily summary of Gen's research activities. Initially the entries were brief, such as "Met advisor on progress of thesis" or "Interviewed respondent #126 at F31", and there were no entries of a personal nature.

As Joe read through the journal, he noticed that the tone of the entries changed over time. At first they were purely a set of clinical observations. These slowly morphed into more passionate observations of the individuals being interviewed and the surrounding area. On the journal's last few pages there were comments from Gen on government money being wasted for projects, such as next year's Exposition, the expansion at the municipal airport, and the refurbishment of the Washington Street Bridge. Then, about two weeks ago, the journal entries abruptly stopped. Joe continued to look through her files and noticed that much of the rest of her work seemed to stop at about the same time. If she'd been constantly busy, but not working on her thesis, it was a good bet that something else was grabbing her attention.

He continued rifling through the desk, searching for whatever it was that had diverted Gen from her thesis. He was about to call it quits, after forty minutes with no luck, when he noticed the tip of a file folder wedged between the side of the desk and the wall. With a bit of difficulty, he slid the folder out. Inside it he found a stack of signed petitions demanding that the city stop the refurbishment of the Washington Street Draw Bridge. It seemed that Gen wanted to use the money that was saved to help the poor of the Red Belt. In addition to the petitions, there was also a portion of an engineering report on the structural integrity of a bridge. The date of the report was from last month. He couldn't find the name of the bridge on any of the pages. "Five-will-get-you-ten," Joe thought to himself, "It's the Washington Street Bridge". He found it impossible to decipher the report's technical jargon, but the handwritten notes on the margins seemed to indicate that the bridge had some serious problems.

It was past 6:00 by the time Joe walked back into his office. Kat was busy working on the accounts, Sid was in his favorite spot, and Mickey was doing some typing on a small table next to the file cabinets. He'd taken typing at De La Salle and was quite a bit faster and more accurate than Kat. Consequently, she frequently had him type up letters and invoices that were going out to clients.

As Joe took his coat off and hung it up on the rack he asked, "Why's it so cold in here?"

Mickey never looked up and kept typing, but nodded toward the open window and responded, "Because Kat's hot."

Sid then add curtly, "Again."

"Seriously?" Joe said as he looked over at his secretary.

Kat began using some papers on her desk as a fan and replied in a defensive tone, "This building can never get the heat right. They always make it much too hot."

From her tone Joe decided it was better not to argue with her and tossed the engineering report on to her desk. Turning to Mickey he asked, "Kid, can you run this over to the professor first thing in the morning?"

"Sure Mr. L." The young man responded with a smile. He looked at the pages with a puzzled expression. "What is it?"

"I think it's some kind of engineering report on the Washington Street Bridge, but it's applesauce to me. I can't make heads or tails out of the technical gibberish. I'm hoping Marty can figure it out."

Kat pulled out the two rubber balls that she'd been working on earlier that day and put them on the desk in front of him. "All done," she said proudly. "Do you want me to keep them in the desk drawer?"

Joe took a close look at them and nodded his satisfaction. "I'll take one and you keep the other under wraps." Joe put one of the balls in his trench coat pocket and then turned toward his investigator. "Sid, we got a new case today. We've been asked to verify the identity of a young woman who claims to be Cyrus McNulty's long lost daughter." Joe went through a few details of the case but Sid noticed that he was a bit fuzzy about his interview with this woman who claimed to be an heir.

"I need you to get over to Fort Wayne tomorrow and spend the day checking out Emma O'Donnell's story," Joe said. "You can take the early morning train." He handed him the file that Theo had given him. "There are three photos in there, two prints of the girl and one of her birth certificate. You can take the file with you, but I'll need to keep one of the photos of the girl." Sid opened the folder and handed his boss one of the pictures. Joe stared at it for several seconds without realizing that a smile had crossed his face.

"Hey Mr. L., I met up with my pal at the Congress Hotel, like ya asked," said Mickey. "He says Mr. Patel had visitors today. A man and woman showed up together. The dame was a real knockout, and the guy looked like he was trouble. Oh, and my pal told me to tell you that this Patel guy is a lousy tipper."

"Ok, thanks, Mickey," said Joe still smiling. "I'll be in my office." He quickly walked through the door taking the picture of Emma with him.

Kat turned to Sid. "So what do you think he was smiling about?" she asked, clearly perplexed. Sid took out the other photo of Emma from the file, made a wolf whistle and held up the picture so Kat and Mickey could see it. "There's your answer," he replied.

Evening

Kat, Sid, and Mickey left the office well after 6:30. Joe stayed behind to try and make some sense out of the three cases he was working on. His method for doing this was to split his time between tossing a baseball straight up in the air, and doodling on a large notepad. The process helped him sort out his thoughts and invariably, he'd come up with a good idea or two. Tonight, however, he had trouble concentrating because thoughts of Emma kept popping into his head.

It was eight o'clock when he pulled up to the Home Run Inn on 31st Street for a pizza, a Chero-Cola and a cigarette. The restaurant was playing a recap of the Sox game on the radio. While he ate, he learned that his team had lost, nine to nothing, to the Phillies.

An hour and a half later, he returned to his place on Warren Street. He found a parking spot a block away, and as he walked toward his apartment his mind once again drifted to Emma. She'd been in and out of his thoughts all day and he smiled subconsciously as images of her flashed through his head once again. He was so preoccupied with these thoughts of Emma that he failed to notice the three men loitering near the entrance to his building. As he approached the men jumped him, and pulled him into the alley next to his building. When the fight began Joe was giving out more punishment then he was getting. Then one of the three men hit him from behind, and the force of the blow caused him to fall to the ground. All three men took turns kicking him. Their blows were aimed mostly at his stomach, but there was also an occasional one to his chest or head.

The beating lasted almost a full minute as three pairs of brown shoes took turns slamming into him. When it finally stopped one of the men bent down and barked at him, "If you know what's good for you, you'll drop the case." With their warning duly given, the attackers each took the opportunity to kick Joe one last time before running out of the alley. Joe stayed on the ground for another minute or two then mumbled to himself, "God I miss Paris." He struggled to his feet and staggered up to his flat.

Ten minutes after the beating ended, he was looking at himself in the washroom mirror, assessing the damage. All in all, he decided, it wasn't so bad. The three guys who'd beaten him had only hit him in the face a couple of times, so there wasn't much visible bruising or damage. They had concentrated the majority of their blows on his mid-section. Once he'd hit the ground, he'd managed to use his arms and legs to shield himself. Consequently, the damage was limited to a few sore ribs and a large number of bruises on his arms and legs. As beatings went, it was a fairly mild one, which convinced him that whoever these guys were, they were amateurs.

Staring into the mirror and examining his face, he thought back to the number of beatings he'd suffered throughout his life. The first memorable ones had been at the orphanage. At the time, Joe had thought that a few of the senior boys delivered some fairly memorable beatings. After being thrown into a Russian jail, however, he found out what a real professional could do.

It had been Rick's idea for the two of them to go into business after the war. Rick had stayed in Paris because he had a death sentence hanging over his head back home. Joe had shipped back and mustered-out in April of '19. A couple of months later a letter arrived from Rick outlining his idea for an import/export business. Joe thought about it for almost five full seconds before deciding to book his passage back over to Europe. Once there, the two of them pooled what little money they had and opened a small office. The company they started cycled between boom and bust half a dozen times over their first five years.

CHAPTER 3 - TUESDAY

By the start of '26, they were riding their biggest boom yet, because the European economies were finally shaking off the effects of the war. Rick had the idea that there would be a strong demand for Russian luxury goods, such as vodka, caviar and furs. As a result, Joe grabbed a boat to Leningrad (as St. Petersburg was now called), in the spring of '26, to negotiate a deal with the Soviet Export Agency. He'd only intended to be in city for a couple of weeks, but just before his departure he was abruptly arrested. After three days in a holding cell he was charged with spying and thrown into the notorious Kresty Prison. It was there that he got his first taste of what a genuine beating was all about. He had never truly known what pain was until the GRU interrogators began to work him over. Sadly, their English wasn't very good, and Joe's Russian was still in its infancy. That meant that the repeated "questionings" rarely served any purpose. It was during one of those sessions that a deep gash opened up above his left eye.

After about a month of beatings, Joe couldn't take the pain anymore. He reluctantly signed a document they put in front of him. The writing was in the Cyrillic alphabet, which he didn't understand. After he signed, the beatings mercifully stopped. Later he would learn that, through this document, he'd denounced other "spies", none of whom he'd ever dealt with or even met.

Joe was eventually tried and convicted of "Wrecking" and transported to a Solovetskii labor camp in Karelia. It was at the camp that Joe learned to speak Russian. When he got there, he'd expected to be housed with convicted criminals, but to his surprise most of the camp was filled with political prisoners. Amazingly, many of them were leftists such as socialists, anarchists and even communists. As he would learn from his fellow inmates, the Bolsheviks who now ruled Russia couldn't tolerate dissent any more than the Czar. Many of their most vocal critics were fellow "Reds" who had fought the revolution alongside them and were now paying the price for failing to toe the party line.

During his time in Solovetskii he lost nearly fifty-five pounds and his health grew steadily worse. After eight months, he became reconciled to the fact that he was going to die in prison. He realized that his only regret in life was he'd never faced his past back in Chicago.

Then, on a clear sub-zero morning in late fall, he was placed in the back of large, unheated, canvas covered truck and driven away. He had expect that something like this might happen, because it was fairly common for a prisoner or two to be trucked off, never to be seen again. The open secret at the camp was that those taken were simply shot and buried in unmarked graves. When they came for him, he was resigned to the fact that it was his turn.

The drive lasted over six hours. When the truck stopped and guards finally pulled him out, he was nearly frozen to death and too weak to stand. Annoyed that their prisoner couldn't walk, the guards dragged him the last hundred yards and literally threw him towards a group of men standing nearby. One of the men in the group rushed forward and caught him just before he hit the ground. "I gotcha, buddy," was all Rick said as he picked Joe up and carried him towards a waiting ambulance. It had taken Rick nearly a year, and every penny he could lay his hands on, to organize Joe's release. It would take Joe four weeks in a Finnish hospital before he could return to Paris. Then, after two more months of convalescence, he told Rick that he needed to go back to Chicago, just for a little while, to come to terms with what he'd run away from.

CHAPTER FOUR

WEDNESDAY

I had a perfectly wonderful evening…but last night wasn't it -Groucho Marx

Morning

Joe's ribs and muscles ached as he pulled himself out of bed and slowly shuffled over to the window to check the weather. It looked like it was shaping up to be a blustery day with an overcast sky. Gingerly, he moved to the washroom. Once there, he examined his face in the mirror to see if the bruising had gotten worse. It had but he was pleased to see that it was better than he'd expected. In fact, the only thing that had actually suffered from the beating was his expensive English suit. His initial thought was to take it to Miss Ella, since she owned four laundries in and around Bronzeville. If he did, however, he was certain she'd ask him what had happened and that was a conversation he wanted to avoid. Reluctantly, he decided to take it to a laundry he knew in Chinatown.

On his way into the office he made a detour over to Canal Street to drop off his suit. The city was extending 22nd Street to improve access to the World's Fair Exposition. The resulting construction was making life extremely difficult for Chinatown. Mr. Huang, the owner of the laundry, gave Joe an earful about the construction and about a "Tong" war that was underway in Chinatown. It seemed Mr. Huang, and other members of the Chinese community, had asked the police to do something about the killings. They told him they didn't want to get involved and "what the celestials did to each other wasn't their concern." Mr. Huang then recited to Joe a Chinese curse, which translated in English meant "may you live in interesting times". Initially Joe didn't think it was much of a curse. As he walked back to his car, however, the man's words began to resonate. With what was happening both in his country and the world, he realized that the consequences of a curse like that could be devastating.

Joe arrived at the Reliance Building a bit later than usual. Crossing the lobby, he headed straight for the open elevator, and to Pudge. "Hey, Joe how's your day going?" said the operator, as the elevator doors sealed them in. "How about those Cubs yesterday, down by two runs to the Giants, and they came back to win it in the ninth by two."

Joe always told people that he didn't know why he hated the Cubs, he just did. The truth was, he knew exactly why he hated them. First, there was the name thing. Initially they were the White Stockings, then the White Sox, then the Colts, then the Orphans – which was a name Joe actually liked – and finally the Cubs. As a kid, that was confusing enough. What came later would be worse. Growing up, the team played just a few blocks away from St. Jerome's, at the old West Side Park. During the season, Joe's world revolved around them. Then, when Joe was a teenager, the team move to Weeghman Field on the north side of town. This was five miles away and, for a poor teenage kid, five miles might just have well been five thousand miles. The day they left it was as if someone had torn Joe's heart out, and it was this betrayal he could never forgive.

Pudge continued talking about the Cubs on the ride up, while Joe had paid absolutely no attention to anything he said. When they finally reached the sixth floor, the doors opened and, as Joe was half way out of the cab, Pudge shouted out, "I tell ya pally this is our year."

Joe immediately froze, then turned back and said in a calm and measured tone, "Pudge, if Jesus and the apostles came down from above and played for the Cubs this season, it still wouldn't be your year."

Somehow Pudge's oversized grin managed to grow even wider. "Not this year, buddy. This year we can't lose."

Joe mumbled an obscenity to himself as he walked away from the elevator, and the feisty Pole yelled out to him, "Have a great day, Joe."

Kat was sitting at her desk, trying to catch up on her typing as Joe entered the office. *"This building needs to get those new modern elevators that work without an operator,"* he grumbled in Russian. Joe first discovered his knack for languages when he was living in Paris after the war. French was the dominant language for business on the Continent, so he picked it up quickly. He also learned to speak German and Italian, because his import/export business was very active in both countries. For all three languages his comprehension was excellent. Sadly, his pronunciation wasn't, because his American accent was so thick.

He'd picked up Russian when he'd been a "guest" there, and he tried to spend some time each week practicing it with Kat. After all, he'd almost died in Russia, so it seemed a pity to lose his ability to speak the language since it was the only thing he took with him when he left. For her part, Kat appreciated the opportunity to speak her native tongue. But while Joe's vocabulary was improving, his accent made it a bit difficult understanding him, at times. Today was going to be a good day to practice because Sid was in Ft. Wayne. Sid hated it when anyone spoke anything but English in the office, because he was always afraid that they might be saying something about him.

"You only say that because you don't like Pudge," replied Kat, also in Russian. *"I think he's sweet."*

"Fortunately, I don't remember asking you," was his surly reply.

When she first started working with Joe she was scared to death of him, and a remark like that would have frightened her. Now, she just smiled and shot back, *"The truth is, you hate anyone who's in a good mood."*

"That's ridiculous," he replied defensively. *"I don't mind if someone's in a good mood. I just wish they'd keep it to themselves."*

"Well, Sid likes him. They're pals. I think they have lunch together a couple times a week."

"I think Sid likes him because he's secretly a Cubs fan," said Joe in disgust. *"He's been trying to hide it from me for years."*

Kat smiled as she shook her head, unable to fathom the American passion for baseball. Joe walked into his office, hung up his hat and coat and sat at his desk. Almost as soon as he sat down, Kat came in carrying a hot cup of strong black coffee and holding a newspaper.

"What's in the news, Kat?" he asked as she handed him his coffee.

She quickly scanned the headlines. *"Capone's off to jail today."*

"Finally!" Joe replied with a shake of his head. *"The bastard was convicted last October."*

"Language, Joseph," she responded, before continuing her sweep through the paper.

"Well, if anyone of us got sentenced to 11 years in prison, we'd have been sent up the same day. Capone gets to hang around his mansion for 7 months."

"The Tsar lives by his own rules," she lamented, and Joe agreed that her Russian proverb was spot-on.

Kat then commented on the next story. *"It looks like the Germans are going to have another election, either in June or early July. The Nazis could win an outright majority,"* she was clearly concerned. *"When Thomas and I were at the pictures on Saturday the newsreels showed the Nazis marching in Berlin."* She reached across the desk and grabbed her boss's hand, then looked into his eyes before adding, *"They frighten me, Joe, and this mad man, Hitler, reminds me of Stalin."*

Joe was also concerned, but decided to downplay the threat, for now. *"I wouldn't worry,"* he assured her. *"Hitler lost the presidency to Hindenburg last month, and I doubt he'll get a majority in the next election. His only route to power is if Hindenburg names him Chancellor. Fat chance that'll happen."* Then he changed the subject. *"What else you got?"*

"This woman, Amelia Earhart, is going to fly to Europe next week. She says she can do it in less than fifteen hours," Kat said in amazement.

"That's a long time to be cooped up in a little tin can," he observed. "Though it would be nice to visit Paris, and be back in less than a week," he added wistfully.

"Oh, I almost forgot, Marty phoned," she said. "He thinks he's solved at least part of the mystery around that rubber ball. He said you should swing by when you get the chance. He's teaching classes for most of the morning, but he'll be in his office after one-thirty." As she spoke, she noticed the bruise on the right side of his face. *"What happened to you?"* she asked in a worried tone. Walking round to his side of the desk, she sat on top and then reached out to examined his face.

"Some guys jumped me last night. They warned me to 'drop the case if I knew what was good for me'."

"Which case?" she asked as she lifted up his chin for a closer look.

"Unfortunately, they didn't say."

"*Well, did you ask them?*" Slowly, she turned his head from side to side to see how badly he was bruised.

Joe shot her a look and snapped back, "*Silly me, I was having such a hell-of-a-good time lying on the ground bleeding, it completely slipped my mind.*"

"*Language, Joseph,*" she reminded him, again. As for his sarcasm, she chose to ignore it as usual. "*You're lucky,*" she observed. "*It's not so bad this time.*" The only visible bruise was small and just along the top of his forehead. Gently, she brushed his hair back to get a better look. "*Not really that noticeable.*"

"*Yeah,*" he agreed. "*They were obviously amateurs. The ribs are a bit sore, but as beatings go, this was a pretty mild one.*"

"*So they told you to 'drop the case', but didn't bother to tell you which one?*"

"*Yeah. My guess is, they've read too many dime store novels. They probably think we work on just one at time. They must have just assumed I'd know which case they were talking about.*"

"*And they actually said '… if you know what's good for you'?*"

"*Yup.*" He took another sip of his coffee. "*That part I remember pretty clearly.*"

"*I didn't know people actually talked like that.*" She shook her head in disbelief. "*It sounds like something from a Cagney movie. You sure you're ok?*" she asked, clearly concerned.

"*I'm fine Kit-Kat. You know I'm indestructible.*"

"*Don't say that, Joseph,*" she snapped angrily. "*One of these days you're going to find out it's not true, and I shudder to think what will happen then.*"

Her reaction was sharp, so Joe decided to quickly change the subject, again. "*Do you know if Sid caught the train this morning?*"

Kat was still upset about his comment, but replied, "*He phoned just after 7:00 from Union Station. He said that he was catching the 7:25 and he told me to tell you not to worry – he knows what to look for. He should get into Fort Wayne by late morning. I told him to check in at the end of the day, just to give us an update on what he's found.*"

"I hope he finds something quickly. The old man doesn't have much time left."

Joe picked up the newspaper that Kat had carried in with the coffee. There was a picture of Gen Ericson on the bottom left half of the front page, with a caption that read "Co-Ed Murdered". *"She was on the front page of the other dailies as well,"* Kat said.

Joe quickly scanned the small article accompanying the photo, but there was nothing new in the story. *"Do me a favor and put the paper in my coat pocket. That's a good picture of the dead girl and it might come in handy later."*

Kat hopped off his desktop and put the folded paper into his inside trench coat pocket before walking back to her desk. Yesterday, when Joe had told her that he was looking into the young girl's death, she'd wondered why he decided to pick up this case. Afterall, he had never met the girl and no one had asked him to look into her death. After seeing the picture in this morning's paper, she knew why he was interested. Wendy had broken off their engagement just a few weeks before Kat came to work for Joe, but she knew what her leaving had done to him. She also could see that this co-ed was the spitting image of the photo Joe kept buried in the bottom-right drawer of his desk.

Joe called from his office to Kat. *"Do you remember the name of that private detective from New York that we helped out last year?"*

"Sure. It was a missing person's case," she replied. *"The guy's name was Manny Goldberg."*

Joe nodded to himself. *"Yeah, that's him. I need you to phone him and see if he'll do so some leg work for us."*

"Long distance is expensive."

"That's ok, we can charge it back to old man McNulty."

"So what do you want him to do?"

"Have him check out Emma O'Donnell's life in New York, the boarding house where she lived, the bank where she worked, the whole nine yards."

"What if he's too busy to take the job?"

"That won't happen if you sweet talk him," he replied with the hint of a smile. *"He was carrying a big torch for you."*

CHAPTER 4 – WEDNESDAY

A wistful look spread across Kat's face. *"He was a very sweet man,"* she said without any further explanation.

"After you talk to him, I need you get ahold of that guy we know in shipping at T&WA, over at the municipal airport." Joe's agency had done some work for the fledgling airline a few months back, because someone was stealing luggage. *"Tell him we have an envelope we need delivered to New York today."* Joe slipped the second photo of Emma into a manila envelope, sealed it, and wrote the detective's name on the outside. *"Be sure to put Goldberg's address and phone number on this before it goes out. Then get Mickey to run it over to the T&WA office at the Muni Airport. It's gotta get there before their last flight out, so if Mickey's pressed for time, tell him to take a cab."*

"A cab is way too expensive," she protested. There had been a time in Kat's life when money had meant nothing to her. Someone else had always handled it, and she'd never even thought about it. Nowadays she was always conscious of how much she had and how much things cost.

"It's ok, we can charge it all to old man McNulty."

Kat shook her head. *"You know Mickey's not going to take a cab, he'll tell us he did, but he'll take the trolley and pocket the difference."*

Joe nodded and replied, *"Probably, but I imagine he can use the extra dough, and as long as I don't know about it and the package gets there in time, it's jake."*

For whatever reason, Joe had a real soft spot for the kid, and Kat smiled at his response. *"Ok, I'll have him run it over just as soon as he comes in."* As she finished speaking, the phone rang. Kat let it ring two more times until finally picking it up and answering, "Argonne Detective Agency." She listened attentively for about a minute, replying "yes" several times to the female voice on the other end of the line. Once she'd placed the handset back into the cradle, she walked back into Joe's office and said, *"That was the Major's secretary, he'd like to see you as soon as possible."*

Robert Maddock, known to many as "the Major", had made his fortune publishing one of the nation's largest and most influential weekly magazines. Over the past ten years he had further expanded his empire which now included newspapers and radio stations. His relationship with Joe, however, began long before he'd made a name for himself in the business world. In October of '18, during the last big push of the Great

War, Joe's 77th Division had orders to advance on the German lines in an area known as the Argonne Forest. During the battle Joe became separated from his unit and was lost behind enemy lines. Avoiding artillery blasts, German patrols, and snipers was no easy task. After nightfall, it became even harder. He'd wandered through no-man's land for hours, searching for the American lines. Exhausted, he sought refuge in a large crater whose only other occupant was a dead soldier lying face down in the mud. At this point in the war, Joe had seen so much death that he paid no attention to the thousands of bodies strewn across the battlefield. Not long after he entered the crater, however, and much to his surprise, the dead man moved. That had been his first encounter with Major Robert Maddock.

Joe turned to Kat and asked, *"Did she say what he wanted?"*

"No, but she said it was very important."

"Ok, I'll head over to his office in a few minutes."

"And don't forget, you promised to phone Mr. Gibbs and give him an update sometime today," reminded Kat.

"I remember," he lied. *"I'll ring him later. Right now, I don't have anything to tell him."*

Joe let out a deep breath and stared at the phone. He had realized yesterday, after giving Sid the background information on the McNulty case, that he hadn't given him a lot to work with. He knew the reason was because he hadn't done his job when he first met Emma. To fix this, he needed to arrange another interview but the idea made him nervous and caused his stomach to knot up slightly. He lit up a cigarette and took a couple of pulls. Then he picked up the handset and had the operator to connect him to her number. After an awkward start to their conversation, he managed to explain that he had some follow up questions. "Would it be possible to meet up sometime this afternoon?" He felt nervous when asking and hoped that this wasn't reflected in his voice.

"I'd love to see you, Joe," Emma replied, clearly sounding pleased at the prospect.

"I'll need about an hour of your time. Would you mind if I dropped by around three or four?"

"That would be swell. I'm going to be here all afternoon and I'd love some company. I'll see you then." After he hung up, his mind continued to hold the image of the beautiful blue-eyed girl, and without realizing it he was smiling once more.

Fifteen minutes later Joe left the office to meet with the Major. The section of Michigan Avenue where he was headed was located on the north side of the Chicago River. In the past, that stretch of road on the river's north side had always been called Pine Street. The Major, however, had been adamant that anything as beautiful as his towering gothic thirty-five stories headquarters couldn't have a Pine Street address. Shortly after the bridge was completed in '28, he got the city to change the name Pine Street to Michigan Avenue. Joe walked into the impressive Art Deco lobby of the Maddock Building and took one of the eight automatic elevators up to a private office on the 26th floor.

Joe entered the palatial private office that at once personified both power and wealth. As he did, a tall man with a decidedly military bearing rose from behind a massive mahogany desk. He grabbed his cane and walked over to greet him. The Major still sported the full moustache that he'd worn in his youth but, like his dark brown head of hair, it was now heavily tinted with gray.

"How are you, Joe?" he asked as he grabbed the outstretched hand in front of him.

"I'm fine, Major," he responded with a smile, "and you, sir?"

"Well, the leg hurts, but hell that's hardly news, is it?" he replied, as he slapped his wounded leg and chuckled. He ushered his guest across the parquet floor, and they sat down in two upholstered high-backed chairs positioned next to a double-sized window. With Chicagoland being so flat and the Maddock building so tall, the view through the windows was incredible.

The Major was an extremely busy man who rarely held meetings that lasted more than five minutes. When meeting with his friends, however, he thoroughly enjoyed a good round of gossip. Typically, these sessions would bounce from topic to topic at a fairly rapid pace. His conversation with Joe went on for over a half hour as the two men shared the latest facts and rumors about people, politics, sports, and world events.

Sooner or later, their conversation always turned to Rick. "How's that friend of yours, he still in Europe?" The Major never failed to ask about him and it always brought a smile to Joe's face. When Rick had been awaiting execution for assaulting an officer, Joe had gone to him asking for help. Maddock had been sympathetic but had told him that there was nothing he could do. Then, on the morning Rick was scheduled to be executed, Joe learned he'd escaped. It didn't take him long to figure out who it was that had sprung his friend. When he went to thank him, Maddock looked him square in the eye and said in a stern voice, "Let's be clear, I had absolutely nothing to do with your friend's escape," then he gave him a quick wink and a smile. The two men never discussed the matter again, but Joe always felt a deep sense of gratitude to him.

"He's fine, sir," Joe replied.

"Staying out of trouble, I hope?"

"I got a letter from him last week and I hear his import/export business is doing very well. Oh, and before I forget, I wanted to thank you for writing that recommendation for Mickey." Joe had carried a wounded and badly bleeding Maddock over a mile through no-man's land, and saved his life. The debt the Major felt he owed him was immense. As one of Chicago's most wealthy and powerful men, there was little he couldn't do for him. What always impressed the Major, however, was that Joe had never asked anything for himself, he only asked on behalf of others.

"Well, to tell you the truth, my secretary wrote it and I'm not sure what she said, but I'm certain it was something appropriate. I did run into Dean Simmons at the Chicago Club last week. He tried to tell me some nonsense about having already given out this year's scholarship money. Now don't you worry, I straightened old 'Fuzzy' out. Did you know that's what we use to call him back in college?" asked the Major with his trademark smile. "That's because he couldn't grow a decent mustache. All he could get was some peach fuzz under his lip," he added with a loud chuckle. "Now if your young man doesn't get what he's looking for from the university, you just let me know."

Joe nodded and added, "I appreciate your help, sir."

"Always glad to help when I can, you know that," he replied with a sincere smile. Then his face turned sad as he quickly switched the subject. "Pity about old man Wrigley, isn't it?"

Joe looked surprised. "What happened to him?"

CHAPTER 4 – WEDNESDAY

"He died at his home in Catalina last night. I hear his son P.K. will be taking over the business, chewing gum, Cubs and all," he said with a laugh. "My magazine is preparing an obit on him right now."

Then the Major changed the subject once more, this time to his least favorite topic, Franklin Roosevelt. He was fiercely anti-Roosevelt and swore to Joe, "There is no way that man becomes president. I promise you that, even if he gets the nomination he won't win. He's a damn socialist for God's sake." Joe just smiled. He'd learned a long time ago that there were two topics where you just couldn't have a reasonable discussion with the Major. One was Roosevelt and the other, oddly enough, was the English aristocracy. It was Joe's theory that the Major had felt slighted by the senior British officers during the war, but whatever the reason, he hated the English upper class.

"Let me get to the reason I asked you here," began the Major. "I need your help. I have a radio station in town called WBM." Joe was well aware of the Major's station and nodded his head. "When we started the damn thing we thought it might help support the magazine. We actually chose the letters WBM because it matched our logo, 'World's Best Magazine'. To tell you the truth, I didn't really think there would be much of a business in radio. I have to tell you, I completely underestimated what kind of revenue radio could produce. I thought the only people who were going to make any money from it were the companies building the damn sets. I missed that one by a mile. The station is actually making quite a profit, and it has the potential to make even more. These new table-top sets are selling dirt cheap, and there's a new company here in Chicago called Motorola that's selling sets for your car. Imagine that, listening to the radio in your car as you're driving along. I can't for the life of me think why anyone would want to do that, but now you can," he added with a shake of his head.

"When we started WBM, ten years ago, there were only a handful of sets out there. Now they tell me there are nearly a half a million sets just here in Chicago, and that number grows daily. Five years ago we were broadcasting mostly music and news, with an occasional sporting event thrown in. But over the past few years, my station has joined the Quality Network, so we've begun to broadcast an evening schedule of programs. We started this new comedy last week called the Lum and Abner show. It's pretty good, if you ask me. Those two guys are a hoot," chuckled the Major. "And these scheduled programs are bringing even bigger advertising revenue. Well, just when I thought I had this radio business all figured out, along comes someone with a new idea. You see, up to now, everyone took as gospel that the evenings were the only time that people would listen to the radio. After all, most people worth their salt are working during the day, and since everyone was working, we couldn't get much revenue from daytime advertising. But wouldn't you know that the people at WMAC, across town, came up with an idea that could drastically increase radio's revenue. They started broadcasting this daily program about a working family here in Chicago. Not a real family, mind you, just some actors reading from a script. The broadcasts began about eighteen months ago, and it's a fifteen-minute drama called 'Day Dreams'. When I first heard about it I thought it was a silly idea. Every weekday, at the same time, people are supposed to tune in to hear about this family and their daily problems. And these stories never end!" exclaimed the Major. "They just keep going and going every weekday."

"My secretary listens to that show."

"Now that's exactly what I'm talking about. The ladies are tuning in every day."

"This is all very interesting, Major, but I can't for the life of me figure out how I'm going to be able to help you with any of this."

"Well, I'm getting to that. I just have to give you some of the 'back-story'," he explained. The Major was famous for his lengthy 'back-stories' and Joe hoped that he would get to the point sometime soon. "This show 'Day Dreams' has got legions of fans, almost all women. I hear that WMAC gets more mail from that show than they do for Amos 'n Andy," he said disbelievingly. "And the advertising revenue is starting to climb. It seems the companies that sell household products like toothpowder and soap have found a way, through this show, to reach the ladies. And when it comes to buying household products, they're the ones that hold the purse strings."

"Well, if the idea is such a good one, why don't you just start your own show?"

"I tried, twice!" explained the Major. "Both shows were flops. It seems that the writing for these daytime dramas has to be done in just the right way. The writers we hired just didn't understand what the women folk want. So I did what any good businessman would do in my position, I hired away the gal who was writing 'Day Dreams'. Her name is Irene

CHAPTER 4 - WEDNESDAY

Fields and the people at WMAC didn't appreciate what they had. They were paying the lady peanuts and I offered to triple her salary, syndicate her new show, and give her a piece of the profits."

"What exactly is 'syndicating a show'?"

"Well now, that's another new idea. What we do is sell the show to other stations. They pay for the right to play a recording of the show, and they get the show for a fraction of the cost if they tried to produce it themselves. We get money from hundreds of stations instead of just one. It's a sweet deal all around."

"Ok, so if you hired Irene Fields it sounds like your problem is solved."

"That's what I thought too, but yesterday the lady calls me in tears and tells me she can't accept the job. My first thought was that WMAC matched my offer, so I convinced her to meet me last night so I could find out what they offered her. Well, after a couple of drinks I was able to coax out the truth. It seems someone is blackmailing her. They have something on her, and she was told that if she leaves WMAC they'll release what they have to the press."

"Did she say what kind of information it was?"

"No, she wouldn't say, but whatever it is, she would do anything to keep it from coming out. She told me last night that the blackmailer has insisted she sign a new five-year contract at WMAC next Monday."

"Do you think the management of WMAC is behind this?"

"WMAC is owned by Giles Brewster," observed the major, "and I've known him for twenty years. He's a hardnosed son-of-a-bitch, but I can't imagine him doing something like this. No, if there's involvement by WMAC it's going to be at a much lower level. What I need you to do is find a way to stop this."

"I'll see what I can do, major, but I'll need to speak to Miss Fields. I'm going to need details that only she can give me."

"I figured that might be the case, so I told her that you would want to see her sometime this afternoon. She's agreed to meet you at WMAC's studios over at the Mart. She has to be there all afternoon." Then the Major's face took on a serious expression. "The woman is frightened, Joe. She's afraid any investigation will cause her blackmailers to release the information. I've assured her that you will be the soul of discretion."

"I understand, sir," he replied. "I'll be as discrete as possible."

The Maddock Building to the City/County Building was a fifteen-minute walk. While it was still cool out with an overcast sky Joe decided to brave the elements, along with his sore ribs, and hoof it over to see Bill Dailey. The walk took him back over the river and west along the upper level of the new Wacker Drive. When he reached La Salle, he headed south, under the 'L' and wound up at an eleven-story office building that consumed an entire block in the heart of the Loop. The building was constructed from huge blocks of granite in a neoclassical style. The east side was used for the County's offices, while the west side hosted the City. Joe entered the City's side of the building fronting La Salle, before walking up three floors to the Treasury Office, where he asked for William Dailey.

Bill Dailey was five foot seven, medium build, with brown hair and eyes. He was born and raised in the Back-of-the-Yards, a section of Chicago adjacent to the Stockyards. Bill had met Joe on his second day at De La Salle High School and they'd been friends ever since. Bill's open and friendly style allowed him to collect friends just as some people collected stamps. Within a year of graduating high school he started working for "Slim" Jim McDonald, one of the city's ward leaders. When Slim became the City Treasurer in '30, Bill became the de facto treasurer. When Cermak became mayor last year, Bill joined the new "Political Machine" he was building in the city's democratic wards.

Bill's secretary led Joe through the maze of corridors, until they reached a private office with the words Assistant City Treasurer stenciled on the door. Joe stuck his head in the office and asked, "How's night school going?"

Bill had been attending DePaul Law School at night since '24. "Believe it or not, I think I'll be done next year."

"So does that mean you and Elli are finally getting hitched?"

"That's the plan," he replied. "So tell me, what brings you deep into the bowels of the city offices?"

"Well, for one thing, I wanted to thank you for writing that recommendation to the university for Mickey."

"You kidding me? He's a De La Salle kid. I was glad I could help, but to tell you the truth, I wasn't sure my recommendation would be worth all that much, so I got the mayor to send one in as well."

CHAPTER 4 – WEDNESDAY

"How did you swing that?" asked Joe, surprised.

"I slipped it in with some routine party correspondence. He signs so much stuff in a day, he rarely pays attention to what he's signing." Bill looked Joe in the eye and smiled, "You could have phoned to thank me, you didn't need to come down, so I'm guessing you're really here for something else? What gives?"

"What can you tell me about this Exposition project?"

"The Century of Progress?" Bill was surprised that Joe wanted to talk about the planned World's Fair. "It's going to draw millions of people if everything goes as planned. It opens next spring on a landfill site south of the Loop along the shoreline."

"I know that part. What can you tell me about the finance and construction?"

"Well, it was conceived as a follow up to the World's Fair held back in '93. Then the depression hit and luckily for the city, it quickly turned into a great public works project."

"I'm working on the murder of the city engineer Fritz Steiner and I understand he was the city's lead engineer on that project."

"Steiner? I thought they arrested some kid for that murder?"

"They did, but I'm looking into the case."

"Ah," said Bill with another smile, "you mean Father Frank has you looking into the case."

Joe simply nodded. He knew that Bill was a devout Catholic and went to mass every day. Other people might kid him about doing free work for Frank, but Bill never would. "I'm looking for possible motives and a ten million construction budget might give some people sticky fingers."

"I see what you're getting at, but I think you're barking up the wrong tree on this one. I'm actually not that involved because a separate corporation was set up to build and run the exposition," he explained, "but I can tell you there are more accountants keeping track of that money than on any project I've ever seen."

"What about the unions? Are they causing any problems on the project?"

"There were some problems a few months back, but from what I've heard they've been settled," Bill replied.

It looked like Bill didn't have anything useful for him, so Joe was about to say his goodbyes when another thought popped into his head. "Is there anything can you tell me about the project to refurbish the Washington Street Bridge?"

Bill looked puzzled. "The Washington Street Bridge project? Why would you want to know about that?"

"I'm also looking into the death of a young girl who was campaigning to stop the bridge's refurbishment, and I'm trying to get some background on the project."

Dailey shuffled through the mountain of paperwork on his desk until he found the file he was looking for. Then he skimmed some of the pages in the file before replying. "Well, that project was put in the budget at the request of the city's Bridge and Road Department. They recommended that the bridge have some refurbishment work done. The project was also being pushed by Congressman Bayles."

"Isn't it a bit unusual for a US congressman to get involved in a city project?"

"No, not really. You see the job is going through because Bayles got some money put into a federal spending bill last term, and that will cover about half the cost. That's one of the major benefits to being a congressman," Bill explained. "They can insert what are called 'earmarks' into spending bills. It's usually not a lot of money, just a little bit of pork to placate the constituents. If you ask me," he added, "I can't see why the bridge would need refurbishment. It was built in '13 and should last for another fifty years. But I'm not going to question both the city's Department of Public Works and a congressman. Especially when half the tab is being footed up by the Feds."

"So what can you tell me about Congressman Bayles?"

"He's a rising star in the Democratic Party and he has his eye on the Illinois Senate seat, which is up for grabs in November. From what I can tell, he has the connections you need to make a run at it. In the last census there were about ten million people in Illinois. Half of them are right here in Cook County. Bayles has built strong relationships here. He got his start years ago in a city job, then won a county election, and eventually a seat in Congress. He's the Democratic frontrunner for the

Senate nomination, and with the Republicans running Hoover again, any Democratic nominee will be a shoe-in this fall."

"Any chance that Bayles is on the take?"

"Come on, Joe," said Bill with a smile. "This is Chicago. Corruption is measured here in degrees not absolutes, he could well have his hand in other people's pockets but if he does, he's quiet about it."

"I don't think I've ever seen him. What's he look like?"

Bill once again rummaged around the stacks of papers piled on his desk and found a campaign flyer that read "Bayles for US Senate". "Here's a picture of him," he said as he handed Joe one of the flyers.

"Can I keep this?"

"Be my guest, I've got hundreds of 'em. We had 'em done in the city's print shop."

"Can you do that?"

"Course not, but like I keep telling ya, this is Chicago. Simply having a law that says it's illegal won't stop anyone from doing it," he explained with a chuckle.

"I may need to speak with Bayles. Do you know if he's back in Washington or here in Chicago?"

"He's in town. He has to be if he wants to wrap up the nomination. The Democratic National Convention gets underway here in about two months so he'll stay close 'til that's over. I heard he was at the Grand Terrace Ballroom just last Saturday. Someone said he was with a gorgeous blonde bombshell." Joe looked surprised but Bill shook his head and said, "What do you expect? His wife's back in Washington and he's a lonely guy."

"If it got out that he was with another woman wouldn't that hurt his chances for the nomination?"

Once again Bill chuckled. "Politicians don't exactly worry about that sort of thing hurting their reputation. In many ways, being seen with an attractive woman helps your reputation. You see, there are unwritten rules that govern the press. The first rule is, the personal life of a politician is never reported. I'll give you an example. One of the front-runners for the Democratic Presidential Nomination is this guy Roosevelt. From what I hear, he has trouble walking and sleeps with his secretary.

Those of us who support Al Smith for the nomination would love the press to report some of that stuff, but they won't. There are a few things that aren't off limits of course," he continued. "Stuff like divorce, homosexuality, drugs are fair game, but personal vices like liquor, gambling and women just can't be mentioned. You'd be amazed what goes on, but never gets reported." It was at this point that Bill noticed the time, and explained to Joe that he was late for a meeting.

Afternoon

Kat was standing in front of one of the file cabinets, sorting through a large stack of papers, as Joe entered the office. She was also sucking on another lollypop.

"*Is that one of the suckers I picked up yesterday?*" he asked, once again speaking in Russian.

"*No, I ate those already, but I picked up a couple more at lunch time. They're called Tootsie Pops and they have a small piece of Tootsie Roll right in the center,*" she said with a satisfied grin. "*I love 'em.*" Joe shook his head. Kat's sweet tooth was in direct contrast to her slim figure, and he could never figure out how she did it. "*What did the Major want?*" she asked.

"*It seems he's trying to hire a woman at WBM and someone is blackmailing her to keep her from joining his station. He wants us to figure out who's doing the bleeding and put the kibosh on it.*"

"*So what's so special about this woman?*" she asked as she continued her filing.

"*She writes that radio drama you listen to, 'Day Dreams'.*"

Kat looked up from her filing and her eyes just about popped from her head. "*Really?*" she shouted in her excitement. Then a series of questions came flooding out. "*Have you met her yet? What's she like? Are you going to meet any of the show's cast? Where do they broadcast? Can you find out what's going to happen to Mary Ellen?*"

"*Hold your horses,*" he snapped, clearly stunned by her enthusiasm. "*We just got the case and I haven't had time to do anything or meet anyone. I'm going over to WMAC's studios this afternoon and I'll meet with her then.*"

"*Can you see if you can get me some autographs?*" she asked, still excited. Joe didn't say anything but shot her a look that showed how annoyed he was. "*Well, only if you get the chance,*" she added defensively. She decided to change the subject. "*So with the addition of this case, how many are we working on right now?*"

Joe began a recap of the cases. "*There's the dead city engineer, Fritz Steiner, and then the murder of this young co-ed, Gen Ericson. So that's two murders.*"

"*Actually, there are three if you count the Greek sailor who's involved in Mr. Patel's case.*"

"*Right, I forgot about him, but for all we know Kyranos was gunned down over a skirt. So let's keep that one out of the murder column for now.*"

"*Ok, so that's three cases,*" said Kat.

"*Then there's the McNulty case, and now we also have this new one involving blackmail. So that's a total of five.*"

"*How many are for paying clients?*" she asked.

"*Three. Patel who fortunately paid us in advance, McNulty, and this new case from the Major.*"

"*Five cases isn't too bad,*" she observed, "*but it would be nice to clear at least one of the them before anything new comes up.*"

Joe nodded his agreement to Kat's remark as he walked back to his office. With five cases they were busy, but it was manageable. In the past they had handled as many as nine cases, but things had gotten pretty crazy trying to keep that many balls in the air. They'd been lucky that one or more of those cases hadn't gone wonky on them. Sitting down at his desk, Joe stared at the note pad he'd scribbled in the night before. As he was reading, he noticed that one of the doodles simply said "Unions". He called out to Kat, "*When you talked to Sid yesterday did he tell you if he got any information on Steiner's relationship with the unions?*"

"*He didn't turn up anything useful,*" she responded, while walking into his office. She sat on the edge of the desk and continued, "*He said that the union guys disliked Steiner, and won't shed any tears that he's dead. But they'd worked out a deal and were getting jobs on the project, so there was no reason for any rough stuff. Do you want me to ask Sid to do some more digging when he gets back from Fort Wayne?*"

"No, Bill Dailey thought the union stuff was settled as well. If that's the case, I just don't see a union angle here. Did Sid mention anything about the German club the Steiners belonged to?"

"He and Mickey came up with 'Bupkis'." Kat couldn't help but smile as she used one of Sid's favorite words. "He said that as much as he'd love to pin a murder on the Nazis, there's no motive. They got what they wanted, took control of the local club, and have merged it into the 'Friends of Germany'. So there's no point to killing Steiner." She glanced over at Joe and asked, "Where does that leave us?"

"Nowhere, and we're running out of suspects."

"You think the kid did it?"

"It doesn't matter what I think, if we don't find some hard evidence they'll fry him for sure."

"Well, we still have the Exposition project, and there must be millions in construction contracts underway."

"Thirty million actually."

Her eyes widened slightly. "That's a lot of temptation. If Steiner became involved in a scheme to skim money, that's a great motive for murder."

"Yeah," said Joe hesitantly, "but Bill Dailey didn't think that was possible. He says there are a boat load of auditors watching how every penny is spent, and their accounting system is foolproof."

"Nothing is foolproof because fools are so ingenious."

"Let me guess, more Russian wisdom?"

"No, that one's from Mr. Kochakian my Armenian butcher." Then she added by way of explanation, "But he's a very smart man."

"So if your butcher's right, maybe Steiner wasn't involved in a scheme, but he uncovered someone else's embezzlement. Then someone killed him to keep him from spilling the beans. When Sid gets back tomorrow, ask him to see what he can dig up on the project. Maybe Steiner left some bread crumbs we can follow."

Just then Mickey entered the office. He was carrying a manila envelope and called out to his boss, "The professor called while you were gone. He asked me to pick this up, and said to tell ya that it's a report on the

Washington Street Bridge. He went through it and wrote some notes for ya, and said that I needed to get them to ya right away."

"Thanks, Mickey," replied Joe, once again speaking English. "Did you get a chance to look around the campus while you were there?"

Mickey entered Joe's office and handed him the envelope. "I sure did, Mr. L. Jeepers it's real swell! The professor told me that I should hear from the Dean's office any day now. He said things were looking pretty good."

"That's great, Mickey, let's keep our fingers crossed." Joe pulled out the engineering report from the envelope, as well as some handwritten notes Marty had made on a separate sheet of paper. The notes referred to different pages of the report. Reading though them revealed that the Washington Street Bridge had some significant structural problems.

"According to Marty," Joe said to his co-workers, "the draw bridge is in danger of collapse, and this so-called 'refurbishment' is nothing short of a complete reconstruction. Mickey, I need you to go over to the Department of Public Works and see if they have any info on that Bridge – when it was built, who built it, that sort of thing." Joe checked his watch, grabbed his hat and coat, and headed for the door. "I'll be back in a couple of hours, Kat. I gotta run down to the Mart and meet up with Irene Fields."

Kat lifted her head and shouted to him as he walked out the door. "If you see any of the actors, don't be afraid to ask for autographs. I hear they love giving them out."

The Merchandise Mart, known simply as "the Mart", is a massive structure built from concrete and steel, and clad with white stone blocks. Although completed just two years ago, it was already a city landmark. Located at the northwest corner of the Loop district, the building covered two city blocks. It also had the distinction of being the world's largest building, comprising nearly four million square feet. The first two floors of the Mart were set aside for commercial and retail activity, while the upper floors of the two eighteen-story wings were a mixture of showroom and warehouse space. The office space was housed in the twenty-five story center tower, and it's on one of the upper floors of this tower where WMAC had its broadcast studio.

After several wrong turns Joe eventually found the WMAC studios, where the station's receptionist pointed him towards Studio C. Once there, he could see a handmade sign on the door that read "Day Dreams". As he entered the studio, a large lighted sign was flashing "On-Air". A nervous woman spotted him and immediately put a finger to her lips. Joe nodded his compliance and took a seat in the back row of the room. There were about twelve people sitting in the room – some in small groups, and some sitting by themselves. All of them were looking through a large plate glass window at the front of the room. On the other side of that window was the soundstage, where seven actors were holding up scripts and reciting their lines into a microphone. Joe could hear them only through speakers mounted in the front corners of the room. It was a strange sensation seeing the actor's lips move but hearing their words come from a completely different direction a fraction of a second later.

Many of the other people in the room were also holding scripts, and seemed to be following along with the actors. One of them, a woman, was visibly upset and without removing the cigarette dangling from her lips whispered to the man next to her, "Damn him, he's ad libbing again. Why is it so fucking hard for the actors to stick to the script?"

After a few more minutes of dialogue, a disembodied voice came over the speaker and proclaimed, *"And so ends another episode of Day Dreams, brought to you by the makers of Super Suds, the only soap created especially for dishwashing. Remember that Super Suds dissolves instantly and completely, protecting the smooth loveliness of your hands. Thanks for listening, and be sure to tune in tomorrow for another chapter of Chicago's favorite daytime radio drama, Day Dreams."* The speaker went quiet for a few seconds, before a monotone voice announced, "We're clear." This was quickly followed by the sound of a loud bell ringing. Immediately the room Joe was sitting in erupted in noise, and the twelve people who had been present raced towards one of the two doors that led to the soundstage.

The woman who had whispered her disapproval now screamed at one of the actors on the soundstage. "Wilfred, the damn line is '… my love for you is ETERNAL'. If I had wanted the character to say 'my love for you will go on and on and on', I would have written that. Let's review what I did write, shall we?"

Joe guessed that this must be Irene Fields.

CHAPTER 4 – WEDNESDAY

"For God's sake, Eddie," shouted the frustrated Irene, "can you get me some God damn actors who will read the script as I wrote it? And Marvin," she continued as she looked over at a weary middle aged man at the other end of the soundstage, "you call yourself a director? Could you please direct these morons so that my characters have at least one of the multiple dimensions I created for them? Don't you think that would be nice, Marvin?" she asked in a mocking tone.

"At least one dimension," repeated a disinterested Marvin without looking up from his clipboard. "I'll make a note of that."

Several frightened actors flew past Joe, scrambling off the soundstage before the writer's wrath was redirected at them. Joe approached the woman and said, "Excuse me, are you Irene Fields?"

"Yes," shouted the writer in reply, before turning to face him. "What do you want?" Clearly, she was about to explode again, as her temper was barely held in check.

"A mutual friend asked me to stop by today and talk with you about a problem you're having."

It took a couple of seconds for Irene both to calm down and register Joe's remark. Then she responded in a much softer voice, "You must be Mr. Lorde."

"That's me."

"You'll have to excuse my outburst just now," she apologized, "but actors are the bane of my existence."

"Perhaps it would be best if we talked in private."

"Yes, of course," she agreed. "Perhaps we can go somewhere where the average IQ is at least above room temperature."

Irene led him down a corridor to an empty office, and the two of them sat down. She lit up another cigarette before explaining, "My office is at the Standard Oil Building, which is just a few blocks away. I come over here for rehearsals and the broadcasts, but I can't write here. There are just too many distractions."

"From your comments back there, I gather the broadcast today didn't go that well."

"It's the damn actors," she complained, after letting out a cloud of cigarette smoke. "It's always the damn actors. I've heard it said that a talented one can mesmerize an audience by creating unique characters that spring to life. Unfortunately, I've never had the privilege of working with any that had talent. In fact, I believe the phrase 'talented actor' is an oxymoron." She was almost shouting as she finished the last sentence, but the tone of her voice lowered slightly as she added, "Or perhaps they're like the Himalayan Yeti. People tell stories about them, but no one has ever actually seen one. Anyway, I can tell you from personal experience that mediocre actors aren't capable of creating shit."

Joe was uncertain how to respond, so he asked, "Is this a bad time, Miss Fields?"

The writer took a pull on her cigarette and said in a calmer voice, "Please call me Irene, and frankly, after that broadcast, I welcome the interruption."

"So what can you tell me about this blackmail attempt?"

"Well, it's like I told Mr. Maddock. I was contacted and told to sign a new five-year contract with WMAC. They said that if I didn't they would release some information that would ruin my life. I'm afraid that's about all I can tell you." She nervously took a long drag off her cigarette, exhaled, then suddenly felt embarrassed. "Excuse me, where are my manners?" she said before holding out her pack of Lucky Strikes towards Joe.

"That's ok," he replied, as he took out his pack of Chesterfields and began searching for a match. Irene instinctively tossed him the red matchbook she'd been using. Joe lit up and was about to throw the matches back, but she held up her hand and said, "Keep 'em."

He took a pull on his cigarette. "Can you tell me how they contacted you?"

"I got a letter in the mail." She reached into her briefcase and took out the envelope. Joe looked at it carefully. It was a standard white letter-sized envelope, the kind you could buy at any stationary store or Five & Dime. There was no address or postmark, just Irene's name, which had been typed on the front. Inside, there was a single typed page on plain bond paper. The contents of the letter were almost exactly what Irene had already described to him.

Joe held it up and asked, "May I keep this for a while?"

"You can keep it forever," she replied sadly.

"There was more than just this letter, wasn't there?"

"I don't know what you mean."

"You just told me that they contacted you through the mail, but this letter has no address or postmark. So obviously it was inside another envelope." Irene looked away. "I realize you don't want to go into the details about the blackmail," he said sympathetically, "but they must have sent you something else, something that would convince you they have the information they claim to have."

She sat silently for several seconds, still not making eye contact. Then she said softly, "I'm afraid I can't be of any further help, Mr. Lorde."

Joe shook his head and replied in a gentle voice, "Irene, Look at me." The reluctant woman slowly glanced up. Once they made eye contact, he continued, "you're going to have to think of me like a priest. If you don't confide in me, you can't be saved." He gave her a second to think about what he'd said before adding, "You gotta give me something more to go on. Can you at least tell me what else they sent you? Was it photos, documents, an article of clothing, a trinket? It would help if I knew what I was looking for."

"Photos," she blurted out before taking another nervous drag on her cigarette. "I was sent photos."

"How many?"

Again a nervous puff, "Ten ... maybe ... I guess. I can't say for sure. I burned them as soon as I saw them."

"You burned them?" he repeated as a question.

Again Irene stopped making eye contact. Looking down at her shoes, she responded softly, "Yes."

"Can you describe what these photos showed?"

Irene looked squarely at her investigator. "They were ..." she paused for several seconds while searching for the right word, then finished her sentence by saying "... private." She took another nervous puff before adding, "And it's imperative that they stay private."

Joe could see that there was a line he couldn't cross and changed his tack. "Do you still have the manila envelope that the letter and photos came in?"

"No," she responded, "I burned it along with the pictures."

"Did you recognize the handwriting on the envelope?"

"No, the address was typed and there was no return address."

"How about the postmark? Did you see where it was mailed from?"

She let out a sigh and some more smoke as she replied, "I didn't think of that." Her hands were now shaking, and she was obviously distraught.

Joe was worried that she could bolt at any minute. "Just a couple more questions," he assured her. "I assume you were in the photos." Irene took a puff and let out the smoke, but didn't answer. "Can you tell me when and where they were taken?"

"They were taken a couple of weeks ago," she replied. "I'm afraid I don't know where. I had gone out for the evening with an old friend of mine, Toddy Frances ... I'm sorry his name is actually Frederick but everyone calls him Toddy. He's the manager of the Majestic Theater over on West Monroe and he's one of my oldest and dearest friends. The two of us met up late one night and went clubbing."

"Was anyone else with you that night?"

"We met a man named Paul at one of the clubs. He was with us the rest of the evening ... and ... he was in the pictures as well," she confessed.

"Does Paul have a last name?"

"Trent," she replied. "His name is Paul Trent."

"Have you had any contact with Paul since the night you went clubbing?"

"No. I haven't seen or spoken to him since."

"Do you have any idea where I can find him?"

"No. If he told me anything about himself, I'm afraid I just don't remember."

"Had you ever met him before?"

"I'd seen him once or twice at one of the clubs, but I'd never actually met him."

"How well do you remember the evening?"

"Only bits and pieces," she admitted. "I do know that I was ... with Paul, but I don't remember where we were or anyone taking photos. I don't even know how I got home. I'm not often drunk, Mr. Lorde, but I was horribly drunk that night."

"Have you talked to Mr. Frances about this situation?"

"Yes, I told Toddy everything. I was hoping he could fill in some of the blanks, but it seems he was so plastered he doesn't remember anything either. This sort of thing happens much more frequently to Toddy than it does to me," she added with a brief and nervous smile.

"What, getting blackmailed?"

"No," she replied clearly annoyed, "getting drunk."

"Since Mr. Frances already knows about this blackmail attempt, would you mind if I talked to him? He might remember a little more about that night."

"Sure, go ahead," she replied. "I'll phone him after you leave, and let him know it's ok for the two of you to speak."

"Do you know which clubs you visited that night?"

"No, I'm afraid I don't, but Toddy might."

"One last thing," said Joe. "Clearly WMAC benefits from this blackmail. Do you think anyone here could be behind this?"

"The station?" Irene thought carefully about Joe's question. "Well, I guess it wouldn't surprise me if that little worm Eddie Collins was involved somehow. He's the producer of the show."

"You think he organized this blackmail attempt?"

"Eddie couldn't organize his pencil drawer, but I wouldn't be surprised if he was involved."

"Why would Eddie, or anyone else, go to these lengths to keep you at WMAC?"

"Do you remember the radio show 'Sam 'n Henry'?"

"It rings a bell, but I can't tell you much more than that."

"It was on a local Chicago station a few years back," Irene explained. "The two guys who wrote and starred in it, Gosden and Corell, were lured away to another station with the promise of syndicating their show. They started an identical show they called 'Amos 'n Andy'."

"Let me guess. The station that lost them lost thousands of dollars?"

"More like millions, actually. Amos 'n Andy is the most popular radio program in the country. It's nationally syndicated and is being listened to by nearly ten million people each week. I'm afraid someone doesn't want that sort of thing to happen with 'Day Dreams'."

"Thanks for talking with me," said Joe, as he rose from his chair.

Irene looked at him, the anxiety showing clearly on her face. "Mr. Maddock has a great deal of faith in you, Mr. Lorde," she said, as her voice cracked slightly. "Do you think you can help me?"

"I'll do what I can, but I can't make any promises."

It was about two in the afternoon when Joe left the Mart and headed south on Michigan to the University of Chicago. When he reached Marty's office, he found him hunched over his desk staring at some papers. "So Kat tells me you figured it out," Joe said, as his friend looked up and smiled.

"Well … yes and no," he replied. "Like I told you yesterday, I wasn't making much progress, so I decided to get a second opinion. I took the ball down to the faculty lounge and showed it to a new professor in the physics department who just arrived from Germany. During the war, the guy worked on deciphering codes and he knew immediately what the ball was, but I still haven't cracked the code."

"What do you mean 'he knew what it was'? I thought it was just a rubber ball," said Joe, with a quizzical look on his face. "Isn't it?"

Marty continued to smile as he held up the toy. "This, my friend, is a European Puzzle Ball."

"A what?" asked Joe, still looking confused.

"A European Puzzle Ball," repeated Marty as if simply mentioning it the first time was somehow self-explanatory.

Joe looked skeptical. "I lived in Europe for eight years. I never heard of a European Puzzle Ball."

"Well, they were all the rage before the war, especially in central Europe. I was told that they stopped making them when the war broke out because of a shortage of rubber."

CHAPTER 4 - WEDNESDAY

"So what exactly is a puzzle ball?" Joe pulled up a chair to Marty's desk and looked more closely at what his friend was holding.

"According to my new colleague, these rubber balls were a type of parlor game," he explained.

Again Joe looked baffled. "Enlighten me?" he asked.

"Well, there's a code here just like you thought, and the key is in these raised markings. When you played the game, you split up into teams. The first to crack the code won."

"So what does the code say?"

"That I don't know yet," replied Marty. "I haven't cracked it. Well, I cracked it, but it turned out to be a simple nursery rhyme, and it's unlikely people would be killing each other over a nursery rhyme. My guess is, there's a second code hidden somewhere in the markings, but I haven't found it yet."

Marty held up the ball while Joe stared at it, still a bit unsure exactly what his friend was saying. "Ok, so how do you play this parlor game?"

"Let me demonstrate," he replied. Marty picked up a pencil and used it as a pointer. "You see the symbols that wrap around the ball?" Joe nodded. "If you look closely you'll notice that most of them are raised but a few are virtually flush. Also, take a look at these two parallel stripes on both sides of the symbols. You see how they run along the top and bottom of the symbols? At first I thought these stripes were just for decoration, but my colleague says they actually have a purpose." Marty continued as if he were lecturing in his classroom. "You'll see that these parallel lines are raised, just like the symbols. Also, like the symbols they vary in height, so that sometimes the lines are quite pronounced and other times they're nearly flush." Marty used the tip of his pencil to point out each item as he referred to it. "That's one of the keys to the puzzle ball. Not all the symbols are part of the code."

"So how do you know which symbols are part of the code and which aren't?"

"That's the really neat part." Joe's friend was clearly enjoying himself. "It's almost impossible to tell just by looking at the ball."

"Wait, if you can't read the code by looking at the ball how do you read it?"

"At each end of the ball there's a small dot, here and here," said Marty still using the pencil as his pointer. He took out an ink pad from his desk drawer and two small straight pins. He pushed one pin into each of the two small dots so that the pins were now sticking out of the ball as if they were poles on a globe, and the stripes and symbols now looked like the equator circling that globe. "Now," Marty continued, "you hold the ball by these pins and then roll it across an ink pad, so all of the symbols circling the ball are covered in ink. Then you roll the ball across a piece of paper and it acts like a miniature printing press and three rows of symbols are printed onto a sheet of paper. But notice that not all the symbols are printed. Only the raised symbols actually get printed, and those parallel lines at the top and bottom of the stripe will keep even some of raised ones from being printed." Marty ran the ball across the paper. "That," he explained with a smile, "is your code." He held up the paper and the code now appeared as a series of grouped symbols with anywhere from one to eight symbols in each group on three lines. "There are twenty-seven groups of symbols, which would mean there are twenty-seven words in the code."

"So you think you can find this hidden code?" Joe asked.

"I think so. I'll let you know by tomorrow."

Joe grabbed his hat and coat and headed for the door. As he was leaving, Marty called out, "I've printed or copied all the symbols so I don't need this anymore." He rubbed the remaining ink off the ball with his handkerchief and tossed it to Joe.

"Can you continue to hold this for me?" he asked as he flipped the ball back.

Marty caught it but was surprised by his friend's response. "Don't you think you'll need it?"

Joe pulled out the fake ball that Kat had made and showed it to him. "I have a copy, and that's all I want to carry around with me for now. No one knows you have the real McCoy, so it's safer with you."

"Pretty smart," he chuckled. "You know, you're not as dumb as you look."

Marty's comment forced a smile out of his friend. "I get that a lot."

CHAPTER 4 - WEDNESDAY

It was mid-afternoon when Joe pulled up to the stage door of the Majestic, in the heart of Chicago's theater district. Being an older theater, the Majestic had been built for live productions, like vaudeville. Up until "talkies" hit the screen a couple of years back, there had always been a strong demand in Chicago for live entertainment. Now it seemed the days of vaudeville were numbered. Most of the live houses in town were, or were in the process of being, converted for moving pictures. Over the past year there had been speculation that the Majestic would soon be converted. However, when Joe entered the venerable old building, he could see that there was no shortage of acts waiting for their chance to audition. In the wings, he spotted a stagehand holding a clipboard and he asked him if he knew where Frederick Frances was. The man took several puffs on a fat cigar, handed Joe the clipboard and a pencil and said, "Write your name and 'turn' in the log. Then take a seat and wait 'til you're called."

"I'm not here to audition," Joe explained, as he handed back the clipboard. "I have a meeting with Mr. Frances."

The stagehand looked him over as he pulled the badly chewed cigar from his mouth and used it to point towards a spiral staircase on the right side of the stage. "Third floor," he instructed. Joe climbed the narrow metal steps to the third floor and walked halfway down a dimly lit hall to an open office door that was labeled "Theater Manager". Peering inside the large well worn office he saw a magician, complete with top hat and tails, doing his act. The performer's audience was a disinterested man seated on the other side of an old oak desk. The man behind the desk seemed far more interested in the paperwork in front of him than the magician.

While continuing to look down, the man said in a deeply sarcastic voice, "Yes, yes, I get it, you've made a handkerchief disappear. How very novel. You've thoroughly amazed me. Now I don't suppose you know a trick that a five year old can't do?" He slowly glanced up from his paperwork.

"Yes sir," said the nervous magician, "this is my best trick." He put his top hat on the desk and began to wave his hands furiously over it while mumbling some incantations. The illusion culminated with him pulling a dove from the hat. Joe assumed that it was supposed to fly away, but instead it just lay there.

"I don't suppose your next trick brings the poor thing back to life?" asked the man behind the desk.

"Somebody killed my bird," cried the grief stricken magician, his lips trembling.

"NEXT!" shouted the manager as the weeping magician exited with his hat and dead bird in hand. As Joe entered the office, the man behind the desk remained seated. His face once again buried in his paperwork. The office was cluttered with boxes and stacks of papers. In a corner there were two old wooden file cabinets, both with several drawers partially open. The open drawers were so overflowing with paper, it was doubtful they could be closed. On the wall to the left of the door was a large oval window that was the room's only source of natural light. To the right of the door hung two posters of stage productions from the Goodman and Selwyn theaters. In front of the desk were two old wooden chairs. The floor made a loud creaking sound under Joe's feet as he approached the desk.

"You must be 'The Incomparable Manteeni'," said the manager, without looking up. "I don't suppose you can bring that poor bird back to life?"

"I'm afraid not," replied Joe, "but I might be able to track down its killer." The man again looked up from his papers, and finally noticed Joe standing in front of him.

"You're not a magician," he observed. "What's your turn?"

"Unfortunately, I don't have an act, but I believe you might have gotten a message from Irene Fields about me."

The man flashed a broad smile, quickly rose from his chair, and walked around his large desk. He was small in stature with a thick frame and a round pale face. "I'm Toddy Frances", he said as he weakly shook his visitor's outstretched hand, "and you must be Joe Lorde. Irene told me you might be stopping by to ask some questions. Please have a seat. You'll have to excuse the office's appearance, but today is one of the two days during the week that I have to suffer through open auditions and everything seems to pile up on audition days. Can I get you a drink? Perhaps a dram of scotch?"

"No, thanks Mr. Frances, it's a bit early for me," replied Joe.

"Please call me Toddy, and it's probably a bit early for me as well, but that's never stopped me before," he said with a laugh. Sitting back down in his chair, he pulled out a bottle of scotch and a glass from the bottom drawer of his desk and poured himself a couple of fingers. Raising his glass in the air, he offered a toast "To the Noble Experiment" before taking a gulp of his drink. He then said to Joe, "Irene tells me you're looking into this blackmail business. I'm not sure I'll be able to give you any more information than she did, but I'll try."

Joe lit up a cigarette and responded, "Let's start with this man the two of you met, Paul Trent. What can you tell me about him?"

"Not a lot I'm afraid. He was a decent looking chap in his late 20's, medium height with a slight build, brown hair and eyes. We met him at the first place we stopped that night."

"Which was …?"

"The Panther Club on Clarke and Randolph. It's in the back of the Sherman Hotel."

"I'm familiar with it," Joe replied. "Had you ever seen him before?"

"I've been trying to remember if our paths had crossed," Toddy replied. Then he added, "It's possible I saw him up in Tower Town a while back, but I'm afraid I don't have any specifics."

"Can you tell me what other clubs you visited that night?"

"Well, after the Panther, our next stop was Chez Paree, over on Fairbanks Court." Toddy stared up toward the dirty ceiling, rubbed his chin and tried to remember more of the evening. "From there … we went uptown to the Green Mill, over on Broadway, and I vaguely remember seeing the palm trees at the Rainbow Garden on Clarke. Sadly, those are the only ones I'm certain of. There might have been one or two others. I do adore both the politics and the jazz at the Dill Pickle. So we might have stopped in, but I can't say for sure. To be honest, it's all a bit of a blur after the Rainbow Garden."

"Irene told me that the photos taken of her included Paul. Can you remember any conversations you might have had with him that night."

"Well, I only remember bits and pieces of any of the conversations we had," replied Toddy. "No one said anything particularly memorable, to be honest."

"Did Paul mention anything about a job, where he lived, or anything of a personal nature?"

"Let me think," Toddy replied as he again stared up at the grimy white ceiling. "I believe he might have mentioned that he was a musician at one of the clubs."

"Any idea what instrument he played?"

Toddy shook his head. "Not that I recall, I'm sorry."

"Anything else?"

"No, that's about all I have, I'm afraid. To be honest, Paul was far more interested in Irene than talking with me."

"So there was an attraction between them?"

"Magnetic," replied Toddy with a smile.

"How long have you known Irene?"

"We first met in early '12, when she was a young playwright and I was an assistant producer. We shared the same dream of working in the theater. She wanted to write the great American play and I wanted to produce it. It's odd really, most people who dream of the theater want to be on stage not behind the scenes, but neither of us ever wanted to be actors. To tell you the truth, we both detest actors. We dreamed of being the ones who created the magic for the stage. When Irene started, she wanted to write for the legitimate theater, but she ended up working in places like this." Toddy waved his arm around his office.

"What does a writer do in a vaudeville house?"

"Well, if you're an act like the Stooges or the Ritz Brothers, and you're constantly traveling from town to town, you have to adapt your material so it connects with the local audience. Sometimes they do it themselves, but more often than not, they hire local talent to come up with it. After all, someone with local knowledge would find it easier to adapt a standard routine so it pleases the natives."

"So that's how she paid the rent?" Joe asked.

"Before this radio gig took off, she couldn't rely on any one job to make enough to pay the bills," Toddy replied. He went on to explain. "From time to time she'd get some gigs writing speeches for area politicians and businessmen. But her bread and butter was the work she did for the *Evening American*, writing obits for them at two-bits each. Without that, she'd have gone bust years ago."

"What she really wanted, however, was to write plays. She did manage to get a few of them produced here in Chicago, one in Milwaukee and then one or two in St. Louis. She is very gifted, but she never had the financial backing to take the shows any further than a local production. We worked together on several shows here in town. Two of them are on the wall over there," Toddy pointed to the framed posters. "I was very proud of them both," he sighed. "They got great notices, but both only ran for a couple of months. It's sad, really. In our youth the legitimate theater was our religion, but we've both fallen from grace."

"Irene made the jump to radio," said Joe. "How come you didn't go with her?"

"Oh, she did try and get me to go into the business several times, but to be frank the whole concept of radio just goes over my head. I'm afraid I paid no attention in science class. To me, producing should be about the stage, lights, scenery, props, and grease paint. Those are things I understand. Enabling disembodied voices to come out of a box just isn't for me. When I didn't make it in the legitimate theater, I ended up in vaudeville. It's not ideal, but I'm comfortable here."

"Are you aware of any enemies that Irene might have made?"

"Well, her ex-agent Herman Roth isn't too crazy about her."

"Did they have a falling out?"

"Herm was fine at getting the old style gigs, but when she started writing for radio, about five years ago, he just couldn't help her. He had no contacts in that business, so every lead she was getting came from her own efforts. Eventually she had no choice but to cut him loose, he was just dead weight. When she finally fired him a little over two years ago, her career really started to take off. Now she's poised to hit the big-time, and I imagine Herm is pretty bitter about being left behind."

"Anyone else?"

"The only other person I can think of is the producer of 'Day Dreams', Eddie Collins. He stands to lose everything if she leaves. Irene thinks he's incompetent, and you can bet your bottom dollar she won't be taking him with her if she jumps to WBM. If you ask me, there's no way the little worm has the guts to do something like this."

Just as Toddy finished his sentence, there was a knock on the door, and a voice from the hallway called, "We have three acts on stage for you, Mr.

Frances." The color on Toddy's face immediately drained away and he let out a soft groan. "You'll have to excuse me, Mr. Lorde," he said before quickly finishing his drink, "but duty calls."

"Thanks for your help," said Joe, as he rose to leave.

"Not at all," Toddy replied with a weak smile. "If you have any more questions you can always reach me here at the theater. The show runs six nights a week 'til ten, but I'm here most nights 'til at least eleven."

After his meeting at the theater Joe took the long drive back up to the McNulty estate to re-interview Emma. He arrived a little after four and parked his car by the guesthouse entrance. Climbing out of his roadster, he was immediately greeted by Emma who was descending the steps at the main entrance. She was wearing a pale yellow sundress, and seemed to him even more beautiful than the first time he'd met her.

Wendy's leaving made Joe vow that he'd never lose his heart again. Now there was this incredible woman who made him forget why he'd made that vow in the first place. He realized that he had to control the feelings he was having, at least while the investigation was underway. What made things more difficult, however, was that she seemed to be attracted to him as well. Joe realized that if he ever let his guard down, even for a moment, he'd fall completely under her spell. If that happened, all objectivity on the case would be lost, which he knew would be a betrayal to Theo.

Emma led him into the house by tugging playfully on his arm. Once inside, she looked back at him and frowned. "You've hurt yourself," she said, clearly concerned. Gently, she brushed his face along his hairline, where the bruise from the night before was visible. "Is it painful?"

Her gentle touch across his forehead caused his heart rate to jump, but he kept his composure and replied, "It's nothing, I just ran into a door."

She examined his bruise closely and admonished him, "You have to be more careful." Taking hold of his hand, she walked him through the house, out the French doors and on to the grounds of the estate.

The sun was out and it had turned into a pleasant spring afternoon. Emma continued to hold his hand as she led him along the path through the garden, down along the lake. Joe forced himself to concentrate on work, and began to ask her the questions he should have asked the day before. Emma willingly shared the details of her life growing up in Fort Wayne. She revealed how, at 17, she met Ken Kevilsen, a piano player who was traveling through town. He had swept her off her feet and she readily agreed to run away with him to New York. This, despite her mother's warnings that their relationship would come to ruin. When she talked about how he'd ditched her four months later, her voice shook slightly. After he split, she thought about going back to Fort Wayne, but decided to stay after landing a job at the downtown branch of the Bank of the United States.

"When the bank went bust last year I started looking for work, but with no luck. If it hadn't been for some money I got from my mom's insurance policy, I honestly don't know how I would have made ends meet," she explained. "You know it's funny, a week ago I was out of work, nearly broke, all alone, and I had no idea how I was going to get by. Now, just look around," she said as she waved her arms across the grounds of the estate. "I'm living on 'Easy Street'. I always thought that if something like this ever happened to me I'd be the happiest girl in the world." She looked at him with sadness in her eyes, "But it's true what they say about money and happiness. One can't buy the other." She smiled and squeezed his hand as they resumed walking at a leisurely pace along the lake shore. Joe continued to ask her questions and she happily responded. They were together for almost an hour before he reluctantly explained that he had to go back into town.

After stopping in the hall to pick up Joe's hat and coat, the two of them walked to his car. When he climbed in, Emma's smile disappeared as she asked, "When will I see you again?"

He hesitated for a moment before replying, "I'll come by tomorrow." Quickly adding, as an afterthought, "I'll have some follow-up questions for you by then."

"You can ring me tonight if you want," she said, once again flashing her extraordinary smile.

"That probably won't be necessary."

"Maybe not," she replied, her voice turning soft and warm, "but please don't let that stop you."

It was well past 5:00 when Joe finally got back to his office. Mickey had visited the Department of Public Works earlier that afternoon to look into the files on the Washington Street Bridge. His handwritten notes about what he found were on top of the desk. Joe sat down, lit up a cigarette, and began to read through them.

When Kat walked in with a stack of correspondence he looked up from his desk and said, "It seems the bridge was built in '13 by Bennett Construction."

"Bennett," replied Kat, "I've heard of them. They're a big company."

"Today they are, but according to Mickey's notes, they were a lot smaller in '13. Back then they had only three employees."

"That must have been a pretty big break for them, getting that bridge contract," said Mickey, as he followed Kat into Joe's office.

"Well, I'll be," said Joe, clearly surprised by what he was reading.

"What is it?" asked Kat.

"It seems that the city's project manager for that job was none other than the right honorable James Bayles."

"Congressman Bayles?" a shocked Kat asked.

"The very same," confirmed Joe. "Bill Dailey told me that Bayles had a city job before he got into politics. Evidently project manager Bayles built a bridge that is now structurally unsound. I'm guessing that back in '13 he and Bennett must have played games with the construction or the specification."

"So, this being Chicago," continued Kat, "it's a fair bet that Bayles, our ambitious project manager, cut a deal with the equally ambitious owner of Bennett Construction. Nearly twenty years, later Congressman Bayles champions a 'refurbishment' of that bridge, which is actually designed to deal with the bridge's structural problems."

"I don't understand," said Mickey. "If the bridge needed structural repairs why don't they just order the repairs? Why disguise it as a refurbishment?"

"Because the bridge isn't even 20 years old," replied Joe. "Major structural repairs for a bridge that age would raise some eyebrows. People would discover that there was something hinky with the original construction. We know that Gen was trying to put the kibosh on the

CHAPTER 4 - WEDNESDAY

'refurbishment' project because I found those petitions in her makeshift office at the Mission."

"But the date on the petitions was over four weeks ago. Why didn't she deliver them to the city?" asked Kat.

"I'm guessing," Joe responded, "that like the good little researcher she was, she did a deep dive into the bridge project and discovered that it wasn't a refurbishment at all, but a reconstruction."

"But if she discovered the truth, why didn't she blow the whistle on the whole thing weeks ago?" asked Mickey.

"There's only one reason I can think of," replied Joe, "she was blackmailing Bayles or Bennett."

"Or both," added Kat who continued, "If we're looking for a motive, blackmail is a good one."

"If we want to be able to prove that Gen was bleeding someone, we need to find out exactly what Bayles and Bennett did back in '13, when the bridge was originally constructed." Joe turned to Kat. "When Sid calls in, have him go to the Department of Public Works tomorrow. Let's see if he can find the specifications the city drew up for the bridge, along with the original contract with Bennett Construction. After we get a peek at those documents, it might be time to have a little chat with Thomas Bennett.

"Well, you can put that idea on ice for a while," Kat replied. "I saw an article in the *Daily News* Society Page last week that said Bennett and his new wife just left on a grand tour of Europe. They're not due back until late November."

Joe cursed softly under his breath and to himself, "So we can't speak to him for seven months?"

Kat added with a smile of satisfaction, "Nothing is worse than waiting or chasing."

Mickey looked confused by her remark, and Joe explained, "That's yet another bit of wisdom from Mother Russia." He went back to the case and added, "So that just leaves us with Bayles."

The room fell silent as they collectively pondered their next move. Suddenly, the phone rang, startling all three of them. Kat smiled, took a breath, and on the third ring calmly answered, "Argonne Detective Agency." A muffled voice could be heard on the other end of the line. Kat responded in a loud voice, "Yes, we accept the charges." A different muffled voice came on the line, and a smile returned to Kat's face. "Hi, are you having fun in Fort Wayne?" she asked, almost shouting. Then after listening for a few seconds she laughed before handing the phone over to Joe.

"So, what did you find out?" he asked Sid. Long distance calls were always a bit garbled so Joe also spoke loudly.

Sid began his summary of what he'd found out, speaking quickly, as these calls were always expensive. "I went down to the Allen County Courthouse here in Fort Wayne, and got into their records. I saw the list of births for '07 and it shows one Emma O'Donnell born at St. Joseph's Hospital in Fort Wayne on March 30th. The mother is listed as Margret O'Donnell and the father as Cyrus McNulty of Chicago. It was clearly the original entry. No one has monkeyed with it, I'm sure of that. I also checked out Margret O'Donnell's death certificate. She died in Fort Wayne on December 10th 1931. Cause of death is listed as a traffic accident. Emma went to school here in Fort Wayne, but only high school graduates get their pictures taken and she didn't graduate, so there's no photo of her."

"She and her mother lived on Williams Street. I checked with their neighbors and several were good friends of Maggie's. They say that Emma left for New York when she was seventeen. They all remember her as a shy mousey girl who fell in love with some piano player who was passing through town. It seems she ran off with the guy, but no one remembers his name. The mother was none too pleased she ran away."

"One of Maggie's friends says that Maggie visited Emma in New York about four or five years ago. She also says that they used to stay in touch through regular letters, and on her birthday Maggie would go to the drug store at an agreed time and her daughter would phone her. The neighbor said that Maggie hadn't talked about either a phone call, or a letter for some time. I showed that picture of Emma you gave me, but I didn't really get any confirmation from that. Just about everyone I talked to thought that the girl in the photo sort'a looked like Emma. But, like I said, she was a shy and mousey teenager when she left Fort Wayne, and the photo was of an older more glamorous woman. So it's no surprise that few were prepared to swear it was her. I couldn't find anyone who thought it definitely wasn't her. Since my train doesn't leave until 9:00 tonight, I'll do a little more digging."

"Great job, Sid," shouted Joe. "I'm going to pass you back to Kat. She has some stuff I need you to run down when you're back. I'll see you in the office tomorrow."

"Ok, boss." As Joe was about to hand the phone over to Kat, Sid shouted back. "One more thing."

"What's that?"

"There was someone else looking into Maggie and Emma not long after Maggie's death," said Sid.

"Did you find out who it was?"

"Yeah, identified himself as an insurance investigator. No one can recall his name or the company he worked for, but there might have been an insurance payout after Maggie's death."

"Ok, thanks." Joe handed the phone back to Kat. Once she rang off, he picked up the candlestick phone on his desk and placed a call to Theo to give him an update.

Joe leaned back in his chair and commenced a summary of what they'd uncovered so far. "Basically, Theo, we have confirmation that the birth certificate is genuine. Maggie did have a child seven months after leaving the McNulty household. The father is listed as Cyrus and the baby girl was named Emma. The young lady staying at the estate generally fits the description of Emma, and some people think the photo we have looks like her as well. Only a few are prepared to swear to it. The last thing we confirmed was that Maggie's daughter ran away from Fort Wayne at age seventeen with a piano player. This ties in with the story we were given by Emma. We're trying to track down the piano player, along with anyone else who knew her in New York. At this point, I'm afraid that's all we got, so far."

"Thanks, Joe," said Theo. "Let me know if you get any new information."

"How's the old man doing?"

"He's sinking fast."

"When I get some information from New York, I might be able to give you a better assessment of the girl's claim. But that may not be until Monday."

"Do the best you can," replied Theo, before the two men hung up.

Almost as soon as he was off the line, Kat stuck her head into his office to tell him that she and Mickey were calling it a day. "Ok, but when you get in tomorrow, I need you to do a couple of things for me." He explained, "According to Irene's friend, Toddy Frances, she had an agent that she fired a while back. His name is Herman Roth and I need you to track him down. Try and get me an appointment to meet him sometime late tomorrow morning. Also, try and get hold of Manny in New York. I need him to try and track down the piano player Emma O'Donnell ran away with. His name is Ken Kevilsen."

"Will do, boss," she replied. After jotting down his instructions, she and Mickey left the office.

Joe re-read the notes Mickey had taken from the Department of Public Works on the Washington Street Bridge project. Once finished, he began to alternate between doodling on his note pad, and tossing his baseball. As hard as he tried to concentrate, however, his mind kept coming back to Emma. When it did, he couldn't help but smile. He hadn't smiled this much in years, and his facial muscles were starting to hurt.

Evening

It was just after 8:00 when he pulled up outside the Dreamland Café on State Street in Bronzeville. The Dreamland had been around for over fifteen years, and was starting to show its age. It wasn't nearly as posh as some of the joints in Tower Town, but Joe liked its older style. With the smell the Stock Yards hanging thick in the air, Joe could tell that the wind was coming from the southwest as he got out of his car. Once inside, he made his way down toward the stage which, like many of the older clubs, wasn't elevated. Instead it was a small area in the front of the room, with a brass rail separating it from the audience. Sam was playing in a trio, and Joe grabbed a table just to the left of the stage. After he sat down, he lit up a cigarette and ordered a scotch. When trio finished, he pushed out a chair for Sam, who was walking over to his table.

"I only caught the end of that, but it sounded sweet," he said.

"We were solid," admitted Sam, as he sat down. "And before you ask, the answer is 'no'," he added with a smile.

"'No to what?" asked Joe with a shocked look on his face.

"Don't try and act all innocent. Rose told me you have her running up to Kenilworth on some case, so it doesn't take a genius to figure out why you stopped by tonight, and the answer is 'no'."

"I came here to enjoy the music," he said, trying to act as if Sam's words had wounded him.

"Look, I'm telling you now that I'm not posing as an irate husband, or pretending to be a stiff, or playing piano in some honky-tonk. So whatever it is you want, I ain't doing it," repeated Sam.

"Fine," replied Joe, "since there's nothing I want you to do, let's talk about the game on Monday."

"OK, where and when do you wanna meet?"

"I'll pick Emma up at *The Defender* at around noon."

"Who the hell is Emma?"

"What?" Joe was startled by Sam's use of that name.

"You said you'd pick up some dame named Emma."

"I did? Well, I meant Rose," he replied defensively. "I'll pick up Rose at about noon." Sam gave him an odd look. "Do you want to meet at Schorling's Park," continued Joe, "or ride with us?"

"I got things to do in the morning," he replied. "Let's meet at the park. So, you going to tell me who Emma is?"

"She's involved in a case I'm working." He quickly changed the subject. "You guys were really smoking on that last set. Who's the white guy on the licorice stick?"

"That's Muggsy Spanier," replied Sam, deciding not to press him about the girl.

"Oh, so that's Muggsy? That kid can play. By the way, you ever hear of a musician in town named Paul Trent?"

"Paul Trent ... Paul Trent," repeated Sam slowly, "can't say I've heard of him. What does he play?"

"Not sure."

"Oh, I get it," Sam said with an all-knowing smile. "That's why you're here, you want me to track down this Trent guy."

"There's a ten spot in it for anyone who can get me a lead."

"I knew you were talking jive," said Sam with satisfaction. "You always want me to do something, but I'll tell you right now I'm not playing anymore stiffs, I hate that. The last time you made me do it, you smeared my face with blood."

Joe interrupted him. "It was catsup," he explained, before adding defensively, "and you got paid a sawbuck."

"I don't care what it was or how much I got paid, the whole thing gave me the heebie-jeebies. I couldn't sleep for a week."

Joe let out a sigh, "Well, no one's asking you to play dead. I just need to get the skinny on this Trent guy."

"For ten bucks, I'll see what I can dig up," he said, as he got up from the table. "Time for the next gang, you sticking around?"

"Can't imagine being any place else," he lied. Joe lit up another cigarette and sipped his scotch before asking, "did you hear if the Sox won?"

"Well they didn't lose," he replied, giving Joe a wide grin. "But that's only because they didn't play. They got rained out in Philly."

Sam moved back towards the stage while Joe took another sip of scotch. "Rained out in Philly," thought Joe. "If that's not the perfect title for a blues song, I don't know what is."

As the next set began Joe noticed a sharply dressed black man sit down at the table next to him. He immediately recognized him as Earl Hines, one of the city's best musicians, and one of the finest band leaders in the country. Known as "Fatha Hines", he was rapidly becoming a national celebrity from his recording and radio broadcasts. A few years back, Earl and another musician in town, Louis Armstrong, had been partners in a Chicago club called the Sunset Café. After the depression hit, the joint was forced to close. Then, last year, serious money was spent on redecorating Earl's club. It reopened under the name "The Grand Terrace Ballroom". Rumor had it that Earl now had Al Capone as his silent partner.

Sam had played with Earl's band many times, and it was through Sam that Joe had gotten to know him. Wednesday was a slow night at the Grand Terrace, so Earl frequently took the opportunity to visit other clubs, listen to the music, and scout for talent. Joe picked up his scotch and moved over to his table.

CHAPTER 4 – WEDNESDAY

"Mr. Private Detective," said Earl, wearing his characteristic smile. "How are you?"

"Fine, Earl," replied Joe, as he shook the bandleader's hand. "What are you doing slumming around here?"

"Always searching for that new sound," he replied, as he looked over at the stage. "And the musicians who can play it."

"Someone told me that you had Congressman Bayles at your club recently?"

"Several times, as a matter of fact. The Grand Terrace Ballroom is the place to be seen in Chicago," he added with pride.

"Was he with anyone?"

"Last Saturday he was with a young lady," Earl replied. "In fact he was with the same one several times over the last couple of weeks."

"You sure it was the same girl?"

"This one was a looker," he responded. "A young blonde chick. A real knockout, and she had class."

The two men fell silent for a couple of minutes as Earl listened to the clarinet solo, and Joe thought about his case. Suddenly a strange thought popped into his head. Reaching into his trench coat pocket, he pulled out the newspaper with the photo of the murdered co-ed.

"This wouldn't be the girl by any chance?" he asked, as he showed the photo to Earl.

The bandleader looked at the paper for several seconds. "That's her all right."

His response startled Joe, and for a long moment he was lost in his thoughts while staring at the newspaper photo. Then he looked up and said, "Are you sure?"

"I never forget a pretty face," he replied with a wink.

"Thanks for the help." Earl nodded and shook Joe's outstretched hand before he went back to listening to the music, and Joe returned to his table.

It had been a wild hunch and Joe had never actually believed that Earl would finger Gen Ericson as the girl Bayles had been with. He leaned back in his chair, tuned out the music, and let his mind race through the facts of the case. It seemed certain that Gen had found out about the problems with the Washington Street Bridge, but if she was blackmailing Bayles, why would they have been dating? There weren't many people who would want to take their blackmailer out to the Grand Terrace Ballroom, regardless of how pretty they were. Maybe she wasn't bleeding him, he thought. Maybe she was going after Bennett instead. There was certainly a lot more money possible from Bennett, but that still didn't explain why she would be dating Bayles. There wasn't much about this case that made sense, but one thing seemed clear, there was more to this young girl's death than anyone had initially thought.

It was just past 9:30 when Joe finished up at the Dreamland Café and headed home to Warren Street. It wasn't particularly late but a cold wind, accompanied by a thin rain, kept most everyone off the street. He found a spot to park about a block away and, after getting smacked around the night before, was cautious as he walked towards his building. The only other person in sight was a man wearing a brown overcoat and a white skimmer hat, approaching from the opposite direction. The man passed just as Joe was turning to climb his building's steps. Before he reached the top of the stairs, he was clobbered with a .45 caliber pistol along the base of his skull.

When he woke up fifteen minutes later, Joe was lying in the same spot as the night before. "Shit," he mumbled in utter disbelief. "Two fucking days in a row." He was furious, but only at himself. Ending up face down in an alley once might be deemed unfortunate, twice might be considered careless, but twice on back-to-back nights was just plain stupid. He stood up slowly and did a quick check of his pockets. He found that the only thing missing was the copy of Patel's rubber ball. He then brushed the dirt off his trench coat and suit as best he could and walked back to the building entrance.

Once inside his flat, he took off his coat and moved into the washroom to splash cold water on his face. He looked into the mirror and spoke softly to his reflection, "God I miss Paris." As he examined himself more closely, he was relieved to see that there appeared to be no additional bruising. He wasn't all that concerned about his appearance, but he knew that if he showed up at work tomorrow with fresh damage, he'd catch hell from Kat. Satisfied that he looked none the worse, he examined his trench coat. Fortunately, it had survived the attack better than his suit had the

CHAPTER 4 - WEDNESDAY

night before. There were a couple of smudges, but some soap and water easily cleaned them up.

It was a few minutes after 10:00 when the urge to call Emma overwhelmed him and he picked up his phone. Instead of a dial tone, however, he heard the voice of a middle aged woman on the line. Marge Kubik was one of five people that shared Joe's party line. She was a nice lady but she was constantly on the phone, usually trading recipes or gossip with friends. "Mrs. Kubik, I need to make a call," he said, trying not to sound too impatient. Joe would have preferred a private line, but it was much too expensive.

"I'll be off in just a moment, Joseph," she assured him in her usual cheery voice.

Ten minutes later he tried the phone again, and this time the line was free. Two minutes after that he was still waiting for a connection to the McNulty guesthouse. When eventually the lines connected he expected the maid to answer, instead Emma picked it up on the first ring. "Hello."

Joe was startled to hear her voice, and hesitated for a second before finally blurting out, "Hi, it's Joe Lorde."

"Hi, Joe, I was so afraid you wouldn't call me tonight," she replied. From the tone in her voice, he could almost feel her radiant smile coming through the line.

"I was just calling because I had a few more questions. It's not too late, is it?"

"Well, that depends," she replied, her voice soft and lyrical. "Is that the only reason you rang me?"

He hesitated again, then leaned back in his chair and said, "It's the only reason I should have."

"Well, I'm really glad you did, whatever the reason," she responded with a playful giggle.

Quickly, he dashed out a couple of questions on a notepad, but over the next two hours of their conversation he completely forgot about them. Finally, towards the end of the call, he looked down at the scribbling in front of him and asked how she felt about finding her father.

"It feels so strange," she replied. "I spent so many years without one that suddenly having a father is an odd feeling."

"I know what you mean," he replied. "I grew up without a family, so the concept is a hard one to grasp. Did your mother have any family in Fort Wayne?"

"No," she replied. "My grandfather moved the family from Gary to Fort Wayne to work for the railroad when my mother was still in diapers. We had no other family in that area, and if there were any relatives in Gary, I'm afraid we lost touch years ago. My mother was an only child, and I'm an only child, and that doesn't make for a lot of relatives." She paused before adding softly, "I think we were made for each other you and I. We're both alone."

"Well, you might end up with a half-brother at the end of this investigation," he replied. "That's not so bad."

"Vance? I still haven't met him, but I hear he doesn't like me very much."

"Well, pretty soon you'll be his closest living relative. You might find he warms up to you then."

"I doubt it. Late this afternoon Mr. McNulty asked me to call him 'Papa' and the nurse told me that when Vance heard, he stormed out of the house. I think if we ever actually meet it'll be like a scene from 'The Scottish Play'."

"It's late," said Joe, finally remembering that he was still conducting an investigation. "I think I have all the information I need for now."

"Will I see you tomorrow?" her voice turned seductive and inviting.

"I'm sure I'll have some additional questions for you," he lied. "I'll ring you and we can go over them."

"I'd like to see you," she said softly.

"I'll phone you tomorrow," he replied before hanging up. After he put the handset back in the cradle, he continued staring at it for nearly a minute.

Once in bed, he tuned his shortwave to Radio INR, a French-language station in Brussels. On Wednesday nights they played jazz, and at the top of every hour they also broadcast the latest European news. With the sound of Louis Armstrong's band playing in the background, Joe wound his bedside alarm clock. He lay in the dark nursing three fingers of scotch, a cigarette, a headache, and sore ribs, all while images of Emma consumed his thoughts.

CHAPTER FIVE

THURSDAY

Even when you're on the right track, you can still get runover if you're just sitting there -Will Rogers

Morning

His encounter the previous night had left Joe with a stiff neck and a large bruise at the base of his skull. Those injuries, coupled with the bruises and welts from his previous beating, meant he was moving far slower than usual. Consequently, it took him forty-five minutes to get dressed, and out the door.

Once he entered the Loop, Joe drove down Wabash to a tobacconist just south of Madison. The street was lined with a variety of small shops, all operating under the shadow of the Wabash "L". The Hawthorne Smoke Shop was wedged between a millinery and a stationary store, and it was one of the few places in town that carried Rothman's cigarettes, an English brand that was Kat's favorite.

It was mid-morning when he finally arrived at his office. Rose was sitting on a chair next to Kat's desk, and Sid was in his usual place on the couch. When Joe entered, he could hear Kat filling Rose in on the co-ed case and, in the background, her office radio had Fred Astaire singing "Night & Day".

"Hey boss," Sid said, as he sat up on the couch. "I went down to the Exposition site first thing this morning and talked to one of the foremen. He said I should go to the project accounting office, so I got there just as it was opening and talked to the chief accountant. He says that if someone was skimming dough off this project, they're doing it in front of an army of bean counters. The guy told me that the bond holders insisted that there be a swarm of auditors all over the place."

"That pretty much confirms what I heard from Bill Dailey yesterday," said Joe.

"So if we rule out money from the Exposition project as a motive, what do you have left?"

"Not a hell of a lot," Joe replied.

"Language, Joseph," Kat fired back.

Joe took out the Rothman's cigarettes from his trench coat pocket and put them on Kat's desk. "Thought you could use these," he said and added, "They were on sale."

She looked at the two cartons of cigarettes, knowing perfectly well that the expensive imported brands like Rothman's were never on sale. "Thank you, that was really sweet. I don't suppose you'll let me pay for them."

Joe ignored her question. "Getting back to Steiner, we don't exactly have a lot of suspects on this one. Where does that leave us?" The room went quiet.

It was Rose who finally broke the silence. "Why was Mr. Steiner in that area to begin with? He was what … a block or so from Haymarket. That's a flophouse district isn't? What would he have been doing there?"

"Maybe he was meeting a friend," suggested Kat.

Joe shook his head and added, "According to his wife, all his friends were either from his office or from his neighborhood."

"Where exactly was he killed?" asked Sid.

Joe responded, "They found his body in an alley off Randolph between Canal and Clinton."

"That's just one block west of the river," said Kat, for clarification. "Is there anything going on around there now?"

"It's not too far from the Washington Street Draw Bridge. Any chance Steiner was involved with that project?" asked Joe.

"I don't see how," replied Sid, "all his current projects are linked to the Exposition in some way."

"So we're back to the Exposition," observed Rose.

The room fell silent again until Joe suggested, "Let's change the subject. Sid, did you come up with anything else in Fort Wayne yesterday?"

"It's pretty much the same stuff I gave you over the phone," he said. "I still couldn't find any relatives for Maggie or Emma. I checked out her church and talked to Father Murphy, the parish priest. He says that he was the one who wrote to Emma to tell her that her mother died. I showed him the picture and he thought it looked like her. Then I talked to six people who went to school with her and showed all of them her photo. The results were pretty much the same as before." Sid flipped open his notepad and read from his notes. "Of the six, four thought the picture looked like her and two weren't sure."

Joe turned to Kat and asked, "You hear anything from Manny in New York?"

"He phoned this morning," she responded. "He wanted you to know that he got the envelope you sent."

"Ok, thanks." Joe walked toward his office. Then he stopped and looked back. "Have any of you ever heard of something called 'The Scottish Play'?"

"The what?" asked Sid.

"'The Scottish Play'," repeated Joe.

"I don't know any Scottish plays," Kat replied. "And you know I love the theater."

"I can't say I've ever heard of it," added Rose. "I'm sure the Scots have written lots of plays, I just can't think of any off the top of my head."

Joe glanced over at Sid. "Hey, don't look at me," his investigator responded, "I'm not much for plays." Then added with a smile, "I'm more a burlesque guy."

"Ok, I just thought I'd check." Joe changed the subject, yet again. "Sid, I need you to see if you can run down a musician by the name of Paul Trent."

"Did you check with Sam?" asked Rose.

"Yeah, I asked him. He's never heard of him."

"Wow, Sam knows just about every musician in town. If this Paul what's-his-name plays here, and Sam doesn't know him, he must be pretty obscure."

"Maybe he plays at one of those Taxi Dance halls," Kat said, adding, "for the dime-a-dance girls."

Joe thought about it for a moment before responding, "I don't think so. Irene's friend said he'd seen him before at one of the clubs."

"Do you know what instrument he plays?" asked Sid.

"Nope. All I got on him is that he's reasonably good looking, slight build with brown hair and he might have played at one of the clubs in Tower Town."

"Ok, boss, I'll dig into it." He grabbed his notebook and wrote down the information.

"What time are you taking Rose out to the McNulty place?" Joe asked him.

"Just before lunch."

Joe looked over at Rose. "What did you tell Arthur?"

"That I was taking the day off to spend it with you," she answered with a smile and a wink.

"He'll be suspicious," he said to himself, clearly worried.

Kat handed Joe a cup of coffee. "I tracked down Irene's old agent."

"And ...?"

"His office is over at the Hall Printing Building on North Milwaukee, but every time I tried to place a call there was no answer."

"North Milwaukee?" Joe was surprised by the location. "Are you sure? That's over in West Town. Not exactly your highbrow location."

"I checked twice, and it's definitely his current address."

"Ok," he replied before taking his one and only sip of coffee for the morning. He grabbed his hat and coat, lit up a cigarette, and headed for the door. "I have some time now, I'll go pay him visit."

"Be nice," Rose called out.

Joe frowned and replied, unconvincingly, "I'm always nice."

CHAPTER 5 - THURSDAY

After several wasted hours trying to track down Irene's agent, it turned out the lead was a dead end, literally. It seems Herman Roth quietly died of a heart attack, nearly four months ago. It was almost noon by the time Joe returned to the office. As he entered, Kat smiled at him and whispered, "You have a visitor. She's been waiting for about thirty minutes," she added. "I let her sit in your office, but I've been keeping an eye on her."

"Who is she?"

"She says her name is Jacqueline Nottingham, but only her name sounds English, her accent is definitely French."

Damn," said Joe as he hung his head down and let out a deep sigh. Sadly, when a married woman showed up at the office it usually meant he was looking at another divorce case. He particularly disliked them because they were messy and sleazy.

Kat fired back, "Language, Joseph," before adding, "Remember, these are the cases that pay the bills."

Upon entering his office Joe was surprised to find a gorgeous brunette standing by the window, staring down at the street below. Typically it was a woman like this that the husband was cheating *with*, not *on*. "Perhaps," Joe thought to himself, "this is about something else."

"I'm Joe Lorde," he said as he walked over to her and held out his hand.

"I'm pleased to meet you, Mr. Lorde," she responded. Then she gave a slight smile and briefly placed the tips of her fingers into his hand before continuing, "My name is Jacqueline Nottingham."

"Please have a seat, Miss Nottingham, and tell me how I can help you." His visitor moved towards one of the two empty chairs in front of his desk. As she crossed the room Joe thoroughly enjoyed the view. She was a real "dish", and was wearing a tight mid-length skirt, a white silk blouse, and a small pillbox hat trimmed with a delicate mesh that dipped down just to her eye level. When she sat in the chair, she seductively crossed her long beautiful legs. The woman had class, there was no doubt about it, and she carried herself with a confidence that so many beautiful women seemed to possess.

"It's Mrs. Nottingham, actually." Her pronunciation was clear and precise but, as Kat had indicated, her accent was unmistakably French.

"My apologies, how can I be of help, Mrs. Nottingham?"

"I believe you may be in possession of something that was stolen from my late husband," she said. The stunning brunette was in her early thirties with a clear, smooth white complexion, full sensuous red lips, and remarkable violet eyes, that were at once both distant and hypnotic.

"Please continue." Joe was intrigued both by the story and the woman.

"There is a small black rubber ball that was stolen from our home in England over six years ago. During the theft my husband was murdered," she explained. "Since his death, I have been trying to retrieve the ball, and I've been informed that it may now be in your possession."

"I do have a ball that matches your description, but there's been a murder committed and I believe the ball was the principal motive for that murder."

"I am prepared to pay one thousand dollars for the immediate return of the ball. In cash, no questions asked."

Joe was caught off guard by the amount of money she was offering. "That's a lotta dough for a simple rubber ball. Perhaps, Mrs. Nottingham, you could tell me what this is about, because I don't understand why people are willing to kill for this ball."

Jacqueline took a silver case from her purse, opened it and extracted a thin dark cigarette. She placed it at the end of a long black enamel holder, delicately perched between the first two fingers of her left hand. She looked directly into Joe's eyes and flashed an alluring smile. It took a second for him to realize what she was patiently waiting for him to do. Quickly, he pulled out the red matchbook from his suit coat pocket, walked around his desk, and lit her cigarette. Again she smiled at him, then took a delicate puff. Joe sat on the edge of his desk, next to her, and lit up a Chesterfield. The right side of his brain was screaming that this dame was trouble, but the left half was thoroughly enjoying itself. It was a sad fact of life that when it came to women like Jacqueline Nottingham, men were rarely in their right mind.

"Have you ever heard of the University of Leuven?" she began.

"In Belgium?"

"Just so, Mr. Lorde," she was clearly surprised that he'd heard of it. "It's one of the world's oldest universities. Before the war its library housed a magnificent collection of priceless paintings, sculptures, and manuscripts. In '14 the Germans invaded Belgium on their way to France. Their path took them straight through the ancient town of Leuven. In order to intimidate the Belgians, they burned the university to the ground, along with its great library and all its contents. Art lovers and scholars the world over were devastated by the loss. What no one knew, however, was that eight enterprising German officers removed many of the most valuable pieces before the fire was set. They hid them, and the location of this treasure was known only to the eight."

"As the war turned into a deadly stalemate," she continued, "four of the officers were killed in the fighting on the Western Front. The remaining four now realized that the conflict could claim them all, so they decided to leave a record of where they hid their prize. The family of one of the officers owned a toy factory where they made a popular pre-war parlor game called a puzzle ball. These balls were embedded on their surface with a set of symbols that formed a code. The winner of the game was the first to decipher the code. It was decided by the remaining four that they would each get a copy of a puzzle ball. Imprinted on the ball would be a code that, when deciphered, would reveal the location of the treasure."

"By the time the war was in its third year all the officers, save one, had died. Sadly, the survivor had been driven to the edge of madness from the constant artillery barrages. I believe it's what you Americans call 'shell shock'," she explained. "When this last officer was hospitalized, he began to tell fantastic stories about the hidden treasure, and the puzzle ball. At first no one took any notice of him since he was, after all, half mad."

"As the war came to a close, a letter arrived at the hospital from the widow of one of the other officers. It seems she'd been told about the treasure by her husband before he died. She was writing to say that she'd lost their copy of the ball, and wanted to know if any of the others had survived. Word spread through the hospital that the wild story about a hidden treasure just might be true. The half-crazed officer kept his copy of the ball in his possession at all times. It was only a matter of time before something terrible happened. Less than a month after the letter arrived, the man was found dead from "unknown" causes and the ball went missing. Then, over the next few months, three of the hospital's orderlies and two nurses were murdered. The ball wasn't seen again for several more months, but during the final days of the war it came into the possession of an antique dealer in Austria. This man sold it to a member of the Hapsburg family. After the Hapsburg dynasty fell, they fled Vienna and took all their valuables, including the ball, with them to Switzerland. Within a year of their exile, the ball, along with some of the former Austrian crown jewels, was stolen in an extremely well-publicized robbery."

"I was in Europe at the time of that robbery," commented Joe. "It was headline news for many weeks."

"Then you know that they never caught the thieves or recovered any of the stolen items," continued Jacqueline. "No one knows what happen to the ball, until it reappeared in Paris three years later. It was there in Paris that my husband Harold acquired it in '22. He spent the next four years trying to break the code, but with no success. Then, six years ago, the ball was stolen from our home in Sussex and my husband was murdered. I've been told that eventually the ball ended up in Istanbul, then went on to Athens and has now turned up here in Chicago."

"So you're attempting to recover the ball so you can recover the treasure?"

"I am not at all convinced that the code on the ball can be deciphered. My husband was an extremely skilled cryptologist. I doubt that there were any codes he couldn't break. It actually was his only real skill, and his one true passion," she lamented. "Like many of the English gentry, much of his family's wealth had been lost. He believed that the treasure of Leuven would restore that fortune. He worked tirelessly on breaking the code, and kept detailed notes on his efforts, but to no avail."

"If you don't believe that the code can be broken, why do you want to retrieve the ball?"

"The local constable back in Sussex was unable to catch my husband's killer," she replied. "If I can get hold of the ball, I intend to set a trap for the murderers by letting it be known that I have it. Then I'll wait for the thief to return."

"Interesting plan, but a bit of a long shot, don't you think?"

"The ball, the code, and the hidden treasure have all become obsessions for quite a number of people, my late husband included. If I can get hold of the ball, I am quite certain that I can lure his killer into the open." She took another puff of her cigarette, exhaled, and crossed her shapely legs again so that her skirt rose up, revealing just a glimpse of her smooth white thigh.

"Well, Mrs. Nottingham," said Joe, as he forced his eyes back towards his guest's face, "I already have a client on this case, so there's not much I can do to help you."

"Surely you can see that I am in a position to pay you significantly more for the recovery of the ball than anyone else," she replied. "Perhaps we can talk about some additional incentives." Her eyes locked on to his and she gave him a smile he could actually feel.

Joe took a breath and allowed his mind to ponder the "additional incentives" she was offering before replying, "Unfortunately, I don't tend to drop clients based on who pays me the most. I will, however, relay your proposal to my client. Perhaps he will want to discuss the matter with you."

A look of disgust registered on the woman's face as she rose from her chair. "You're making a terrible mistake," she snapped in an angry tone as she stood and grabbed her purse and fur stole.

"Perhaps, but it's not my first, and I doubt it'll be my last." Anger flared in the beautiful woman's gorgeous eyes. Without saying another word, she abruptly turned and stormed out of his office.

"Well, she was pleasant," Kat remarked sarcastically, as she walked back into his office.

Joe took a pull on his cigarette and nodded in agreement. As he exhaled, he asked, "Did you catch her story?"

"Yes, but can we believe any of it?"

"It seemed to have more truth to it than what Patel was trying to feed us, and it does fit what we know about the ball," he added. "But I doubt she wants to recover it so she can trap her husband's killer. She doesn't strike me as the 'grieving widow' type."

"I remember the 'rape of Belgium' by the Boche," she said, using the French slur for Germans. "The papers in St. Petersburg were filled with atrocities like the burning of the library at Leuven."

"What does your intuition tell you about her?" Joe had learned from experience that Kat had excellent instincts about clients.

"There's honey on the tongue but ice on the heart."

"I assume the translation is she's not to be trusted."

"Never," was Kat's response. Then she explained, "That one's far more dangerous than the typical hoodlums you go up against."

"Well, I don't have time to deal with Mrs. Nottingham right now," he said, has he rose from his desk and grabbed his hat and coat. "Hold the fort, Kat. I'll be back in a couple of hours."

"Where are you off to now?" she asked as she walked over to the window and pulled it open.

"I want to go back to the Mart and talk to Eddie Collins, the producer of 'Day Dreams'," he replied. "He has a lot to lose if Irene leaves his show, and I want to see how he reacts to some difficult questions."

When Joe arrived back at WMAC's studios, he found a crowd milling outside the lobby entrance. He pushed his way to the front towards a young patrolman at the door. "Can you tell me what's going on here?" he asked.

"Sir," replied the cop, clearly annoyed, "we'll let you know what's happening just as soon as we can. Now please wait in the hallway like everybody else."

Joe looked past the lobby doors and could see Sean O'Halloran, a detective he knew from the 1st Precinct. Sean was a tall, good looking guy with thin sandy hair that always looked as if the wind had gotten hold of it. Most everyone who dealt with him thought he was a genuinely nice guy with a big smile and a bigger heart. Joe liked him because he was honest, and because he was one of the few cops he dealt with that wasn't a twit. For over two years now Joe had made sure to send all of his collars over to Sean, and this had allowed him to lead his division in major arrests and convictions. Consequently, he'd received four commendations and two promotions.

CHAPTER 5 - THURSDAY

Joe caught Sean's eye and the detective walked over to the door, whispering something to the cop who had stopped him.

"Sorry, sir," said the officer apologetically. "You can come through." Joe crossed the lobby and walked towards Sean, who was standing outside one of the soundstages.

"What are you doing here?" Sean asked.

"I'm working a blackmail case. What's going on?"

"A girl was found dead on one of the sound stages," he replied. "It's odd there's a blackmail attempt and a death at the same station. Any chance our cases are somehow linked?"

"I don't like coincidences either," agreed Joe. "Why don't we share what we can, and see if there's any possible connection." Sean nodded in agreement, and the two men walked into Studio A. When they entered Joe spotted a body on the floor and detected the unmistakable odor of gunpowder still hanging in the air.

"It seems the victim was shot in the head, but here's the twist," said Sean, "she was shot with blanks."

Joe flashed a quizzical look. "If she was shot with blanks, how could she be dead?"

"Well, according to the coroner, the discharge from a gun barrel, when it fires a blank cartridge, has quite a kick to it. If your hand is directly in front of it, the force can rip off a finger or two. If you're dumb enough to fire it into your temple at point-blank range, it can kill you."

Joe looked at him in disbelief. "That's possible?"

"That's what the man tells me," replied Sean. The two of them were now kneeling on the floor of the sound stage next to the corpse.

"What was her name?"

Sean flipped through his notebook and replied, "Betty Parker." Reaching out, he pulled the sheet off the body to reveal her lifeless form. She was wearing a modest plaid skirt with a white button down cotton blouse. Joe guessed that she was about twenty-five. Neither her round face, nor her figure were particularly attractive, and her dark hair was cut in a short bob with tight curls. Basically, she was Betty Boop without the sex appeal. The powder burns and bruising from the gun barrel discharge were clearly visible on her right temple.

"How many shots were fired?"

"At this point we're guessing just one shot, but only because that's how many empty shell casings we found," replied Sean.

"Did Betty work here?"

"Part time. She did some freelance work for the station, filling in on weekends. She also did some work on commercials, singing jingles, that sort of thing."

"So how do you think this went down?"

"If it turns out only one shot was fired, and we can't find any signs of foul play, my money is on either an accident or suicide."

"Any witnesses?"

"No, no one. Seems these studios are sound proof. No one heard or saw anything."

"Who discovered the body?"

"One of the technicians," replied Sean. "He came into the room to do a sound check and discovered her body about forty-five minutes ago. We're not sure when she died, but the coroner is guessing around 10:00 this morning. So does this have anything to do with your case?"

"I don't see how. My case deals with one of the radio shows here at the station. Seems someone is trying to blackmail one of the people involved with the show, using some compromising photos taken a couple of weeks ago. I can't go into too much detail, but I can't see how it has anything to do with this girl. I can tell you that no one with her name or description has come up in the investigation so far."

"Well, maybe we're just dealing with a coincidence."

"It's possible I guess, but I still don't like it."

The two men parted company and Joe agreed to let Sean know if his blackmail case became connected in any way to the late Betty Parker. He left the soundstage and headed back to the lobby to look for Eddie Collins. After speaking to a few people, he learned that Eddie had left the building. He managed to track down the 'Day Dreams' production secretary and explained to her that he'd been "authorized" to meet with Eddie tomorrow morning. After a bit of convincing, she agreed to enter it in his diary.

CHAPTER 5 - THURSDAY

"Who should I say the appointment is with?" she asked.

"Just tell him Giuseppe needs a few minutes of his time," he responded, before heading for the elevator.

Afternoon

After leaving the Mart Joe drove over to the Maxwell Street Market, just off Halsted, to grab a couple of hot dogs. It took him well out of his way, but he'd had a taste for a dog all day and it was well worth the detour. Forty-five minutes later he was back at his office, tossing his baseball and scribbling notes. After another thirty-five minutes of getting nowhere he was interrupted by Sid.

"I thought you'd gone to pick up Rose?" Joe asked, surprised at seeing him.

"She hasn't phoned in yet."

Joe checked his watch and shook his head. "It shouldn't be taking her this long." He looked back at Sid and changed the subject. "Before I forget, I need you to get me the low down on Betty Parker. She's a gal who died earlier today at the WMAC studio over at the Merchandise Mart."

"Wait," interrupted Kat, clearly concerned about what Joe was asking Sid to do. "Are we taking on another case?"

"I don't think so," he replied. "Betty was found dead on one of the soundstages at WMAC, and we need to know if her death is somehow related to our blackmail case."

"Ok," was her reluctant reply, "but the last thing we need right now is another case."

Sid quietly nodded his head in agreement, so Joe explained, "I don't like coincidences, so we need to confirm that Betty Parker wasn't involved in this blackmail. Once we know she wasn't, we won't spend any more time on it."

"You got it, boss", replied Sid, jotting down the name of the dead girl in his notebook.

"What did you dig up on the Washington Street Bridge?" Joe asked. Sid responded by dropping a copy of the Bridge report on the desk.

As Joe picked it up Sid explained, "All I could get was a carbon copy." Joe scanned the pages. Most of them were slightly smudged, not unusual for carbon copies, but overall it was legible. "I gotta run it back to the Hall of Records before they close for the day. You know it's funny, at first I tried to get this from the Department of Public Works. That's where the original should have been, but here's a surprise, it was missing."

After Joe finished skimming through the document, he read the summary page carefully. The report's conclusion was clear. The Washington Street Bridge was in need of serious repair. He lowered the report and looked up at Sid. "This proves there's a big problem, but it doesn't say how it happened. What we need to do is compare the Engineering Department's original construction specs with the ones that were in Bennett's contract."

Sid gave his boss a big smile. "I'm way ahead a ya," he replied, before dropping two more documents on Joe's desk. "These also gotta be back to the Hall of Records before they close. And just like that other report, the original documents were supposed to be kept at the Department of Public Works but they were also missing. It's pretty hinky if you ask me. I'll bet ya dollars-to-donuts that someone lifted those originals, but didn't know the city kept copies." The practice of keeping duplicates of key documents was a legacy of the great fire, and these duplicates were now stored in an off-site at the Hall of Records.

It took a few minutes to read and compare the city's original specifications, drawn up in '12, with Bennett's construction contract from the same year. The conclusion, however, was clear. Bennett's contract specifications were much lighter than those filed in the city's project outline.

"According to these documents," Joe explained to Sid and Kat, "the bridge's specifications were changed prior to the contract being signed, but the cost of the bridge stayed the same." Bennett Construction saved about fifteen grand over the original budget. Also, having the lighter specs meant that Bennett could finish the job quicker. That earned him a bonus of five grand."

"How did they think they could get away with it?" asked Kat.

"Back in '12 there wasn't as much heavy traffic going over the city's bridges," explained Sid. "It was mostly horse drawn buggies and wagons. The number of cars and trucks was pretty small when compared to today's traffic."

CHAPTER 5 - THURSDAY

"Bayles must have believed the bridge was over engineered. He probably thought he could cut corners on the specifications and no one would ever know."

"Bennett needed the money from the job to kick start his new construction company, and Bayles needed the money to start his political career," explained Sid.

Joe nodded his agreement and added, "but Bennett was smart. He had his contract drawn up with the lighter specifications. That way, if there was ever any trouble, he couldn't be blamed. He left all the risk with Bayles."

"But didn't someone check Bayles' work?" asked Kat.

Joe flipped through the documents looking for the supervising engineer. He paused on the final page and looked up, his face registering his surprise. "I was just telling Sean how much I hate coincidences."

"What coincidence?" asked Sid.

"It seems the person who signed off on Bayles' work was our dead city engineer Fritz Steiner. From what we know about him, he was a straight shooter. My guess is that he trusted Bayles and didn't check what he was doing. He probably didn't know that Bayles had cut corners on the specs."

"Steiner's body was found in an alley off Randolph," Kat said to both men. "That's just a block and a half away from the Washington Street Bridge. Do you think he might have met Bayles down by the bridge the night he was murdered?"

"We were wondering what he was doing there," Joe replied.

"Hold the phone," interrupted Sid. "Are we saying that that the death of Fritz Steiner is somehow linked to the murder of that co-ed?" He rubbed his forehead before looking over at Joe, "But there's no evidence they ever met, yet alone knew each other."

"No, but they may have stumbled across the same thing," surmised Joe. "Steiner, like Gen, must have discovered that Bayles altered the contract specs. His wife said that he'd been upset at work lately. We've assumed it was because of the Exposition project, but we haven't been able find any issues with that. So what if something else was wrong? What if he finally discovered that Bayles had altered the bridge specs, and confronted him?"

"If Steiner had threatened to blow the whistle on the bridge 'refurbishment', the shit would hit the fan," concluded Sid.

Kat gave Sid a disgusted look, "Why would anyone throw something like that at a fan, it's revolting?"

"It's just a saying," responded Sid with a smile.

"Americans have such odd expressions," she replied as she shook her head. "Bayles would have lost the Senate nomination if it came out that he'd swindled the city. So … what? He killed Steiner and that poor girl to keep them quiet?"

"It could be," Joe replied. "We need to have a conversation with Mr. Bayles and see what he has to say for himself. We just gotta figure out where and when we can corner him."

"As it turns out," Sid opened his small notebook and thumbed through the pages, "I think I have a pretty good idea. According to a pal of mine over at the Federal Building, when the right honorable congressman is in town, he's usually at Erma's partaking of their afternoon tea." Erma's was a small coffee shop a few blocks from the Federal Building. It offered its regulars an afternoon "tea" which consisted of watered-down scotch served in tea cups.

"All right," said Joe, "Let's meet up at Erma's at 4:30." He turned towards Kat. "Have you heard anything from Manny in New York?"

"No, and I've placed a call to him at least half a dozen times. But don't worry, I've been calling person-to-person so at least we're not getting charged for the calls."

"Keep trying," he replied. "We need to get an update from him."

The phone rang and Kat walked to her desk to answer it. After less than a minute she hung up and called out, "That was Rose. She's ready to be picked up."

Joe looked at his watch and shook his head, as Sid left to pick up Rose.

"How long was she there?" Kat asked.

CHAPTER 5 - THURSDAY

A scowl crossed Joe's face as he replied, "Almost four hours." He knew that there was no way her investigation should have taken that long. "Did she mention anything about a young man named Adam?" he snapped.

"No," replied Kat with a smile, "but she did seem to be in an awfully good mood."

"Damn," he muttered under his breath, before storming back to his office.

Kat shot back quickly, "Language, Joseph."

Joe grumbled a response to Kat that she couldn't hear and spent the next few minutes sulking in his office, trying hard to think up a couple of good lies he could tell Arthur about how Rose met the McNulty gardener. Eventually he resigned himself to his fate, picked up the phone, and placed a call to Theo to give him an update on his case. "I'm afraid I've got nothing new since yesterday," he said. "But at this point my gut tells me she's the real McCoy. We're still digging, but so far we've found nothing that indicates she's not legit."

"Thanks Joe. Keep working as fast as you can. The old man is close to giving up the ghost."

"I'll try and give you an update early tomorrow."

Joe's next call was to Emma. The phone rang only once and, as before, she answered herself. "Hello."

"It's Joe Lorde. I was just calling to see how you are."

"I'm ok I guess, but I am going a little stir crazy," she admitted. Joe hadn't really thought about it from her angle, but he suddenly realized how hard it must be for her. She'd been cooped up in the McNulty guesthouse for days and her only activity had been visiting a dying old man.

"Do you have some glad rags?"

"Just one dress with me."

"Well, what d'ya say you get dolled up and I get you out of the house tonight. Just for a few hours."

"You mean it?" she asked excitedly.

"Why not? We could both use a break. I'll pick you up at quarter past seven." Emma squealed with delight.

As soon as Joe put down the phone, he started having second thoughts about taking her out. He couldn't "date" someone he was investigating, could he? The more he thought about it, the more he realized he'd made a mistake. He knew he should cancel, but he also knew that he didn't have the heart to do it. After thinking about what he should do for several minutes, he called out, "Kat, can you get me a table for two at the Grand Terrace Ballroom for 8:00 tonight?"

"A table for two?" she replied, clearly surprised by his request. In all the years she'd worked for him she'd never made him reservations before.

"Yeah, I'm taking Emma O'Donnell out, as part of the investigation."

Kat got up from her desk, walked toward his office and poked her head around the corner. "And what part of Miss O'Donnell are you planning to investigate?" she asked with a smirk.

"Just get me the reservation," Joe shot back, not appreciating her attempt at humor.

It was 4:30 when Joe met up with Sid at Erma's Coffee Shop, located off Wills, under the shadow of the "L". The two men scanned the late afternoon crowd, looking for Congressman Bayles. They soon spotted the handsome, sandy-haired politician sitting alone in a booth sipping his "tea". After Joe and Sid slipped into the opposite side of his booth, Joe began to give Bayles the Reader's Digest version of their investigation into the Steiner murder. As Joe spoke the congressman became more and more agitated. When he got to the killing of Genevieve Ericson, the congressman's face was pale and drawn. By the time Sid showed him a copy of the recent engineering report, the congressman was nearly apoplectic.

"I don't know what any of this is about," said Bayles with no conviction, before adding meekly, "None of this has anything to do with me."

Joe showed him a copy of the original specifications for the bridge drawn up in '12, as well as the alternate ones that Bayles had written into the construction contract. "Can you explain the discrepancies between these documents?" he asked.

The congressman was now sweating heavily. "I told you, I have no idea what you're talking about." The man started to get up, but Joe yanked down sharply on his arm, forcing him back into his seat.

CHAPTER 5 - THURSDAY

"We know you altered these specifications, and that Steiner found out about it, so you killed him." Bayles began to show signs of panic, and tried again to pull away but Joe's grip was too firm.

"When Gen Ericson discovered your secret," added Sid, "she threatened to expose you, so you killed her as well."

"Face it, congressman, you're caught," concluded Joe.

"No," cried Bayles, "you can't tell anyone. You don't understand ... you don't know what'll happen to me ... to my family. It's the Third Period, for Christ sake! You have to believe me, I never wanted any of this, you understand, don't you? I never wanted any of it."

Bayles was by now terrified, so Joe decided to try and calm him down. He eased his hold on the man's arm and said, "Relax, pal, this is Chicago. This kind of stuff happens all the time. Get a good lawyer and you'll come out a hero."

"No, they won't let it be all right. I told you, it's the Third Period. It was never supposed to go this far, you have to believe me." The frightened congressman broke away from his accusers, raced out of the coffee shop, and back toward the Federal Building. Joe and Sid tried to follow, but lost the fleeing politician on the crowded city sidewalks.

"Where do you think he's headed?" asked Sid.

"You got me ... but he shouldn't be too hard to track down." He pointed to a building across the street and said to his investigator, "There's a payphone in Woolworth's. I'll give Sean a call, and fill him in. Something tells me the police are going to have a few questions for the congressman."

"I need to take these documents back to the Hall of Records. I promised my contact I'd get them back today, and they close at five," explained Sid.

"Ok, but tell them to keep those reports locked up. It looks like they're now evidence in two murders. Are you going back to the office after you drop off the documents?"

"Yup," replied Sid.

"Tell Kat I'm going to see Walt at the coroner's office. I want to talk to him about how Betty Parker died over at WMAC studios."

It was quarter past five by the time Joe parked his car on Polk Street in the Hospital District. Unfortunately, the wind had shifted and was now coming out of the southeast. This caused the smell of the Stock Yards hit to his nostrils as he opened the car door. Ignoring the smell, he headed down the alley towards the office entrance.

"Got a minute?" he asked as he stuck his head into Walt's office.

"Sure," mumbled his friend through yet another cigarette dangling from his lips.

"What's wrong? You look like hell."

"I'm going to pop the question to Jodi. I made reservations at seven-thirty tomorrow at that place you've talked about, the Grand Terrace Ballroom." Then Walt add, "I'm so nervous, I can't eat or sleep."

"You'll do fine. All you gotta do is let the words come out. She'll take care of the rest."

"You didn't drop by to shoot the breeze," said Walt, "you here to see another 'guest'?"

"Yeah, but I can take care of it another time". Joe could see how wound up his friend was, and didn't want to push him.

"Don't be silly. Working will take my mind off tomorrow. Who are you looking for?"

"There was a girl who died over at the Mart today, her name's Betty Parker."

"Oh, that one," Walt said, without needing to look at the 'Guest List'. "We've all been talking about her since she came in. They just finished her up a little while ago." Walt got up from his desk and led Joe down the corridor to the cooler. Once inside, he walked over to a drawer, rolled out the slab, and pulled back the sheet to reveal the young woman's head.

"What do you think happened?" Joe asked, as both men stared at the lifeless face.

"Good question. There's no clear evidence of foul play, but there are a few things that are odd."

"Such as?"

"Well, for one thing there seems to be some light bruising on both sides of the victim's left wrist." Walt lifted up the dead woman's arm and pointed to two small bruises. "It looks like someone grabbed her by the wrist like this," he said as he used his hand to demonstrate.

CHAPTER 5 - THURSDAY

"Is there anything else?"

"Yeah, if you look closely at her temple you can see that there appears to be a wide area where the burn mark occurred. This might suggest two different shots were fired. If there were two shots, then this is definitely a murder. A suicide would only involve one shot, because after the initial shot you'd be incapable of firing a second one."

"So if there were two shots, someone else must have pulled the trigger," Joe summarized.

"Yeah, but based on what we can tell from the wound it's impossible to say with certainty if one or two shots were fired."

"Could you tell from the gun if it was fired more than once?"

"Nope. The person on the soundstage who's responsible for the gun, they call him the 'Prop Master', never bothered to clean it after it was used during the rehearsal. There was only one spent shell when the cops found the gun. Their theory is that it was only fired once, but it's possible it was fired multiple times and then reloaded. Another odd thing was that some skin and blood were found under the fingernails of the victim's right hand."

"Can you tell whose?"

"No, under the best of circumstances you might be able to match a blood type, but that could only tell us whose blood it *isn't*. Unfortunately, these samples are much too small for us to do any testing. As for the skin, there are no tests that can match a skin sample to an individual, regardless of how much skin we have to test."

"Still," said Joe, "if she had skin and blood under her nails she may have fought with someone".

"Maybe, but that could have been several hours before her death. Besides, for all we know, she could have gotten the skin and blood under her nails while scratching some guy's back during sex."

"You ever see someone killed with a pistol that shoots blanks?"

"Nope, can't say I have," replied Walt, "but I did look in the files and there was a case back in '22 where a man died in the same manner. Apparently the victim was an actor, and was horsing around with several people backstage. He pretended to shoot himself in the head with a gun loaded with blanks. No one was really sure if he intended to pull the trigger or the gun went off by itself. There were about ten witnesses, and all of them said it was an accident."

"Anything else you can tell me about Betty's death?"

"Well, without some additional evidence, I can tell you that the coroner is going to rule it either an accident or a suicide."

Joe walked back with Walt to his office. He checked his watch and realized that it was getting late, so he said his goodbyes. "Have a good time tomorrow night."

"Thanks. You think she'll say yes, don't you?" Walt was clearly looking for Joe to reassure him.

"Relax," he replied, giving his friend another brief smile. "What woman could say no to a handsome devil like you?"

Before heading back up to Kenilworth to meet Emma, Joe had to pick up his good suit at the laundry and go back to his place to change. Despite the detours, he still managed to pull up to the guesthouse at seven-fifteen on the dot. He rang the doorbell and the maid ushered him in to the main hall. Joe stood there for almost fifteen minutes, becoming more and more annoyed as the time dragged on. Finally he heard Emma's voice. "I'm sorry I'm so late," she said as she stood at the top of the marble staircase. As if by magic, the annoyance he'd felt moments before melted away, replaced by a smile that spread from ear to ear.

She was wearing a pale peach-colored dress that came halfway up her calf. The fabric clung to her curves and the color enhanced her complexion. She kept her eyes squarely on him while gracefully descending the long stairway. As she approached Joe moved towards the staircase, unable to take his eyes off her. When she reached the last step, she stumbled slightly and Joe instinctively reached out to catch her. Emma fell into his arms and he held her close for several seconds, his arms wrapped firmly around her waist, and hers gently around his neck. She giggled and apologized for being so clumsy. The detective in Joe suspected that the fall had been staged, but the man in him couldn't have cared less.

The Grand Terrace Ballroom was just off South Park Way on East 35th in Bronzeville, and the look of the place lived up to its reputation as being Chicagoland's hottest night spot. The building had originally been constructed as a garage back in '09. Today, it housed one of the country's

CHAPTER 5 - THURSDAY

best known "Black & Tan" clubs, where many of the country's top entertainers headlined.

While Joe and Emma were being shown to their table, Earl Hines and his house band were playing one of their biggest hits, "57 Varieties". Earl spotted Joe as he was being led through the club and, once the set was done, he came over to greet him. The two men shook hands as Earl looked over at Emma.

"Mr. Detective, who is this lovely creature you've brought to my club?"

"Fatha Hines," said Joe, "I'd like you to meet Miss Emma O'Donnell."

Emma giggled slightly as Joe introduced her. "I'm a big fan," she said with a smile.

"Well, lovely Emma," began Earl with characteristic charm, "this is my club, and anything you want you just let me know."

Earl had to move through his audience before the next set. He was the host as well as the band leader, and needed to engage with as many people as he could. He said his farewells and started to leave, but Joe pulled him aside.

"Earl, I need a favor," he said.

"What can I do?"

"A guy named Walter Dorfman is coming here tomorrow night to propose to his gal. Could you arrange to have his tab picked up for the night?" He slipped Earl twenty dollars, "if this doesn't cover it you just let me know, and I'll take care of the rest. And if it's not too much trouble, could you dedicate a song to them after he pops the question?"

Earl gave Joe one his trademark smiles and replied, "Happy to, but how will I know when he pops the question?"

"When the girl screams, you'll know. Oh, and let's keep this just between us? If Walter asks who paid, just tell him he won a contest or something."

The band leader gave him a nod and a quick wink. "Always a pleasure, Mr. Detective," he added, before moving on to the next table.

The night seemed to fly by as Joe and Emma talked easily for hours. She teased him about how he tried to look so stern all the time, and during the evening she made him laugh more than he had in years. He talked about his time in the army, his time in Paris, and how he ended up a private detective. He also told her about how much he disliked guns.

"To be honest," he explained, "it's bullets I really hate. Whenever I'm in the same room with a loaded gun, I have this intense desire to take out the bullets. I guess I learned to hate them during the war. They just scare the hell out of me."

Emma talked about growing up in Fort Wayne, and their dreary house on Williams Street. "Both my grandparents died by the time my mom was twenty, so she moved to Chicago to try and get work. I guess she always felt that Fort Wayne was home. When she got into 'trouble,' it was just natural for her to go back there. It's funny, Mom always loved Fort Wayne, but from the time I was a little girl I dreamed of living anywhere else. I couldn't wait to leave."

"I may not have agreed with her about Fort Wayne, but she was right about one thing," she said with a forced smile. "The guy I ran off with turned out to be exactly what she said he was. I guess she figured that after my romance was over I'd come home, but I changed when I went to New York. I was shy and timid when I was growing up. Coming to the city taught me that there was so much more to life than being frightened all the time. The city was so exciting, I just couldn't get myself to go back to Fort Wayne. Mom never liked New York and she only came to visit me there once. We tried to keep close through letters and an annual phone call. I always told her that I'd come visit, but I never did," she said sadly. "I guess I'll have to live with that for the rest of my life."

"How did you find out she'd died?"

"I got a letter from Father Murphy, our parish priest. He got my address from an insurance investigator and wrote to me that Mom had been killed in a traffic accident. Three weeks after his letter, he sent me two boxes with all her personal things. It was in one of those boxes that I found my birth certificate. At first, I was reluctant to contact Papa. I was so afraid he'd deny he was my father. Then I finally got up the nerve to come to Chicago. I'm glad I did. If I had waited, I would never have gotten the chance to see him before he died."

"Have you talked to Vance yet?" Joe asked.

"I've been at the estate for five days now, and I haven't even gotten a glimpse of him," she said with sadness in her voice. "When Mom died I felt so alone, but when I found out I had a brother, I was excited. I thought maybe I wouldn't be alone anymore. Vance doesn't seem to feel the same way."

There was a deep sadness that showed on her face and Joe wanted to do something to cheer her up. He stood, stretched out his hand towards her, and asked, "May I have this dance?"

Emma's infectious smile flashed across her face. "I'd love to," she replied, as she took his hand and followed him down to the dance floor.

"When I was younger I wasn't a bad hoofer," Joe explained as he took her in his arms, "but I have to warn you, I'm a bit rusty."

"It's just like riding a bicycle," she whispered into his ear. "Once you've learned how, you never forget."

Joe's ribs and neck were still fairly sore, thanks to his "dance partners" from the two previous nights. Now, holding Emma in his arms and moving with the music, the only thing he could feel was her body against his. Normally when a house photographer approached, Joe would waive them off. This time, he let the girl snap a photo with the two of them dancing. Then he made a mental note to himself to make sure he got a couple of prints.

It was well after midnight when Joe pulled his Roadster back up to the guesthouse. Typically, when a fella took a gal out on the town there would be, at a minimum, a kiss at the end of the evening. Not a peck on the cheek, mind you, but a serious kiss. He'd been thinking about that kiss since he saw her come down the staircase, but an inner voice kept warning him that if he ever locked lips with Emma, she'd own his soul. He knew he couldn't let that happen, not yet.

Joe escorted her from his car towards the guesthouse entrance. When Emma started climbing the steps to the front door she suddenly spun around to face him. The extra height of the step put her full red lips just below his. He had planned to avoid getting this close, but her sudden turn caught him off guard. He took a half step back, and her luscious lips began to pout in response. "Don't you find me attractive?" she asked sadly.

"We can't have this conversation. Not while the investigation is still on."

"Then why did you take me out tonight?" she asked angrily, before turning away from him.

"I shouldn't have, but I knew you'd been cooped up in the guesthouse day after day, and I just wanted you to have some fun," he explained.

She looked back at him and her smile returned. "I did have fun," she admitted. "I had a really swell time. Can't you come inside?" Her voice turned warm and seductive as she added, "We could make some ... coffee. I make really good coffee." Her eyes looked straight into his as she reached over and gently stroked his hand.

Joe was usually slow to pick up on the signals that women gave, but even he understood that she wasn't talking about coffee. "I can't, but even if I could I ... haven't ... well ... 'made coffee' in a while."

"It's just like dancing, really," she said, as her fingers continued their journey up his arm. "Once you know how, you never forget. I bet the two of us could make really great coffee together, and we could make cup ... after cup ... after cup."

Joe was now deep into her captivating blue eyes. As she spoke, he could feel the tips of her delicate fingers running up along his shoulder. His body began to react accordingly, and he realized he wanted so much to be with her. Every male instinct he possessed told him he should go inside with her, but he also knew what he had to do. "I can't, I'm sorry," he said, before taking another half step back. "Not while the investigation is going on. It just wouldn't be right." He added, "I'd better go now," before turning and walking back to his car. After opening his door, he looked back to see her she still standing on the porch. "I'll ring you tomorrow," he called out, as he climbed into his coupe.

"Joe," she replied. "I had a wonderful time tonight."

He sat in the driver's seat, still looking at her on the front step and whispered to himself, "Me too." As he watched her walk into the guesthouse, he let out a deep breath, started his engine, and headed back to Warren Street.

Later that night powerful images of Emma swirled through his head, and even after a cold shower he couldn't fall asleep. He spent half the night in bed smoking cigarettes, listening to Jazz over his shortwave, and thinking about 'making coffee' with Emma.

CHAPTER SIX

FRIDAY

When you have lost everything, even hope, life becomes a disgrace and death a duty -W.C. Fields

Morning

Thirty minutes after Joe finally nodded off, the phone rang. He desperately wanted to ignore it, but the phone just wouldn't stop ringing. Eventually he gave in and picked it up.

"Someone better be dead," he grumbled into the handset, still half asleep.

"Give that man a cigar," said the voice on the other end of the line. At first Joe couldn't quite place the voice, but after some of the sleep drained from his head he realized it was Billie Breslau, a reporter from the *Trib*.

Joe's brain and voice were still compromised by the deep sleep he'd been in. "Why are you calling me in the middle of the night?" he groaned, rubbing his eyes.

"I just thought you'd like to know that Congressman Bayles had a late night snack that didn't agree with him."

"Yeah," he replied, still somewhat groggy. "What was it?"

"A .38 caliber bullet." Joe was now wide awake. He quickly swung his feet around and sat up on the edge of the bed. The reporter continued. "I slipped a couple a bucks to the flatfoot that found the late congressman. He tells me the guy wrote a suicide note and confessed to killing both Steiner and that co-ed from the University of Chicago. Then I remembered that I saw you calling on the widow Steiner earlier this week.

And that detective pal of yours, O'Halloran, told me yesterday you were looking into the co-ed's murder. So, I figure you might be able to give me some inside scoop ... what gives, Joe?"

Normally Joe didn't talk to the press, but he owed Billie a favor from a few months back. It was obviously payback time, so he proceeded to fill him in on what he knew.

"Wow," Breslau responded once Joe had finished. He could hear the reporter scribbling furiously in his notebook. "Now there's a story I didn't see coming. A double murder to cover up a crooked construction deal. That poor bastard Bayles had obviously been hanging around Washington too long."

"What do you mean?"

"This is Chicago, Joe," replied Breslau. "If politicians around here started whacking people just because someone found out about their shady business deals, the Loop would be a ghost town. Still, this is going to make a hell of a story."

"Can you do me a favor and keep my name out of it?" Joe had learned the hard way that name recognition from publicity might bring in a few more clients, but it made it a lot harder to actually investigate.

"You got it."

Joe added as an afterthought, "Hey Billie, any chance you know what the 'Third Period' is?"

"Christ," replied the reporter while shaking his head, "you've never been to a Black Hawks game?"

"That's what I thought you'd say."

"I gotta run, they're going to want to stop the presses for this one. Thanks for the scoop, Joe," he said, just before the line went dead.

After the call Joe felt certain that he'd never fall back to sleep, but amazingly he passed out almost immediately. Consequently, when the alarm clock at his bedside went off at 8:00 it jolted him from a sound sleep. When he arrived at his office on State Street, he found Kat sitting at her desk, Rose in the chair next to her, and Sid in his usual spot. The three of them wore slightly stunned expressions while listening to the radio's news bulletin recapping the story about the suicide of Congressman Bayles.

CHAPTER 6 - FRIDAY

"So ya heard," he said in a matter of fact tone, while walking into his office.

The others followed him in. "Billie Breslau broke the story," said Kat. "Did you give it to him?"

"He phoned me last night to let me know Bayles was dead and that he'd left a note confessing to both the Steiner and Ericson murders. I owed him a favor. You remember, from that thing in that place with that guy, a couple of months ago." Kat and Sid both nodded and Joe continued, "So I filled in the missing pieces."

"Well, I for one think we did a great job," said Kat with pride. "We cornered an embezzler and double murderer, and he committed suicide."

"I suppose."

"You suppose?" she repeated, astonished by her boss's remark. "Look, he cheated the city, used the money to launch his political career, and then killed two people to cover up his crime."

"He confessed in the suicide note, for goodness sake," agreed Rose. "Case closed."

"What do you think, Sid?" asked Joe.

"Well, I guess I agree with the ladies," he replied halfheartedly. "But there is something hinky about this case and it bothers me. I can't put my finger on it, but it's there."

"I agree," said Joe. "Yesterday, when he was at Erma's, Bayles kept referring to 'they'. He'd said 'they' wouldn't leave him alone and 'they' wouldn't let it be all right. I wonder who 'they' are? And then there was the comment about it being the Third Period. What was he referring to?"

"Maybe he meant that time was running out for him," said Sid. "You know, maybe he was using some kinda hockey metaphor."

"We'll probably never know," added Rose. "It looks like he took that secret to his grave."

"Did you hear about the other big story?" Kat asked. "They found the body of the Lindbergh baby." Charles Lindbergh was arguably the most famous American on the planet. The kidnapping of his young son back in March had electrified the country.

"Yeah, I heard it on the BBC last night," Joe responded, saddened by the news. "That's gotta be real tough on his family."

Tears began to well up in Kat's eyes as she said, to no one in particular, "Losing a child is the worst thing that can happen to someone."

Sid unconsciously let out a deep sigh. "I'm glad we weren't working that one."

"My money is on the nurse," said Rose, clearly fascinated by the case. "I think it was an inside job and I read she gave conflicting accounts of what happened that night."

Joe decided to change the subject, and looked over at Sid. "You dig up anything on Paul Trent?"

"I came up with bupkis," Sid answered. "I was up most of the night and hit a couple dozen clubs looking for a lead, but got zilch. How about you, you dig up anything on Irene's ex-agent?"

"Well, if we want to talk to him, 'digging up' will definitely be required. It turns out it was a trip for biscuits. The guy died a while back, so it's safe to say he's got an iron clad alibi."

"It seems to me," said Rose, "WMAC has the most to gain by her staying. My guess is they're behind it somehow."

"It's hard to believe that this blackmailer would tell her to sign a new contract with WMAC just because he thinks they're good people," agreed Sid. "Someone there must be involved."

"Well, the Major said that the top guy wouldn't do this," said Joe. "So, if WMAC is involved, it must be someone lower in the ranks. The most logical guy is the producer, Eddie Collins. He has the most to lose if she leaves."

"But there's no way to know if he's involved or not," replied Rose.

"The cat knows whose meat it's eaten," added Kat.

Rose wrinkled her nose. "The cat knows what?"

"It's Russian," explained Sid. "She's got a million of 'em." He turned to Kat, "You want to decipher that for her?"

Kat always felt it was unnecessary, believing that, like all her proverbs, the meaning was self-evident. She sighed, and turned towards Rose, "It means Eddie Collins knows if he's involved or not."

CHAPTER 6 – FRIDAY

"If he's involved the last thing he'll want to do is tell anyone about it," replied Sid.

"He will if someone can convince him that it's the right thing to do. Alright," Joe added, "let's change gears. Rose, what did you find out over at the McNulty estate yesterday?"

"Well," she said, as she perched herself on the edge of the desk, crossed her legs, and took out a small notepad from her purse. "Cyrus is not particularly loved by the staff. There are, however, a few who've been with him for a long time and they seem fairly loyal."

"Did you get them to open up about Maggie?" he asked.

Rose glanced through her notes and began to summarize. "Only three of the current staff actually knew Maggie, but everyone I talked to at the estate had heard rumors about the affair. It was also common knowledge that Maggie was pregnant before she left. According to the cook, who's been there thirty years and just loves to gossip, Maggie was madly in love with Cyrus. She said Mrs. McNulty was so busy with her various charities and social activities that she was completely oblivious both to her husband and the affair."

"What about Emma? Do the staff believe she's Maggie's daughter?"

"Well," Rose flipped a page in the notepad, "the three that knew Maggie sure seem to think so. The cook, the chauffeur, and the downstairs maid all think so. They say that she's the spitting image of the Maggie they knew, both in looks and personality."

"Anything else?"

"Yes," she responded. "It seems that Emma has been visiting Cyrus three or four times a day since she arrived. The nurse told me that she sweeps into his room like a fresh breeze. She reads to him, sings him songs and just simply lifts the old guy's sprits."

"Yeah," agreed Joe, "she can have that effect on someone."

Rose continued, "The nurse also said that her visits are making Mr. McNulty's last days much happier than they would have been. She told me that Cyrus is very weak and might not make it through the night. She said that his son, Vance, won't even bother to walk down the hall to see him. The chauffeur called him a vulture, and said that he was just waiting for his old man's death."

"That it?"

"Yup," she responded with a smile. "I think that's all of it."

"Thanks, Princess, that was really great."

"Jeepers, you mean it?" she was clearly thrilled to be helping on a case. "You're not just saying that, are you?"

"No," he responded earnestly, "that was good stuff. But maybe you can look in that notebook of yours and tell me one last thing."

"Sure," she gushed, "what do you need to know?"

"Why exactly did it take you four hours to dig up that information?" Upon hearing Joe's question, as well as the tone in his voice, both Sid and Kat decided it was better to quietly leave his office, and closed the door behind them.

Rose pretended to be startled by his comment. "Whatever do you mean?"

"I mean," he explained in an exasperated tone, "how much time did you spend with Adam the gardener?"

Rose was in no way intimidated by his size, booming voice, or intense glare. "Now you wait just one minute," she shot back. "I had every intention of not talking to him just like we agreed, but then I found out from the cook that he grew up at the McNulty estate."

"You lied to me," he replied angrily. "You promised to stay away from the gardener."

"Well, you lied first," she said with a smile. "He's never been sick a day in his life, and he was also a great source of information. His grandfather was the McNulty's handyman, George, and it was George who went to Fort Wayne to see Maggie twenty-five years ago. Besides, if you want to get technical about it, I promised to stay away from the gardener, and it turns out he's not the gardener." Rose's voice began rising in excitement. "He's just helping out because of the staff shortage. He's actually a graduate of Tuskegee, and he's waiting to find out if he's been accepted to medical school, and he doesn't have a girlfriend, and he's as cute as a bug's ear." It was obvious that Rose was smitten by her new love interest.

In the front office Sid and Kat could hear Joe shouting, and he continued this for several minutes. Eventually Rose strolled out of the office and

CHAPTER 6 – FRIDAY

said, still smiling, "I don't see the point in discussing this with you any further, at least not until you've calmed down."

"I am perfectly calm!" yelled Joe.

"Don't be silly," she replied sweetly, "you're about ready to blow your wig. We can discuss this again once you've had time to settle down." She turned towards Kat and gave her a wink, then looked over at Sid. "Would you be a dear and run me back to *The Defender*?" Sid looked at his boss, who was still fuming but silently nodded.

Joe warned Rose, his voice just below a bellow. "You think I'm bent, just you wait 'til Arthur gets wind of this. You bring your 'gardener' to the house, and he'll chew him up and spit him out before he gets past the front door."

Rose grabbed her coat, blew Kat a kiss, and turned back towards Joe. "I'll see you Sunday," she said in a chipper voice before heading out the door with Sid.

Joe stood there for several seconds before turning towards Kat. "Did you see the damn look in her eyes?"

"Language, Joseph," was Kat's quick response.

Joe ignored her and continued, "God help us, she's in love again."

Kat smiled and replied, "Love and eggs are always best when they're fresh."

"Put a cork in the Russian wisdom, Kat. I'm not in the mood," he snapped as he shook his head in disgust. "When Arthur finds out how Rose met this kid he's going to chew me up as well," he added woefully, before slowly walking back into his office.

Kat waited a few minutes for him to cool down before pouring a cup of coffee and taking it into him. "How was the 'investigating' last night?" she asked, as she handed him the cup.

Joe decided to let her comment slide, lit up a Chesterfield, and took a sip. "Did you hear anything from Manny in New York?"

"I talked to him about an hour ago. He's come up with nothing that contradicts the girl's story. He said he tracked down the bank branch in lower Manhattan where Emma worked as a teller, but it went bust a while ago and the building is vacant. He also found her landlady, and she confirmed that the girl in the photo is Emma. She was positive on the ID.

The landlady said that Emma has been renting a room at her boarding house for over six months. She also confirmed that she'd been working at the Bank of the United States until it went bust. Manny said that he also talked to several of the other women who live at that boarding house, and they all positively identified Emma from the photograph, as well. The only negative thing said by anyone was when the landlady complained that she was two weeks behind on her rent. He confirmed that he was trying to locate the piano player that Emma ran away with. So far, no luck. He said that he's still tracking down some leads, and promised he'd check back in later today." Kat started to walk back to her desk, but paused for a moment to add, "Don't forget you have a meeting over at WMAC at 11:00 this morning."

Joe nodded, then picked up his phone's ear piece and placed a call to Theo. After a brief word with his secretary, Mary, he was put through.

"Anything new?" asked Theo.

"We've been able to confirm that Emma lived at the address she gave in New York," said Joe. "And it seems she did work at the Bank of the United States before it went bust last year, just like she said. Unfortunately, we can't speak to anyone at the bank because it's now just an empty building. We also finished up our interviews in Fort Wayne, and we've talked to several of the staff at the McNulty estate. The bottom line is still the same, there's nothing definite, just more circumstantial evidence that tends to point to the girl being legit."

"You expect to get any more information?" asked Theo.

"We might, but my gut says we aren't going to find anything more concrete than what we have now."

"OK, thanks. If you find out anything that contradicts what you've learned so far let me know. Otherwise, you don't have to worry about providing any more updates."

After hanging up, Joe's next call was to Emma and the two of them spoke for nearly an hour. He had only intended to speak to her briefly, but like the other times he'd phoned her, he had a difficult time saying goodbye. By the end of the call he'd agreed to meet her at the guesthouse later in the afternoon. Once he hung up, he spent some time scribbling on his case notes and tossing his baseball. Without realizing it, he was humming while he did both.

CHAPTER 6 – FRIDAY

It was just past 11:15 when Eddie Collins got back to his office. A short, disheveled man in a poorly fitted gray suit, he was just forty-two but looked much older. Eddie also had bad teeth, which kept him in constant pain and were the principal reason for his surly attitude towards everyone. His normally acerbic mood was even worse today because he'd been working on equipment changes to the soundstage since 6:00 this morning.

Walking into his office, Eddie immediately spotted a man dressed like a hood, sitting behind his desk. Eddie rolled his eyes and mumbled in disgust. One of Irene's new storylines required them to cast someone to play a gangster, so it was hardly a surprise to see some poor deluded fool actually dress for the part.

"Who are you, and why are you sitting in my chair?" he demanded, as he moved to a large table adjacent to his desk and dropped off a stack of publicity stills. The table had piles of paperwork and Eddie began searching through them. "Actually," he said without looking up, "forget what I just asked. I don't want to know anything about you, just get out."

Joe was once again dressed in his "gangster" suit and playing the hood. "We had an appointment at 11:00 and you're late. I don't like to be kept waiting."

Oh, God, thought Eddie, this one was playing the tough guy to the hilt. "Look, whoever you are, my secretary made your appointment without checking with me first. I'm busy today, so like I said, get out."

Joe rose from behind the desk and began to move toward the door. Eddie suddenly found what he'd been searching for and held it up in triumph. "Gotcha," he shouted, but as the word came out Joe grabbed him by the throat and slammed him up against the wall. In almost the same instant, he flicked open his stiletto and held the thin blade less than an inch from Eddie's eyeball.

"Don't move," commanded Joe, in a deep, hushed voice. Even though he couldn't breathe, the terrified producer did as he was told. He hoped that by doing so, the intruder would ease his vice-like grip.

"I want you to listen to me carefully, because I don't like to repeat myself. Some very important people in this town are extremely bent about you blackmailing Miss Fields. I'm sure you had no idea she'd those kinds of friends, but she does. The people I work for have given me two choices," Joe said calmly. "I can either kill you and then search for the photos and negatives you're using to blackmail her. Or you can simply give them to me, in which case you get to live. Now I'm going to loosen up on your throat just a bit, so you can answer. If you try and scream, I'll jam this knife clear through your eye socket and into your brain. Is that clear?" The frightened man nodded his agreement, and Joe's hand eased its grip. "Now, where is the stuff on Miss Fields?"

"I don't know what you're talking about," Eddie's voice was raspy as he gasped for air. "I swear I don't."

"Well, then," Joe replied coldly, "I guess it's choice number one, isn't it?" He tightened his hand around the producer's throat and pulled the knife back in preparation for thrusting it through Eddie's eye. The horror on the pudgy man's face was obvious, as he shook his head in protest. Then he soiled himself. During the war many men faced with going "over the top" had done the same thing, but Joe hadn't smelled that particular byproduct of fear for many years.

"You have something else you want to say?"

Joe realized that he'd taken Eddie as far as he could. If he didn't crack now, then either he didn't know, or he was willing to take his secret to the grave. He eased up on the producer's throat, and as he did Eddie took a huge gulp of air before blurting out, "It wasn't my idea."

"Bingo," thought Joe. He quickly replied to the frightened producer, "What wasn't your idea?"

Everything Eddie knew about the blackmail of Irene Fields came gushing out, in between sobs and gasps. "I got a call about three or four weeks ago. He never gave his name and I didn't recognize his voice. The guy says that Irene is planning to leave WMAC and start up a new show on WBM. I knew if she left my show wouldn't survive. The caller says that for five grand he can guarantee that she stays put for five more years. At first I didn't believe him, but then he says I got nothing to lose. If Irene stays I pay the five 'G's'. If she doesn't, I don't pay a cent. I'm desperate to keep her, so I figure what the hell. Then a couple of days ago I get another call from the same guy. He says Irene is ready to sign a new contract. I can't believe it. She's suddenly prepared to sign for a fraction of what she said she wanted. The guy tells me to get the new contract to her right away, and he'll make sure she signs it on Monday. He also says

CHAPTER 6 - FRIDAY

that I gotta give him the five 'G's' on Monday or she won't sign. I've been working all week to pull the dough together." Eddie's crying had eased up, but the smell from his trousers was getting worse.

"How do you contact this mystery caller?"

"I don't. He calls me."

Joe released the man's throat and closed his stiletto. "Ok, Eddie," he said, as if he was talking to a frightened child. "I need you to do something for me."

"Sure, anything, you name it," he replied weakly.

"I want you to continue to deal with whoever's been calling you. Do you understand?"

"Yes," confirmed Eddie, as his voice cracked.

"Under no circumstances are you to tell him that you and I had this little chat. When this mug calls again I want you to agree to anything he asks, but I also want you to phone this number." Joe handed Eddie a piece of paper with his office number on it. "Now, are you sure you understand what I want you to do?"

"Yes," repeated Eddie again.

"I'm leaving now, Eddie, and I want you to wait here for five minutes. Then go clean yourself up. After that, I want you to think about how close you came to meeting your maker."

"Yes," Eddie promised, his voice still shaking. "I will."

Joe opened the office door, then stopped and turned back towards the frightened producer. "You ever hear of a show called 'The Scottish Play'?"

"You mean 'Macbeth'?" he asked in a trembling voice.

Joe gave the little man a dark stare. "I'm not an idiot Eddie, 'Macbeth' is an English play."

"I know, I know," replied the producer now trembling, "but it's set in Scotland. Actors believe it's bad luck to say the word Macbeth, so they always refer to it as 'The Scottish Play'."

"You wouldn't lie to me, would you, Eddie?" Joe flicked open his knife again.

"Oh God no," he exclaimed loudly, "it's a damn acting superstition, really. They have lots of them, you gotta believe me."

"Ok, Eddie, I'll take your word for it, but if I find out you lied to me …"

"No, I swear on the soul of my mother," replied the frightened producer.

Once again Joe closed and pocketed his stiletto. "Now remember what I said about waiting for five minutes." The producer nodded his head rapidly to indicate he knew his instructions. Joe started to leave but stopped again when he spotted the stack of publicity photos that Eddie had placed on the nearby table. It looked like several of them were autographed by the entire cast. He turned to the frightened man and asked, "Is it jake if I take one of these autographed pictures?"

"Sure, sure, take it," said the producer, almost in tears. "Take anything you want. Everything's jake."

"Thanks, Eddie, that's really swell of you." Joe grabbed one of the signed photos and walked out.

After leaving the WMAC studios Joe headed back to his office. When he entered, he saw Kat working on her filing, while Sid was again laid out on the couch, his eyes closed. Joe slammed the door and Sid leaped up, startled by the noise. Kat giggled, but when she saw how he was dressed the smile immediately left her face.

"Why are you wearing that suit?" she asked, knowing full well that he only wore his "Italian" suit when he was pretending to be part of the Outfit.

"I paid a visit to Eddie Collins, the producer of 'Day Dreams'. I needed to convince him that confession is good for the soul."

"So you did your Italian number on him?" chuckled Sid.

"The poor man," said Kat sympathetically.

"I wouldn't feel too sorry for him, Kat," Joe was annoyed by her attitude. "He admitted he's planning to pay someone five 'G's' to get Irene to sign a new contract."

"Who was he going to pay?" asked Sid.

"He didn't know. He got a phone call offering a new five-year deal in exchange for the dough."

"Did you scare him badly?" Kat was concerned.

"Let's just say he'll need a change of underwear, but like Frank always says, 'When you dine with the devil, don't be surprised if you're on the menu'."

"But you weren't even sure if he'd dined with the devil," complained Kat. "For all you knew he wasn't involved."

"The cat knows whose meat it's eaten," replied Joe, throwing Kat's proverb back at her. "He was the one person we were sure would benefit from Irene staying at WMAC. The odds seemed pretty good he was involved somehow."

"Well, I for one don't like it when you do that sort of thing," she complained. "It smacks of the GRU." The Soviet secret police were a sore subject for Kat, and for Joe as well. "And one of these days you're going to find yourself in trouble for pretending to be part of the Outfit."

Joe walked toward his office and replied, "No worries Kit-Kat. You know I'm indestructible."

"For goodness sake Joseph, stop saying that," she said sharply. Her Russian accent thickened as her voice rose in anger. "No one is indestructible, and I wish you'd stop pretending you are."

Joe was startled by her reaction and decided to quickly change the subject. "The next time you talk to Manny, ask him to flash Emma's picture around some of the local talent agencies. I think she might have tried her hand at acting."

"Maybe you should try your strong-arm tactics on her," Kat replied, still fuming.

It was obvious that Kat was upset, and Joe was worried. It seemed that lately she was much more emotional, and he wasn't sure how he should respond. To calm the waters, he decided to use his newly acquired trump card. He pulled out the autographed picture of the Day Dream's cast, and laid it on her desk. "I told Eddie you were a big fan of the show, and he wanted you to have this."

She looked at it, then sighed and gave him a smile. "Eddie wanted me to have this did he?" she asked, not buying his ridiculous explanation. She got up from her chair and walked over to him. "The next time you strong-arm poor Eddie, give him this for me," she said, and kissed him on the cheek.

"Somehow I think he'd rather get that directly from you." Sid was anxious to get the conversation back to Irene's case. "So if the show's producer isn't the blackmailer, who is?" he asked as he followed Joe into his office.

"Unfortunately, we don't have a long list of suspects," Joe replied.

"There was her former manager, Herman Roth," said Kat as she joined them in Joe's office, "but the poor man passed away."

"I'm not sure we should count this producer fella out just yet," added Sid.

"I don't know Sid, he was happy to pay the blackmail money, but I don't see him as the guy who set this up. "

"Well there's the mystery man, Paul Trent," continued Sid. "We know he was in the actual blackmail pictures with Irene. She admitted that."

"He's definitely involved somehow, but we're still missing a piece of the puzzle. I got a hunch that we're close on this one."

"Your elbow is close, but you still can't bite it," said Kat.

Sid thought about her proverb then lifted his arm up and attempted to bite his elbow. "What-da-ya know," he remarked, "She's right."

Kat didn't want to smile, but couldn't help it. "We may be close," she added, "but that doesn't mean we can solve this. Without finding Paul Trent, we're nowhere."

"Well, if we can't find this Trent guy, maybe we can find his accomplice," reasoned Joe.

"Why do you think there's someone else involved?" Kat asked. "Maybe Paul Trent acted alone."

"He couldn't," Sid pointed out. "Someone had to take the pictures. Trent couldn't have been in the photos and taken them as well. If Eddie Collins didn't take the pictures, then there's someone else involved."

Joe looked over at Sid. "Did you find out anything about that dead girl, Betty Parker?"

Sid opened his note pad and began to summarize his findings. "I spoke to some neighbors, her parents, three friends, and a couple of co-workers at the radio station. From what I found out, Betty was twenty-five years old, an only child, and worked at her dad's dry goods store over on Division Street in Humboldt Park. Not surprisingly, their business has been struggling these last few years and it's been tough sledding for the family.

CHAPTER 6 - FRIDAY

Betty didn't smoke or drink, she sang in her church choir on Sundays, and was by all accounts a nice girl from a good family. She was no great beauty. She did have several boys sniffing around over the last few years, but no current boyfriend. She loved to sing and was pretty good at it. Everyone I talked to said she had a great set of pipes. That was what she did at the station," explained Sid, "she worked on jingles."

"Sean said something about jingles too. What are they?" asked Joe.

"Jingles," replied Kat, "are those singing ads on the radio, like ... Have You Tried Wheaties? The best breakfast food in the land." Her attempt at imitating the radio tune missed the mark because she was hopelessly off key.

Sid started to laugh. "Let's hope she sang better than that." Kat chose to ignore his comment.

Joe was trying to hold back a smile and replied, "Yeah, I've heard 'em. I just didn't know they were called jingles."

Sid continued, "They're on the radio all the time, pitching different products. One of the studio guys told me that Betty made a few extra bucks at WMAC singing 'em. He said she had perfect pitch and a great range. That made her voice ideal for jingles."

"So what jingle was she working on at WMAC when she died?" Joe asked.

"Well, that's just it. There were no recording sessions set for the day she died. No one knew why she was at the station."

"Had anyone you talked to ever heard of Paul Trent?"

"Nope, I dropped that name on everyone, but got bupkis."

"Anything else?"

"Nah. That's about it, and I gotta say, I just don't see the connection between Betty and Irene's blackmail."

"Me neither," agreed Joe.

Kat spoke up, "Maybe it's a good thing that we can't find a link between the two."

"What do you mean?" asked Sid.

"Well, we have a lot on right now. If there's no link then we can drop the investigation into that poor girl's death, and concentrate on our paying clients."

Joe knew she was right. They didn't need to start another case. He thought about it for a minute then asked Sid, "Before we walk away from this one, do me a favor and check with Betty's family. See if she kept a diary or a journal?"

Sid looked surprised. "Sure boss, but what makes you think she did?"

"Someone told me recently that people who keep secrets liked to write them down. Check out her home, and let's see if she wrote anything down."

"Ok boss, you got it."

Joe looked at the papers on his desk and began to review his notes. Typically, when he started doing this, people would leave him alone. This time Sid and Kat remained in his office. After a few seconds of them staring at him, he looked up and asked, "What?"

"Pudge is missing," Sid replied sadly.

"Good," Joe replied, before looking back down at his notes. But his two co-workers didn't budge and after a few more seconds he reluctantly looked up again. "Ok, tell me what you know."

"I was coming in to the office this morning," explained Sid, "and I saw the building manager talking to Pudge's wife. Seems he didn't come home after work yesterday, and no one's seen him."

"Maybe he hit the jitter sauce and went on a bender. Or he's shacked up with some dame. If it's only been a day, it's probably nothing."

Sid shook his head, "He's married with three kids, Joe. His wife says he's never failed to come home before, and she also says he doesn't drink."

"That's enough to make me suspicious right there. If I were a Cubs fan I'd be drunk all the time."

"C'mon, Joe," pleaded Kat, "Can we look into this, please?"

"Weren't you just telling me that we had too much on our plate?"

There was pain visible in Kat's eyes and he could see that tears were welling up. "This is different. He's a friend and he needs our help."

CHAPTER 6 - FRIDAY

Joe sighed, took a drag off his cigarette. "Ok, fine, but let's give it another day before we jump in."

"You got it boss," agreed Sid. He was grateful that Joe had agreed to look into the disappearance, but disappointed that they couldn't get started sooner.

Afternoon

The Marshal Fields clock indicated that it was just past noon as Joe hopped the State Street Trolley and headed south. He got off twenty-five blocks later and walked into the Pekin Cabaret where a small crowd had gathered to grab lunch and listen to music. Sam was just off to the left of the stage, talking with several people. Joe sat down at a table towards the back, ordered a couple of egg rolls along with a Chero-Cola, and listened to the quartet on stage. Ten minutes later Sam sat down next to him.

"Any luck finding this Trent guy?" Joe asked as he took his cigarettes from his pocket, pulled one from the pack and then slid it over to Sam.

"Afraid not," Sam answered as he grabbed the pack and tapped one out. "No one's heard of him." Joe tossed him a matchbook and Sam lit up. He took a drag and blew out a long thin stream of smoke before making a sour face. "I don't know how you can smoke these things," he said. He stared at the pack of Chesterfields and then back at the cigarette. "They burn your throat. You should try a desert horse, they're a lot smoother."

"Camels have no flavor," Joe replied. He took out two dollars from his wallet and put it on the table. "Thanks for checking."

"I can't take this. I didn't find out anything."

"Don't worry, I'm getting paid on this one. Besides, I appreciate you asking around."

Sam tossed the matchbook back, and picked up the money. "Always happy to help," he said with a smile. He was expecting some kind of snide remark in response, but instead Joe was staring at the matchbook. It was bright red on both sides with a black dot on the back. It had been given to him by Irene when he had met her at the Mart. On the inside there were two printed words "The Spot". Matchbooks had become a fairly common form of advertising over the past few years, and most upscale restaurants and clubs were giving them away. After staring at it for several seconds Joe turned to Sam and asked, "You ever heard of a joint called The Spot?"

"The Spot," Sam repeated to himself before taking another drag on his cigarette. "It doesn't ring a bell. Let me check with some of the guys." Joe watched as Sam went down to the stage, and talked with several other musicians. Eventually he connected with the guy playing the skins. A few minutes later he came back to the table. "Gene says he's heard about a club called The Spot. He says it's up on the Near North Side. Somewhere on Clarke, between Division and Elm. It's a private joint, members only."

Joe took out a five spot and tossed it on the table. "I gotta run Sam. Can you give that to Gene, and thank him for me?" he asked.

"Will do," Sam replied, but Joe was already halfway towards the club's front door.

The area of North Clarke Street that Sam had steered him to was made up of three and four story stone and brick structures. They were all pressed against each other, which made the block an uninterrupted line of buildings. The street level was mostly retail stores, with the upper floors typically office or commercial space. There was also a scattering of apartments, churches, and social clubs thrown into the mix. At this time of day the street was buzzing with activity. There were quite a number of housewives doing their daily shopping. There were also delivery trucks parked at various points on both sides of the street, with men hauling ice, meat, dry goods, dairy products, and vegetables to the retail shops. Adding to the confusion were several horse drawn rigs hawking rags, pots, and brushes from the backs of their wagons.

Joe spent the next few minutes walking up and down the busy street searching for The Spot. Eventually he concluded that there was no outward sign of where the club's entrance was located. He parked himself beside a small butcher shop in the middle of the block, leaned against the building, lit up a Chesterfield, and waited. He figured that sooner or later there was bound to be some sort of activity on the street that revealed the club's location. While he wasn't sure what that would be, he was confident he'd know it when he saw it. Twenty-five minutes and two and a half cigarettes later, he saw a black man carrying a base fiddle case into a building at the far end of the block. Joe walked over to the building's front door, opened it, and climbed up a steep set of stairs that led to a red door. He knocked and almost immediately an enormous man with no neck appeared. The man was so massive that when he stood in the doorway he blocked any view of the inside.

"This is a private club, and you're not a member."

"I'm thinking of joining, so I'd like to speak to the manager."

The man gave Joe a large grin that showed he was missing a few teeth, then abruptly slammed the door shut. He waited a few seconds before knocking once more. The big man answered again and spoke in a flat monotone voice, "Don't make me hurt you." Then, with far more speed than seemed possible, he reached out and grasped Joe's throat. "It's time for you to leave, and don't come back." The man's huge hand squeezed his victim's neck, just as Joe had squeezed the frightened producer's neck only a few hours before. Joe, however, was no Eddie Collins. He responded with a hard kick into the giant's knee which caused him to release his grip and scream in pain. He gave the bouncer a second kick into his groin, and the man crumpled to the ground like a child's rag doll.

"That's enough," commanded a female voice. Joe looked over to see a woman whose pantsuit, shoes, hat, and lipstick were all a matching shade of red. It was the same blood red that was on both the club's front door and the matchbook in Joe's pocket. Stepping away from the now whimpering giant, Joe moved towards the sea of red. "I'm sorry about that, but I don't like to be choked."

The red lady walked over to her bouncer to check that he was alright. When satisfied, she turned to Joe and asked, "Why is it you men feel the need to act in such a brutal fashion?"

It seemed clear that she didn't expect him to answer her question, so Joe continued, "I'd like to speak with the manager, please?"

"What is it you want," she asked as she turned and walked back into the club. The tone of her voice registering her annoyance.

Joe followed her and, surprised by her response, asked, "You're the manager?"

"It gets worse," she replied, as she looked back at him with a wry smile, "I'm also the owner."

There weren't many women owning or running clubs in Chicago. Nevertheless, Joe felt a bit embarrassed that he'd jumped to the wrong conclusion. "My apologies," he said, "I clearly made the wrong assumption."

"I get that a lot," she replied, her comment forcing a flicker of a smile on Joe's face. She was a tall, gaunt woman of about forty with black hair and very white skin.

She continued into the club with Joe still following. "My name is Harriet Simms. Please excuse your reception back at the front door," she said. "There's been a death in our family here at The Spot, and I'm afraid it's put us all a trifle on edge. Even poor Oscar back there isn't quite himself," she added as she glanced back at the front door.

Walking through the dimly lit club, Joe could see that only about twenty percent of the tables were occupied, which he attributed to the early hour. On a small, well-lit platform that served as the club's stage a man was singing. On closer inspection, he realized that something was odd about him. It took a moment to register, but eventually Joe realized that the singer wasn't actually a man. It was a woman impersonating one. He glanced around the club once more and noticed that all the patrons were women.

"Based on how you're dressed, you're either the police, or here for the weekly collection," observed Harriett. "Which is it?"

"I'm not here to collect for the Outfit, if that's what you're asking," he replied, deciding he'd get more cooperation from her if she assumed he was a cop. "I've been assigned to a case," he began and then he took out a notepad and pencil from his inside coat pocket. "I'm afraid I can't provide any specifics at this point, but may I ask who died?"

Harriett turned and looked him in the eye before saying with sadness, "Paul Trent. Did you ever hear him sing?"

Joe stopped in his tracks, startled by her remark, and asked, "Paul Trent is dead?"

"Yes, Paul died yesterday but we just found out late this morning. Such a wonderful voice with a great range."

Joe mumbled to himself, "A great range." The proverbial wheels spun in his head as he worked to put the pieces together. He took a deep breath and let it out as a long sigh before adding, "Paul Trent was a stage name?"

"Yes, of course."

"And Paul's real name was Betty Parker?"

"I believe that's the name he used. He performed here at the club as 'Paul' for several years. He was a favorite of many of our members." As the red woman spoke the words, Joe suddenly realized that it was Irene's fear of having her relationship with another woman made public that so frightened her. That was what the blackmail was all about.

"I'm afraid Betty may have been involved in the case I'm investigating. And this may have led to her death," he explained. "Did she keep anything here?" He figured it was a long shot, but maybe the blackmail material was kept at the club. "Any clothing or personal items?"

"Paul shared a small dressing room with our other performers. Would you like to see it?"

Joe nodded, and followed Harriett to a windowless room behind the stage. It was small, just as Harriett had said, and stuffy, with a strong smell of mothballs. Inside were three tiny dressing tables, each with its own mirror. Harriett pointed to the table that Paul regularly used, and Joe searched it carefully but didn't find anything useful. Opposite the dressing table was a rack of men's clothing, and his host noticed him staring. "Paul's items are on the right side of the rack." Joe went through the apparel, but only found a half pack of cigarettes and another red matchbook. He spent some time questioning Harriett about Betty's personal life but from her answers it was clear that she really only knew her as 'Paul', and had little knowledge of her personal life.

"Thanks for your help," Joe said as Harriett walked him back toward the front door. He could tell that she was shaken up by the singer's death. While she escorted him to the exit, he tried to think of anything to say that seemed appropriate. Finally, when they reached the entrance, he said, "I'm sorry I beat up your doorman."

"Oscar is a good man and it's unfortunate that the two of you came to blows. He's a very valuable member of our family here at The Spot. You see the 'Jam' out there don't accept how we choose to live our lives, and I doubt they ever will."

A look of confusion crossed Joe's face and he asked, "Who are the 'Jam'?"

"Oh, I'm sorry. It's a term we use when referring to what you might think of as 'normal' people."

"Why do you call them the 'Jam'?"

Harriet looked at him and hesitated for a second before replying, "You don't want to know." She continued, "As I was saying, there are many ignorant people who would think nothing of destroying this club, and its members. We need a good soldier to guard our door, and for many years now Oscar has been our guardian."

Joe tipped his hat to his host, and turned to walk down the stairs. Harriet called out to him, "I trust you'll find poor Paul's killer." Her comment caused him to stop in his tracks halfway down the steps. After a brief hesitation he turned around and stared up at the woman.

Harriet was surprised by his action, "Was there something else?"

Joe continued staring. After a few more seconds he muttered, mostly to himself, "Find Paul's killer."

Harriet, still standing at the top of the staircase, was confused by his statement and unsure what she should say or do. Joe, who had been lost in thought, pulled himself back to the present. "My apologies, but sometimes I'm amazed by my stupidity."

"Sadly," began Harriet, "the members of my club are all too familiar with the stupidity of men." She added with a smile, "But I can't tell you how refreshing it is to meet one who's willing to admit it." The woman's comment forced a broad smile from Joe and again he tipped his hat to her before heading back down the stairs.

It was just past two in the afternoon when Joe got back to his office. As soon as he arrived he filled in Kat, Sid, and Mickey on his visit to The Spot.

"No kiddin', this lady writer likes gals?" asks Sid.

Kat gave him a stern look. "I'm not sure that's something we should be talking about," she said in a disapproving voice as she tilted her head toward Mickey.

"It's jake, Mrs. M," the boy replied with a smile. "It's nothing I haven't heard before. In fact, my Aunt Cozy likes women. She's my Dad's half sister and my Mom says she likes 'em because she's half English. Mom says no Irish woman would do something like that."

Sid grinned, replying, "That ain't right."

'Yeah," agreed Mickey, "But if I told Ma that she'd box my ears."

CHAPTER 6 – FRIDAY

Joe shook his head, remembering the number of times he'd had his ears 'boxed' while growing up. Then he pulled the conversation back to the case. "The answer to Sid's question is yes."

"So, Betty, or Paul, killed herself because she felt ... what ... guilty about the blackmail?" asked Kat.

"I don't buy the suicide angle," responded Sid. "If she'd felt guilty, she had plenty of time to stop the blackmail scheme."

Joe agreed. "You don't kill yourself from guilt when you have time to make things right. I think she had a falling out with her accomplice, and that's who killed her. Maybe Betty wanted to back out or maybe she wanted a bigger cut, but for whatever reason she fought with someone on that soundstage. That's how she got bruises on her arm, and skin and blood under her nails. There was a struggle, then Betty broke free and tried to leave, but when she turned her back the accomplice picked the gun up off the prop table, put the muzzle to her temple, and pulled the trigger."

"If her back was to the killer she probably didn't even know it was happening until it was too late," added Sid.

"Well, with this information the police will have to treat Betty's death as a murder investigation," said Kat.

"Ah ... that's where it gets tricky," lamented Joe. "If we give them this information then Irene's secret will be out. The cops will never keep a lid on it. The detective in charge will sell it to one of the dailies and she'll be ruined."

"Plus," added Sid, "let's not forget that our client has the best motive to kill Betty. The police will just say she was trying to keep their affair secret, and pin the murder on her."

"So what do we know?" asked Kat, hoping someone would summarize the case.

Mickey was happy to oblige. "Well, it looks like our mystery man took pictures of Irene and Betty together," he began, "then Betty and her accomplice had a falling out on the WMAC soundstage and that person killed her."

"But we have no idea who that is," said Sid, adding, "but we know it was a man because Eddie Collins said it was a man's voice he heard on the phone."

"Maybe the accomplice wasn't a man," suggested Kat. "Remember that Betty was a male impersonator, so it could have been her, or even someone she worked with at The Spot, that made Eddie think he was talking to a man."

"I hadn't thought of that," replied Joe.

Sid nodded his head in agreement, then added, "As far as we know, Irene had never met Betty until the night the pictures were taken. So, it's unlikely Betty knew that Irene was on the verge of signing with WBM. That means whoever the accomplice is had to be the one who knew that Irene was on the verge of signing with WBM. If they knew that, it's likely they also knew how important she was to Eddie Collins. My guess is, the accomplice is the one who set up the whole blackmail scheme."

The four of them sat quietly for several minutes pondering the case while Kat's radio played "Stardust" softly in the background. Finally, Joe broke the silence. "Sid, have you ever heard of someone being shot with blanks?"

"Nope, that's a new one on me."

"So our mystery person fights with Betty," said Joe, "and when she pulls free, the killer grabs a gun that fires blanks and shoots her in the head. Why in that split second did the killer choose to use a gun that fires blanks?"

"Maybe the killer didn't know the gun shot blanks," replied Kat. "Maybe he thought it was a real gun."

"But if that were the case, he or she wouldn't have bothered to push the barrel up to Betty's temple. The killer would have just shot her in the back of the head," responded Sid.

"Good point," agreed Joe. "The killer must have known the gun shot blanks. Why else press the nose of the barrel against her temple? And since he did, he must have also known that a gun that fires blanks could kill under the right circumstances."

"So how did the killer know that a gun that shoots blanks could kill someone?" asked Mickey.

CHAPTER 6 - FRIDAY

"When Walter was reviewing the autopsy, he told me there was another person killed in a similar manner back in '22. He didn't have any information on it, but he said there were a number of witnesses that saw the whole thing." As Joe was explaining, Mickey pulled out a purple lollypop and began to suck on it. "Is that one of those Tootsie Pops?" Joe asked.

"Sure is. Kat has a drawer full of 'em. She gave me one yesterday. They're really great. They have a piece of chewy candy inside," Mickey explained.

Joe shook his head, "You're gonna rot your teeth eating those things kid." Turning towards his investigator he asked, "Sid, can you try and dig up the old police records on that death back in '22? I want to find out who those witnesses were. Maybe one of them learned a trick they decided to use ten years later."

"You got it, boss." Sid hopped off the couch and grabbed his hat and coat.

Joe turned towards Mickey. "When I was at the Majestic Theater on Wednesday I noticed that people auditioning signed a log. That might be something all the theaters do. I want you to check the Majestic log, and then the logs at the other vaudeville houses in the Loop, and see if Betty Parker's name shows up anywhere. I doubt she would have posed as Paul Trent except at The Spot, but while you're looking check for that name as well."

"You got it, Mr. L," shot back Mickey, his face registered confusion. "But if it turns out she auditioned somewhere how's that going to help us?"

"Well, it's a long shot, but if we find out she'd been auditioning at one of the theaters we can check to see if any of the staff at that theater is connected to WBM or WMAC. Maybe we'll get lucky and find our missing blackmailer."

After Mickey and Sid left, Joe grabbed his hat and coat and headed for the door. Before leaving he stopped at Kat's desk and asked, "Do you have that second copy of the puzzle ball you made?"

Kat opened her bottom drawer, reached into the back, and pulled out the black rubber ball. She handed it to him and asked, "Where are you off to?"

"I think I'll stop by the library. I want to ask Claire some questions about this Leuven treasure that the Nottingham dame was talking about." With

Joe's departure the office was now empty, and Kat took advantage of the opportunity to open the office window closest to her desk.

It was cloudy but mild outside when Joe left the Reliance Building and headed east on Washington Street towards Chicago's Public Library. The library had been officially opened in '97, but its origins dated from the great fire in '71. It was in the aftermath of that fire that the generous people of England donated over eight thousand books to Chicago. Their mission was to help replenish the shelves of the city's library, destroyed in great the fire. Notable donors included Alfred Lord Tennyson, Robert Browning, and Prime Minister Disraeli. Even Queen Victoria made donations, personally signing several dozen books, most of which were still in the stacks. The irony in all of this was that Chicago didn't have a public library before the fire. Determined not to be embarrassed, the city quickly established one, eventually building an imposing block long, five-story granite and bluestone structure along Michigan Avenue. In the end, however, the most impressive thing about Chicago's Library wasn't its size, its design, or the number of volumes it housed. The most impressive thing was its librarian.

Dr. Claire Gibbons was only thirty-five years old when she became Head Librarian in '25. She was born in Canada and raised by parents who were both full professors at McGill University. From an early age, the importance of education had been emphasized in her family. Her two younger brothers and her older sister all received doctorates and now held impressive research and academic positions. Claire, however, was the black sheep of the family. Not because she failed to graduate from the most prestigious schools; on the contrary, she received a bachelor's degree from McGill, a master's from Yale, and a doctorate from Oxford. What made Claire the black sheep was that all of her family had concentrated on the hard sciences, while she had been drawn to a subject that would become known as Library Science.

Joe had first met her back in '29 when she'd helped him locate some information for a case he was working. He soon learned that it didn't matter what the subject was, she always seemed to know which books would lead you to the answers you were seeking. There was, however, one problem with Claire; she didn't suffer fools gladly. Joe respected her a great deal, and for some reason the feeling was mutual. He had no idea why she liked him. Perhaps it was because they shared a knack for languages. Whatever the reason, he always enjoyed meeting up with her, and she always greeted him warmly.

Joe entered the library through the Washington Street entrance and climbed the steps to the main hall. It was so quiet that as he walked his footsteps echoed through the chamber. His path took him past the main desk and up the center hallway's impressive stone staircase to the second floor administrative area. Once there, he approached the office marked "Librarian" and could hear the distinctive sound of Enrico Caruso singing Handel's "Ombra mai fu". It was one of Claire's favorites. She adored opera and the library's extensive collection of 78's gave her the chance to indulge her passion.

Joe knocked on the door and after a few seconds the sound of the music stopped. He heard her voice respond, "It's open," and as he entered, he saw Claire standing next to the gramophone on the other side of the room. She was a pleasant woman with black wire rimmed glasses and salt and pepper hair.

A smile instantly spread crossed her face. "Joseph, what a pleasant surprise," she said as she crossed the office to greet him. "Why didn't you let me know you were coming? You're lucky I happened to be in today, otherwise we might have missed each other."

"Claire," he replied with a bemused look on his face, "it's three o'clock on a Friday afternoon. Where else would you be but at the library?"

"You make it sound like I never take any time off. Why, Amos and I took a Friday off just a couple of weeks back to spend the day together. It was really quite lovely," she said with a smile. Amos was an art dealer in town and had been her devoted companion for over ten years.

"That was almost two months ago, Claire, and you didn't take the day off. It was Good Friday. The library was closed."

A frown crossed her face as she realized he was right. "I need to spend more time away from work," she said to herself as she shook her head.

"Don't we all?"

"Well, do have a seat," she insisted. Joe sat in one of two chairs next to a small side table and away from the large neat desk which dominated the room. "Is this a social call? Or is there something you need help with?"

"A bit of both actually."

"A good friend of mine in London sent me some Earl Grey, and I was just about to make some," she said happily. "Fancy a cuppa?" Joe nodded his agreement. She opened her tin of Jacksons, measured out several spoonfuls into the teapot, and added boiling water. She detested the American invention of the tea bag, and devoutly believed there was only one way to make a proper cup. She carried her tea set over to the table, and sat down in the chair next to Joe, where they continued their conversation while the brew steeped.

"I was hoping you might be able to give me some information," he began. "Are you familiar with what happened to the library at the University of Leuven, during the war?"

Claire switched from English to French. *"You mean what the Germans did to it?"*

"Yes," replied Joe now also speaking French. He'd expected that she would take the opportunity to speak French. She found so few people in Chicago who spoke it well enough to hold a conversation. Consequently, she never failed to take the opportunity to practice when he was visiting. Despite the fact that Joe's thick American accent sometimes made it difficult to understand him, she enjoyed their conversations.

"Of course," she replied, *"the burning took place soon after the Germans crossed into Belgium in August of '14. When the Belgians resisted the invasion, the Germans were so incensed they chose to terrorize the population into submission. One of the steps they took was to burn the university and its library to the ground. Some of Europe's oldest and rarest books, along with countless manuscripts, were lost in that fire. Centuries of culture and knowledge vanished in a senseless and ruthless act,"* she shook her head in disgust. *"The burning of that library was just one of many brutal acts by the Germans to try and break the will of the francs-tireurs. The tactic didn't work, of course."*

"Someone recently told me a story," explained Joe, *"about a few German officers who took many of the library's most valuable treasures and hid them before the buildings were torched ..."*

She interrupted him with a spontaneous chuckle before adding, *"That old tale?"* She then explained, *"That story began to circulate even before the war ended. So many irreplaceable works were lost in the fire. I think the story was told more as a wish than as fact. Unfortunately, it's a myth, a* mere dream of historians and librarians. Their 'Holy Grail', if you will. I'm afraid no one has ever proven that something like that actually occurred."

"Besides the books and manuscripts that were lost, do you know of anything else that might have been destroyed?"

"I don't understand what you mean," she replied. "What else but books and manuscripts would have been lost in the library fire?"

"I heard there were priceless paintings, and other works of art kept in the library before the war."

Briefly Claire changed the subject and the language. She pointed towards the flowered teapot and asked in English, "Shall I be mother?" Joe nodded, and as she began to pour, she returned to his question and to speaking in French. *"The library wasn't a museum and I've never heard anyone talk about priceless artwork being kept there. I was lucky enough to have visited the university before the war. I was studying at Oxford and several of us took a trip to Louvain. It was truly a magnificent library but I don't recall seeing much in the way of artwork, other than a few rather ordinary tapestries and an occasional unimpressive portrait."*

"Those rare books and manuscripts that were lost are often referred to as priceless," said Joe. "If they were suddenly discovered would they be worth a great deal of money?"

"A great deal of money, now that's a relative term," she said with a wry smile. *"On a librarian's salary most everything seems to be worth a great deal of money. If you're asking me if their monetary value was high, I shouldn't think so. When people refer to the lost items as priceless, they tend to be speaking more from an historical and academic perspective. I suppose many of the books and manuscripts would have had some monetary value, but I doubt anyone would get rich selling them, especially nowadays."*

"What do you mean 'nowadays'?"

"Well, since the start of the depression, the demand for rare books has plummeted. When people are short of money they don't spend what little they have on books, no matter how rare. If someone saved any of the best books and manuscripts from the library," continued Claire, "it would mean more to scholars than to anyone else."

"Well, I have another question for you, on a different topic," Joe said. "Have you ever heard of something called a 'Puzzle Ball'?"

A broad smile swept across the librarian's face as she took another sip of tea and switched to speaking in German. "*I was at a party once in Berlin before the war,*" she said, fondly remembering the experience. "*After dinner and several rounds of drinks, someone brought out a puzzle ball, and we split into four teams. I had never seen one before, and it was really quite amusing.*"

"*What can you tell me about them?*" he asked, also in German.

"*Well, it was made of black rubber and it was about the size of a cricket ball, only lighter. There were some raised symbols on the surface. What you did was rub the ball on an ink pad and then roll it across a piece of paper. Then the ball's raised symbols would print onto the paper. These symbols formed a coded message, and the first team to decipher the code won the game.*"

"*Was the code difficult to break?*"

"*Not really, once your team figured out which of the printed codes was the correct one.*"

"*I don't understand. Wasn't there just one code on the ball?*"

"*Yes, but it wasn't as simple as it sounds. Since the ball was round you couldn't be sure where the starting or end point was. You also weren't sure if you'd printed it upside down or from right to left. So, you needed to print out the code a number of times onto different pieces of paper, and it took a while to figure out which printed code could actually be deciphered.*"

"*Does this look like a puzzle ball?*" Joe held out the copy that Kat had made.

"*Yes,*" she replied as she took the ball from his hand, but then her smile quickly faded. "*The markings on this ball aren't raised. So you can't print the code.*"

"*The ball you have there is a copy of an actual puzzle ball,*" he explained.

Claire handed it back to him, clearly not interested in a copy. "*It took my team about two hours to crack the code but I'm afraid we finished second.*" Joe sensed that even after all these years she was still disappointed at not having won the game. "*I think we could have done better,*" she lamented. "*But unfortunately, my German wasn't strong enough back then so I wasn't as much help to my team as I should've* been. *It was a wonderful party game and a wonderful night,"* she said with a wistful smile. Then her facial expression changed to one of concern. *"You know, Joseph, it's really quite difficult to comprehend the Germans. Individually or in small groups they are wonderful people; generous, compassionate, intelligent. As a nation, however, they are capable of terrible things. It seems their current fascination with National Socialism could lead them in a regrettable direction."*

With that remark the conversation drifted away from Joe's cases and centered on what was happening with the rise of the Nazis. Claire stayed current by having many of Europe's most prominent newspapers delivered to the library each week. These included *The Times*, *Le Monde* and the *B.Z. am Mittag*. She knew that Joe also stayed current by listening to European short wave broadcasts in the evening. It was one of reasons she enjoyed talking with him so much. From their discussion about German politics, they moved on to other world events, and continued chatting for nearly an hour. All the while drinking tea and slipping easily between English, French, German, and Italian. Finally, Joe looked at his watch and apologized for his short visit.

As he rose to leave, he turned towards Claire and said, "By the way, I want to thank you for taking the time to write that letter of recommendation for Mickey."

"He's such a nice boy. I was glad to be able to recommend him. After I sent the letter, I called the Dean over at the university. Fuzzy and I went to graduate school together at Yale and he's a dear friend."

Joe bent down and kissed her on the cheek. As he started to leave he added, "Oh, one last thing. Any chance you might know what a reference to 'the third period' means?" Claire was about the answer, but Joe cut her off by adding, "Besides the final period of a hockey game."

She immediately smiled and replied, "Well of course, as a good Canadian, that would have to be my first guess." Then she thought for a moment before adding, "I suppose it might be a reference to the Communist Party's belief that the world has entered the final phase of the workers revolution."

Joe wasn't sure what she was referring to and asked, "What can you tell me about that?"

"From what I've read, the Communist doctrine states that with the start of the current economic depression the world has entered what they're calling the 'third period'. During this time, the resulting civil unrest will culminate in a global socialist revolution."

"Besides global revolution, is there anything else that happens during this 'third period'?"

"The faithful believe that upon entering the 'third period' there can be no deviation from strict discipline and adherence to Communist doctrine as laid out by the Party leaders. Those who deviate must be purged. Unfortunately, that's about the limit of my knowledge on the subject. Was that helpful?" she asked.

"It might be, but to be honest I'm not sure," he replied with a smile. "Thanks for taking the time to talk with me."

"You know you're always welcome, Joseph."

Joe left her office and retraced his steps through the library and out the Randolph Street exit. Once on the street, he walked back towards the Reliance Building. He crossed under the eastern tracks of the "L" at Wabash, before turning left on State, and past the front windows of Marshal Fields. All the while he was deep in thought. In fact, he was so caught up, he initially didn't notice that he'd picked up a tail. Then, at the corner of Washington and State, while waiting for the light to change, he glanced back at the Marshal Fields display windows and finally spotted the guy in their reflection. He couldn't see the man's face clearly, but the combination of the brown overcoat and a white skimmer hat were all the warning he needed. When the signal changed, he crossed Washington and continued down State with his tail still in tow. A block later, he turned left at Madison and then left again into a small dark and dead-end alley.

The man in the brown overcoat briefly lost sight of his mark because of the dim light. Then he caught sight of a door closing about twenty yards ahead. Fearing he might lose him, he cursed to himself and rushed towards the door. When he reached the door he raced through it, still hoping he could catch up to his mark. Just as he crossed the threshold, the door slammed back into him. The unexpected force caught him completely off guard, throwing him backwards. He landed flat on his back, and both his head and his skimmer bounced off the dirty pavement with a dull thud. The man lay there for several moments, stunned from the impact. He was vaguely aware that someone was frisking him, but he was too dazed to resist.

Joe searched the mug lying on the ground and pulled out his wallet. Checking the man's ID, he was surprised to see who'd been following him. He saw that the man was packing heat, two nickel-plated .45 caliber Colts. He quickly unloaded them, tossed the bullets away, and put one pistol in each of his two trench coat pockets.

"On your feet Sweet Pea," Joe ordered before kicking the guy just a little harder than necessary. The man slowly regained his faculties and as he staggered to his feet Joe threw him back his wallet. "So what's 'Honey Boy' Morris doing in Chicago?" he asked. "I thought you ran with the Purple Gang out of Detroit?"

Honey Boy was of medium height and build, with black hair and a boyish face. He was also clearly surprised that his mark had made him. "I'm doing a private job," was his explanation.

"Who for?"

"Go fuck yourself."

Joe's initial instinct was to slap him around a bit, as payback for the beating he took the other night. He resisted the urge, and decided instead to continue questioning him. "Are you working for the Nottingham dame or the little guy, Patel?"

"Go spit," replied the gangster.

"Why were you tailing me?"

"Someone wants to see ya."

"Ok, so let's go pay 'em a visit, but remember Sweet Pea, I have both your gats."

It took just five minutes to walk to the Palmer House on Monroe, between State and Wabash. During that time, Joe had his right hand in his trench coat pocket holding one of the empty .45's. This kept Honey Boy from making any moves to get his guns back. Joe could tell that with each step closer to their destination, the gunman was becoming more agitated. Once in the hotel, the gangster reluctantly led him through the ornate lobby to the elevators and up to the twelfth floor. When they reached room 1232, Joe knocked on the door.

"Come in," a woman's voice called out from inside.

"You first," said Joe to the hood. "This ought to impress the hell out of your boss," he added with a smile. The anger that had been evident in Honey Boy's eyes now changed to rage as he opened the door. The two men entered the well appointed parlor of a two room suite. Jacqueline Nottingham was sitting on a sofa chatting with Avaj Patel. "Sit down over there, Sweet Pea," Joe said mockingly to the gangster as he waved the pistol at an empty chair to the left of the sofa. At first Jacqueline didn't notice that her hired muscle wasn't in control of the situation, but she soon saw the look on the man's face and turned towards Joe.

"*I told you he was a savage*," said Patel in French. The little man was disturbed by the pistol that was now pointing in their direction.

"You wanted to see me?" Joe asked in a casual voice.

"I trust we're not going to conduct this meeting at the point of a gun," said Jacqueline.

"The idea didn't seem to bother you when your gunsel was going to be the one holding the gun," he replied. "What did you want to talk about?"

"As you can see," said Jacqueline, "Mr. Patel and I have joined forces. I believe you still have something that belongs to us. I simply sent Mr. Miller here to collect you, so that we could discuss the return of the item."

"Your goon over there took the ball from me the other night," Joe said as he glanced toward Honey Boy. "I still have the lump on the back of my head from when he introduced himself."

"Please don't play games, Mr. Lorde. We both know the ball Mr. Miller recovered was a fake." She took out a thin, dark cigarette from the silver box on the coffee table, then put the cigarette in a black enameled holder, and waited for a light.

Joe let several awkward seconds pass before taking out the red matchbook and tossing it at her. "You'll excuse me if I don't light it for you."

Jacqueline lit her cigarette before saying, "You can put that gun away. You needn't be concerned. Neither Mr. Patel nor I have any intention of taking hostile action towards you."

"It's not you two I'm worried about," he replied as he again glanced at Honey Boy, who was seething in his chair.

CHAPTER 6 - FRIDAY

As she drew a breath through her elegant holder, Joe took advantage of the momentary pause in the conversation to again admire the beauty sitting in front of him. She wore a clingy beige silk blouse with a tight black skirt that rose well above her ankles. There was a slit in the skirt that ran part way up her right leg, revealing just enough of the black silk stockings she was wearing to fire the imagination and give a guy a lot of ideas. As a woman doing battle in a man's world, she was well armed.

"Now, what is it going to take for you to turn the ball over to us?" she asked with a cool and alluring smile.

"I'll tell you what, Mrs. Nottingham. You bring five grand to my office tomorrow morning and I'll give you the ball."

"You are a thief!" shouted Patel, who suddenly sprung to life from the sofa where he'd been sitting quietly. "I paid you to retrieve that ball for me and now you dare to try and charge us for it again." The little man's face grew crimson with anger, but Joe ignored him.

"Like I said, you bring the dough, and I'll bring the ball."

"Why can't we just conclude our business now?" she asked impatiently.

"Because I've put the ball in a safe place, and I can't pick it up 'til tomorrow morning," he explained.

"We can't trust him," said Patel, again speaking in French.

"On the contrary," she replied in the same language, *"I'm very encouraged. He has finally stated his price, which means, once we agree terms, he's prepared to deliver us the ball. He has no idea the true worth of the ball, so his price is easily met."*

"Surely you don't intend to pay this scoundrel?"

"We need the ball to crack the code, and we need to crack the code to find the treasure, therefore the recovery of the ball is paramount. If he tries to double cross us we'll have the voyou take care of our friend here."

"What if he doesn't bring the ball to the meeting tomorrow?" asked Patel.

"He's a hard man, but I think he might have a weak spot. If he doesn't keep his word, we'll use his secretary as leverage. She seems to be one of the few people he actually cares about."

"What if you're wrong, and he doesn't care what we do to her? He doesn't seem to be interested in your 'charms'. How will we get him to give us the ball?"

"Trust me, he is very interested in my 'charms'. He happens to be a man who can control his base urges better than most, but he's still a man. Given a little time I could easily persuade him, and I believe I'd thoroughly enjoy that," she said, giving a flirtatious glance over her shoulder toward her prey. "But sadly we don't have the time. There are others searching for the ball, and we need to secure it as soon as possible. If he doesn't care about his secretary then we'll find someone else. There's always someone or something that can be used as leverage."

"You will have to excuse us," said Jacqueline as she reverted back to English and turned towards Joe, "but Mr. Patel, and I were just considering your proposal."

"Yeah, I figured you were doing something like that," he lied.

"We agree to your terms. We'll meet you at your office tomorrow morning. Shall we say nine o'clock?"

"No," replied Joe, "we shall say ten o'clock. I need my beauty sleep."

"Very well," confirmed Jacqueline, "and please don't disappoint, Mr. Lorde. I'm not someone to be trifled with."

Joe pulled out the second Colt from his trench coat pocket and tossed both guns onto the sofa next to Patel, who instinctively jumped back in fear. "For the meeting tomorrow, let's leave the hardware at home," he said as he walked towards the door.

The instant his back was turned Honey Boy leaped for his pistols. When Joe reached the hallway door, he heard the gunsel shout, "Don't move."

Joe stopped and turned back to face the room. "You're not still steamed about me taking your two shiny toys away, are you?"

"You're a real funny guy, aren't you?" said Honey Boy, "a regular W. C. Fields."

"Mr. Morris," said Jacqueline sternly, "please put down your weapons. We need him alive."

"Don't worry about your precious rubber ball, I'll find it," said Honey Boy, "and I won't need him to do it."

CHAPTER 6 - FRIDAY

Firmly she shouted at him, "Mr. Morris, stop this at once!"

"This has been loads of fun," Joe said to Honey Boy, "and although I'd love to stay and chat some more, I've got real work to do." He winked at the thug before adding, "Cheer up Sweet Pea, I'm sure we'll see each other tomorrow." He turned his back on the gangster and his twin Colts and opened the door.

Click ... Click. The two pistols pointed at Joe's back both failed to fire and Honey Boy momentarily stared at his guns trying to figure out what had gone wrong.

"Even if you had bullets, I doubt you would have hit anything," said Joe as he shut the door behind him.

"You fucking piece of shit," screamed the hoodlum. Almost immediately there were two loud thuds against the hotel room door as the enraged gangster threw his empty pistols. Joe smiled to himself as he walked towards the elevator. It was now obvious who had gunned down the Greek sailor, and he wanted to make sure that Honey Boy was at tomorrow's meeting. After their encounter today, he felt certain that no power on earth could keep him away.

It was late afternoon by the time Joe got back to the Loop. When he walked through the door of his office, an excited Mickey jumped up from the table where he'd been typing and exclaimed, "Mr. L, I got it! I got it! The University of Chicago sent me this letter," he said, holding it in his hand and waiving it in the air. "I got the scholarship. I can't believe it." His hand was shaking slightly as he handed the letter over to his boss. "I just can't believe it."

Joe took the letter and read it. "That's great news, Mickey," he replied with a big smile while patting the young man's back.

"Wait 'til I tell Mom. She's going to bust a gut, but I know she's going to be worried about how I'm going to pay for books and stuff."

"Don't worry about that," said Joe reassuringly. "Father Frank tells me that you're eligible for a scholarship from St. Jerome's. It should cover all your other expenses. Besides, you're still going to be working for us, right?"

"You bet, Mr. L."

"Look, I want you take off and go tell your mom the news, and under no circumstances do I want you in here over the weekend." Mickey frequently came in on Saturdays to do some filing and typing that Kat had set aside for him. With the Nottingham dame looking for 'leverage', the last thing Joe wanted was for the kid to be anywhere near the office when Honey Boy and company showed up. "I mean that Mickey. I don't want to see you back here until Monday, is that clear?"

"Crystal boss," the young man replied as he picked up his stuff from the table where he'd been working. The jubilant youth shouted out to everyone in the room, "I'll see ya all on Monday," before racing out the door.

"I suppose you're going to tell me that you didn't have anything to do with him getting that university scholarship?" asked Kat in a disbelieving tone. "And I've never heard you mention anything about a St. Jerome's scholarship."

"I don't have any juice with the university, you know that," he replied, "and as for the St. Jerome's scholarship, I believe that's a fairly new thing that's still being set up."

She shook her head and smiled. She wasn't sure how, but she knew he'd arranged both awards. "Oh, before I forget, Miss Addams phoned and asked if you could stop by Hull House early next week. From the tone in her voice I think something is upsetting her."

"I ran into her earlier this this week and she didn't mention anything." Jane Addams was not someone who cried wolf. If she need him, it must be something important. "Something must have come up," he said, mostly to himself. "Remind me to get over there Monday morning."

Kat wrote a note to herself, and asked, "How was your meeting with Claire? You spent a long time there, was she any help?"

"She confirmed that a lot of people believe in the treasure of Leuven, but she also said she didn't think it existed. As for how long I was gone, I ended up meeting with Nottingham and Patel," he added.

"Both of them ..." she responded, clearly startled, "... at the same time?"

"Yup," he answered as he walked back into his office and sat down behind the desk. "It seems they've joined forces."

CHAPTER 6 – FRIDAY

Kat followed him to the office, but remained in the doorway. "How did the meeting go?"

"You mean besides the fact that their hired muscle tried to kill me?"

"Someone tried to kill you?" she repeated with deep concern in her voice.

"It was nothing I couldn't handle," he said calmly. "Besides, you know I'm indestructible." Joe regretted saying the last word the moment it left his lips.

"Jesus Christ Joseph, stop saying that," she shouted, her Russian accent suddenly so thick he could barely understand her words. "You're not indestructible. No one is."

In the four years he'd known her, he had never heard her swear. Caught off guard by her outburst, he thought carefully about what he should say next. "Relax Kit-Kat," he replied softly, hoping to calm her down. "I had everything under control."

His reassuring words didn't help. As her eyes flared with anger, she immediately shouted back at him in Russian. *"What happens when one of these days things get out of control? What happens when you make a mistake?"*

He was in uncharted waters, never having seen her like this, and he fumbled for words. Finally, he blurted out, "I guess ... I'll pay the price." Those turned out to be the wrong words.

"Damn you, Joseph," she screamed, hurling her coffee cup at him. The cup missed, but skipped off his desk and smashed against the wall just below the window. Tears welled up in her eyes as she continued. *"If you get yourself killed, you won't be the only one who pays the price! What happens to the people who count on you? What happens to Sid? Does he crawl back into the bottle? And Mickey, how will he pay for college, or help support his family? What about the people that care about you like Father Frank, Rose, or Miss Ella? Did you ever think about any of them?"* Kat was now in a full-on rage with tears flowing down her cheeks. *"And what happens to me? I won't be thrown back into the gutter again. I won't walk down a filthy alley for two dollars, or scrub toilets on my hands and knees. I won't live that way again, do you hear me? I won't! I won't!"* Her sobbing was now uncontrollable, so she covered her face with her hands and ran out of his office.

Joe sat at his desk, stunned. He knew there had to be something he could say that would make things better, but so far everything he'd tried had backfired. Hearing the office door slam, he got up and went out to the front room, but she was gone.

He walked solemnly back to his desk and sat down. After a few minutes, he lit up cigarette, took a pull, held it for a moment, and then gently released a long stream of smoke. Sitting in his chair, he tried to sort out what had just happened. Kat was right, of course – he did have a lot of people in his life. Far more than he ever imagined. For as long as he could remember, he had planned to live his life alone, never needing anyone. He hadn't intended to have friends or loved ones, and he'd never wanted to be responsible for Kat, Sid, Mickey or anyone else, for that matter. How he'd ended up with so many people counting on him or caring for him? He took another long draw off his cigarette and said softly after letting out a stream of smoke, "God I miss Paris."

He was on his second cigarette and still lost in thought when the office door flew open and an excited Sid called out. "Hey, boss, I just saw Kat in the lobby and she was in tears. I tried to talk to her but she ran away." When he entered Joe's office, he spotted the broken cup on the floor and a stream of the coffee dripping down the wall. "What gives?" he asked.

"I'm not really sure, Sid," was his boss' response, accompanied by a heavy sigh. Getting up from the chair, he pulled out his handkerchief and began wiping the coffee off his desk and the wall. "I said something and she went all squirrely on me." Once he finished cleaning, he went back to his chair. "I'll phone her at home later and try to square things," he said, more to himself than to Sid. After a few minutes of silence, while his investigator was picking up the pieces of the cup, Joe asked almost as an afterthought, "you find out anything?"

"Yeah," responded the investigator, as he tossed the cup fragments into the waste basket. "I managed to see the old case file on that accidental death ten years ago. The one caused by the gun that shot blanks. The guy who took the shot to the head was an actor. It happened at the Goodman Theater on East Monroe. I read the account from the police file and got the names of the witnesses," he added as he held up his notepad. "Unfortunately, there's only one name on the report that has anything to do with our case."

CHAPTER 6 - FRIDAY

Joe pulled himself away from contemplating his life, and forced himself to respond to his investigator. "Well one name's better than nothing."

"Not this time," he replied. "It's Irene Fields. According to the file, it was her play that was running at the Goodman."

"So for the death of Betty Parker, Irene had both a motive, and the knowledge of how to kill with a gun that shoots blanks."

"I hate to say it, but she's the best suspect we got." Just then the office phone rang. The two men looked at each other, unsure who should answer it. Then Sid smiled, grabbed the neck of the phone, and put the earpiece to his ear. After listening for a second, he handed it over to his boss and whispered, "It's Mr. Gibbs."

"Yes, Theo," said Joe, as Sid quietly left his office.

"I'm at the McNulty estate," Theo explained, in a calm and serious voice. "I just thought you should know that Cyrus died at about one o'clock this afternoon. I also wanted to tell you that your job is done. Just before he died, Cyrus acknowledged his paternity of Emma and signed a document making her an heir to his estate."

"How did you finalize that so quickly?"

"He had me draw up the papers several days ago," he explained. "He was convinced that Emma was his daughter from the first moment he laid eyes on her. When you didn't turn up any evidence to the contrary, he decided to move forward. He was afraid that Vance might try to drag the issue out in court after his death."

"I'm sure that didn't please Vance very much."

"Well, actually he isn't as upset as you might think."

"How's that?"

"To put salve on Vance's wounds, Cyrus took an extra one million dollars from the trust and moved it back into his estate."

"Could he do that?" Joe was surprised.

"While Cyrus was alive, he could do whatever he liked," explained Theo. "Now that he's passed, the board has assumed total responsibility for the trust. With the extra million that Cyrus added, a conservative value on the estate is now just a bit over two million. That means Emma and Vance will each get at least a million, which is the same amount Vance was going to inherit before Emma showed up. To keep Vance from trying anything after his death, he had him sign a separate agreement acknowledging Emma as his half-sister."

"Why would Vance agree to that?"

"Well, look at it from his point of view," explained Theo. "He could sign the agreement and get one million guaranteed, or he could fight it in court, and potentially lose everything. For a guaranteed million bucks, he decided to acknowledge Emma."

"Looks like the old man did a pretty good job of painting him into a corner."

"Yeah," agreed Theo. "Vance was never a match for his old man."

"Is Emma aware of the change?"

"She knows. Cyrus instructed me to tell her immediately after his death.

"How's she holding up?"

"She's upset. She just found her father and now he's dead. All in all, she seems to be holding up. By the way, Cyrus also left instructions that his will should be read at 4:00 in the afternoon on the day after his death. I'd like you to come, if you can."

"I'll be there," Joe replied.

His next call was to Emma at the guesthouse, and she answered almost immediately. "I just heard," Joe said. "I'm sorry."

"I guess it's not exactly a shock," she said sadly, "but still I wish we had had a little more time. I know we talked about getting together later, but I'm going to have to ask for a rain check. I'm really sorry," she added with a slight tremor in her voice.

"I understand," he responded sympathetically. "Did you finally meet Vance?"

"Yes. I was up at the main house just after Papa passed and Vance came up and introduced himself. He needed me to meet with a lawyer from the trust, and sign a briefcase full of papers."

"Was he at least being civil?"

"Actually, he was very polite," she replied, "but I think he believes I put some kind of spell on our father." Emma's comment suddenly made the solution to one of Joe's cases appear painfully obvious. His mind began to race through the facts, and her voice drifted off into the distance. Eventually he heard her calling out to him. "Hello? Hello? Joe, are you still there?" This pulled him back to their conversation.

"Yes, sorry," he replied, adding by way of explanation, "Vance has it all wrong. It isn't a spell, it's a magic trick."

Emma was confused. "What's a magic trick?"

"Look, I'm really sorry, but can you please hold the line for just one minute?" Joe put the phone down on his desk without waiting for her response. "Sid," he called out, "I need you to do me a favor."

"What can I do boss?" he responded as he walked back into Joe's office.

"I need you to organize a magic trick for me." Sid's face registered his confusion while Joe rapidly scribbled an address on a piece of paper, and handed it to his investigator. "I need you to phone Walt and have him meet me there at ten-thirty sharp. Be sure to tell him, he has to bring his medical bag."

"No problem, boss. I'll phone 'em now."

"Thanks," he replied. He picked up the phone on his desk and returned to his call with Emma. "I'm so sorry, I had to arrange something."

"I can tell you're busy," she replied, and Joe could tell from her tone that she was annoyed at him for putting the phone down. "The reading of the will is tomorrow afternoon, and I was hoping you'd be there?"

"Mr. Gibbs just asked me and I told him I'd come," he replied. He looked at his watch and realized that he needed to get ready for his magic trick. "Look, try and get some rest and we'll talk tomorrow."

There was a pause on the line before she said softly, "I miss you."

He hesitated before replying, "I miss you too."

After his call with Emma, Joe shook thoughts of her out of his head, picked up the phone and placed a call to Sean O'Halloran at the 1st Precinct.

"What shift are you on tonight?" he asked Sean after he answered the phone.

"I'm on until eleven."

"Good, I have a couple of collars for you, and there's going to be another one tomorrow morning."

"I don't know, Joe. I'm getting an ear full from my lieutenant."

Joe was taken back by his friend's response. "What's he complaining about? Is he upset your arresting too many people?" he asked as a joke.

"Basically, yes," replied Sean. Then explained, "He knows I'm getting tips from you, and he's telling me that the other guys are getting pretty steamed about it. He says I gotta start sharing the collars."

"Ya gotta be kidding me?" Joe was annoyed at the absurdity of the idea.

"I wish I was," Sean replied, "but if I don't want to end up working the graveyard shift 'til I retire, the lieutenant says I gotta spread the wealth."

"Ok, but can we sort this out another time? There's definitely something we need to deal with tonight, and if my hunch is right, there's a second one tonight, as well."

"Alright," said Sean reluctantly, "but after this we're going to have to spread these collars around to some of the other guys."

"Ok, fine," Joe agreed reluctantly.

After discussing his plans with Sean, Joe's next call was to Marty at his office on campus. "Any luck with the code?"

"The only message I can get out of this ball is a nursery rhyme."

"A nursery rhyme? You mean like, 'Mary had a little lamb'?"

"Humpty Dumpty, to be precise."

"You sure?"

"Yup, I printed it out every way you can imagine. I even looked at the symbols that were not printed out, just to see if there was a hidden code. I'm pretty sure that the only code on that ball is Humpty Dumpty."

"Well, it doesn't make a lot of sense, but I appreciate your working on it. I need to get that ball back. Can I send Sid around to pick it up from you?"

"No problem," replied Marty, "my wife's going to be glad I've stopped working on the damn thing. She says I've become obsessed."

As Joe hung up the phone, he couldn't help but wonder if Marty had missed something. Was it really possible that the only code on the ball was a child's nursery rhyme?

CHAPTER 6 - FRIDAY

"Sid," yelled Joe. "I need you to get something for me."

"You name it, boss," he responded as he came back into Joe's office.

"I need you to get over to Marty's office at the university and get that ball back from him. Keep it with you tonight but don't go home. People have been killed for that thing, and I don't want you taking any chances."

"Don't worry, boss, I'll spend the night at a hotel."

"I need you to bring the ball here before 9:00 tomorrow morning, and be careful when you come into the office. I got shanghaied today by one of the Purple Gang, a hitter named Honey Boy Morris."

"Honey Boy!" exclaimed Sid. "Isn't that the hood that always wears a skimmer hat and carries two nickel plated revolvers?"

"The very same," Joe replied.

"He's bad news, but I thought the Purple Gang only worked out of Detroit. What's he doing here?"

"He seems to be providing muscle for this Nottingham dame. So I need you to make sure that Kat doesn't come into the office tomorrow." Both men knew that she liked to come in on Saturday for a couple of hours to catch up on filing and invoices. The last thing Joe needed was to have her there when tomorrow's meeting took place.

"She won't like it boss, but I'll make sure she stays home."

Evening

It was nearly 7:00 and growing dark outside when Professor Maximilian Somerfield returned to his office. After entering he heard someone say softly, "You must be very disappointed, Max."

The unexpected voice caused the professor to jump back. He turned towards the sound and saw a dark figure sitting behind his desk. The man was slightly illuminated by the red glow of a cigarette he was smoking. "Who are you and what the devil are you doing here?" Somerfield demanded.

"I hope you don't mind, but I let myself in," said Joe, before taking another pull from his cigarette. "I'm not sure you remember me, but we met earlier this week when I told you I was looking into the death of Gen Ericson."

"Yes," replied the annoyed professor as he switched on his desk lamp, "and during that encounter I made the mistake of assuming you were with the police. Are you familiar with the old academic adage 'When you ASSUME you make an ASS out of U and ME'? Since our little chat the other day, Mr. Lorde, I've learned that you're not a cop. I don't intend to let you make an ass out of me again. Now leave my office at once or I'll phone the actual police."

Joe ignored the threat and took another drag on his cigarette while remaining seated behind the desk. "Like I said, you must be pretty disappointed. You see, I know the whole story."

"I really don't care what you *think* you know." Somerfield walked to the front of his desk and picked up the telephone. "And I don't have to listen to any of this."

"If you're calling the cops you can save the nickel," said Joe. "They should be here in little while. You see I know the congressman didn't kill either the city engineer or Gen Ericson. And, I know that you arranged both of their murders, though I doubt you did the deeds yourself," he added.

"You're out of your mind," said Somerfield, the disdain in his voice was thick.

"Let's start by discussing the missing city documents, shall we?"

As Joe began his explanation, the professor put the phone down and looked over at his file cabinet. Several of the drawers were open, and his faced registered his anger. He turned back towards Joe and snapped, "Those were locked."

"Yeah, but those file locks aren't all that difficult, are they?" asked Joe as he opened the manila file in front of him. He pulled out the signed originals of the engineer's report, the Bennett Construction contract, and the City's original bridge specifications. "I have to say, I was pretty surprised to find them all filled under 'Bridge'," Joe shook his head in amazement. "I suppose that means you never expected anyone to connect you to the murders. To be honest with you, I never would have suspected you if it hadn't been for a couple of slip-ups you made. The first one was when you told me that you hadn't seen Gen for several months, but I had seen the two of you together the day of the Peace Pledge rally."

CHAPTER 6 – FRIDAY

"That's hardly proof of anything," Somerfield walked over to his file cabinet and shut one of the drawers. "You just misunderstood what I said."

"Possibly, but then during our meeting you also said something odd. You said you hoped Gen's *killers* would be caught. I've been doing this job for a number of years now, and I've handled more murders than I care to remember. During all those investigations, the people I've met frequently ask me to catch the *killer*, but you didn't. You said, *killers*. You used the plural, not the singular. I didn't catch it at first because there actually was more than one killer. But the police never released that information. It was something you shouldn't have known."

The professor smiled, then laughed before replying, "If that's the extent of your evidence you're wasting my time."

"There's more actually. There's also the issue of the brown shoes."

"I'm not sure I even own a pair of brown shoes," Somerfield said, still wearing a bemused look on his face.

"I didn't say they were your brown shoes," Joe responded, then continued, "A few nights back, several people were kicking me in an alley, and all of them happened to be wearing brown shoes. Over the past few weeks there was only one place I'd been where all the men were wearing brown shoes. It was here on campus during the Peace Pledge Rally. So, if the brown shoes that were kicking me are the current college fashion, well you were the only one on campus that I had talked to about this case. QED, you must have sent them. It's thin, I'll grant you, and that's probably why I didn't think of it right away."

"This is absurd. What possible motive would I have to kill Gen?"

"Excellent question Max," Joe replied, adding "You don't mind me calling you Max, do you?"

Any vestige of professor's previous smile immediately drained from his face as he delivered his quick and icy retort, "No one calls me that, because it's not my name."

Joe ignored his response and continued, "My hunch is, Max, you're a recruiter for the Communist Party." Somerfield stiffened noticeably at the accusation. "And I figure Gen was one of your recruits. After all, you told me she was a 'good soldier' and believed wholeheartedly in the cause. She was a member of the party, which as it turns out, is the same party you're also a member of." Joe picked up a wallet-sized card and then dropped it back down on the desk. "I found your membership in one of the file drawers over there."

"It's not against the law to be a member of the Communist Party," Somerfield pointed out.

Again Joe ignored him and continued, "Gen discovered the problems with the bridge while she was doing her field work. She told you that Congressman Bayles was vulnerable. You ordered her to get close to him, that's why they were together at the Grand Terrace Ballroom. You were sure you had enough incriminating information to turn him, but you forgot that this is Chicago. Corruption just wasn't the motivator you needed to snare him. Then Bayles told Gen that Fritz Steiner wasn't going to play ball on the bridge 'refurbishment', and you saw your chance. You had Steiner killed. Then told Bayles that you had all the information on the bridge, and enough evidence to link him directly to Steiner's murder. You told him you owned him, didn't you? That's why he was telling me, when I met him at Erma's, that 'they' wouldn't leave him alone. You and your 'soldiers' were the 'they' he was referring to."

The professor, still standing by the file cabinet, said indignantly, "Proof, Mr. Lorde? Your fairy tale is meaningless because you have no proof."

"Oh, I'm sorry, Max," said Joe in mock apology. "Did you think I was telling you about the evidence I've collected? That's my mistake. I was just explaining how I got to this point. To tell you the truth, I don't have all that much evidence yet, but with the information I picked up from your files today I should be able to get the police to start their investigation. Once that happens, the evidence should be easy to collect. Your arrogance let you believe that no one would ever suspect you. Which is why you kept the information on the bridge and your Communist Party card in your file cabinet. I suspect that the pictures of poor Gen that you used to blackmail Bayles are in this office somewhere. Then, there are your 'soldiers' here on campus. They're just kids really, and when the cops lean on them a bit it's a good bet they'll fold just like the Cubs in '06."

Maximillian turned away from the detective so that he was briefly facing the file cabinet. When he spun back around he was holding a gun. It was a Baby Browning .25 caliber pistol and the professor looked at Joe with an air of utter contempt. "Believe it or not I had this filed under 'P' for pistol," he said with a smile.

Joe paid no attention to the threat posed by the gun, and continued. "There's still a couple of things I don't understand, for one – why did she have to die? Why did you eliminate one of your own dedicated soldiers?"

"Gen was a revisionist, a Trotskyite who had become a danger to the party and the revolution. I realize that you are blissfully unaware of the fact that we have entered the Third Period."

"You mean the final stage leading to global revolution and the ultimate triumph of the dictatorship of the proletariat?" Joe replied.

The professor was clearly taken aback. "Full marks, Mr. Lorde. It seems I may have underestimated you."

"I get that a lot."

"The Party requires all revisionist elements be purged during the Third Period. Gen had been warned many times that the ideas she was espousing deviated from the party line. Nevertheless, she continued to ignore those warnings. Do you appreciate irony Mr. Lorde?" The professor continued, not waiting for an answer. "I always have. For some reason that's beyond comprehension, Gen believed it was perfectly acceptable to discuss and debate the Party's decisions. That is the root cause of revisionism, and revisionism must be stopped or the will of the party will be corrupted. I had just been given orders to purge revisionists like Gen, and I was struggling with how I was going to do this. Then she came to me and told me that she planned to do something about the bridge. That silly girl had someone analyze the engineering report and became worried that the bridge might collapse. Now do you see the irony? We had just killed Steiner to keep him quiet about the bridge, and one of my own agents was picking up Steiner's cause. She told me that she was going public with the bridge's problems. I had repeatedly instructed her that the revolution was our primary concern. She was told that we couldn't do anything that would jeopardize it, or for that matter our new asset, Bayles. My God, the man was the odds on favorite to take a senate seat in November. We were going to own a senator, and that stupid bitch was worried about a few peasants. It was an easy decision on what to do next. We got the congressman drunk and took photographs of him in bed with Gen. Both before and after she was killed."

"She was a good soldier," said Joe who slowly let out a sigh. "She believed in the party and in you. She had no idea, when she jumped into the sack with a drunken congressman, that you intended to kill her and frame him for her murder."

"Her death served two ends," Somerfield continued, choosing to ignore Joe's comment. "We purged a dangerous revisionist threatening our movement from within, and at the same time we secured our control over the congressman. She wanted to serve the party and had told me many times she was prepared to give her life for the cause. Well, she did both."

"Only your plan backfired. You pushed Bayles too far, and he shot himself."

"No, the plan worked perfectly," replied the professor bitterly. "I'm afraid you have to take responsibility for his suicide. After Gen's death I showed the congressman the incriminating photos and I made it very clear who was in control. I explained that we were now in the Third Period so there was no room for mistakes. He was warned that if he was responsible for any breach of security, he and his entire family would pay the price. Sure he was frightened, I expected that, but he was manageable until you blundered in and pushed him over the edge. He phoned me after your meeting. It seems he made the same mistake I did, and assumed you were a policeman. He told me that the police knew everything, and he said he was going to confess. I tried to calm him down, and explained that we could still manage the situation, but he kept talking nonsense. Eventually, I made it clear to him that if he went to the police I'd eliminate his wife and children. I thought I had regained control, but of course he went and shot himself."

"Like I said earlier, you must be very disappointed."

"I was ... I am," said the professor sadly, "but I'm about to feel a whole lot better." Somerfield raised the pistol and pointed it directly at Joe's head. "You should have heeded the warning I sent you the other night."

"Oh, I'm glad you mentioned that, Max. In the future, you might want to tell your 'soldiers' that private detectives can't make a living just working one case at a time. So in the future, please ask them to make their warnings a bit more specific."

"I'll be sure to remember that," said Somerfield with a smile. "Goodbye Mr. Lorde."

CHAPTER 6 – FRIDAY

Click ... Maximillian had pulled the trigger, but his gun failed to fire. He slid back the barrel to chamber a fresh round and pulled the trigger again. Click ... again nothing happened.

"If you'll recall, I searched your file cabinet before you got here," Joe explained calmly. "By the way, you misspelled the word 'pistol'. There's only one 'L'." He showed the professor the bullets he'd taken from the gun and poured them from one hand into the other. "I have this bad habit of unloading guns. Loaded ones make me nervous."

Joe collected the papers and reports on the desk before walking towards the office door. At the same time the professor moved swiftly from the file cabinet to his desk. As Joe reached the office door, he heard the sound of a desk drawer opening. "Turn around," the professor commanded harshly. Joe did as instructed, and saw that Somerfield was now holding another pistol, a Mauser. "I have to admit, you're far more clever than I thought."

"I get that a lot."

"It never occurred to me that anyone, yet alone someone like you, could have put all the pieces together and followed them back to me. Allowing you to continue on this case was a mistake – one I intend to rectify immediately," he said. Then he raised the gun and pulled the trigger. Click ...

"Did I mention I was here for thirty minutes before you arrived?" Joe pulled some additional bullets from his coat pocket and again poured them from one hand into the other. The professor's face flushed with anger as he tossed the gun on to the desk and fell back into his chair.

Joe opened the office door and started to leave but turned to face the professor once more. "There's one last thing. If you had to kill Gen, why have her raped as well?"

"That was not my doing," he replied adamantly. "I never authorized that, and let me assure you that the men responsible were severely reprimanded."

"Severely reprimanded," Joe repeated sarcastically. "Well that's something, isn't it. I'm sure if Gen knew that she'd feel a whole lot better."

He turned and again began to leave when the professor said loudly, "When you see her, offer her my apologies." Joe looked back and, unbelievably, the man was holding yet another gun. This time it was a .38 snub-nosed revolver.

Joe let out a sigh, accompanied by a soft laugh. "Perhaps, Max, you're not as smart as I thought you were. I'm not sure why you'd think that I'd leave that gun with any more bullets than the other two." Once more, he pulled some bullets out of his coat pocket and poured them from one hand into the other while shaking his head in dismay. "Now, as much as I've enjoyed our little chat," Joe said mockingly, "I think I have all the information I need. I still have to try and solve another murder tonight. Oh, and if you'll excuse me for just a second, I think the police have finally arrived."

Joe left the office and walked quickly down the hall. The professor, his defeat clearly visible on his face, tossed his third gun on to the desk and once again slumped back into his chair.

Several minutes passed before Joe returned, accompanied by Lieutenant Sean O'Halloran. Behind them were two uniformed officers. Joe then explained to Sean that the professor was responsible for the deaths of both Gen Ericson and Fritz Steiner. The two uniformed officers moved to arrest him, each grabbing an arm, while Joe handed the folder with the reports and the construction contract over to Sean.

Joe picked up the Mauser off the professor's desk. "When I heard that Gen was killed with a 7.63 caliber bullet, my first thought was a 'Bolo' Mauser." He turned towards the professor. "You undoubtedly got this from your Russian handler. The Bolo is very popular in the Soviet Union." He turned back to Sean, handing him the pistol. "You might want to have Walt Dorfman from the coroner's office check to see if this is the gun that killed Gen Ericson." Looking back at Somerfield, he explained, "There's something they call ballistics now, Max. What do ya wanna bet they'll be able to match that gun to the bullet that killed Gen."

"Nothing you do here will stop the revolution," said the professor weakly, but with conviction in his voice. "A Workers' State will be established. It's inevitable."

Joe showed little interest. "Did I mention to you Max that I was a guest of the Soviet Union back in '26?"

The professor's eyes widened with disbelief. "Is that true?"

"I'm afraid so."

CHAPTER 6 – FRIDAY

"That must have been glorious," said the professor, his face showing his envy.

"Glorious," repeated Joe as he rubbed the scar above his left eye, "isn't exactly the word I would use."

Joe picked up the third gun that the professor had held on him from the desk. "Oh, and to answer your question from earlier," he said with a smile, "I do appreciate irony." The professor's face drained of color as he watched the private detective spin the cylinder of the .38 special and empty out the bullets one by one into the palm of his hand.

"But you showed me the bullets!"

"Oh that. I just showed you the .25 caliber bullets a second time. You assumed they were from the .38. Now, what was it that you were saying earlier about not letting ME make an ASS out of U ... again?" He put the .38 and its bullets into his trench coat pocket, before approaching Somerfield and clocking him with a hard right.

Sean watched as his suspect crumpled to the floor, slightly startled by the uncharacteristic use of force from his friend. "What was that for?" he asked.

"That was for having a young defenseless girl raped and murdered." The professor slowly pulled himself up so that he was now on his hands and knees.

Sean nodded his head in agreement, but added, "I thought it might have been payback for the beating you took the other night."

"Nah," replied Joe as he slammed his foot into the professor's stomach causing him to collapse back down to the floor. "That was payback for the other night."

Somerfield gulped for air and called out in a weak voice. "You all saw that. This man attacked me. I'm pressing charges. I want him arrested for assault."

The three policemen in the room began to laugh. As Sean helped Somerfield to his feet, he handcuffed him and said with a wry smile, "You're going to find out what a real assault is soon enough professor. The boys at the Cook County Jail will be more than happy to teach a class on the subject for you."

[Case Epilogue] Torre Porcini, the youth originally accused of Fritz Steiner's murder, was released from jail the day after the professor was caught. Grateful that he didn't get the chair for murder, he swore to both his mother and Father Frank that he'd never break the law again. That oath lasted less than four months. Over the next six years, Torre would be in and out of trouble for various petty crimes. Eventually, in late '38, he was caught trying to steal a car. This was a relatively new line of work for him, and one that he wasn't very good at. Up before an uncompromising judge, Torre was given the choice of four years in prison or three years in the army. He chose the army. In late '41, two days before his three years were up, the Japanese bombed Pearl Harbor. His enlistment was automatically extended until the end of '45. During the war he was assigned to a medical unit and became an army corpsman. He may not have been very good at stealing cars, but he turned out to have a gift when it came to saving lives. After the war he used the GI Bill to go to college, and then on to medical school. Eventually he would take a post at the Mayo Clinic in Rochester where he became one the most talented surgeons in the country.

Maximillian Somerfield was charged with two counts of murder and a number of lesser charges including blackmail and rape. The Mauser was confirmed to be the gun used to kill Genevieve Ericson. As Joe predicted, it didn't take the police more than a couple of hours to pick up several of the professor's "soldiers" on campus. After interrogating one young man for just thirty minutes, they soon had the names of everyone involved. At Somerfield's arraignment the judge refused to grant him bail. A prominent Chicago attorney took up his case, and in a second hearing, two days later, he managed to get the judge to set bail at $35,000. Typically, such a huge sum would have been far too much for a college professor to raise. The socialist community, however, rallied around their local hero, who they viewed as being framed by the capitalists. They started a fund both to secure the professor's bail, and pay for his defense. Hundreds of socialists throughout the Midwest pooled their money to get Somerfield released, including Joe's two communist neighbors, whose frequent and loud philosophical discussions routinely interrupted his sleep. They contributed their life savings of $134.73 to the cause. Later they would explain to Joe that the professor was obviously being framed, because no one in the movement could ever harm a "Fellow Traveler".

CHAPTER 6 – FRIDAY

The combined efforts of the Midwest socialists paid off, and they raised $57,387.14, which they turned over to the professor. After making bail, Somerfield gave a rousing speech on the courthouse steps, attended by nearly two hundred supporters. In his speech he stated that he would not only prove his innocence, but he would also put the truly guilty on trial. Namely, the "greedy industrialists who daily suppressed and exploited the working class". Immediately after the speech he walked down to the cab stand adjacent to the courthouse and was driven straight to the new municipal airport. There he boarded a T&WA flight to New York, which landed just in time for him to catch a boat for Europe. He arrived in Moscow some six weeks later and was given a hero's welcome.

With the $22,000 he had left from his defense fund, Maximillian lived very well in the new Soviet Union. After six months, however, he was arrested by the OGPU and sent to Moscow's Lefortovo prison. He was never told why. In '36 he was finally put on trial, accused of being a Revisionist and a Trotskyite. Initially he denied all the charges, but after five minutes of interrogation he "confessed" to his crimes and denounced a series of people he'd never met. For this "cooperation" he was given ten years in the Sevvostlag labor camp. He never made it there. Instead, Somerfield was sent back to Lefortovo. After six months he was driven to a wooded area a hundred miles outside Moscow and shot in the back of the head with a Bolo Mauser. It's not known if he appreciated the irony.

It was about ten-thirty when Toddy Frances entered his office. The evening performance had finished, and, as usual, he had returned to wrap up some paperwork before heading home. When he entered he was startled to see three men waiting for him. Two were standing by his desk, and a third was leaning against the back wall. He recognized one of the men by his desk as the private detective working for Irene, but he didn't know the other two.

"Mr. Lorde," said Toddy casually, "I'm afraid I'm not used to having visitors this late."

"Well unfortunately, Mr. Frances," replied Joe, making a point of addressing him by his surname, "this isn't a social call."

The empresario hesitated for a moment. "Perhaps you could introduce me to your friends?"

Joe ignored the man's request. "We know the whole story, Mr. Frances. These gentlemen are here to take you into custody."

Toddy, who was clearly taken aback by the remark, responded, "What on earth are you talking about?"

"We know that you and Paul Trent, or should I say Betty Parker, conspired to bleed Irene Fields. Your friend Irene told you in confidence that she was on the verge of hitting the big time. She was about to sign a deal giving her a nationally syndicated radio show that would be launched by WBM. With the Majestic set to be converted into a movie house, you saw your opportunity to make enough money to survive the collapse of vaudeville."

Toddy moved towards the oval window that dominated his office and nervously lit a cigarette while Joe continued. "I imagine it didn't take you long to hatch your plan. You met Betty during one of your open auditions here at the theater. We checked your log, and her name appeared in it nearly three months ago. It seems likely that the next time you saw her was when she was singing at The Spot nightclub. Even though she was dressed as a man, you recognized her and all the pieces came together."

The theater manager stared out the window and took another draw from his cigarette while small beads of sweat began to form along his brow. "You knew Irene's 'preferences' and you knew that Betty was just her type. For her part, Betty needed the money. Her family's business was dying and squeezing some dough out of some well-heeled woman she didn't know seemed like a good idea. So you arranged for the two of them to meet. You knew how lonely Irene was, and you also knew how scared she was that someone would discover her secret. You made sure that Irene had too many drinks in her when you introduced her to Paul Trent. Then, just as you planned, sparks flew. With Irene so drunk that she didn't know what was happening, the three of you went someplace quiet and you took photos making sure that they were as explicit as possible."

Toddy loudly protested, "You can't prove any of this. If you don't stop this immediately I'll sue you for libel."

"Actually, you'd have to sue me for slander," explained Joe. "You can only sue for libel if the accusation is in writing. Either way, truth is an absolute defense." Joe reached down next to the desk and picked up a large manila folder and threw it onto the top of the desk. The corner of a photograph was clearly visible. "We found these after a thorough search of your office," he explained. "My apologies, but you might find your house and car a bit disheveled. We searched them as well."

Toddy looked at the envelope before replying, "That proves nothing. I was looking for those photos just as you were. I found them first, that's all. I remembered who Paul Trent really was and went to Betty's dressing room at The Spot. I found the photos there," he explained, his voice shaking slightly. "It's clear that Betty was the one blackmailing Irene, not me."

"Nice try, but no cigar," was Joe's acerbically. "Did you know that Betty kept a diary?" Toddy's face went ashen and he stood with his mouth slightly open. Joe took a black journal with red trim from the drawer and dropped it on the desktop. "Seems she wrote in it every day," he said as he pulled the journal closer. "Not every detail, just the highlights." He opened it and flipped through the handwritten pages. "It's all in here, Mr. Frances. The whole blackmail scheme, and the last entries dealt with how she'd changed her mind. The two of you set up a meeting at the Mart."

"I was never anywhere near the Mart the day she was killed," insisted Toddy.

"Really?" said Joe in disbelief. "Did you honestly think you could make it into a building as busy as the Mart without being spotted? It didn't take us that long to find a couple of witnesses."

"I've had to go to the Mart many times for business," he responded nervously. Your witnesses are just confused about which day I was here, that's all," but from the tone in his voice it seemed that even he didn't believe his defense.

Joe ignored his comment and continued. "When the two of you met at the Mart you decided to speak on one of the soundstages, so you couldn't be overheard. Your talk turned into an argument and then into a fight. You grabbed her by the wrists but she resisted. During the struggle she scratched your arm. She broke free and tried to leave. It was at this point that you saw the gun laying there on the prop table. In a moment of panic you grabbed it and shot her in the temple."

"You can't prove that I was on that soundstage with her."

"Actually, we can. Let me introduce to you Detective Sean O'Halloran from the Chicago police department." Sean, who had been quietly listening to Joe's summation, took out his badge and ID and waived it at Toddy. "It seems the Bureau of Investigation in Washington has opened a new laboratory that's dedicated to fighting crime. It creates new scientific tests and makes them available to the local police around the country. One of those new tests can match blood and skin samples. The small traces we got from under Betty's fingernails can be put under a microscope and I'm fairly certain they'll match your blood and skin perfectly. That, Mr. Frances, will put you on the soundstage with Betty at the time of her death. In order to take the blood and skin samples we are going to need your right arm."

"Your right forearm, Mr. Frances," demanded Sean in his most official voice.

"I don't have to submit to this," said Toddy indignantly, as sweat poured off his brow.

"I'm afraid you do," replied Joe as Sean grabbed hold of Toddy's right arm and pinned it against the wall. He ripped open the sleeve of the man's white dress shirt, exposing the underside of his wrist. Joe rubbed Toddy's exposed skin with his handkerchief, removing some theatrical makeup and revealing three parallel scratch marks.

"I would now like to introduce you to Dr. Walter Dorfman," Joe said. Walt stood, took out his official ID and showed it to Toddy. "Dr. Dorfman works for the county," Joe explained, being careful to omit the fact that he worked at the Coroner's Office. "He will be taking of the skin and blood samples." Walt lifted up his black medical bag and placed it on top of the desk.

"This is crazy," said a frightened Toddy.

"I knew you had done it when I read that the dead actor in '22 had been working on a play, and he'd shot himself in the head with a gun that fired blanks. It was the same play that you have a poster of here in your office." Joe pointed to the poster hanging on the wall and continued, "That's how you knew that a gun that shoots blanks could kill. You'd witnessed it firsthand. Face it, Toddy," said Joe sympathetically, "you're caught."

Sean could tell that the suspect was about to crack so he released his grip on the shaking man. Toddy walked over to the desk chair and collapsed. He was so defeated that the truth flowed out of him like scotch from a tipped-over glass. "I didn't plan to kill her," he began. "I made the mistake of telling her that Irene had hired you, and she got cold feet and wanted out. I told her to be strong and everything would be ok, but Betty was a mess." Toddy bent down, put his head in his hands, and continued, "The more I tried to calm her down the more unraveled she became. I told her that all we had to do was hold out until Irene signed her new contract on Monday." He was in tears as he continued, "but she was petrified that her parents, and the people at her church would find out about her double life."

Then the empresario looked at Joe and asked, "What was I supposed to do? Vaudeville was dying and my theater was going to be converted to a movie house. I had no place to go, nowhere to turn. Am I supposed to stand in front of a factory during a shape-up, or line up at a soup kitchen for one meal a day? I'm nearly 50 years old for god's sake. You tell me Mr. Lorde, what was I supposed to do?"

Joe walked over to the defeated theater manager and put his hand on his shoulder. "How did Betty die?" he asked.

"After she pulled away from me she started to leave the soundstage. I panicked," Toddy explained. "I couldn't let her ruin everything – not when we were so close. I had to stop her. I saw the gun on the prop table, grabbed it and without even thinking I placed it against her head, and pulled the trigger. She was moving so the gun jiggled slightly when it went off. At first I thought I hadn't killed her, but after a minute her breathing stopped, and she was dead. Then I put the gun in her hand and left."

"You could have found a more imaginative place to hide the photos and negatives," Joe said to him. "Once we began to search it didn't take long to find them."

"I wasn't planning on keeping them here for long," explained Toddy. "I had rented a safe-deposit box at the Harris Bank on North Michigan but there was a run on that bank this week. I got worried that if the bank went under, I wouldn't be able to get access to the box."

"Mr. Frances, I'm placing you under arrest for the murder of Betty Parker," said Sean as he pulled out his cuffs.

While the detective placed the restraints on Toddy's wrists, the dejected man looked over at Joe. "When I first met you, Mr. Lorde, I didn't think you'd pose much of a problem. Obviously, I underestimated you."

"I get that a lot."

"Joe," said Sean as he held out his hand toward his friend. "I'm afraid I'm going to need those photos of Miss Fields and Betty Parker as evidence."

"These photos?" he asked as he grabbed the manila envelope that he had lain on the desk. "Unfortunately these aren't the photos you're looking for." He pulled out the contents of the envelope to reveal two 8 x 11 pictures of him dancing with Emma at the Grand Terrace Ballroom, along with ten blank pieces of typing paper.

"Where are the photos?" asked Sean. As he spoke, Toddy instinctively glanced toward his file cabinets.

Joe pointed to a garbage can next to the desk. Inside the can were the ash remnants of a fire that had burned out a while ago. "Someone burned the photos, I guess."

"That's destroying evidence," snapped Sean angrily.

"Your suspect just confessed in front of three witnesses," said Walt. "You don't need that evidence. In fact you don't need any evidence at all."

"Well, I'm afraid I'll need Betty Parker's diary," insisted Sean.

Joe picked up the journal from the desk. "This doesn't belong to Betty. We did search for a diary, but didn't find one."

"Whose diary is it?"

"It's not a diary," explained Joe. "These are field notes on a sociology study a young co-ed was doing in the Near West Side of town."

"You lied to me!" Toddy realized he'd confessed to a murder when there was no evidence against him.

"I don't think of it as lying to you," explained Joe. "I simply performed a magic trick and did what any good magician would do. I diverted your attention and made you see what I wanted you to see. You knew you were guilty. All I had to do was make you think you were caught, and I was sure you'd take care of the rest." Sean escorted the stunned Toddy out of the office and off to the station.

CHAPTER 6 – FRIDAY

Walt looked over at Joe and smiled. "That was pretty slick," he said. "But, if you remember what I told you the other day, there are no tests that can match skin or blood samples."

"Yeah, I remembered, but Toddy was a man of the arts and never paid attention in science class. So, unfortunately for him, he didn't know."

Walt looked puzzled and added, "There's still one thing I don't understand. If you didn't have Betty's diary, how did you know she was getting cold feet and wanted to call off the blackmail?"

"I didn't," responded Joe. "It was a good bet that Toddy never intended to kill her. If he had it's unlikely he would have used a gun that shot blanks. So if the murder wasn't planned then why would it have occurred?"

"Because they had a falling out of some kind," answered Walt.

"That was my guess," agreed Joe. "I had no idea what they fought about, but I was sure they fought over something. All I had to do was keep it vague. I was confident that if Toddy thought Betty had put the reason in a diary, he would just assume we knew the truth. As with any magic trick, the object was to keep Toddy from looking too closely at what was actually happening. If I could do that, I could lead him where I needed him to go."

"Well, I gotta head home. I promised Jodi I'd stop by this evening and it's already late."

"So how did it go last night?" Joe asked.

"I'm engaged!", Walt replied with a boyish smile. "I'll tell ya the whole evening was fantastic. Just after she said 'yes' the band leader dedicated a song to us. How he knew we'd just gotten engaged is beyond me. And you want to know the topper?" he continued excitedly. "The club picked up the tab for the whole evening. Here I thought it was going to cost me a week's pay and it turns out I won some sort of contest. It didn't cost me a thing." Walt walked to the door, then stopped and turned back towards Joe. "By the way, I wanted to ask you if you'd be my best man."

Walt's request caught him by surprise. "You must have someone better than me you can ask?"

"You've been like a brother to me. I don't think I would have made it through those years at St. Jerome's if it hadn't been for you." Walt had expected Joe to have difficulty responding to his request so he added, "You don't have to give me an answer straight away. We can talk about it later." He started to leave but turned back again and asked, "You coming?"

"In a few minutes. I need to make a call." Joe watched as Walt walked down the hall and descended the narrow spiral staircase. Closing the office door, he went over to the two wooden file cabinets. He checked behind one cabinet and didn't feel anything, but when he reached around the second one, he felt something taped to the back. Carefully, he removed a large manila envelope from its hiding place. Inside he found the pictures and negatives of Irene and Betty. Joe walked over to the metal wastebasket that held the ashes of some writing paper he'd burned earlier. He took the red matchbook from his pocket and used its last match to set fire to the envelope. As the fire took hold he dropped the burning mass into the metal basket. He then opened the bottom left drawer of Toddy's desk and took out a bottle of scotch, along with a glass. He poured himself three fingers of a delightful single malt, then slowly emptied the remainder of the bottle into the flaming waste basket, causing the fire to flare up. Leaning back in the desk chair, Joe sipped his drink and watched as the fire completely consumed the basket's contents.

[Case Epilogue] – Toddy Frances pleaded guilty to second degree murder. The Major used some of his considerable political influence to make sure that Irene's story did not come out during the trial. In exchange for his part in keeping Irene's secret, Toddy's sentence was reduced to twenty years in prison. When he was paroled in '48, Toddy was sixty-four years old. With the continuing decline in live theater, coupled with the fact that Toddy was a convicted felon, it was hardly surprising that he had trouble finding a job. He ended up working in a new business that sprung up after the war. He may never have understood radio, but he caught on quickly to the potential of television. He started by producing plays for TV. These received excellent notices from critics, even though there were only a couple of hundred TV sets in the Chicago area at the time. Eventually he moved to Hollywood where he produced several television series including a western and a crime drama.

Irene Fields started a fifteen-minute daytime radio drama at WBM which was syndicated nationally. Just as Eddie Collins had feared, 'Day Dreams' folded soon after she left.

Irene made a lot of money in what became known as "soap operas" and later moved two of her successful radio shows to television. In '42 Irene met a woman named Edith, who became her life-long partner. At the height of Irene's career in the mid-50's, Edith was called to testify before the House Un-American Activities Committee because she'd been a member of the Communist Party. Edith refused to provide any names to the House Committee, and Irene's relationship with Edith became public. Irene refused to break off the relationship and was blacklisted.

The two women moved to a small town about fifty miles outside Portland, Oregon, and it was there that Irene began to write again. In the early 70's, her plays were "discovered" by a professor at Berkeley. A number of them were staged on campus and eventually in San Francisco. During the final years of her life, Irene went back to doing what she had always wanted to do – making magic on stage.

CHAPTER SEVEN

SATURDAY

There are few things better than sex, and many many things that are worse, but there is nothing like it! -W.C. Fields

Morning

It was just after sunrise when Joe arrived at the Reliance Building. Because it was Saturday all the elevators had been shut down, so he had to hoof it up five flights of stairs. When he got into his office, he locked the door behind him. Then he went to his desk and angled the chair so he could keep an eye on the entrance. He took off his trench coat and took out the .38 snub nose pistol along with the six bullets that he'd liberated from Professor Somerfield the day before. After reloading the gun, he put it back into the right hand pocket of his coat. He didn't like the idea of having a loaded gun in the office but with Honey Boy Morris coming over not having a loaded gun seemed far more dangerous.

Since Kat wasn't going to be in, he'd brought some coffee in a thermos and he poured himself a cup before lighting up a Chesterfield. To kill time, he started to wade through the bills, invoices, and correspondence that she'd left on his desk for review. At around 8:30 he set aside the paperwork, picked up his phone, and phoned her at home.

"Morning," he said warily, unsure what kind of mood she'd be in. Kat knew immediately who it was, but her only comment was "ummm", her standard response when she was angry. "Are we ok, Kit-Kat?" he asked apprehensively.

She ignored his question and snapped back, "The only reason you don't want me to come in today is because you're planning on doing something stupid."

"I'm not planning anything stupid, I promise you. I just can't vouch for what other guy might do."

"You know how I feel about the chances you take."

"I'm always careful."

"Ha!" she interrupted. "A man is judged by his deeds and not his words."

"Look, I didn't call to upset you. I phoned to see if everything is jake."

After a moment she let out a sigh and responded. "We're fine, and I'm sorry I got so mad yesterday. I just seem to be a lot more emotional lately, and you taking all these unnecessary risks upsets me. By the way, Sid phoned this morning and told me that Pudge still hasn't come home." She waited for a second before adding, "I'm worried about him, Joe, and so are Sid and Mickey."

"Ok, I think he lives up near Pulaski Park. I'll send Sid to meet up with his wife later today and we'll see if we can track him down."

"Thank you." Her emotions made her voice crack slightly as she added, "Remember, God keeps those safe who keep themselves safe."

"Come on, Kat, you know I'm indestruc ...," Joe paused and then said simply, "... I'm careful as mice."

"I wish I could believe that," she replied in a somber tone. "If the scythe hits a rock, call me."

"I assume that's another Russian thing."

She let out a deep sigh before explaining, "If the shit hits the fan, call me."

Joe's next call was to Theo, at his home. He wanted to try and explain his relationship with Emma, even though he wasn't really sure he could explain it to himself. After a customary greeting, Joe said, "I need to tell you something Theo. I have ... feelings for Emma." He was having trouble finding the right words but continued. "Now that the investigation is over, I'll be at the reading of the will as her ... friend."

There was a pause on the line before Theo replied, "I had a hunch that something was up. Just answer me this, Joe. Did your feelings for her interfere with your investigation in any way?"

"No, you have my word, Theo. I would never have let that happen," he answered earnestly.

"That's good enough for me. Thanks for calling and letting me know."

After finishing the call with Theo, Joe continued reviewing the correspondence that Kat had left for him. It was just before 9:00 when his muscles instinctively tensed at the sound of keys jingling in the hallway. The office lock disengaged, the door swung open, and Sid walked in. Joe released the gun from inside his trench coat pocket, threw the coat back over his chair, and walked out of his office to greet his investigator. "Did you get the ball?"

"Sure did, but I thought I saw that client of ours, Mr. Patel, along with a couple of other people sitting in a car across the street from the office."

"Did they spot you?"

"I don't think so, but I can't be sure. Just to be safe, I didn't go through the main entrance. I came around through the back alley instead."

"Good," said Joe. "Now you need to scram out of here before our guests arrive. Then wait outside the building until the police get here. I placed a call to Sean at home late last night, and he's bringing plenty of back up. He said he'd try and be here before 9:30. When they arrive, you hustle 'em up here fast."

"Will do boss." Sid reached across Kat's desk, opened a drawer, and took out a Tootsie Pop. "You try one of these?" he asked with a smile as he put it in his coat pocket for later.

"Now you're eating 'em too?"

"Kat gave me one the other day, they're great." As he was talking, he took out the rubber ball he'd gotten from Marty and placed it on the desk. "Speaking of Kat, you two ok?"

Before Joe could answer, Honey Boy Morris walked through the office door followed closely by both Patel and the sultry Jacqueline. The goon didn't have any guns visible, but from the bulges under his arms it was obvious he was wearing iron. Joe quickly put the ball in Kat's Tootsie Pop drawer and momentarily considered making a run for the gun back in his office. Realizing he'd never make it, he looked at the gunman and said in a surly tone, "You're early."

"We saw your stooge there duck around the back," replied Honey Boy, "so we thought it was a good time to come up."

CHAPTER 7 - SATURDAY

Joe snapped back at the thug, "I wasn't talking to you, Sweet Pea." With his gray eyes seemingly glowing with anger, Joe turned toward Sid and yelled, "I paid you to do one simple thing and you let them follow you up here, you stupid fucking twit." With no warning, he slapped Sid across the face with the back of his hand. The force of the blow caused the smaller man to stumble backwards towards the open office door. "I should know better than to hire a lousy washed-up rummy like you." Joe approached the stunned man and again smacked him across the face. Blood flowed freely from Sid's upper lip and nose as he stumbled through the open door into the hallway. "Get out of my sight, you damn yid," Joe shouted as he raised his hand to strike Sid yet again. Before he could deliver the blow, the bruised and bloodied man fled down the hallway to the stairwell.

Patel, speaking French, whispered softly to Jacqueline, "*As I've told you, he's a barbarian.*"

"*But he has the ball. I saw it when we came in,*" she replied. "*Let's conclude our business and get out of here as quickly as possible.*"

"I believe you have something for me," said Joe as he regained his composure. Patel took out an envelope and placed it on the desk. Joe picked it up and inside was a thick stack of one hundred dollar gold certificates.

"And you have something for us as well," said Jacqueline. Joe finished counting the money then reached into the drawer and placed the rubber ball on the desk. Jacqueline and Patel leaned down to look at it.

"Is this really the one?" asked Patel softly.

"Yes," she whispered in response, "I do believe I finally have it."

She reached slowly for the ball, but just as she was about to touch it a loud voice from behind her barked out an order. "Get away from the desk." Jacqueline and Patel spun back towards Honey Boy. He had pulled out one of his twin pistols and was pointing it in their direction.

"What do you think you're doing, Mr. Morris?" an outraged Jacqueline demanded.

"I *think* I'm taking the ball," he replied with a smile. Reaching across the table, he grabbed the ball and slipped it into his overcoat pocket. Then he turned his attention towards Joe. "I'll take the five G's as well," he said as he motioned with his pistol for Joe to drop the envelope on the desk.

"You might as well leave the ball," said Jacqueline. "It has no value to you."

"Who knows?" smirked the thug as he picked up the envelope full of cash. "Maybe I'll crack the code and find myself a treasure. The way I see it, even if I can't figure it out, there always some sap who's willing to shell out plenty of dough for it. Either way, I can't lose."

Honey Boy turned his attention back towards Joe. "I have a score to settle with you." As the gangster moved towards him, Patel reached into his suit coat pocket and pulled out his 9mm pistol. Honey Boy responded quickly to the threat by pivoting to his left and firing four rounds at the little man. Patel was hit just once but collapsed to the floor. The altercation between the two men gave Joe the opportunity to race back into his private office. As he did, the thug spun back to his right and fired two quick bursts at him. Both shots missed their mark. Once in his office, Joe grabbed his trench coat and threw himself behind his desk, while pulling the snub nose out of his coat pocket. Honey Boy followed him into his office firing two more shots which slammed through the desk, again missing their target.

"The word on the street is, ya hate guns and never use 'em," said Honey Boy with a laugh. "I kinda wish ya had one now, this fight would be a lot more fun."

Joe reached around his desk and fired two shots in the direction of the gangster's voice. One bullet lodged into the door frame in front of the goon and the other knocked the white skimmer hat off his head. "Careful what you wish for, Sweet Pea."

The gunman responded by firing two more times in Joe's direction, ripping into the desk but not quite hitting his mark. Joe fired another shot that again struck the door frame, then two more shots in quick succession, with one shattering the frosted glass that formed the top part of his office door.

Once again Honey Boy let loose a burst of shots that were followed by a series of metallic clicking noises. Joe recognized the sound of new ammo clips being loaded into Honey Boy's .45's and realized that in all the commotion he'd lost track of how many shots he'd fired. More importantly, he'd lost track of how many he had left. He opened his snub-nosed, rotated the chamber, and saw that he had just one unspent round.

CHAPTER 7 – SATURDAY

He let out a deep sigh and rolled his eyes up towards the ceiling. "God I miss Paris."

Suddenly the room exploded with the sound of gunfire and flying wood chips as Honey Boy, now firing from both his pistols, emptied the magazines into Joe's defenseless desk. When the shooting stopped he could hear the same metallic clicking sounds, indicating that the gangster was reloading his pistols yet again.

Joe's mind raced as he tried to come up with a plan. Honey Boy seemed to have plenty of ammo. What's more, at the rate he was firing even a terrible shot like him was bound to hit something or someone eventually. After racing through his options, Joe pulled back the trigger on his revolver and quietly rotated the cylinder so that his remaining bullet was no longer the next round in the chamber but was instead the last round. Rising up from behind his desk, he pointed the pistol toward the doorway and began pulling the trigger. Click ... click ... click ... click ... click ...

A huge grin stretched across Honey Boy's face as he heard the hammer in Joe's pistol repeatedly strike the empty shell casing. The thug finished reloading his guns and strolled into the office to find Joe standing behind his bullet ridden desk pointing a .38 at him. Honey Boy stood with his pistols down by his side, a smug grin on his face.

"If you move a muscle I'll kill you," Joe said calmly, training the revolver at the head of the thug.

"You'll kill me with what?" laughed Honey Boy contemptuously. "You're empty."

He gave the gangster his icy stare. "I reloaded," he lied.

"Ya made a sucker out of me with an empty gun once already. Do ya really expect me to fall for that again?"

"In case you hadn't noticed, this is my office. And here's a news bulletin for ya, Sweet Pea. I keep the ammunition for my gun here." Joe fired his last round inches from Honey Boy's ear then opened his left hand and flashed the bullets he'd taken from Professor Somerfield's 25 caliber pistol. You could almost see the wheels turning in the gangster's head as he stared into Joe's cold gray eyes and tried to figure out if he was telling the truth. Joe wasn't certain that the goon was going to buy his con so he gave him a wicked smile and pulled the hammer back on his empty pistol. "I still owe you for the beating in the alley the other night. So please, just give me an excuse to kill you." The thug was locked into Joe's gaze for what seemed like minutes but was in reality just a few seconds. Honey Boy let out a breath he'd been unconsciously holding, and dropped his guns to the floor. Joe grabbed a pair of handcuffs from the top drawer of his damaged desk. As he approached the gunman, he kicked both of the man's pistols to the far end of the room. He then took his .38 revolver, opened the cylinder, and slowly spun it, letting each empty cartridge fall to the desk in front of the gangster.

A wild look swept across Honey Boy's face as he watched the spent shells fall on the desk. "You piece of shit," he screamed while throwing a haymaker at Joe's head. Joe had been hoping the gangster would do something stupid like this. He easily countered the punch, then thrust his knee up into the man's groin, causing him to double over screaming in pain. Grabbing the hair on the back of Honey Boy's head, he slammed his forehead onto the top of the desk. The thug went limp, dropped to the floor, and Joe removed the rubber ball and the five grand from the unconscious man's pocket. He then lifted him up off the floor, tossed him into a chair, and swiftly handcuffed him to the radiator.

With his gangster problem solved, Joe put the empty .38 into his trench coat pocket, walked into the front office, and knelt down beside Patel to examine him. The little man was still breathing, so Joe carefully moved him to see how badly he was hurt. It was at that point he heard a female voice behind him. "Stand up, please." He looked over at Jacqueline Nottingham, who was aiming Patel's 9mm at him, and complied.

"Don't you think we should help your partner?" he asked.

"Our partnership was a temporary arrangement at best," she replied while glancing down at the unconscious Patel. "It looks like this is the perfect time to dissolve it," Jacqueline's voice was cool and all business.

"Why don't you let me call for an ambulance?" he asked as he reached for the telephone.

"Don't touch that," commanded Jacqueline. "The bullet just grazed his skull. He's not in any danger. Now I'll take the ball," she demanded. Joe could sense from those violet eyes that she would have no compunction in shooting him on the spot. He placed the ball on the edge of Kat's desk and pushed it in her direction. It wobbled slowly towards the French beauty. As she grabbed it, the secret of the puzzle ball finally dawned on Joe.

CHAPTER 7 - SATURDAY

"Have you ever had a Tootsie Pop?" he asked.

"A tootsie what?" she replied, confused by the question.

"A Tootsie Pop," he explained. "It's like a lollypop. I hear they're delicious. There's probably one in the desk drawer in front of you, if you want to try one."

"I have no interest in sweets, but I will take the five thousand dollars you recovered from Mr. Morris." Joe tossed the envelope on the desk.

"Unfortunately, I have to decide what to do with you, Mr. Lorde. I'm fairly certain that you won't let me walk out of here. And now I know that I can't trust the services of Mr. Morris," she said disappointedly, looking over at her handcuffed goon. "So I don't have the means to stop you." A sexy smile spread across her gorgeous face. "It's a shame really. There's much about you that I find extremely compelling, and I imagine there's a lot going on underneath that hard boiled exterior you maintain. I believe it would be immensely pleasurable getting behind that façade of yours and exploring all that you have to offer." The smile left her face as she added, "but I just can't have you chasing me, can I?" She raised the pistol to eye level. "Nothing personal mon cher ...," click ... the Savage 9mm had no bullet in the chamber.

"I guess Patel didn't tell you. It seems he never keeps a round chambered." Jacqueline tried to pull the bolt back to set the next round, but it wouldn't budge. Joe reached over and calmly took the gun from her hand. Jacqueline, realizing any resistance was pointless, released her grip. "These Savage pistols are temperamental things," he explained. "I told Avaj they had a tendency to jam. Especially if you pull the trigger when there's no round in the chamber." He wiggled the trigger back and forth while pulling on the bolt. After only a few seconds he was able to clear the jam and chamber the next round.

"*Violà*," he said with a smile as he switched to French and pointed the 9mm at the lovely lady. "*Now you see, it's good as new.*"

Jacqueline let out a sigh and smiled as she replied, also in French, "*I see that I underestimated you, Mr. Lorde.*"

"*I get that a lot.*"

"*Perhaps you and I can come to some sort of ... arrangement.*" Almost like magic, she turned off the cold hard persona of only moments ago and flashed a seductive smile. Her violet eyes now seemed to glitter as she spoke.

Joe couldn't help but admire her swift transformation. *"You're good, you're very good ... but as tempting as you look, I don't think it bodes well for a relationship when it starts with one person trying to kill the other. Now, the ball and the money please,"* he said as a command, rather than a request. Jacqueline set both on the desk and Joe put them in his pocket.

A moaning sound could be heard coming from the floor next to Kat's desk, and Patel slowly staggered to his feet. "What happened?" he asked in a stunned voice.

"You were shot," explained Joe.

"Yes," Patel became angry as he remembered the events. "By the *voyou* she hired." He pointed an accusing finger at Mrs. Nottingham. "Where is Mr. Morris? Did he take the ball?"

"No, the ball's safe and Honey Boy is cooling his heels in my office." Patel looked through the office door and saw the now conscious thug sitting in a chair, handcuffed to the radiator and rubbing his aching forehead.

Suddenly there were noises in the hallway. A moment later Sid, still bleeding from his earlier beating, entered the room, along with several uniformed policemen and Detective Burt Callahan.

Joe leaned over to Sid and whispered, "What the hell is Burt doing here? Where's Sean?"

"When Callahan showed up I rang Sean from the lobby pay phone and asked what gives," explained the investigator. "He said something about his lieutenant insisting that he share his collars. He said you knew about it."

Joe remembered their conversation from yesterday and mumbled under his breath, "Great, just great."

It took twenty minutes to explain to Detective Callahan what was going on. Eventually he seemed to grasp the situation and placed Jacqueline, Patel, and Honey Boy under arrest.

"Ok, so where's this ball you've been talking about?" Joe pulled it out of his pocket and placed it on the table. "Now what is it again?" asked the detective, still confused.

CHAPTER 7 - SATURDAY

"It's a puzzle ball." Sid wanted to add a sarcastic "genius" to the end of his sentence, but thought better of it.

"Right, and it holds the key to a buried treasure?"

"No, it doesn't," said Joe, his tone revealing his irritation. "They only *thought* it did," as he spoke he pointed to the suspects in the room. "But they got it all wrong. The ball isn't a clue to a treasure. The ball is the treasure."

"What? The ball is the treasure?" repeated Patel. "That's ridiculous."

Joe began to explain. As he did, Patel, Jacqueline, Sid, Callahan, and Honey Boy, who was now securely cuffed to one of Chicago's finest, gathered around Kat's desk. "When you came into my flat, Avaj, you spun a story about a rubber ball that belonged to an Indian prince."

"Yes, but none of that was true."

"To be precise, none of the ancient history was true. You mentioned that the ball belonged to the Hapsburgs, and after the war it was stolen in a well-publicized robbery in Switzerland."

"That wasn't true, either," admitted Patel.

"Actually, it wasn't far off from the truth," corrected Joe. And it was where your story and Mrs. Nottingham's came together. By the way, I have a friend at the university who managed to crack the code."

"He did?" Jacqueline exclaimed excitedly. "What did it say?"

"It's the Humpty Dumpty nursery rhyme, but in German."

"Yes, yes," she said in a dismissive tone and a wave of her hand. "My late husband discovered that years ago, but that's not the true code. There's another code hidden in the symbols on the ball."

"The ball has no hidden code, and there is no treasure of Leuven. That was all a myth that grew up after the war. It was the ball that was the treasure all along, or rather the ball hides the treasure."

"What the hell are you talking about?" demanded Callahan.

"It so simple, really, but I didn't figure it out until just before you showed up, Callahan. The ball is a Tootsie Pop."

Joe pulled out the switch blade from his coat pocket and flicked it open. "I couldn't figure it out for the longest time. On the one hand people were willing to kill for this thing," he used the blade to point to the ball. "But on the other there was no evidence that the treasure ever existed. It all finally made sense when I rolled the ball across the desk and noticed it was wobbling. Then I recalled that a friend of mine, who had played a parlor game with a puzzle ball many years ago, said that it was lighter than a cricket ball, which is about the same weight as a baseball. This one, however, is heavier. That's when I realized that we're dealing with a Tootsie Pop."

"You're speaking in riddles," complained Jacqueline.

"It's a new type of lollypop," explained Joe as he pulled one out of Kat's desk drawer and unwrapped it. "You see it looks like a typical lollypop, but what makes it special is what's inside." Joe put the lollypop aside then took the ball from the center of the desk and began to cut a deep straight line around the circumference.

"What are you doing?" yelled Jacqueline. "Stop him!"

Callahan moved toward him but Joe raised his hand. "Relax Burt, I'm authorized," he said with a smile. He continued cutting until he had completed the circle. He then twisted the two halves of the ball in opposite directions until they separated. "Just like a Tootsie Pop," he said has he pulled the two halves apart. "There's something sweet and tasty in the center." Sid let out a long low whistle as all eyes focused on a huge, flawless yellow diamond embedded in the left half of the ball. Joe then added, "I think we're looking at the Tuscan Diamond."

"The what diamond?" asked Callahan.

"The Tuscan Diamond," Joe repeated. "It was one of the crown jewels of the Austro-Hungarian Empire. When the Hapsburgs fled Vienna at the end of the war they took their valuables with them, but in one of Europe's most famous robberies thieves stole most of crown jewels including the Tuscan Diamond. Nobody ever figured out how the stones managed to disappear, but it seems this one was hidden inside an ordinary rubber ball."

"Then the ball never led to the treasure of Leuven?" asked Jacqueline sadly.

"I'm afraid not."

"All those years my husband spent searching for the treasure, and he had it in his hands the entire time," she said in disbelief.

CHAPTER 7 – SATURDAY

"What's a stone like that worth?" asked Sid.

"Well, at the time of the heist the papers said it was worth a million bucks," replied Joe.

"Are you kidding me?" said Callahan. "How can one rock be worth that much dough?"

"It's one of the largest diamonds ever found and it's the largest yellow diamond in the world," Joe explained.

"How do you know all this?" asked Callahan.

"I lived in Paris at the time of the heist," replied Joe. "The papers were full of the details of the robbery and the missing jewels."

"But how did you know the diamond was in the ball?" asked Patel.

"I didn't," he replied. "But the only reason a solid round object would wobble as it rolls across a desk is if something was throwing its balance off. It was then I realized that whatever it was people were chasing it was undoubtedly inside the ball and not on the outside. I didn't know what was in there, but it stood to reason there was something."

"Officer," Jacqueline flashed her beautiful eyes and smile at Detective Callahan, "that ball and the diamond belong to me. They were stolen from my home in England six years ago."

"Is that a fact, ma'am?" Callahan moved closer toward the beautiful woman.

"I doubt you'd have a legitimate claim to the stone," responded Joe. "The Tuscan Diamond belongs to either the Hapsburgs or to the Austrian government." Then he added, "and Mrs. Nottingham is involved in the murder of a Greek sailor named Kyranos, who was killed last Saturday."

"I had nothing to do with that," she said indignantly.

"You did, you did," insisted Patel. "She had her *voyou* over there kill him, because she thought he had the ball."

"That's ridiculous," said Jacqueline in a soft voice as she pressed her long slim body against the side of Callahan. "I could never do such a thing."

"Ya got no evidence I killed anyone," said Honey Boy.

"I think we have plenty of evidence on you, Sweet Pea," replied Joe. "You tried to kill me here in my office and we have the bullet holes to prove it.

And there's this new thing called 'ballistics' which will allow the cops to match your gun to the slugs taken out of the dead Greek." Joe turned towards Jacqueline and explained, "Once we nail your hired muscle, he'll either give you up or get the chair."

"This is all some kind of terrible mistake," she said to Callahan. Her French accent was more pronounced than it had been moments before, making her sound more vulnerable, and even sexier. "Everything here is so confusing. I just don't understand how things work in America." She appeared completely helpless as she looked up into the eyes of the police detective.

"Now don't you worry none," replied Callahan soothingly. "I'm sure we can get all this straightened out."

"Don't be a sap, Callahan," said Sid. "You're not going to fall for that load a malarkey, are ya?"

"When I want advice from a drunk I'll talk to my old man. Now, I'm in charge of this investigation," Callahan declared, "and no one is getting railroaded on my watch. We're all going down to the station and I'll figure out who gets charged with what."

Joe took out the envelope with the five grand and handed it to the detective. "This is the money they were using to purchase the ball from me." Giving Callahan an envelope with money was inviting trouble. However he didn't want Nottingham claiming he was hiding it, so there didn't seemed to be another option.

The detective looked at the cash then did a quick count before giving off a slow whistle. "There must be two G's in here," he said with a smile. Joe realized that the detective intended to pocket most of the cash.

While giving Callahan his intimidating stare, Joe grabbed the envelope from him and took out one fifty dollars. "This should cover the cost of repairing my office," he explained before handing the envelope back.

The detective glanced around the room surveying the damage before shrugging his shoulders and pocketing the envelope. He ordered the two uniformed officers to take Honey Boy and Patel down to the station in the patrol car. Then he walked over to Joe and held out his hand. "I'll take the diamond with me," he said, shooting a nasty look at Joe. "I don't want you getting 'sticky fingers'. You and the wino need to follow us down to the station. I gotta lot of questions for you." Joe reluctantly gave

CHAPTER 7 - SATURDAY

up the rock. He watched as the detective pocketed the stone and escorted Jacqueline out of the office.

Once all their visitors had left, Sid also surveyed the damaged office. "Kat's not going to like this one little bit," he said. "I can't wait to see you try to explain it to her," he added with a smile.

The expression on Joe's face registered his deep concern. "You ok?" he asked Sid, referring to the beating he'd given his investigator. From the moment Honey Boy had come through the door, Joe knew he had to get Sid out of there or he'd become the "leverage" that Jacqueline had been talking about the day before. Acting like he detested Sid sent the message that his investigator had no value. He had to be brutal to carry the con, and it was the only idea he could come up with on the spur of the moment.

"Never better," Sid replied with a wide grin.

Joe examined the cuts and bruises on the older man's face, and felt horrible about what he'd done. The only thing he could think of to say was, "I'm so sorry."

Sid put his hand on his friend's shoulder, "Don't sweat it, boss. I knew why you were doing it. The fact is, you getting me outta there probably saved my life." Joe appreciated Sid's words but still felt miserable. He wanted to say something more but couldn't think of anything. Finally he held out his hand. Sid gave him a big smile and as he grasped Joe's hand he said softly, "Let's not tell Kat." The two men nodded as they shook hands.

[Case Epilogue] – Honey Boy Morris was found guilty of murdering the Greek sailor Kyranos and got "the chair" in the fall of '34. Avaj Patel was released after spending a week in jail and was never charged with a crime. He went back to Europe where he opened an antiques business in Paris. Among dealers and collectors he was known to specialize in stolen property, although he was never arrested.

Patel was able to avoid prosecution in Chicago because Detective Callahan, Jacqueline Nottingham, and the Tuscan Diamond all vanished. After Jacqueline left Joe's office with Callahan she continued to play the innocent victim. Her wide-eyed act, coupled with her sultry beauty, easily convinced the detective that they should find a quiet place where they could "talk" about the case. Holed up in a small hotel at the south end of the Loop, the lovely Jacqueline gave Callahan better sex than he'd ever imagined possible. After just two hours the detective went dizzy with a dame, readily agreeing to abandon his wife and three children. Burt and the stunning French beauty left for Rio de Janeiro, along with the diamond and five thousand dollars. The missing detective became headline news in Chicago. It was widely assumed that he'd fallen victim to foul play, something Joe never believed for a second.

The loving couple arrived in Rio five weeks after they left Chicago and for Burt Callahan it was the happiest time of his life. It took them three weeks to line up a diamond cutter who could break up the large yellow stone. However, when Jacqueline learned that cutting up the diamond would sacrifice half of its potential value, she began to have second thoughts. The night before the diamond was to be cut the happy couple enjoyed a lavish dinner and several bottles of expensive champagne. The next morning Jacqueline boarded the first class section of the S.S. Stella Polaris and sailed for Europe. Sadly, Burt Callahan wasn't able to accompany his sweetheart. His body was discovered two days after she sailed, when a maid at the hotel disregarded the room's Do Not Disturb sign. An autopsy revealed that the unidentified dead man had consumed a large quantity of champagne, laced with strychnine. A brief investigation followed, but the authorities were never able to identify the deceased or question any suspects. In the end, Detective Burt Callahan was buried in an unmarked grave.

After landing in Bordeaux, Jacqueline took a train to Zurich. Using the discrete services of a large Swiss bank, she made contact with numerous potential buyers. Eventually she identified one and settled on a price of 4.6 million Swiss francs. Sadly, Jacqueline died in an "accident" the night before the sale was to complete. The Tuscan Diamond disappeared and to this day it is still missing.

Afternoon

Because Detective Callahan failed to show up at the station Joe and Sid spent several fruitless hours waiting before being allowed to leave. By the time Joe got back to Warren Street, he had just enough time to shower and change before motoring to Kenilworth for the reading of Cyrus' will.

He pulled up to the McNulty's circular driveway at 4:00 on the dot. Once inside the house, he was ushered into the crowded main hall by one of

CHAPTER 7 - SATURDAY

the maids. He immediately spotted Emma standing at the other end of the room, wearing a simple black dress along with a stylish black hat and gloves. Even though it was a somber event he couldn't help but smile when he saw her.

Emma hurried over to him, wrapped an arm around his, and gently squeezed. "I'm so glad you're here," she said, the relief evident in her voice. "I've had the jitters all day, but I feel so much better now that you're with me." About thirty people were gathered in the entry hall, including many of the household staff. Vance was also there with several people in tow.

"How's everything been going?" Joe asked her.

"Well, Papa passed early yesterday afternoon and it's been hectic ever since. There's been an endless stream of phone calls from people sending their condolences. You could tell that few of the callers actually cared that he'd died. In fact, I think some of them were actually pleased. I'm afraid Papa wasn't a very popular man."

"Have you set the plans for the funeral?"

"Papa was very specific about how he wanted his funeral. He planned a short, modest service at the Union Church in Kenilworth and a simple burial. He'd purchased a double plot at the Lake Forest Cemetery many years ago, and Vance's late mother occupies half of it. We found out today that Papa recently purchased another plot at the same cemetery. But this new plot is at the other end of the property and his instructions were quite clear. He's to be buried at this new site instead of next to his wife. Poor Vance was really upset when he found out."

"How's Vance been treating you?"

"Better than I expected," she replied with a smile. "He's been very civil, and I take that as a good first step."

Just then, Theo asked that everyone move into the library so they could begin. The staff had arranged several rows of chairs for the guests to sit. Emma, with Joe escorting her, moved to the front row. The reading began with Theo recapping Cyrus' plans for his funeral. The will went on to state that he was to be buried within four days of his death and, as Emma had said, laid to rest in the recently purchased plot. Theo then read off a list of monetary gifts left by Cyrus to some of the staff.

Halfway through the will Cyrus lamented the passing of George Monroe, his loyal employee for thirty-five years, and left the sum of $8,500 to George's grandson, Adam. On hearing this, Emma leaned over and whispered, "He's planning to go to medical school you know."

Joe rolled his eyes and muttered to himself, "If he lives that long."

Theo then finished the reading with the words, "the balance of the estate including all property, cash and stock will be split evenly between his heirs, Vance McNulty and Emma O'Donnell." With that statement, the reading was complete. Joe looked over at Vance and saw a huge smile across his face. He had expected Vance to be bitter about everything but, quite to the contrary, he seemed to be a pretty happy guy. Joe escorted Emma out of the library and back into the hall. Once there, a still smiling Vance approached the two of them and asked if he could speak to Emma privately. She walked back into the library with Vance as Theo came up to Joe.

"I was instructed by Cyrus to give you this." Theo handed him a thick white envelope. Joe peaked inside and saw a stack of twenty dollar bills. "It's eleven hundred and eighty dollars."

"You over paid me. I was only supposed to get the thousand dollar bonus if I could prove or disprove Emma's claim before Cyrus died. I didn't do that."

"Cyrus believed that since you couldn't disprove her claim it was all the proof he needed. He appreciated your efforts." Joe hesitated to take the money and Theo continued, "If you don't take it, it'll just go back to the estate. I think the two heirs have plenty, don't you?"

"Why wouldn't it go to the charities?"

"The moment Cyrus died, the money in the trust became the responsibility of the board," explained Theo. "Everything that wasn't specifically put into the trust is part of the estate, and will go to the heirs."

"Is that why you didn't mention the trust in the will?"

"Precisely. It's separate from the estate. By the way, I have another case I'd like you to take on."

"What is this one about?"

"Have you ever heard of Samuel Insull?"

CHAPTER 7 – SATURDAY

"Damn, Theo," replied Joe, clearly surprised. "First Cyrus McNulty and now Samuel Insull, who's next? Rockefeller?"

Theo ignored Joe's remark and continued. "There's been a break-in at Insull's house in Vernon Hills."

"Did the thieves get away with much?"

"Nothing of monetary value," replied Theo. "However some very important papers *might* be missing. Let me give you some background. Samuel Insull is being investigated by a congressional committee on the activities of his 'holding companies'. Insull invented the concept of a holding company."

Joe looked at the lawyer with a blank stare. "Humor me Theo, pretend I have no idea what a holding company is."

Theo laughed and explained, "A holding company is an entity that doesn't actually employ people or sell products. It exist simply to own large chunks of other companies. They borrow money from banks to buy stock in these other companies. When the value of this stock goes up, they borrow even more money, and buy even more stock. They have no assets other than the stock they've bought. Through several of these holding companies Mr. Insull now controls half a billion dollars' worth of Chicago-based firms. Among these companies are the "L" and the electric company. Unfortunately, the value of the stock in the holding companies he owns was hit hard by the market crash in '29. So his holding companies' debt to the banks is now greater than the value of the stock they hold. Several of Mr. Insull's holding companies might go broke, and that will ruin a lot of people. To make matters worse, if Roosevelt wins in November the pressure on the guy will intensify because one of Roosevelt's key supporters in Illinois is Harold Ickes. Let's just say that Ickes and Insull don't play well together."

"So you want me to recover the missing papers, which I assume have something to do with these holding companies?"

"I can't confirm or deny that any papers are missing, or even exist. The only thing I can tell you is that *perhaps* some papers were stolen, and *if* they were, I need you to recover them. Also, Mr. Insull and his wife are not aware that there was a break-in at their house because they are both out of the country. If Mr. Insull *was* in the country, he could be served with a congressional subpoena compelling him to testify before congress.

Since he's *not* in the country, he can't be served. So, *if* you happen to see someone you *think* is Mr. Insull when you're up at this house investigating the break-in, rest assured it isn't him. Even if the guy looks like him, talks like him, and walks like him, it's not him." Theo gave Joe a quick wink then smiled.

Joe shook his head and returned the smile. "Ok, I'll try and get up to Vernon Hills on Monday morning. When I'm there, if I run into a Samuel Insull impersonator, should I throw him out of the house?"

"No, and don't throw out the woman who's impersonating his wife, Gladys, either," chuckled Theo. "You'll have to excuse me. I have to go talk to Adam about paying him the money Cyrus left him."

As Theo left, Joe looked again at the envelope with the cash and grinned. The extra thousand bucks he'd just received should be more than enough to set up the new scholarship at St. Jerome's for Mickey. He pocketed the envelope just as Emma returned from her meeting with Vance. "Everything jake?" he asked.

"Yes, everything's fine. I was afraid he wanted me to sign more papers for the trust."

"What did he want?"

"Oh, he just wanted to talk about setting a date for the trust's first board meeting. He sure was in a good mood."

"Remarkably good," agreed Joe.

Evening

Most of the people who had gathered at the main house for the reading started to drift away almost immediately after it was over, but a few lingered for a while. Emma and Joe left the mansion shortly after the last guest departed. It was nearly 6:00 when he pulled his car up to the guesthouse and walked Emma to the front steps. As they reached the door, she turned and gently put her arms around his neck but then abruptly pulled away.

"What on earth is that?" she asked, clearly startled by the lump she'd felt as she pressed her body against his.

"Oh, sorry," he responded, showing her the revolver he had in his pocket.

She giggled. "I thought you didn't like guns."

CHAPTER 7 - SATURDAY

"Actually, it's bullets I hate, but I needed this earlier today for another case I was working on."

"Well you won't need it now," she said softly as she slipped the gun back in his coat and moved her delicious red lips toward his. He hesitated initially because he'd been struggling to maintain control for days, but now with her body pressed against his he could no longer think of a reason to resist. He pulled her closer, moved his lips just inches from hers, and finally they kissed. She pressed her mouth urgently against his and wrapped her arms around his neck. As she did, what little resistance remaining inside him completely evaporated.

Their kiss was long, deep, and passionate, but rather than relieve the pent up desire inside him it only intensified. They continued to kiss for several more minutes until, eventually, Joe whispered in her ear, "Is that offer to make coffee still open?"

The clock on the nightstand by the large four poster bed showed 10:10 pm. They had been "brewing coffee" for over three hours, and Joe was exhausted. As much as he wanted to continue laying with her, he knew he couldn't stay any longer. She was now an heiress, and held a place in Chicago society. There were appearances that had to be maintained, which meant he needed to leave before the hour grew later. Reluctantly, and quietly, he got up. After dressing, he sat on the edge of the bed for a few minutes, gazing at the beautiful woman who was still sound asleep.

In the years that had passed since his heart had been broken there had been times when his need grew so strong it overwhelmed him. When that happened, he had sought relief in the arms of different women. During those times he could see only Wendy's face. Afterwards, when the deed was done and the need fulfilled, there would still be the ever-present emptiness clawing at him. Tonight, though, there had only been Emma, and the emptiness he'd felt for so long was gone. He gently brushed back the soft red hair from her face and kissed her tenderly on the cheek before leaving the guesthouse.

It was pitch black outside and raining heavily during his drive back to Warren Street, but Joe was thinking more about Emma than the weather. He pulled up to his building at 11:00 pm. When he entered his apartment he heard his phone ringing and raced to answer it. He had thought it might be her, but it was Kat.

"I've been trying to get hold of you all evening," she explained, "but your line's been busy the whole time."

"Sorry, Kat, that was probably Mrs. Kubik on the party line. That woman can talk for hours." In truth he was glad the line had been busy, otherwise he'd have had to explain to her why he hadn't picked up. He wasn't ready for that yet.

"Well, Manny phoned me from New York. He said that your hunch about checking the theatrical agencies paid off. It seems Miss O'Donnell tried her hand at acting and had been using the stage name Margot St. Clair. She landed some minor parts in a few plays, but nothing you'd call a serious role. Her current bio says that she's from Boston, but according to Manny a lot of young actresses from the mid-west claim to be from Philadelphia or Boston. They think it makes them sound more sophisticated. He found a secretary that works at one of the agencies who said she thought Emma's original bio listed her home town as Wayne 'something-or-other' in Indiana."

"Was it Fort Wayne?" he asked.

"Manny said that initially the woman was saying Waynesburg, but then admitted that she was probably mixing that up with Pittsburgh."

"For Christ sake," he replied, shaking his head.

"Language, Joseph," she retorted.

"But Pittsburgh is nowhere near Indiana," he said, in his defense.

Kat continued, "I did point that out to Manny and he said that to a New Yorker any place past Jersey City is pretty much the same place. The only thing the woman was sure of was that it had 'Wayne' in the name. He also pointed out that we were lucky she remembered Margot at all. He said the talent agency gets hundreds of girls coming through each week, and the secretary typically doesn't remember any of them."

"So why did she remember her?"

"Broadway gossip," Kat explained. "Word was that Margot St. Claire was seeing some producer a while back. The woman at the agency liked to keep tabs on who was sleeping with whom."

"Thanks for the update Kat. You'll be happy to know that we can close the books on this one, and we got paid already."

CHAPTER 7 - SATURDAY

He was about to hang up when Kat added, "Don't forget about tomorrow. You missed last Sunday and Rose telephoned me today and made me promise to remind you to be there."

"Damn," he said to himself under his breath, though apparently not soft enough.

"Language, Joseph," she replied.

"You didn't happen to hear the score of the Sox game today?" he asked, changing the subject.

Kat had thought he might want to know. "They got shut out, six to nothing."

He hung his head in despair. That was eight losses in a row. This was shaping up to be one lousy year.

After he finished with Kat, Joe lay in bed. Despite the fact that he was exhausted he couldn't sleep, so eventually he stopped trying. Resting an ashtray on his chest, he finished off a pack of cigarettes while listening to Jazz being broadcast on Deutsche Welle from Berlin. It was pouring rain outside and he could hear thunder and see flashes of lightening through his bedroom window. He paid little attention to either the storm or the music from his radio because his thoughts were of Vance, Cyrus, the Trust, and Emma. Even though the case was closed he had this uneasy feeling that something was wrong. Somehow this case just didn't add up. He took another long drag on his cigarette, slowly exhaled, and then it hit him.

"It doesn't add up," he mumbled to himself, "it's all about the math." He sat up on the edge of the bed, knocking the ashtray to the floor as he reached for his phone. Because of the late hour, Mrs. Kubik wasn't on the line, so he was able to immediately place a call to Theo, at his house. His wife answered, making it clear that she was none too pleased about being awakened, before handing the phone to her husband.

"Do you have any idea what time it is?" Theo, like his wife, was not happy about the interruption to his sleep.

Joe ignored his question. "What happens to the trust now that Cyrus is dead?"

"For Christ sake, Joe, I've explained this to you several times," he snapped. "The board will run the trust."

"But there will now be seven votes on the board, right?"

"Theo was still a bit groggy from sleep, but thought for a moment and replied, "Yes. The three charities each have one vote apiece, and Emma and Vance as co-chairs of the board will have two votes each. So yes," repeated Theo, "three plus four, makes seven. Now I'm going back to sleep."

"If Vance wanted to liquidate the trust and distribute the money to himself, what would he need to do?"

"What?" Theo was angered by the stupid question and unwilling to put up with it any longer. "I'm hanging up. If you want to talk about this, you can phone me in the morning."

"WAIT!" shouted Joe into the line. "Just humor me, please. It's important. What would Vance have to do?"

Theo heard Joe's plea and pulled the handset back to his ear. "He would need to have a majority of the board members vote with him. There are now seven votes on the board, so there needs to be at least four votes for any distribution to be made."

"So it's possible that Vance could trick Emma into liquidating the trust?"

Theo's eyes suddenly popped wide open and he shot up in bed. "Yes," he replied softly.

"Emma told me that Vance had her sign a bunch of papers."

"That's not possible," said Theo. "Steven Simkins from my firm is the attorney for the trust. He's the only attorney the trust has ever had, and he hasn't drawn up any papers for the trust in weeks."

"Did you know the people who were with Vance at the reading of the will today?"

"I knew one of them. He's an attorney who represents Vance. He was the one who reviewed the letter Vance signed, acknowledging Emma as his half-sister."

"Of course, how could I have been so blind? Cyrus didn't outsmart his son." Joe rubbed his forehead and continued, "it was the other way around. Vance never intended to deny that Emma was his sister. He needed Emma to be his sister. Even if the old man hadn't moved the extra million into his estate, Vance still would have accepted Emma as his sister. He needed her votes."

CHAPTER 7 – SATURDAY

"You mean he was planning this?"

"Most likely from the day she showed up at the house," explained Joe. "He could do the math. He knew right away that if Emma was accepted as an heir she would get two votes on the board. Her votes could tip the balance in his favor. What do you want to bet that Emma was conned into signing papers distributing the money in the trust to Vance?" asked Joe.

"If he had those papers signed just after Cyrus died on Friday," explained Theo, "they might have had time to get to the bank and transfer money on the same day."

"If they did try and pull a fast one and raid the trust after the old man died, do Emma and the board have any recourse?"

"Possibly," replied Theo, "if Emma was tricked into signing those papers she could claim fraud."

"But how could we prove it?"

"Well, it may not be too difficult, actually. If all the money in the trust was suddenly transferred to Vance it shouldn't be too difficult to demonstrate to a judge that it was done through fraud. Unless …," Theo's voice suddenly trailed off.

"Unless what?"

"… unless Emma doesn't file a complaint," continued Theo.

"Of course she'll file a complaint," insisted Joe.

"Precisely," said Theo, "and Vance would be an idiot not to know that."

"So how could he stop her?"

"If she were to die in an accident, she could never claim that Vance had tricked her into signing."

Suddenly it became clear to both men that Emma was in grave danger. With her death Vance's revenge on his father would be complete. He would have gotten the millions that he felt were rightfully his, and also murdered his father's bastard child.

"Theo, you live closer than I do. Can you get to the guesthouse right away?"

"I'm on my way," he replied and there was a click as the line went dead.

Joe tried to phone Emma next but there was no answer, so he got hold of the operator and asked to be connected to the Kenilworth police. Once through, he gave his name and asked the officer on duty to send a patrol car to the McNulty guesthouse, explaining that a woman's life was in danger. He then threw on some clothes, grabbed his coat, and ran out of his apartment.

CHAPTER EIGHT

SUNDAY

How ridiculous and how strange to be surprised by anything which happens in life -Marcus Aurelius

Morning

It was well past midnight as Joe raced his Ford towards the McNulty guesthouse in the teeming rain. The roads were slick and he almost lost control of his car twice. After turning north, along Sheridan Road he could see that there was an accident up ahead. Fortunately, it was just an overturned Speed Wagon blocking the southbound lane and it didn't slow him down much. The traffic heading southbound, however, was badly snarled.

Six minutes later Joe pulled up to the guesthouse where he found several police cars and a fire truck parked out front. His heart sank deep into his stomach when he noticed smoke coming from the upstairs windows. He dashed from his car through the rain and into the guesthouse. Inside the main hall several firemen were moving up the marble stairs. In the center of the room, laying on the hard stone floor, was a body covered by a white sheet with a police officer kneeling beside it. Joe was too late. He walked slowly towards the officer, knelt down beside him, and asked, "Do they know what happened?"

"It looks like an accident," explained the policeman. "A fire started upstairs. The victim was racing out of the bedroom, tripped in the upstairs hall, and went right over the second floor banister," he said, pointing to the balcony two floors up. "Then landed here and broke his neck."

"*His* neck?" Joe repeated.

"Yeah." The officer pulled back the sheet to reveal the face of Vance McNulty.

"Where's the woman who was staying here?"

"I'm not sure. I just got here a few minutes ago, but I know that some people went up to the main house," he replied.

Joe ran back to his car and raced up to the mansion. There were two patrol cars in the circular driveway as well as Theo's car. When he entered the building, he saw Theo standing in the hallway next to two uniformed policeman and a plainclothes detective.

"Is she ok?" Joe asked urgently.

"She's fine," Theo assured him. "She's shaken up, but fine."

The relief on Joe's face was obvious as he took off his hat and coat and asked anxiously, "Where is she?"

"In the library," Theo answered. Joe ran to the library and found Emma sitting on a leather couch with a drink in her hand. He tossed his hat and coat on an empty chair and Emma immediately put down her drink and rushed towards him. She was wearing a beige silk dressing gown with a matching robe and was shaking slightly as she threw her arms around his neck.

"I never should have left you tonight," he said.

"How could you know? How could anyone have known?" she replied as tears welled up in her eyes.

Joe looked at her, wiped away the tears, and kissed her softly on the lips. After holding her for several minutes, he walked her over to the couch where they sat down.

"I really needed this," she said as she picked up the glass and took a full gulp. "Good thing Papa kept some bourbon here in the library."

"What happened?"

"When I woke up, you had left. So I went down to the kitchen to fix something to eat. That's when the phone rang. I thought it might be you, but it was Vance. He said he had something he wanted to talk to me about and asked if the maid was there. I told him it was her night off. He said it would only take a minute and would I mind if he came over. It was late, but he said it was important, so I agreed. Five minutes later he was at the front door." She paused, took another sip of her drink, and continued. "He told me that in the past when he visited Papa he always stayed at the guesthouse. This time, because of Papa's failing health, he decided to stay at the main house. He said the last time he stayed here he'd left some important papers in one of the closets upstairs, and asked he could go and get them. I told him to go ahead, so we went upstairs together, but before I realized what was happening, he pushed me into a closet and locked the door." Her hands were trembling as she paused to take another sip of bourbon. "At first I just thought he was being mean. I banged on the door and yelled at him to let me out. After a few minutes I smelled smoke and I became really scared. Then I heard a scream and that's when I panicked. I started screaming as well, and then I began pounding and kicking the door as hard as I could, until it suddenly popped open."

Joe could see that her hands and feet were red and swollen. "I couldn't see any flames, but there was thick smoke everywhere," she continued. "I covered my mouth and ran out of the house. Just as I came out a police car pulled up the driveway. I didn't even know that Vance was dead until the policeman told me there was a body in the main hall. They also said that you had sent them," she added with a smile. "How did you know I was in trouble?"

"It took a while, but it finally dawned on me," he answered. "It was those papers he had you sign after Cyrus died. They transferred all the money in the trust to Vance. He needed you to sign them. He also needed you to die in an accident, so you couldn't claim later that you had been tricked. Your 'accidental' death in a fire was just what he needed." Emma shivered slightly and Joe wrapped his arms around her, partly to warm her but mostly to protect her.

While he was holding her, Theo walked in. "I've talked it over with the police and they've agreed that Emma can come down to the station first thing tomorrow morning to give her statement. They want the two of us to go with them to Wilmette and give ours tonight."

As Theo walked back out to the hallway, Emma pulled on Joe's arm and begged, "Joe, can't we stay together, please? You could give your statement tomorrow when I give mine."

"It's ok, Dollface," he replied as he rose from the couch, putting on his hat and coat. "I'll be back before you know it, and I'll make sure they park a couple of patrol cars here until I'm back."

Emma's face showed how frightened she was. She stood up and hugged him. "I really don't want you to go," she said, pleading with her eyes.

"Now don't you worry about a thing," he replied with a smile. "I'll be back in no time, and when I am you can tell me all about Margo St. Claire." He had meant the last part as a joke, but he could feel Emma's body stiffen when he said the name.

"I'm afraid I don't know who that is," she said, turning her head and stepping quickly away from him.

"I'd be a pretty poor detective if I hadn't found out about your life in New York," he replied, still smiling.

Emma grabbed a cigarette from the silver box on the table in front of the couch, lit it, and took a long drag. "I have no idea what you're talking about," she professed nervously. Her response was not what Joe had expected. Was she concerned that people would think less of her because she'd been an actress?

"I know all about it," he said before he turned and called out into the hallway. "Theo, I need to talk with you before you leave."

As he was about to call out again, Emma quickly stubbed out her cigarette, raced back to him, and wrapped her arms around him. "It's all ours now darling. Don't you see, all of it is ours," she whispered. Joe's mind raced as he tried to make sense of what she was saying. Again, Emma pleaded to him softly. "We have everything we could ever want, sweetheart. Don't spoil it now."

From the hallway, he heard Theo call back to him. "Did you need me for something?"

Joe continued to stare at her, completely baffled, but managed a reply to Theo. "Yes, you can't go yet – there's a problem you need to know about."

"I'll be there in a minute," Theo answered as he continued to speak with the police detective.

Suddenly Joe realized what Emma was saying. All of the money from the trust had been transferred to Vance and since she now was his only living heir, she would inherit everything – the stock, the cash, the houses, the yacht. The entire ninety million. But why was she so afraid? What had he said that caused her to rush to him like this? When the answer came to him it was like a punch in the gut. "Margo St. Claire isn't your stage name," he said to her softly. "It's your real name."

The room fell silent and there was a pause that seemed to hang in the air for an eternity. Joe was staring into her eyes, and she back into his. Then … CLICK. The sound was unmistakable. Joe looked down at the left side of his coat, where he could see the bulge from the snub-nosed revolver pointing at him from inside his pocket. CLICK … CLICK … CLICK. Emma's face froze as she realized that the pistol was empty. She immediately released it, letting it fall back into his coat, before stepping away from him.

After a few more seconds of silence the stunned private detective said softly, "I did tell you that I hated loaded guns."

Once more, silence dominated the room while the two of them continued to stare at each other. He with a wounded look on his face, and she with fury flashing in her eyes. Moments later Theo entered the room and asked, "What is it you wanted to tell me?" The last few words of his sentence trailed off as he registered the tension in the room.

Joe turned towards him and letting out a breath that he'd been holding for nearly a minute. "Well, I wanted to tell you that there's a bad accident on Sheridan Road that we need to avoid, but it seems there's something else I need to tell you." Emma watched as Joe's face slowly drained of all emotion. The same instincts that had enabled him to push aside the horror of Chance's death during the war now took control as he pushed aside the intense pain of her betrayal. His eyes returned to the woman who, just moments before, he was certain he'd fallen for. He cleared his throat before continuing, "Theo, I'd like you to meet Margot St. Claire." From that moment Joe never again referred to the woman in front of him as "Emma".

"I'm guessing Margot here is from Waynesburg, Indiana. It is Waynesburg, right Margot?" he asked, without waiting for an answer. "I actually had a case with a runaway from Waynesburg a while back. It's not much of a town really, just a couple of crossroads. If that's where you're from, it shouldn't take the police long to find someone who'll recognize your photo."

Theo had no idea what was happening, but when he heard the word "police" he waved the detective and the two uniformed officers into the library. Within seconds, all four men were standing in the doorway listening to Joe.

"Besides hailing from Waynesburg," he continued, "Margot is also an actress who was living in New York. It was there that she met Vance McNulty." Joe's mind was now rapidly piecing together the case from the clues that had always been there. Everything began to make sense now. Everything fit. "It started when Vance got ahold of his father's journal a while back. He read the part about the affair with the maid, and about having a half-sister. I first suspected that Vance had seen the journal at our initial meeting. He mentioned his father's 'Irish whore' and the fact that the woman had been a maid. From what I'd been told he shouldn't have known anything about Maggie. He also ridiculed his father's attempt at poetry, yet Cyrus told me that the only poem he had ever written in his life was in his journal. So it seemed fairly obvious that Vance had read it. I have to admit," he explained as he looked over at Theo, "his reading the journal didn't seem to be all that important. I just couldn't see how he would benefit from his half-sister suddenly appearing. The answer, however, was right in front of me the whole time. You see, Vance decided that if he couldn't stop his father from putting his inheritance into the trust, he would take control of the trust. To do that he needed to control the board, and to control the board he needed another relative. What made the plan so perfect was that he actually did have a half-sister. If he brought in the real Emma, however, she'd have a legitimate claim to the estate. So, even if she went along with his plan, he'd have to split the money with her. His solution was to bring in a fake Emma and, through her, gain the extra two votes he needed to take control of the trust. Then, all of the money would be his."

"He used his contacts in New York to 'cast' for the role of Emma. Margot here got the part." Joe looked over at her, "You know, I never would have thought about you being an actress if you hadn't made that comment about 'the Scottish play'. Looks like Macbeth really is bad luck." Margot was sitting in a chair, nervously puffing on another cigarette and trying to ignore his summation.

"Vance had to find just the right girl," Joe continued. "He had no idea what the real Emma was like, but Cyrus' journal described Maggie in loving detail. So he decided to model Emma after her. Margot was perfect for the role, and she and Vance prepared and rehearsed their parts carefully. They had Margot pose as Emma for many months in New York, getting a room at a boarding house and making friends with everyone in the building. Vance even hired someone to pose as an insurance investigator looking into the traffic accident that killed poor Maggie. The investigator collected all the background information on Emma and Maggie's life in Fort Wayne. This fake insurance guy also made sure to give the local priest Margot's address in New York. That way the priest could send her the box of Maggie's personal effects, which included Emma's birth certificate."

Joe looked over at Margot and admitted, "Your meticulous preparation and rehearsal paid off. In all our conversations and hours we spent together you only made one mistake. You said that your mother and her parents moved to Fort Wayne from Gary when she was just a baby, but the town of Gary didn't exist when Maggie was little. It was built by a steel company in '06. That slip up should have made me suspicious, but by the time you made that mistake you already had me wrapped around your finger. I just couldn't see anything past your stunning blue eyes."

"Vance wasn't nearly as well rehearsed as you were," Joe continued. "Besides making the mistakes that showed he'd read his father's journal, he also slipped up when he called Emma a 'tart from New York'. There was no way he should have known you'd been living in New York. Supposedly he hadn't even talked to you. Was it Vance who was the producer you were rumored to be having an affair with?" Joe asked, not really expecting a response. "What did he promise you, Margot? Money, fame on the stage, or maybe a bit of both? Not a bad payout, but it wasn't what you wanted, was it? I'll bet you realized the first time you heard his plan that after Cyrus was dead and the trust was stripped, all that stood between you and ninety million was Vance. So you had to make sure that something unfortunate happened to him," he said coldly.

Margot rose from her chair and faced the men in front of her. "I don't have to sit here and listen to this fairy tale. This has been a very traumatic evening for me and in case you've all forgotten someone tried to kill me. I've been shattered by the experience. If you'll excuse me, I'm going upstairs to lie down."

Margot began to move forward but the police detective said firmly, "Please take a seat, Miss. This is a criminal investigation and you aren't at liberty to leave at this time. Go on, Mr. Lorde." Margot reluctantly fell back down into the chair.

"When Cyrus died Vance didn't need to trick you into signing the papers that stripped the trust. That was all part of the plan, and it worked perfectly. The reading of the will was Vance's moment of triumph. That's why he seemed so happy. He had already raided the trust and transferred the funds on Friday. He had the last laugh on his father and he just couldn't contain his excitement."

Margot continued to squirm in her chair, clearly uncomfortable. She was aware that all eyes in the room were squarely on her, and she pulled hard on what was left of her cigarette while staring down at her shoes.

"Vance pulled you aside after the reading of the will because he wanted to see you tonight," Joe continued. "That's when you put your plan into motion. You arranged to meet him late in the evening at the guesthouse. You made sure to give the maid the night off so when he showed up you'd be alone. Vance must have been celebrating for hours before he arrived. I'll bet he was so blinded by liquor and lust that he didn't even realize you were maneuvering him to the railing on the second floor landing. Once he was in position, you simply pushed him over the banister. Then you started a fire to make it look like he tried to kill you, and even pounded and kicked on one of the closet doors until your hands and feet were swollen. I have to admit, that last bit was a nice touch," he said with a hint of admiration.

Joe continued, "There was no reason for anyone to suspect you. After all, it was Vance who had arranged everything. It was Vance who had laid out the plan, Vance who hired the attorneys to write up the documents, Vance who had hired the phony insurance agent, and in the end it was Vance and not you who stripped the trust. As far as everyone was concerned, you didn't even know that the trust had been raided."

"You know it's really quite funny," he said with a shake of his head. "At first we all thought the old man had outsmarted his son, and then we thought the son had outsmarted his father, but all along it was really you who had outsmarted everyone."

"You have no proof for any of this," Margot protested loudly.

"I don't think it will be all that difficult to prove, Margot. Like I said earlier, Waynesburg is a small town. And it shouldn't be too hard to find people back in the Theater District in New York that can identify you and confirm your relationship with Vance. Then again, you knew that, didn't you? Which is why you tried to kill me just now, after you heard me say your real name."

With Joe's last statement, the detective from Kenilworth had heard enough, "I'm afraid I'll have to place you under arrest on suspicion of murder, ma'am. You're going to have to come with us down to the station."

Joe approached Margot, took hold of her harm and pulled her out of the chair. "Hey, look at the bright side, kiddo," he said sarcastically, "now we get to go down to the station together, just like you wanted."

Margot looked at him with utter contempt. "No, the bright side is that I won't have to let you touch me again," she said angrily, before spitting in his face.

Joe used his handkerchief to wipe himself off. "She's all yours," he said as he used her arm to push her over towards the detective.

After several hours at the police station the pain Joe had felt when he learned the truth about Margot began to subside, and he had Margot herself to thank for that. After her arrest she stopped playing the role of "Emma", and her true personality came to the surface. Gone was the girl who brought sunshine into any room and spoke with a soft lilt in her voice. In her place was the cold, calculating, venomous woman that she truly was.

Joe arrived back at his flat just before sunup. He lay awake in bed smoking his Chesterfields and thinking about what had happened that night. It wasn't simply Emma's betrayal that kept him from falling asleep, however. There was something else gnawing at him. Something that made him question who he was and what he believed. Laying there, he could hear her voice whisper to him over and over, "It's all ours now darling ... we have everything we could ever want." And that was the rub. If she hadn't tried to kill him, and had continued to be "Emma", would he still have done the right thing? He wanted to believe that he would have, but deep down he wasn't so sure. If, as they say, every man has his price, then it may well be that Emma and ninety million was his.

[Case Epilogue] – *First thing Monday morning Theo took the necessary legal actions to have the ninety million dollars Vance stripped from the trust returned. Once that was done, he hired Joe to find out what had happened to the real Emma O'Donnell? Her neighbors in Fort Wayne confirmed that she'd indeed gone to New York, so Joe had Manny start a search for her there. Within a week he'd tracked her down. It seems that when Emma ran away from home with her piano player, she had in fact found her prince charming. The two of them had gotten married in New York not long after they ran away together. When Manny found her, she was five months pregnant with their second child. Emma and her mother had not spoken for several years because they had fought when Maggie had found out about the marriage. Until Theo broke the news to her, Emma didn't know that her mother had died or that Cyrus McNulty had been her father. At the time of their marriage, her husband had given up the life of a traveling musician and had started a small business tuning and repairing pianos. Unfortunately, the Depression had taken its toll and his business had failed. The young couple was desperate for money, so the news that Emma had inherited a two million dollars estate, with an annual salary of $65,000 was, to say the least, hard to believe. It took Theo quite a bit of persuading to get Emma to understand that she was now on "Easy Street".*

As Joe had predicted, it didn't take long for the police to confirm Margot's identity and hometown. As the investigation continued, the police were able to confirm virtually all of the facts that Joe had laid out, including the affair between Margot and Vance. After talking with the maid who had been working in the McNulty guesthouse, they learned that Margot had even measured the height of the second floor hallway banister.

Margot stood trial for fraud and murder in fall of '32. The prosecution's case was strong and they had numerous witnesses testifying against her, though Joe wasn't one of them. The prosecutor felt that his case was strong and that Joe's relationship with the defendant would compromise his testimony. He also worried that putting Joe on the stand would allow the defense to spin his testimony into a "lover's quarrel".

Upon seeing all the evidence, Margot's attorney agreed with the prosecution. The case against his client was far too strong and he urged her to cut a deal to avoid the death penalty, but Margot would have none of it. The principal witness for the defense was Margot herself. When she testified she again assumed the persona of Emma. Using the sweet and alluring voice that had easily seduced Joe, she admitted to the jury that she had pretended to be Cyrus' illegitimate daughter. She explained that she didn't do it for money, but to make an old man's last days on earth happy. Cyrus' journals weren't destroyed, as he had instructed, because they became evidence in the murder case. The defense was able to read passages to the jury that spoke of the old man's anguish over casting out his true love. Margot made herself out to be a young, naive girl from Waynesburg, Indiana who had been tricked by Cyrus' evil son in his ruthless attempt to get his hands on his father's millions. She was a compelling witness and made the whole thing sound like a terrible misunderstanding. In the end, the all-male jury found her not guilty on all charges.

After her release from jail Margot had no desire to stay in Chicago, sharing Vance's opinion that it was a "cultural desert". She had already tried New York with no success, so she headed west to Hollywood. When she arrived, she changed her name to Vivian St. Cloud. Just a few months after stepping off the train, she met and seduced a very successful movie producer, fifteen years her senior. The producer was married at the time but that didn't stop the couple from beginning a torrid affair. Five months after a "mysterious" telephone call alerted the producer's wife about the affair, the couple divorced, and Vivian was married. After her wedding she quickly settled into a rich and glamorous lifestyle. She and her husband were "happily" married for forty-two years and Vivian had three children – none of them his.

Late Morning

"Shit," Joe muttered under his breath after looking over at the alarm clock by his bed. He'd forgotten to wind it last night, so it had stopped several hours ago. He glanced at his wristwatch, saw that it was 11:20, and realized that he was going to be late. "Shit, shit, shit," he repeated, this time in a much louder voice. It took him forty minutes to get washed, shaved, dressed, and out the door. The heavy rain from the previous night had ended several hours earlier and racing down the apartment steps he was greeted by a warm sun and crystal clear skies. There was also a fresh breeze that kept the smell of the Stock Yards well to the south.

Early Afternoon

On a beautiful Sunday afternoon it was fairly common for people to pack the family into their car and head to a park or the countryside to enjoy the scenery and fresh air. Unfortunately, these "Sunday Drivers" were easily distracted and very slow. Consequently, getting stuck behind them as Joe currently was meant the journey to the Kenwood section of the city was taking longer than normal. He tried several alternate routes, but every street seemed to be blocked by the same old black Ford, packed with people, and slowly motoring in front of him.

While stuck in traffic, he thought about what promised to be a busy week ahead. Theo needed him to go to Vernon Hills to start an investigation into Samuel Insull's missing papers. Then, Jane Addams over at Hull House needed to see him, and Miss Addams was not the sort of person to ask for help unless it was a serious issue. And finally, Pudge was still missing, and god only knew what that was about.

Eventually he pulled up to the beautiful three-story brick home near the corner of 48th Street and the South Parkway. He quickly climbed out of his car and dashed up the steps to the front door. It was 1:15 when he finally entered the house. Looking down the hallway past the stairs he could see and hear people at the oversized kitchen table. There were several conversations going on simultaneously, with occasional laughter sprinkled through the voices.

Joe walked toward the kitchen and above the conversations he heard Miss Ella call out. "Is that you, Joseph?"

"Yes, ma'am."

All conversations stopped, and half a dozen different voices called out to welcome him. Then Miss Ella added, "You do realize, Joseph, that Sunday dinner starts at one?"

"Yes ma'am. I'm sorry. I had a late night last night."

"Were you with Emma?" asked Rose with a sly smile. Sam and Arthur made an "ooooh"' sound in the background after she spoke.

"As a matter of fact, I was. It's a long story," he added as he entered the room.

Miss Ella's large kitchen was bright, cheerful, and filled with delicious aromas. She was sitting at the end of a table that seated eight, and her

CHAPTER 8 - SUNDAY

husband Arthur was sitting at the opposite end. Rose and Sam were both on the far side of the table with an empty chair between them. Aunt Ester and Uncle Willie, along with someone whose back was turned toward Joe, were seated on the near side.

Joe walked over to Miss Ella and gave her a kiss on the cheek, then did the same to Aunt Ester before shaking hands with both Uncle Wille and Arthur. He moved towards the empty seat and, as he approached, he looked over at Rose and saw that she wore an even bigger smile than usual. Only then did he see why.

"Joseph," said Miss Ella, "I'd like you to meet Adam Monroe. Rose has invited him to join us today. They met at the White City Roller Rink, earlier this week."

It was the same young man who Joe had met briefly at the McNulty estate. He immediately glanced over at the smiling Rose who winked at him before adding, "Isn't it just swell that Adam could join us for Sunday dinner?"

"Just swell," Joe replied as he flashed Adam a half smile. He leaned over and kissed Rose on the cheek. "Very clever, Princess," he whispered in her ear.

"You know, Joseph," said Aunt Ester, "Adam is a graduate of Tuskegee, and he's going to attend medical school in the fall."

"He's one of the Talented Tenth I keep telling you about," added Arthur. "You mark my words, it's young men like Adam here who are going to lead our next generation."

"You don't say," replied Joe, who could see that Rose's eyes were now fixed on Adam.

Sam looked up from his mashed potatoes with a quizzical expression on his face. "Am I missing something?" he whispered to Joe.

"I'll fill you in later," Joe quietly replied.

Ella May Hughes looked across her table as the people in her kitchen laughed, talked, and enjoyed themselves. It seemed surreal now, as she looked back on it, like a wonderful dream laced with a horrific nightmare. The only world she had known had come crashing down the night those hooded men rode up to their farm, lynched her husband and burned their farm to the ground. When she fled Tylertown, Mississippi, and arrived in

Chicago, she had just four dollars and twenty-seven cents in her pocket and a child in her arms. Walking out of the old Central Station and onto Michigan Avenue she was cold, tired, hungry, and so very frightened. With no idea where to go, or what to do, she was convinced that God had forsaken her. But it was when everything seemed hopeless that she found hope. At the station a man from the Salvation Army had told her about Hull House, and it was there she found sanctuary and began to plan for the future. A future for herself, for her son Samuel, and for her unborn child.

When she gave birth several months later, the horror of that murderous night in Mississippi came racing back with the realization that the baby wasn't her late husband's. Instead, he was the son of one of the hooded men who had raped her. Her initial reaction was horror and rejection, but it was Jane Addams and Father Frank who counseled her that the sins of that wicked night shouldn't rest on an innocent child. They told her that in time she would come to understand this. At first, she didn't believe that could ever happen but as she watched the boy grow she came to realize that they were right. Both Joe's height and build were gifts from her father. It was his eyes, however – her mother's powerful gray eyes – that made Ella May finally understand.

Five years after arriving in Chicago Ella May met, fell in love with, and married Arthur Hughes. The two of them built a wonderful life together, and in '09 their daughter Rose was born. At the urging of Jane and Father Frank, Ella May stayed a part of her son's life, and it was Father Frank who had found a way to bring her family together many years later, when Joe returned from Europe.

Joe sat down between his two siblings and began to fill his plate. He soon became immersed in the conversations at the table. Sunday dinner was the one time when, without realizing it, the pain, frustrations, and even heartache of the previous week could for the moment be set aside. It was the one time of the week when he felt the most joy, the most relaxed, and the most love. It was also the one time of the week when he didn't miss Paris at all.

THE END

FIELD NOTES

Chicago – As an overview, there are 3.4 million residents in America's second largest city – half of the total population of the State of Illinois. It sits at a crucial junction of the country's main transportation links, with the convergence of key water, rail, and road networks. Stretching to the west for a thousand miles are the Great Plains, which provide much of the country's farming and meat production. And for seven hundred miles to the east lies the bulk of the industrial, financial, and political infrastructure of the nation.

The city of Chicago is broken up into neighborhoods with most dominated by a different ethnic group. Irish, Italian, Jewish, Ukrainian, Armenian, German, African, Hispanic, Polish, Chinese, and Russian, just to name a few. In short there's a place for everyone, and everyone is in their place.

Politics – The mayor of Chicago is Anton Cermak. He's only been in office for 13 months, but the democratic "machine" he's building will run the city for generations. Cermak replaced "Big Bill" Thompson, the leader of a long serving and hopelessly corrupt Republican administration. Thompson also had close ties to Al Capone and the Outfit. Corruption runs rampant in the city at virtually all levels. As mayor, Cermak wants to crack down on corruption. His main goal, however, is to implement a progressive agenda that will try to combat the effects of the Depression. In response, his opponents have organized a "tax strike" which discourages businesses from paying their city taxes. This lack of tax revenue severely impacts the mayor's ability to advance his agenda. Regardless of its revenue problems, however, there is an air of political excitement in the city in anticipation of the Democratic Presidential Convention, scheduled to start next month.

Herbert Hoover is the president of the United States. Unlike many who have held the office, Hoover is educated, highly accomplished, and extremely well traveled. Originally from a small town in Iowa, he graduated from Stanford University and went on to live and work on four continents. During the Great War, he ran the U.S. Food Administration. After the war, he took up the cause of hunger in Europe and became internationally renowned for his humanitarian efforts. His politics at that time were progressive, supporting minimum wage, union organizing, the forty-eight-hour workweek, and the elimination of child labor. Now, as president, Hoover has become far more conservative. In '32, he is urging voters to reject the notion that government intervention can save the country from the Depression.

Most people in the country blame Hoover for the current problems. They mock him by calling the shanty towns that are springing up "Hoovervilles", and by using slang terms like "Hoover Flags" to denote someone's empty turned-out pockets.

World's Fair – A Century of Progress, the official name for the Chicago World's Fair, is currently under construction, and it's scheduled to open in May of next year. It's a follow up to Chicago's previous World's Fair, the immensely successful Columbian Exposition, which opened in '93. This earlier exposition was nicknamed "The White City" because all the buildings were clad in white stucco, and the entire fair was spectacularly illuminated by over two hundred thousand electric bulbs, powered by Nikola Tesla's AC equipment.

For the new exposition, the city officials designated 400 acres of reclaimed land along Lake Michigan and south of the Loop. Unfortunately, you won't be able to see it while you're here, as it's not going to open for another year. The cost for the construction of the site will be over ten million dollars, and the total cost of the fair will exceed thirty million. The city was incredibly lucky, because the financing for the fair was completed the day before the market crashed in '29.

The Great Chicago Fire – The fire started on the 8th of October, 1871, and burned for two days. According to the locals the fire started when Mrs. Catherine O'Leary was milking a cow in her barn on DeKoven Street, on the south side of the city. The cow supposedly kicked a burning oil lamp onto a pile of hay, which quickly ignited. Aided by months of drought and strong winds, the fire moved swiftly north, consuming all of what would become the Loop. It then leapt across the north bank of the Chicago River and burned all the way to Belden Avenue, on the city's north side.

After the fire Chicago became a different city. Its architecture changed dramatically, as wood structures gave way to those of stone, brick, terracotta, and steel. A new streamlined building design developed, known as the "Chicago School", with world renowned designers such as Daniel Burnham, John W. Root, Louis Sullivan, and Frank Lloyd Wright leading the way.

The Great War – To a remarkable extent, the mass slaughter that engulfed Europe from 1914 to 1918 barely touched the United States. Total American losses totaled just over 115,000, while many European countries saw more than ten times that number. Even more striking, the number of civilians killed in the war was nearly 7 million, while the number of American civilians that died was less than 800. Consequently, the impact of the war on the American people was minimal when compared to their European counterparts. So, and not surprisingly, Americans didn't have the deep scars that the majority of Europeans carried with them.

For the American veterans, the horrors they experienced during the war were never understood by the vast majority of their fellow citizens. Only those who had served seemed to understand, and this meant that many veterans formed a bond with their fellow soldiers that would last a lifetime.

The veterans of the Great War are scheduled to receive a bonus payment from the federal government in '45. With the Depression biting hard, many veterans have called for these payments to be made immediately. To strengthen their demand for an early payment, a call has gone out from veterans groups for a "Bonus Army" to be formed. This "Army" plans to march on Washington DC to pressure the government to make the payment in '32. You might see a few passing through Chicago during your stay, as tens of thousands from every corner of the country are descending on the capital. Once there, they intend to remain until their demands are met.

Prohibition – The Eighteenth Amendment of the Constitution established the prohibition of alcohol in the United States. The amendment was ratified by the required number of states on January 16, 1919 and, in accordance with the terms of the amendment, commenced one year after ratification at midnight on January 17, 1920. The Volstead Act was the law that enabled the enforcement of the amendment. It was passed by congress on October 28, 1919 (over Woodrow Wilson's veto) and it too went into effect on January 17, 1920.

Prohibition is still the law of the land, but after more than a decade the people of the country are weary of what's been termed the "Noble Experiment". Consequently, if you want a drink during your stay don't worry, the law is widely flaunted and liquor is easy to come by.

The Gangs – In the days before Prohibition, the numerous gangs in the city had been small and ethnically based, with their operations centered around gambling. All of that changed when the Volstead Act was passed in '19. "Big" Jim O'Leary – yes, it was his mother that started the Great Fire – had run the Irish gang. Like most of the older bosses, he couldn't see the opportunities that prohibition offered. Consequently, many of his men joined up with O'Banion's "North Side Gang". These "Northsiders" quickly gained control of the northern half of the city by either absorbing or eliminating their competition. Meanwhile, Jonny Torrio and his lieutenant Al Capone ran the Italian gang. After they reorganized into "the Outfit", they took control of the southern half. For nearly a decade the two gangs battled in an on again, off again turf war. The apex of this struggle occurred in early '29 when the Outfit, now run by Capone, struck the Northsiders, now run by Bugs Moran, on February 14th. In what became known as the "Saint Valentine's Day Massacre", seven workers at the SMC Cartage garage were lined up facing a wall and mowed down with Thompsons submachine guns, or what the press liked to call "Chicago Typewriters". Each body was hit by at least six shots, with some being hit by as many as eighteen. The Northsiders never recovered from this attack. Over the next few years, the dust gradually settled and the Outfit controlled the city.

Chicago River – The Chicago River flowed from west to east and emptied into Lake Michigan. There were two issues with the river. The first was that the city was only marginally higher than the river. This meant that the land was often wet and suffered from poor drainage. The problem was so bad that the City's first nickname was the "Mud City". Besides the swampy conditions, the poor drainage also led to health problems, culminating in the cholera outbreak in 1854, which killed one out of every fifteen residents.

To solve this drainage problem, a unique solution was employed – they raised the city. Building by building, and street by street, the entire city was raised anywhere from three to six feet off the ground. This allowed for sewage and drainage lines to be laid, ultimately solving the mud problem.

The second issue was the river's slow speed. During the city's early years this wasn't much of a problem. With the development in '64 of the Chicago Stockyards, however, it became a serious issue. This was because the new stockyard was dumping so much waste into the river it became known as "Bubbly Creek" due to the gaseous byproducts of the waste bubbling up to the surface. This mess moved very slowly through the heart of the city, and the smell of the decomposing waste permeated the entire area.

To solve this problem, the city chose another unique solution. In 1900, the course of the river was permanently reversed. Considered one of the engineering marvels of its day, changing the direction of "Bubbly Creek" sent the waste (and the smell) west, away from the city.

Entertainment – While you're in town you have to spend at least some of your nights sampling the nightlife. Chicago offers some of the hottest nightclubs in the country. Many of the swankier clubs like the Boulevard Room, the Empire Room, the Panther Club, and The Grand Terrace Ballroom frequently showcase major talent and host nationwide radio broadcasts. "Speakeasies", usually smaller and not as posh, are omnipresent in the city and its suburbs. They get their name because patrons typically have to whisper a password at the door to gain entrance. The better establishments, like Chez Paree, the Green Mill, the Dill Pickle, and the Friar's Club offer music, typically jazz, the blues, or popular favorites from Tin Pan Alley. These joints generally serve an "honest" drink. The smaller places, sometimes called "Blind Pigs", offer limited or no entertainment, and can be guilty of serving watered down liquor, or even "bathtub" gin.

The city has dozens of newspapers, almost too many to count. There are numerous dailies with some editions published in the morning while others are published in the afternoon. The most popular dailies are the *Chicago Tribune* (morning) and the *Chicago Daily News* (afternoon). Besides the dailies there are also weekly and monthly publications. A number of these papers are published in different languages (Polish, German, Ukrainian, Greek, etc.).

Moving pictures have exploded in popularity since the advent of "talkies" in '27. This revolution in entertainment was a threshold that once audiences crossed they had no interest in going back. By '30, less than a quarter of the theaters in the country were equipped to handle sound, but by the start of '32, virtually every theater had converted.

An offshoot of "talkies" is the rise in popularity of the newsreel. These short films are produced by news services such as Pathé, Paramount, and Movietone. Running for ten minutes, just before the feature film, the newsreels cover the top stories of the week, and are now being shown in virtually every movie theater in the country. They are giving Americans a view of the world, in sight and sound, they've never had before.

Radio is changing the way virtually all Americans spend their evenings. Up until recently, the radio business was comprised of independent stations, each broadcasting their own programs. Over the past few years, however, four major "networks" have developed, each broadcasting an evening program schedule. This allows local stations to offer quality news, sports and entertainment programs at a fraction of the cost of producing them individually. It is also attractive to larger advertisers who can reach customers in all the major population centers through these networks. For the American people, it means that wherever you live you can listen to the same music, news, entertainment, and sporting events.

With both talkies and radio now consuming much of the average person's evenings, the demand for live productions, particularly vaudeville and burlesque, has declined sharply. Not surprisingly, many of the theaters that catered to live productions are undergoing conversion to accommodate "talkies".

Sports – Chicago has professional teams in all of the major sports – baseball, football, and hockey.

Baseball – The most popular sport in the country is baseball, and that's true in Chicago as well. There are said to be two "major" leagues – the National League and the American League. Chicago, like many of the larger American cities, has one team in each league – the Cubs in the National League, and the White Sox in the American League. While you're visiting you might want to catch a game, but if you do be careful how you speak about either club. Fans are passionate, and there's a strong rivalry between the clubs. Which is funny really, because they've only played each other once, in the World Series in '06.

In addition to the National and American Leagues, there is also the Negro National League, and many consider it to be the third "major" league. Chicago has a team in the NNL, the Giants. They have been the most dominant team in the league for the last few years, and they are favored to win the NNL pennant in '32.

Football – Chicago has two teams in the National Football League, the Bears and the Cardinals. Both teams are founding members of the league. Neither team has been particularly strong, with each winning just one championship since the league was formed in '20.

Hockey – The sport of hockey is popular only in the northern states of the country, but it's almost a religion in Canada. There are 9 teams in the league, 5 from the US, and 4 from Canada, but 90% of the players come from Canada. The league is divided into two divisions, the American Division and the Canadian Division. The Black Hawks are Chicago's National Hockey League team and they play in the American Division.

The Depression – Undoubtedly the single most important thing to remember while you're in town is that this city is reeling from the effects of the "Great Depression", or more simply, the Depression. The stock market crash of '29 ushered in this economic disaster, and three years on from that collapse there's been a rising tide of business closures and bank failures that threatens to swamp everyone. Unemployment is said to be 30%, but for some ethnic groups the rate is closer to 50%. Legions of the unemployed wait each morning outside the factories that are still operating for the start of the "shape-up", when the factory's foreman selects his day laborers. It's a sad fact that only a few of the men waiting will be chosen, but for those who are it means 25 cents an hour for ten hours of back-breaking work. In addition to the crowds of men at the shape-ups, there is also a seemingly endless stream in line at the soup kitchens dotted throughout the city. These soup kitchens are run by private charities, with most getting their support from various religious groups, while a few others get support from men like Al Capone.

While the Depression for most of the country started in September of '29, for the nearby farmers it began in the mid-20's when crop prices crashed. To make matters worse, decades of poor farming practices coupled with a persistent drought created the perfect conditions for massive dust storms. These storms, known as "black blizzards", impact the entire mid-west and occasionally drift all the way to the east coast.

The effects of the Depression weigh on the city like the loss of a loved one, but time can't seem to lessen the pain – it only serves to pull more people into the misery. There is no "safety net". People are expected to fend for themselves, and the very real fear of losing your job hangs over everyone's head. Throughout Chicago a feeling of desperation is in the air, and it's becoming more and more intense with each new bank failure and factory closing.

Lorde of Chicago

CHICAGO 1932

FIELD NOTES
LOOP DISTRICT

Made in the USA
Monee, IL
19 August 2022